Praise for the American River Trilogy

"O'Connor's writing is lyrical and bold, suffused with the sensibility of painters and pianists. She is a master of still-life renderings of meadow, mountain and mood, and of sheer action ... A meditation in novel form on the agonies and ecstasies of the great American experiment at a crucible moment."
  —Greg Dawson, Author of *Busted in Bloomington* and *Hiding in the Spotlight*

"The complex relationships and family crises effectively parallel the turbulence of the era that provides the backdrop for addictive melodrama."
  —Kirkus Review

"O'Connor's talents in keeping track of the threads of major plot lines enable her to map individual experiences onto a national epic."
  —Blazing World, OnlineBookClub.org

"*American River: Currents* has a most urgent message for everyone living in today's turbulent times where immigration issues are on everyone's lips. The book is a strong reminder that we are all the same people, united on this lonely planet, Earth."
  —Kislany, OnlineBookClub.org

"Contemporary fiction is one of my favorite genres, especially when it is mixed with themes of family and history. American River encompasses everything I love about literature; it has plenty of family love, twists and turns galore and brilliant, unconventional characters."
  —The Redheaded Book Lover Blog

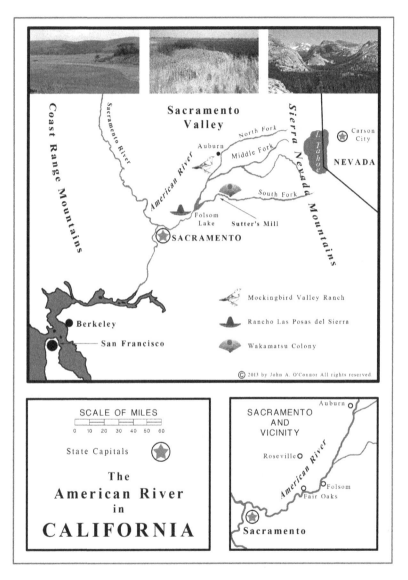

Mockingbird Valley Ranch

Rancho Las Posas del Sierra

Wakamatsu Colony

SCALE OF MILES

0   10   20   30   40   50   60

State Capitals

The
American River
in
CALIFORNIA

SACRAMENTO
AND
VICINITY

Auburn

Roseville

American River

Folsom
Fair Oaks

Sacramento

Map of the American River

American River: Confluence

BOOK THREE OF THE AMERICAN RIVER TRILOGY

Mallory M. O'Connor

ARCHWAY
PUBLISHING

Archway Publishing books may be ordered through booksellers or by contacting:

Archway Publishing
1663 Liberty Drive
Bloomington, IN 47403
www.archwaypublishing.com
1 (888) 242-5904

ISBN: 978-1-4808-6819-9 (sc)
ISBN: 978-1-4808-6818-2 (e)

Library of Congress Control Number: 2018958072

Print information available on the last page.

Archway Publishing rev. date: 9/17/2018

For Nate, a true Californian. We miss you, amigo.

ACKNOWLEDGEMENTS

First off, I'd like to thank my readers for taking the time to explore my work. A work of art—whether it's a painting, a symphony, or a novel—is is dead without an audience. Art is meant to communicate, so thank you for your attention.

Second, I want to thank my good friends—you know who you are—who have encouraged me and offered their suggestions and expertise. I am forever in your debt.

And to my son Chris: you're a heck of an editor, Rico!

CAST OF CHARACTERS

The McPhalan Family

Owen McPhalan – Cormac's grandson and patriarch of the
  McPhalan family (deceased)
Marian Archer McPhalan – Owen's ex-wife
The McPhalan children:
Mary Katharine McPhalan (Kate)
Alexandria Archer McPhalan (Alex)
Julian Francis McPhalan (deceased)
Cormac McPhalan Fitzgerald (Cory) – Kate and Carl's son

The Morales Family

Jorge Morales – Mexican immigrant and self-made successful
  businessman
Rose Fitzgerald Morales – Jorge's wife
The Morales children:
Carlos Estevan Morales (Carl Steven Fitzgerald)
Silvio Morales
Allison Morales

The Ashida Family

David Ashida – First generation Japanese American (Issei)
Connie Yoshinobu Ashida – David's wife
David and Connie's son:
Tommy Ashida
Emiko Namura Ashida – Tommy's wife (deceased)
Willie Ashida – David's brother
Pearl Ashida – his wife (they have four children, Tommy's cousins)

Others

Stefan Molnar – Hungarian émigré and classical piano superstar (deceased)

Jean Molnar – Stefan's widow

Jerry McClosky – Carl's music agent

Marty Swanson – Alex's boyfriend

Armand Becker – Santa Barbara doctor and patron of the arts

Veronique Becker – Armand's wife

Chris Malacchi – Kate's best friend

Nick Vecchio - Canadian-born sculptor/video artist and Marian's second husband

Jon Fisher – Marian's New York art dealer

Kyoshi Namura – Emiko's father

Natsumi Namura – Kyoshi's wife

Roberto Gonzales – wealthy Mexican businessman and patron of the arts

Tatiana Gonzales – Roberto's wife

Francisco Gonzales – Roberto's son

PART I

CHAPTER

1

Mockingbird Valley Ranch
Near Auburn, California
June 1970

Kate McPhalan was sitting at the breakfast table at Mockingbird Valley Ranch, reading *The Sacramento Bee* and sipping coffee, when the phone rang. Consuelo, the housekeeper, started to pick up, but Kate shooed her away. "I'll take it. Hello?"

"It's me." Kate's sister's voice was small and shaky.

"Alex?"

"I need to talk to you."

Kate carried the phone to the table and sat down. "All right."

There was a long pause, and then Alex said, "Can I come and see you?"

"I guess so."

"You don't mind?"

Kate thought for a minute. "I *do* mind, but I think we should talk. Where are you?"

"Santa Barbara."

"What are you doing there?"

"It's a long story, but I've been staying with Jean Molnar."

"Jean Molnar?" Kate said in surprise.

"We've gotten to be friends. I'll explain later. Could you pick me up at the airport this afternoon?"

"When do you get in?"

"Around three."

"I'll be there."

Kate had to fight to keep the shock from her face when she saw her sister coming toward her in the hallway of the terminal. Alex had always been slender, but now she was wraith-like, eyes like dark pools in the snowfield of her face. Kate gave her a hug and could feel bones through the thin fabric of Alex's dress. "You look a little bushed," Kate said diplomatically. "Let's get your luggage, and we'll head for home."

"This is it," said Alex as Kate took the single overnight bag. Another surprise. Alex never went anywhere without at least four suitcases.

"How's Jean doing?" Kate asked as they walked into the glare of the parking lot. "I haven't heard from her since Christmas."

"She's getting married."

"Really?"

"His name's Wright Westmorland."

"Armand's friend?"

"You know him?"

"I met him once a few years ago." Kate didn't add that Stefan Molnar had played a recital at the Westmorland's posh seaside mansion. The memory flooded back to her—the pale blue of the sea, the scent of jasmine, Stefan at the piano playing Mendelssohn. Gently, she put the memory aside.

"What happened to the first Mrs. Westmorland?" she asked.

"Messy divorce," Alex replied. "Seems she was having an affair with the chauffer. You know rich people. They just move on to the next best option."

"That's interesting news," Kate said. "I'm happy for Jean. How's Janos?" she added. She remembered Jean and Stefan's son at three—blond, energetic, and into everything.

"Beautiful. And smart. He wants to be a race-car driver. But that's this week." Alex glanced around. "Where's Cory?"

"At school. He'll be home around four. We just had a party for his fifth birthday. Can you imagine?"

"That's really nice. I can't believe. . ." The words seemed to catch in Alex's throat, and Kate glanced at her sister in time to see a tear spill from the corner of Alex's eye.

"Alex," she said, "what's wrong?"

"Let's go home please," Alex whispered.

That evening, dinner over and Cory tucked into bed, Kate and Alex sat in front of the fire, nursing a final glass of wine. "I had to get away from Marty," Alex said. "Nikki was so right about that bastard. I hope he drowns in a sewer."

"How did you happen to move in with Jean?"

"I called Armand from LA and asked if I could come see him. I'd been living on champagne and dexedrine for weeks, and I guess Armand could tell how fucked up I was. So he invited me to visit. I didn't know that Jean was in Santa Barbara. I didn't intend to see her, but the Beckers insisted we go to lunch. Jean and I got into this heavy conversation about Stefan and me and you and. . . everything."

Alex paused and gave Kate a wary look.

"Go on," Kate prompted.

"I guess I never really thought of Jean as a person. She was just sort of *there* in the background. I had all these ideas about her, and they were all wrong. Anyway, I told her that I thought I'd go back to New York, but she didn't think I was in any shape to travel. So she asked me to stay with her for a couple of weeks and try to sort things out. I was afraid to go back to LA. I tried to call Mom, but she and Nick had gone back to Mexico. Jean wanted to call you, but I told her not to."

"Why not? You know I would have tried to help."

Alex looked down at her hands and muttered, "I figured you'd never speak to me again after what I did in Lenox."

"You told the truth in Lenox," Kate said evenly. "You were pretty crude about it, and it wasn't pretty. But it was the truth."

"Damn it, Katie," Alex said, her voice thin and raw. "I've done everything *wrong*. It's my fault Stefan died."

Kate stared at her sister. "How can you say that? It was an accident."

"It was my punishment."

"For what?"

"I seduced him. I made him break promises. He even said so at the time. He loved you, and I was so jealous and wanted to hurt you." She squeezed her eyes shut. "I would have done anything to have Stefan—*anything*! That's why I was so horrible to you, and now I've destroyed your marriage and—"

"Good grief, Alex," Kate said wryly, "you certainly give yourself a lot of credit."

Shock wiped the pain from Alex's face. "Meaning?"

"Everything's *your* fault? Sounds like you could damn near single-handedly destroy the world."

"But I—"

"Listen, my dear. Stefan had broken a lot of promises before he ever met you. He hurt you as much as you hurt him. And as for my marriage, Carl and I had been drifting apart for years. What happened in Lenox was just the final straw." Kate gave her sister a half smile. "Sure, you've hurt people. You've been selfish and irresponsible. But it's not your fault that Stefan died, and it's not your fault that Carl and I have gone separate ways." Kate shook her head. "I won't have you taking more credit for our disasters than is due."

Alex gave a laugh that turned into a sob. "Then you don't hate me?"

"No, I don't hate you."

Alex threw her arms around Kate's shoulders. "God, I've been such a dope. All my life." She pulled away and buried her face in her hands. "Damn! I can't seem to stop crying."

"It's okay," Kate said, stroking the tangle of blond curls. "You've got a lot to cry about, hon."

"I loved Daddy," Alex sobbed, "and I never told him so. And I miss Julian. And oh, God, I miss Stefan so much! I can't stop thinking about him. I figured if I stayed stoned long enough I'd stop hurting, but it didn't do any good. And every time Marty touched me, I'd go crazy. I felt like such a whore." She raised an imploring, tear-streaked face. "Could I just stay here with you for awhile?"

Such a child, Kate thought. *Such a little girl*. "Of course you can. There's plenty of room."

Alex took a deep, shuddering breath and rested her head on

Kate's shoulder for several minutes. Small night sounds murmured: the trill of crickets, the distant lowing of cattle, the muted cooing of doves. "Maybe Stefan was right after all," Alex murmured. "Maybe I didn't really love him. Maybe I don't know what love is. I loved my fairy tale of him. Maybe I've never had any real feelings, just fabrications."

"Not even with your music?"

"That's the closest I've come. When I played, everything was real. When I stopped, I got lost."

Alex straightened up and took a gulp of wine. "When I was little," she continued, "I used to wake up in the morning and think, *Who will I be today?* I'd choose a storybook character and pretend that's who I was. Then one day when I was about thirteen, I woke up and said, 'Why don't you be yourself?' That's when I realized there was no *me*. Scared me so much I didn't know what to do. So I started cutting myself. At least the pain was real."

"Good God," Kate said. "That's awful. Didn't Mom try to get you help?"

Alex shook her head. "She didn't know. I was pretty good at faking accidents." For several minutes they were silent, watching the fire. Then Alex said, "You know, I used to think you were crazy for loving this place. But maybe you weren't so crazy after all."

CHAPTER

2

An hour later, Alex climbed into bed and tried to remember when she had last slept in this room that had once been hers. Maybe the weekend when Carl and Kate were married? Seemed like ages ago.

She got up and opened the window. The night air was cool and soft, and there was a fragrance—something that she remembered from her childhood, a sweet perfume. Roses? Jasmine?

She lay back down and hugged the covers around her. Such a simple pleasure, this feeling of being warm and safe and embedded in a place surrounded by family and memory and history. There was a sense of belonging that she had never consciously missed and now wondered why. In light of what she had recently been through, she could see that a sense of security was invaluable. And fragile.

She hadn't told Kate the whole story. Yes, she had broken off with Marty Swanson and yes, she had called Armand and asked for sanctuary and yes, Jean Molnar had come to her rescue. But she had omitted the details of that terrifying week. Just thinking about it made her flinch and cower and curl up into a fetal position with her eyes shut. After a minute, she was able to breathe again and keep her thoughts steady enough to review the episode that still seemed too bizarre to believe.

First had come the fight. There had been lots of those, but this particular evening had been especially ruthless. She couldn't even remember exactly what she and Marty had been fighting about—something as irrelevant as the music being too loud—but it had escalated quickly to an all-out battle that had advanced from name-calling to throwing things. She remembered throwing an expensive bottle of cabernet sauvignon at him and watching it explode against the wall like a blast of blood.

Then they were struggling, grappling like two wrestlers, and he had his hands around her neck. She tried to scream, but couldn't. She managed to punch him in the stomach and he gasped for breath and grabbed the phone and started to call the police, but she yelled at him and ripped the cord out of the phone jack. He retreated down the hall. She ran after him and when he slammed and locked the bathroom door she kicked it hard enough to shatter the wood.

Next, she ran into the kitchen and started taking everything out of the refrigerator and throwing it as hard as she could against the wall—mustard, pickles, mayonnaise, a bottle of Dom Perignon—splat, whack, crash, slosh. So satisfying.

But then the police showed up—Marty must have called them from the bedroom—and after Marty claimed that she had threatened him with a butcher knife somehow they decided to arrest her, HER, for "domestic battery." They pulled her hands behind her and cuffed her and herded her out to the squad car and off they went through the smoggy darkness to the Los Angeles County Detention Center.

She remembered a large, overly bright room with uniformed people everywhere and "civilians" being herded about to different cubicles where they were "processed." Clothes were removed, jewelry confiscated, any semblance of individuality stripped away. Her picture was taken. Her fingerprints catalogued. "Who's the female?" she heard a voice say. She didn't hear the answer, but glanced up and saw a uniformed woman staring at her. She lowered her head and wondered if the woman had recognized her. Probably not —she seemed an unlikely fan of classical music.

Next, Alex was "interviewed" by a "nurse" who asked questions about her medical history. Did she have high blood pressure, kidney problems, seizures? Sexually transmitted diseases? Did she drink? Take drugs? Which ones? "Let's see your arms," said the nurse. "What are these scars?"

"I broke my wrist. They used pins to hold my bones together."

"Hmmm," the nurse said skeptically.

She sat in a small cell for about an hour. The cubical was dark, but the door was glass so she could see the large room beyond. She asked a guard for some water. He told her to shut up.

After a while, they put her in a larger cell—six bunks, a toilet-washbasin combination. No windows, just a dim light on the back wall.

There were two women in the cell. They stared at Alex and whispered to each other, but she ignored them and lay down on the bare plastic mattress. She pulled the thin blanket around her and stared at the wall. There was no way in the world that this could be happening to her. But it was.

For the next six hours, Alex tried to sleep, but couldn't. Her cellmates were quiet, but the jailors constantly shouted and babbled, disembodied voices in a chaotic chorus of nonsense. Doors slammed every sixty seconds. Somewhere in the distance a garage door grated again and again, metal on metal.

At some point the fluorescent light in the ceiling went on and a guard came and shoved "breakfast" through the door. Alex watched from the bunk as her cellmates gobbled up whatever it was. A little later she had to use the toilet.

The two young women eyed her curiously. "Honey," one of them said, "you sure don't look like you belong here. What the fuck are you in here for?"

Alex looked at the woman. She was thin and angular with ragged black hair down to her shoulders and a pinched face that Alex thought made her look like a rodent. "I threw a wine bucket at my lover," Alex replied.

Both of the women gaped at her and then burst out laughing. "No shit?" the second woman—a heavily made-up bleached blond with a round face and plump legs and arms—crowed. "Man, that is so fucked up! I can't believe they locked you up for *that!*"

The women introduced themselves. "I'm Carrie," said the thin one, holding out her hand. "Parole violation. Third offence." This was said in the same casual way one might say, "I'm Fred, assistant office manager."

"And I'm Faith," said the other woman. "Shoplifting."

"Alex," she said. "Ummm. . ." *Concert pianist? Ex-concert pianist? Fucked up basket case?* "Ummm. . . domestic battery."

Introductions completed, Faith and Carrie amused themselves for an hour by looking through the little glass panel in the cell door and discussing the physical attributes of the guards. "Tall and skinny," Carrie noted. "Bet he's hung."

"You never know," Faith countered. "I had this guy once, little fat dude. Had the biggest pecker you ever saw. Called him my frog prince."

After a while one of the guards came in and walked all three women down the hall for a "hearing." The "judge" was on a TV monitor. Each prisoner was called to come forward, the charges were read, bail was set or not.

"I'm releasing you on your own recognizance," the judge told Alex. "But, you are to have no contact with the victim or I'll put you back in jail. Understood?"

Alex nodded. "Yes, sir."

She was taken to another cell where she sat by herself for several hours until the guard came and gave her a bag with her clothes and told her to get dressed.

And just like that she was taken to the entrance and released into a blazing hot, cloudless Southern California summer day. She had no money, no identification, no regular shoes (she'd been in her house slippers when she was arrested) and was wearing a white silk tank top and a pair of blue velvet slacks.

And she had no idea where she was.

A sidewalk ran along the edge of the treeless street in front of the detention center. Behind the concrete buildings she could see an elevated freeway. She headed toward what she thought might be north and tried to think of a plan. Where could she go?

She couldn't contact Marty or any of his friends, and she hadn't met anyone outside his circle since arriving in Los Angeles six months before. In the free-range constant party-time lifestyle that Marty had introduced her to, there didn't seem to be *friends*, just *players.* She had hooked up for an evening with several different guys, but couldn't even remember their names. Her other life—the one that she had lived before Stefan's death and "the accident" that had ended her concert career—seemed like a distant mirage, and she was lost in an empty desert of isolation.

Exhausted, dizzy, her skin already reddening from the relentless sun, she staggered along the sidewalk. She hadn't had anything to eat or drink for at least fifteen hours, and she wondered what would happen if she fainted. Would anyone stop and try to revive her or would she just be left there on the sidewalk to die?

The road curved to the left and she saw a deserted schoolyard behind a chain-link fence. The school was closed for the summer, but if she could get through the fence there might be a water fountain. Thirst pulled at her.

She found a gate and went into the long open corridor that served as an outdoor hallway for the classrooms. Finally, she spotted a water fountain and gratefully gulped down the lukewarm fluid. She splashed water on her burning face and arms and sat down in the shade, trying to decide what to do. Was there anyone at all that she could turn to?

Her mother, Marian? But she was off in Mexico with that new boyfriend of hers. Kate? Kate was at the other end of the state and had a child to take care of and a ranch to run. And why would Kate help her anyway after what happened in Lenox? The memory of that Christmas Eve washed over her—Carl and Marian's panic, Alex's furious revelations about a decade-old love affair, Kate's initial disbelief that slowly turned to comprehension. *How could I have been so awful?* she thought. *What did I hope to gain?*

She glanced around the deserted schoolyard. What had happened, happened. Too late for regrets. She had to think about what to do NOW. Who could help her? Who *would* help her?

Rube? She hadn't seen or talked to her former agent for over a year. And he was in New York for God's sake.

Then she thought of Armand Becker, Stefan's friend and mentor. Armand and his wife, Veronique, lived in Santa Barbara. That was only two hours away. Would Armand remember her? She'd met him several times, but that seemed like ages ago. In another life. But she decided he was her best hope. Perhaps her *only* hope.

She got to her feet and headed back to the sidewalk. If only she could find someone who would let her make a phone call.

And suddenly there it was before her—a church. Old. And Spanish. Like a mission. And there was a woman just opening a door marked "Office." Alex hurried forward. "Ma'am? Excuse me. Hello!"

The woman turned and gave Alex a look of dismay. "My goodness," she exclaimed, "where did you come from?"

"Long story," Alex said, "but I really, *really* need to use your phone. Would that be okay?"

The woman—a short, round Hispanic woman with black hair and pretty brown eyes—led Alex into the building, told her to sit down, and brought her a glass of cold water. "Just dial nine for an outside line," the woman instructed as she set the water down in front of Alex.

"It's long distance," Alex told her, "and I don't have any money."

The woman shrugged. "Unless you're calling overseas, don't worry about it."

Santa Barbara information gave her Armand's phone number. She tried the office number first but got an answering machine. She dialed the home number and waited. On the sixth ring a woman answered, "Hello."

Feeling suddenly uncertain, Alex said, "Ummm, hello? Is this, ummm, who am I speaking to?"

"This is Veronique Becker," the woman replied. "Can I help you?"

I hope so! Alex thought. Aloud she said, "Hi Veronique. This is Alex. Alex Archer." Would Verrie remember her?

"Alexandria," Veronique exclaimed. "Where are you, *cherie*? It's been ages since we heard from you. How are you?"

"Ummm," Alex said, "I'm in trouble." She went on to explain the basics of her predicament and ended with, "If you don't want to get involved in this mess, I'll understand. I just couldn't think of anyone else to call."

"Poor darling, of course we'll help you," Verrie said. "Just tell me exactly where you are and I'll send Sanchez or Gabrielle to pick you up."

Alex glanced at the Mexican woman who was working at her desk on the other side of the office. "Where am I?" she asked.

"You are at St. Lucy's Catholic Church on Hazard Avenue in East Los Angeles. But," she smiled sympathetically, "I overheard your story. Let me give your friend the directions how to get here."

3

Santa Barbara, California

That night, Alex sat with Armand and Verrie and told them the whole story of her accident, the spiral into chaos, the fiasco in Lenox, and the dissolution of the past six months.

"The first thing we must do is to get your legal problems resolved," Armand said. "I'll get to work on that in the morning. Meanwhile, please make yourself at home."

Alex glanced at Verrie, then back at Armand. "I don't want to intrude," she said. "I feel like such an idiot."

"Nonsense," scoffed Verrie. "You are our guest and we will take good care of you."

And they did. By the end of the week, a friend of Armand's, a lawyer in Los Angeles, had visited with the State Attorney. Shortly thereafter, the charges against Alex were dropped and the restraining order was rescinded. Armand sent Sanchez to pick up Alex's belongings at Marty's house, and just like that the whole ugly episode was over.

Except for the panic attacks and the nightmares and the flashbacks. Those would continue for a very long time.

"Aunt Alex? Are you awake?"

Alex opened one eye and saw Cory, her five-year-old nephew, standing in the doorway. Sunlight was streaming in through the window, burnishing the terra cotta floor tiles. *Oh, that's right*, she thought. *I'm at Mockingbird. I'm safe. At least for now.* She stared at her nephew. Goodness, he'd grown. How could six months make such a difference?

"Hi," she said.

Cory came in and stood solemnly next to the bed. "Consuelo wants to know if you want breakfast," he said.

Alex blinked. "Okay. Sure."

Cory nodded. "I'll tell her yes."

"I'll be right down," Alex called after him.

She rumaged through her bag and found a pair of grey slacks and a blue tee shirt. She dressed quickly and went downstairs. Kate and Cory were at the table and Consuelo was bringing a stack of pancakes and bacon from the kitchen. "Coffee?" she said to Alex.

"Please."

"Sit," said Kate, pointing to the chair across from her. "How did you sleep?"

"Great." Alex yawned and hunched her shoulders. "I guess I was really tired." She studied the plate in front of her. Pancakes. And bacon. How long had it been since she'd had a real breakfast?

When they had finished eating and Consuelo was clearing the table, Cory jumped up and said, "I've got to practice piano. Want to watch me, Aunt Alex?"

Alex glanced at Kate.

"He's taking lessons," said Kate. "His teacher says he's got real talent."

Alex rolled her eyes. "Jeez. Here we go again." She smiled at Cory. "Sure, I'd be happy to watch."

Kate decided to leave them alone and went upstairs to her study, while Alex sat down on a chair next to the piano. Cory played some scales and then pulled out a Muzio Clementi Sonatina book. "My teacher says these are really good to practice," Cory announced.

"I remember them well," said Alex.

"Mama says you play really good. Why don't you play something?"

"I *used* to play," Alex replied. "I don't any more."

"How come?"

"I hurt my hand."

Cory frowned. "But you got two of them."

Alex laughed. "Yeah, but one of them doesn't work."

"Which one?"

"The left one." She held it out. "See? It's all stiff."

Cory looked thoughtful, then brightened and said, "I know. I'll play the bottom and you play the top."

"I . . . uh . . ."

"Come on." He scooted over and patted the bench next to him. "Please?"

She hesitated for a minute, then sat down beside him. "All right, maestro. Which one do we play?"

"I like this one," Cory said, pointing to the open score.

"Okay, Clementi's Sonatina Number three it is."

"Ready?" Cory cried, putting his hands on the keys.

"Whoa," Alex said. "Not so fast. First we need to take a look at the score."

"Why?"

"So we get a better idea of what the composer wants. The composer created the music and our job is to interpret it. But we have to check first to see what the composer expected. So, tell me, number three is written in what key?"

Cory studied the score. "C major?"

"That's correct. And how many movements are there in this piece?"

Cory turned the pages, tilted his head. "Three?"

"Right again. How are we going to know how fast to play each movement?"

Cory looked at her. "Get the teacher to play it first?"

"You're a sly devil," Alex said with a laugh, "but there's an easier way. The composer tells us. See? Right here it says 'allegro.' Do you know what that means?"

"Fast?"

"Good. But now we have another problem. How loud should it be?"

"'F' is for loud and 'P' is for soft."

"Correct. 'F' means *forte* in Italian and 'P' means *pianissimo*. Okay?"

"Aunt Alex?" Cory said, "how do you know all this stuff?"

"Same way I got to Carnegie Hall," Alex said with a smirk. "Practice, practice, practice."

When Kate came downstairs an hour later, she found them still at the piano. "Try this fingering," Alex was saying. "Fourth finger on G. Yeah, that's it. Better? Let's take it again from the top."

Oh my God, she thought. *Cory's gotten her to try.* Kate smiled to herself as she turned around and tiptoed back upstairs.

CHAPTER

4

Sacramento, California

"I wish you wouldn't go down there tonight," Rose said one balmy evening as Jorge prepared to leave for a Farm Workers rally in the nearby town of Stockton.

"I must show my support," Jorge replied firmly.

"But I don't understand," Rose protested, following him to the door. "Isn't it bad enough that you're fighting the growers and the labor contractors and the illegals brought in to break up the strikes? Do you have to take on the Teamsters too?"

Jorge paused with his hand on the door. "*Them* most of all," he said.

"But why are you fighting the Teamsters?" Rose asked.

Jorge sat his clipboard down and looked at his wife. "Listen to me, Rosita. The Teamsters don't represent the field workers. Cesar says they were brought in to *suppress* the Chicano movement."

"But they're a *union!*"

"Yes, but they want to do away with the worker's meetings. They want to disband the shop stewards and the ranch committees that workers can go to with complaints. The Teamsters would send their representatives into the fields, but they do so mostly to collect dues. They would bring back the labor contractors and do away with the hiring halls. And the hiring halls were the most basic reform. They help stabilize the work force and give the field hands what they never had before, the chance for a steady income so they can make a permanent home for themselves and their families. This is why we oppose the Teamsters. If anything, they are allied with the growers. The workers must control their own affairs, or all we have tried to do will have no value."

Rose studied him unhappily. "But why get yourself mixed up in it? For goodness sake, Jorge, you could get hurt."

"That's why I must go," he explained. "We need strong numbers to support the protest. There must be people willing to make a stand." He picked up the clipboard. "Surely, I can give them a few hours of my time."

Rose hugged him hard. "Be careful. Don't do anything foolish."

He kissed her cheek. "Don't worry. I just want to show my support. I'll be home around midnight, so don't wait up for me."

But I always do, Rose thought as she watched him leave.

Less than two hours later the phone rang. Rose hurried to answer. "Hello?"

"Rosa?"

"Yes."

"There was. . .a bomb," an hysterical female voice informed her. "The car, it was was torn to shreds. Three men were killed instantly, but Jorge, I think he is still alive. The driver of the ambulance said so."

"Where did they take him?" Rose cried. "Which hospital?!"

"Sacramento, I think," the woman said. "The one here is not so good. I must go."

Rose began to shake uncontrollably. "Thank you for calling me."

"God bless, Señora," the woman said.

Someone was pounding on the door. Rose's only thought was that it would be the same two uniformed men who had come to tell her that her son, Silvio, was dead. Angels of death dressed in olive drab. "No," she whispered, "not again."

But it was Father Malone. "Rose. . ." he began but he could see that she knew.

Her hand flew to her mouth. "Is he—?"

"Still alive," the priest said. He put his arm around her. "Come. I'll take you to the hospital."

As they drove through the dark streets, Fr. Malone explained that on his way to the meeting, Jorge had stopped to talk to the men in the car when the bomb exploded. He was thrown clear of the wreckage and the fire that followed.

"How bad is he, Father?" Rose asked. In the eerie blue of the streetlights she saw him swallow.

"He's still alive," he repeated doggedly.

Rose took a deep breath and tried to push away the panic that was rising like a flash flood. She willed herself not to cry and began to pray silently.

Father Malone stayed with Rose in the waiting room. They were both silent, trying not to think of what might happen, but not able to avoid thinking of it. Finally, a doctor came through the door and asked them to follow him into an office.

"We have him stabilized," the doctor said. "He lost a lot of blood, but his vital signs are good."

Rose jumped to her feet. "Can I see him?"

"Not yet," the doctor replied. "We have him prepped for surgery. Fortunately, he was outside the vehicle, so there appears to be limited pulmonary or hollow viscus injury—meaning his lungs and other internal organs weren't impacted by the blast. He has several broken bones and other wounds from flying debris, but overall he came through pretty well, considering."

Rose took a deep shuddering breath as Father Malone put his arm around her shoulders. "Thank God," she said weakly.

Somehow, her mind was working very calmly. Just as it had when the news of Silvio had reached her. "Do you have some change you can lend me, Father? I have to make some phone calls," she said.

During the six hours of surgery that followed, Rose called Kate, then Ali. Carl was in London for a performance, Ali said. But she would try to reach him. Called out of an early rehearsal at Albert Hall, Carl informed the management that there was a family emergency, hastily re-packed his bags, got a cab to Heathrow, and booked the first available flight to California.

CHAPTER

5

Rose and Ali greeted Carl when he got to the hospital and told him that his father's prognosis was good. It would take time, but Jorge should make a full recovery.

The doctor let them stay in Jorge's ICU room. Ali finally convinced Rose to take a short break and visit the cafeteria, but Carl stayed behind.

He closed his eyes, trying to relieve the ache that had settled there. The dull hum of the fluorescent lights lulled him and he dozed, vaguely aware of the periodic quacking of the hospital intercom, footsteps passing outside the door. There seemed to be a weight hanging above him, something huge and pressing. He started awake, his heart thumping. In the sickly light the sheets looked grey, but they continued to slowly rise and fall. Jorge was still alive. Blankly, as though in a dream, Carl read the name on the chart at the foot of the bed. "Morales, Jorge. Male. Age 52."

Morales. When had he renounced that name and why? Was it when he moved from Arizona to California and, still sick with grief over his grandparent's death, he became determined to keep Gramps' name? No, that wasn't it. The name Fitzgerald had already become part of him even before Gramps died. When had he decided? Exactly when? Carl hadn't thought about it for years, but suddenly it seemed important. Rubbing his eyes with the back of his hand, he saw the name Morales written in his mind. Then he remembered.

He had gone with Gramps to the university to get something— perhaps a music score—from Grandpa's office. Carl was six years old. It was cool inside the building. Cool and dim. In the hallway outside the office was a glass case filled with trophies and Carl stood looking at the golden statues while he waited for Gramps.

Then a rough voice called out, "Hey there! *Hola! Que hay*! What are you doin'?" A bulky, red-faced man stomped toward him, waving a nightstick. "*Que estas haciendo, chico?*"

Frightened, Carl stood wordlessly staring at the guard.

"How'd you get in here?" the gritty voice repeated. "What you doin' here?"

Carl was too scared to speak.

"*No habla Englas?*" the guard grunted. "What's your name, chico? Que esta—"

"Carlos," the boy managed to quaver.

"Car what? Speak up, boy!"

"Carlos Morales."

"Morales, huh. So what the hell you doin', Morales? Go on. Get outta here!" When Carl didn't move the guard raised his stick. "Go on, ya little wetback bastard. Pronto!"

"What's going on out here?" Gramps appeared in the office doorway. "What's the problem, officer?"

"No problem, perfessor. I was just tellin' this little spic to take a hike. Found him sneakin' around here by the trophy case."

"That little spic happens to be my grandson," Andrew replied coldly.

The guard opened his mouth, then closed it. Taking off his hat, he mopped at his face with a faded handkerchief. "Oh. I uh—" He jammed the hat back on his balding head. "We've had a lotta vandalism, sir," he muttered. "Kid said his name was Morales, so I just—"

"Never mind," Andrew said.

"Right. Good day to you, sir." The guard hurried away down the hall.

Andrew hugged Carl and patted his shoulder. "It's okay. Don't cry. Look, if anyone asks you again, just tell him your name is Fitzgerald, okay? Then they'll know you're part of the family. Will you do that for me? That's a good boy. Now, now. Don't cry. He's gone. You're safe now."

Carl stared at the figure on the hospital bed. He had convinced himself that by taking his grandfather's name he was somehow honoring Gramps, keeping his name alive. *But it was cowardice all along*, he thought hopelessly. *Just plain, dumb cowardice.*

Carl found his mother, Rose, and his sister, Ali, in the family lounge. He was not surprised to see Kate there—he knew that she was close to both Rose and Jorge. But it was a bit of a shock to find Alex there as well. He greeted them both, then sat down next to his mother, eager to tell her about what he'd remembered, the reason he'd taken his grandfather Fitzgerald's name. She listened, but didn't appear to share his enthusiasm. He faltered to a stop and sat looking at her, trying to gauge her reaction.

"I really don't know why you're bothering to tell me this," Rose said, her voice brittle with fatigue. "Isn't it a little late for explanations?"

Carl felt the dull, stupid heaviness of his own exhaustion. The insight had seemed a revelation, but maybe she was right. "I just thought it might explain something," he offered.

Her face was blank, but suddenly her eyes grew cold. "All these years," she said flatly. "All these years you rejected him, and now you come up with some paltry excuse for your bigotry?"

"I didn't—"

"I don't *care* about your explanations! Where were you all those years when he needed you? He tried and tried, but never once would you let down that stubborn, stupid arrogance." She stared at him, red-eyed and shaking. "You and my father. Neither of you is half the man Jorge is. I don't even know why you're here. You never wanted to be part of this family. Why don't you just go back to New York!" Rose buried her face in her hands and began to sob.

Kate and Allison, Carl's younger sister, both rushed forward to comfort Rose. Carl stood up and mutely looked at the three women, trying to decide what to do. They sat, huddled together on the sofa, embracing each other, comforting one another in hushed, low tones.

Desperate, he glanced around and found Alex looking at him from across the waiting room. She had on a rumpled, tan trenchcoat that belonged to Kate. Carl stood there for a moment staring at her in a kind of blank dismay. Then he broke away from her eyes and looked down at his mother.

"Come on, Rose," Kate was saying. "Ali and I will take you home. You need to get some rest."

"I won't go," Rose choked.

"Please, Mama," Ali implored. "The doctor says he can't do any more. We just have to wait. You haven't slept in almost two days and you're exhausted."

"I won't leave," Rose repeated.

"Then at least let us take you downstairs," said Kate. "The nurse says you can lie down on the sofa there. Come on, let me help you."

Kate and Ali guided Rose to her feet. Carl stepped forward to help, but Kate stopped him with a look and said, "We'll take care of her."

He nodded woodenly and watched them move off down the hall. Fatigue and humiliation covered him like a heavy blanket. Then he felt a light touch on his arm. "Hey," Alex said gently. "Why don't we go for a walk. I could use some fresh air."

CHAPTER

6

Outside the hospital, a thick haze had descended over the valley, and the late afternoon light was muted. Carl and Alex walked silently side by side for several blocks. Finally, Carl said, "She really hates me."

"She's tired," Alex replied. "Overwrought."

Carl shook his head. "I don't blame her. God, I've been such a fool."

"We're all fools, luv," said Alex.

"Think so?"

They were walking through a park. Rose bushes sported bright pink blossoms. Ahead, the dome of the capitol emerged from the gloom. Carl stopped and looked at Alex. "Can I buy you a drink?"

"You know a good place close by?"

"The best."

The original Casa Morales was five blocks south of the capitol. It was a modest adobe structure with a red tile roof and a hand-painted sign that announced *Casa Morales, A Taste of Old Mexico.* When they reached the weathered wood door Carl paused. "You know, I haven't been in here for at least fifteen years."

"Better late than never," Alex said.

They were quickly seated in a booth near the white-walled bar. A heavy-set man with graying hair and a thick mustache came out from behind the counter and hurried toward them. "We pray for your papa," he said.

Carl looked at him in amazement. "How did you know who I am?"

A huge grin captured the swarthy face. "How could I *not* know you? All over your papa's office, nothing but pictures of his famous son. I would know you anywhere, maestro!" Then his face darkened with concern. "Any news?"

"He's hanging on."

"Then he'll be okay. He's one tough man, your papa."

"You must be Gus," Carl said. "Jorge—my father—spoke of you often."

Gus laughed. "Nothing good, I hope."

"Everything good, I'm afraid."

"Well," Gus said, "now that you're here, what will you have? Or did you just come here to talk with this pretty lady?"

Carl introduced Alex and said, "What will you have, Alexandria?"

"I'll bet you make one heck of a margarita," Alex said to Gus.

"You bet. Fresh limes and the best tequila. None of that packaged stuff."

"On the rocks, please," Alex said.

Carl said, "I'll have the same."

While Gus was making the drinks, Carl told her, "I'm going to call the hospital and let Ali know where to reach us."

"Good idea."

When he came back to the table, Alex was already sipping her drink. "That's what I call a margarita," she told him as he dropped into the booth.

"Told you this was the best place in town."

They studied each other guardedly. Then Alex smiled and said, "So, Mr. Fitzgerald, what are you going to do with me?"

Carl stared at her for a moment, then grinned. He remembered that day in Lenox more than a decade ago when Marian had first introduced him to her daughter. "God, I was scared to death. You were what, twelve?"

"Eleven."

"Going on thirty."

"I was a prodigy, remember?"

"You were a force of nature, Miss Archer."

"Used to be."

She set her glass down and was quiet for a moment, then looked up and said, "So, what's going on in the Imperial City? I've kinda lost touch."

"Overkill as usual," Carl replied. "Serkin was at Carnegie Hall last week playing Beethoven for the bicentenary. The BSO did a new Dahl saxophone concerto—very intriguing. Stockhausen's going to be around at the end of the month to conduct a new work with the Philharmonic." He sipped his drink, then grinned. "And of course my new chamber orchestra has done a series of brilliant performances."

"What were you doing in London? Kate said you had to rush back when you heard about Jorge."

"Do you know Alan Hawthorne?"

"The composer? I've heard of him."

"Music Group of London was doing a new piece of his, and I was supposed to work with them. I've been doing a lot more with smaller groups since I got to New York. I really enjoy it."

Alex looked down at her hands. "That's something I've missed."

"What?"

"That feeling of belonging. It's like being a part of a tribe, you know? I thought I could live without it, but now I'm not so sure." She picked up her glass and swirled the liquid.

Carl studied her for a moment, then asked, "Why did you quit?"

"You know why I quit. I can't play."

"There are other things you could do."

She looked up at him sharply. "Like what?"

"Teach. Compose."

"Right. Those who can, do. Those who can't—"

"Teaching's a gift, Alex. And you have a fantastic background for it."

"Or, I could just pretend that performing is unnecessary. Become a hermit like Glen Gould." She finished her drink and put the glass aside. After a minute, she continued. "I had this strange dream the other night. I was in a great hall, like a cathedral. And Stefan was there. He was writing something, but I couldn't see what it was. I kept asking him to show it to me, but he just ignored me and I got furious. I shouted and stomped around and threw a regular fit, but he acted like he didn't know I was there. So I sat down and waited. I was determined that I wouldn't leave until he shared that writing with me.

"At first I was really impatient. But the longer I sat there, the calmer I got. Like all the confusion was slipping away. There was a grand, beautiful stillness. Like a little *pausa*, you know? That space between the music that makes the next note so much fuller? And I thought, 'This is the silence between the music of my life.' When I looked around, I realized I was alone. Stefan was gone, but that was all right somehow. I felt... peaceful."

Carl didn't respond for a moment. Then he said, "Have you really tried?"

"Tried what?"

"To play."

Alex looked away.

"Aren't there any therapies? Surgeries? Anything?"

She started to get up, but he caught her arm. "Listen to me, Alex. I know a doctor in San Francisco. He's been doing some exceptional work with musicians. He's at the Medical School. I think you should at least go talk to him."

"No!" She shook her head. "It's over."

"I don't believe that."

"Why not?"

"If you won't do it for me, then do it for Stefan. He was your teacher. You owe him something."

She lowered her head. "I owe him a lot."

"Here." He took out a pen and wrote the name on a napkin. "At least go talk to him."

She looked at the name, then nodded slowly and put the crumpled paper into the pocket of her coat. "Maybe."

Carl sat back and looked at her, a smile wiping the fatigue from his face. "Good," he said. He tipped his glass at her and finished his margarita.

"Maestro!" They heard Gus calling from across the room. "Quickly. Your sister is on the telephone."

The smile evaporated. "God almighty," Carl said as he got to his feet and hurried to take the call. A moment later, he came back to the booth. Alex tried to read his face but it was blank. Her heart sank.

"Is he—?"

Carl slapped a five dollar bill down on the table. "Come on," he said, grabbing her arm. "He's conscious. The doctor thinks he's going to be fine."

"Then why are you looking like that?"

"Ali said he was asking. . . for me. For *me*!"

"What's wrong with that?" Alex said, running to keep up with him.

"Nothing. Just. . . Oh, what the hell. Come on I've got to get to him right away!"

Jorge blinked up at the face bending over him, trying hard to bring it into focus through the haze of drugs. "Carlo?" he murmured. "Is that you Carlo?"

"Si, Papa. I'm here."

Jorge attempted a smile. "Carlo, twenty years it has been since you called me Papa."

"I know." Carl's voice was a rough whisper.

Jorge's hand inched across the surface of the sheet and trapped Carl's with his own, pressed gently. "Strong," Jorge murmured. "Even when you were little, your hands were so strong. Such wonderful hands."

"Don't try to talk, Papa. The doctor wants you to rest."

Jorge's hand tightened on Carl's. "You will be here when I wake up?"

"I'll be here. I promise."

"Rosita? She is here too? And Ali?"

"They're right outside."

Jorge's eyes closed, then drifted open. "I saw Silvio," he whispered. "He waved to me."

"Shhh," Carl said. "You need to rest."

Jorge struggled to speak. "No. I must tell you. He is all right, do you understand?"

Carl swallowed. "No."

"He loves you," Jorge said.

Overwhelmed, Carl put his head down on his father's shoulder. "I love him too," he said brokenly. "And you, Papa. I love you too."

In the hall outside the room, Carl found Rose and Ali huddled together. Rose smiled wanly when she saw her son and reached out to take his hand. "I'm sorry," she said. "I was so tired." He put his arms around her.

"Evening, folks."

A doctor dressed in blue scrubs came toward them. "I have good news."

The three figures gazed at the doctor in frozen expectation.

"Mr. Mortales has multiple contusions and several broken ribs, but the surgery was successful and there was very little damage to internal organs. There was a problem with fluid. We were concerned about pneumonia, but that's much better this evening, and there's no sign of any secondary infection. I'm certain that with a little rest and some physical therapy he'll be back in shape in a month or so."

Rose began to cry.

"Thank God," Carl breathed, hugging his mother tightly. "Thank God."

CHAPTER

7

Mockingbird Ranch
August 1970

"I had no idea things were this bad," Kate muttered, looking up from the ledger book. "Daddy must have spent a fortune on that last campaign."

Jaime, the ranch foreman, stood before her, twisting his hat unhappily. "Not just that, señora," he said. "Production was down last year because of the blight, and costs were up. We had to keep spraying the trees to stop the infection. Then in August we couldn't find enough pickers. The gypsies, they have all left and legal workers from Mexico are harder to find since the bracero program ended." He shook his head. "Labor. Irrigation."

He enumerated the problems on his fingers. "Taxes went up again and fertilizer and parts for the equipment. Madre! The prices they charge these days. I've tried to keep costs down, but that is hard to do."

"I'm not blaming you, Jaime," Kate said, sighing. "Obviously, growing pears just isn't a money-making business any more."

"The combines are the problem," Jaime said. "The small growers are being squeezed out. Your father always said it would be like this."

After the foreman left, Kate sat staring glumly at the ledger. Had it really come to this? Her great-grandfather's ranch, her father's pride and joy, reduced to a hobby farm supported by returns from real estate investments? How could a productive ranch be useful primarily as a tax shelter? How could you lose this much money growing food when there was a starving world out there? It didn't make sense.

I'll have to think of something, she told herself. *I hate the idea of running a deficit, but I won't consider selling. If I can just cover taxes and labor costs. . .* Maybe the income from American River Estates would cover the deficit. Ned Warren had approached her about selling her share of the project to him, but she would have to pay taxes on the payout. What should she do?

She snapped the book shut. She would wait until after the harvest, and then make a decision.

The mockingbird's singing woke her just as the sun was lifting above the mountains to the east. Kate lay still, listening to the bird's crazy chorus, savoring the air perfumed by acacia blossoms, their cotton candy scent wafting in through the open window. For just a moment, it seemed as though she had never left, that the events of the past decade had happened to someone else. Or never happened at all.

Downstairs, Consuelo greeted her with hot popovers and a bowl of fresh plum jam. "Where's Cory?" Kate asked between bites.

Consuelo laughed. "He and my Teresa, they been gone for an hour already. Took the horses and headed for the hills. I told them to be back in time for lunch."

Memories whirled as Kate finished her breakfast—the hills, the trails, the wine-dark smell of blackberries. "I think I'll go for a walk," she told Consuelo.

The family cemetery called to her and she wandered among the graves, reading the headstones. "Angus Randolph McPhalan. Maude Cahill McPhalan. Patrick Arthur McPhalan, a brave soldier, age twenty-one. Moira Moore McPhalan. Gone but not forgotten." Her voice broke a little as she read, "Julian Francis McPhalan, 1941-1963." And next to it, "Owen Everette McPhalan, 1908-1969." Her brother and her father, estranged in life and now lying next to each other for eternity.

She sat down beside a clump of golden poppies. Quail called to each other from the orchard. A monarch butterfly fluttered among the wildflowers. "Well, Pooh," she said, using Julian's old nickname. "Here I am. I left for a while, just like you said I would. But now I'm back. Maybe this time for good."

Julian had come home too, she thought, and wondered if his soul was peaceful now. Lying back, she looked up through the branches of the oak tree at the boundless California sky. Someday, she too could lie quietly, without regret, beneath the hard red clay. *But first,* she thought, *I need to figure out what I'm doing. I've made a new beginning, but where do I go from here?*

Two days later, Kate got a phone call from Carl. He was in LA and would like to visit her and Cory before returning to New York. Alex had recently accepted a position at the Music Conservatory in San Francisco and was in the City searching for an apartment, so the guest room was available. Why not?

When Carl arrived the next day, Cory ran to meet him as he stepped from Jaime's car. "Look Mama," Cory squealed with delight. "Daddy's a hippie!"

Kate stared with amused disbelief at the bearded stranger who stood before her. His hair was nearly shoulder length, tousled as ever, flecked with grey at the temples. Over the past two months, he had been completely transformed—familiar yet unfamiliar. Like an old friend she hadn't seen for years.

"Where are your love beads?" she teased.

"That's Ozawa's trademark," he said with a grin. The Japanese conductor was known for his casual style.

Kate tilted her head. "Actually, you look more like Arthur Nikisch," she joked, refering to the bearded Hungarian conductor.

"Better not tell them that at Boston."

"Oh, I don't know. Maybe they'd want to grab you now that Leinsdorf's left."

"I'm not their type," Carl said easily. "Besides, I like New York."

"Then I'm glad for you," Kate said. They looked at each other until she turned away. "Come on in. Do you need help with your luggage?"

"I'll get it later."

After lunch, Cory led Carl around the ranch, excitedly pointing out the vegetable garden, the corral for the mare Kate had given him, the tree house that Jaime had helped him build. The hills were turning red-gold in the setting sun when Kate saw them walking toward the house—a tall dark-haired man and a small blond-haired boy. She went to meet them. Carl paused and looked around at the deep green pastures, the orchards, the thickets of roses and wild mint. "Great place for kids," he said.

"Yes," said Kate.

"Better than the city, I suppose."

"I've always thought so."

They walked on silently for several minutes while Cory ran ahead. Then Kate said, "I've enjoyed watching Cory re-discover all the things I loved about this place—the river and the bluffs, the old trees and the tracks of birds and foxes. Did he tell you we've been going camping?"

"Yes. Said you'd be going again this weekend."

"So beautiful in the high country this time of year."

"I can imagine."

That evening she fixed a simple supper. Afterward, Cory fell asleep on the couch, leaning against his father and Carl carried him gently up to bed. When he came back, Carl poured himself a glass of wine and sat down opposite her. "Okay," he said. "Now we talk. When are you moving to New York?"

There comes a moment when you realize that delusions can no longer be permitted. "I'm staying on at Mockingbird," she told him.

"I won't accept that, Kate." Those beautiful dark eyes, so stubbornly refuting her.

"I belong here," she said quietly.

"You're my wife," he replied. "You belong with me."

"Not enough, Carl. Never was."

His brow furrowed. "I don't understand. What do you want from me? I know I've made mistakes. We've been through all that." He got to his feet and began to pace. "I'm to blame. I know that. And I'm sorry, so sorry." He stopped and looked at her. "I promise I'll make it up to you somehow."

"I'm not blaming you," she said. "I'm not asking for apologies or promises."

"Then what do you want?"

She let her breath out in a long sigh. "I want to find out who I am."

Exasperation sharpened his voice. "You've had every chance. Did I stand in your way when you wanted to finish college? I even let you get a job—"

"Listen to what you're saying, will you?" she cried. "You *let* me? Did I need to get *permission*?"

"I didn't mean—"

"It's not about what *you've* done, Carl," she said. "It's about what I *haven't* done. I don't want a life by default." As though her anger had brought the image into focus, she shook her head. "Oh, Carl, we're caught in the wrong time. Maybe *every* time is the wrong time, I don't know. But we've gotten caught in between, somehow. Things are different now."

He looked baffled. "What are you talking about?"

"I thought when I married you that I was a very liberated person. But you're not liberated just because you sleep with a man before you marry him or because he agrees to *let* you go to school."

Carl started to interrupt, but Kate raised her hand. "No, let me finish. The only way for any of us to be really liberated is to find out who we *really* are and live a life of our own choosing. I married—" The realization hit her like a shock wave. "I married the Royal Astronomer!"

"The what?"

"The prince. The knight in shining armor. I was supposed to live happily ever after. But it doesn't work like that. I married a life, and then I woke up one day and realized that the life was *yours*. *You* had the life, and I was just an. . . an *afterthought*."

"But what am I supposed to do?" he exclaimed. "Give up my music, my career? Is that what you want?"

"I don't want you to give up *anything* that's yours. But I have to think about what's *mine*. I want my own life and I don't think we can find a way to share. I need to be *here*. I need to be at Mockingbird. This is where I *belong*."

"I know you love this place," he said, "but does that mean you can't spend time in New York? You could come out here for the summer. Maybe I could—"

"Don't you see?" she cried. "What you're *saying* is the problem."

"What am I saying?"

"Mockingbird's not a vacation cabin. It's a way of life."

"But you don't always have to be here. Jaime and Consuelo can take care of the place."

"You're not listening to me!"

"Damn it, I'm trying to!"

She closed her eyes for a moment, then looked at him and said, "I don't know yet who I am, but I know one thing. Who I am is somehow tied up with this *place*. This piece of land. And I have to stay here until I've resolved this for myself."

He sat down and folded his arms. "I wish it had been Molnar," he said.

"What?" she asked, surprised.

"I'd have known how to deal with that. How to fight for you." His voice was muffled, as though his throat was holding back the words. "But how do I compete with. . ." His hand encompassed the room. "With all of this? I don't even know where to start."

Silently, she watched him struggle with his thoughts. Then he looked up and said, "What about Cory?"

"We'll work something out. Maybe he can stay with you part of the year."

"Kate," he said slowly, "are we talking about a divorce?"

"I don't know," she said.

"Is it really over for us?"

"All I can tell you is that I'm staying here. This is my home."

"And nothing I can do will change your mind?"

She shook her head.

"I can wait." The hope in his eyes saddened her. Suddenly he got up and put his arms around her, kissed her hair, ran his fingers along the side of her neck. She shuddered slightly and closed her eyes, felt his warm breath on her cheek. "Let's go to bed," he whispered.

"I don't think we—"

"Please?" His arms tighted around her, pressing her close. "It's been almost half a year."

She took a deep breath. "It won't change my mind."

"I know, but I just love you so damned much. For just a while, couldn't we be the way we used to be?"

She savored every instant—the feel of his body against hers, the silky tangle of his hair, the new delight of his beard. There was a gentleness and a sobriety to their lovemaking that made it almost a ritual.

Sometime before dawn, Kate woke and lay watching him for a long time as he slept. When she woke again it was light and the bed was empty. She sat up with a start, then heard the shower and slowly lay back down. He came in already dressed and said he had an early plane to catch. Jaime would drive him into Sacramento.

"Do you want coffee?" she asked, as she started to get up.

"Jaime's driving me to the airport. I'll get something there." He sat down on the edge of the bed. "I'm leaving for Salzburg at the end of the week, but I'll call before I go. Tell Cory I love him."

She nodded, not trusting herself to speak. He started to say something, then simply grasped her in his arms and held her tightly. "You'll come back to me," he whispered brokenly. "I know you will."

He kissed her and she smiled at him through tear-filled eyes. She heard his footsteps going down the stairs, heard the door open and close, his steps on the patio, the creak of the gate, the car starting.

And then he was gone.

CHAPTER

8

Santa Barbara, California

The Becker's patio was just as Kate remembered it, the swaths of bougainvillea, the wine barrels filled with lavender and geraniums, the worn terra cotta tiles. Before lunch, she had gone for a long horseback ride through mesquite-covered hills and meadows filled with wild nasturtiums, had dismounted and sat for a while in the eucalyptus grove where she and Stefan had talked. It seemed as near as yesterday and as far away as the beginning of time. Seven years. Seven, Stefan had always said, was the magic number.

"Would you like some more tea?" Verrie's voice interrupted her thoughts and she glanced up at the older woman's handsome face. Although she was not born in France, Veronique exhibited her French ancestry with her immaculate sense of style. Everything—the hair, the makeup, the clothes—always "just so."

"Please," Kate responded.

Verrie poured the tea and sat down next to Kate. "Now then," she said, "you must tell me how your work on Stefan's biography is proceeding. Armand and I are so pleased that you're working on such a wonderful project."

"I just hope I can do him justice," Kate said with a nervous laugh.

"I'm sure you will." Veronique smiled encouragingly.

Kate told Verrie about the painstaking research, the hours spent pouring over every scrap of paper she could find, every concert program and news clipping that Stefan had left behind. The interviews with colleagues and former students, with managers and rivals, the famous and the obscure.

"I want to be really thorough," Kate explained, "because I want the book to be more than a journalistic profile. I think, and my editor agrees, that what I can offer is a very *personal* portrait of the man, intimate without being sensational or lurid." She smiled. "I'm certainly not going to publish all those torrid love notes he got from his admirers."

Verrie laughed. "And I'm sure there were hundreds of them."

"Thousands," Kate agreed.

"You know," Verrie said, "he really was one of the most charming and charismatic men I've ever known. There are a lot of attractive men in the world and a number who are also quite talented, but Stefan was special. And he could break your heart with that smile of his."

"Yes," Kate said. "I know."

Verrie patted Kate's hand. "Well, my dear, sounds like you've really done your homework. I can't wait to read the results."

Kate shook her head. "I have tons of material, but there's still one piece of the puzzle that's missing, a very important piece."

"Oh? And what is that?"

Their eyes met. "Prague," Kate said.

Verrie nodded. "Prague."

Kate leaned forward. "I think I have a good grasp of his childhood in Budapest before the family moved to Czechoslovakia. Jean was able to tell me something about that, and so were several of his musician friends who had lived in Europe before the war. There were even a few photos, and a wonderful letter from his father in honor of Stefan's concert debut when he was six.

"But then there's this big empty space for the next five years. Just bits and scraps, not enough to make sense of. And there's no one left from that period. His mother, his father, his brother are all gone. Even the records have disappeared. I've talked to several people who were there at the time, even some who were interned in the camp at Terezin. But I can't find out *anything* specific about what happened to Stefan. He never spoke of it to Jean or to anyone else as far as I can tell. I'm totally at a loss." Kate's eyes searched Verrie's face. "Can you help me? Can you give me any leads?"

Veronique leaned back and folded her arms, her grey eyes fixed on the distant edge of the sea. She was silent for several minutes. Then she turned back to Kate and said, "There is one person who might know what happened during that period of Stefan's life."

"There is?" Kate said excitedly. "Who?"

"Armand," said Verrie.

CHAPTER

9

"Do you mind if I record this?" Kate asked. Late afternoon light streamed through the double windows that framed a view of the garden outside Armand's office.

Armand shook his head. "No, but I must insist that you destroy the tape after you have decided what to include in your book."

Kate's eyes widened. "All right."

Armand turned away from the window and sat down in the leather lounge chair next to his desk. Kate took a seat opposite him across the glass coffee table and set up her tape recorder. Then she glanced at him and said, "I'd be happy to send you the manuscript if you like. You can take out anything you find inappropriate."

Armand nodded. "Fair enough. However, before we start I should tell you that I have only a few more weeks to live. So you may have to serve as editor."

Kate stared in disbelief. How could this tall vibrant man with his bronzed skin and thick silver hair be dying? "I'm. . . sorry, Armand. I—"

He waved his hand dismissively. "Please. I didn't mean to alarm you, but you need to know exactly why I decided to do this interview." He paused and studied her. "Stefan was not formally a patient of mine, but I feel that what I am prepared to tell you today could be a breach of confidence. Still, if you are to present an adequate portrait of the man, it is imperative that you understand the depth of his neurosis. Therefore, I will tell you what I know." He gestured toward the recorder. "So, are you ready with your machine?"

"All set." Kate pushed the record button.

Armand paused for a moment, then began. "Stefan's family left

Budapest in 1939 just after Stefan's sixth birthday and only a few weeks prior to the German occupation. His father, Martin, had been offered a position at Charles University in Prague, and they thought they would be safer there than in Budapest. Maya, his mother, was from a well-to-do Czech family and they supposed that they would be immune from persecution. Unfortunately, they were wrong. The Nazis sealed the borders shortly thereafter, and for the next six years the family was trapped until the city was liberated in 1945.

"Now then, Maya's maternal grandfather had an estate outside Prague, and the family took refuge there. Stefan's father joined the Resistance almost immediately and went underground. The family did not see him again until 1945. They had occasional news of him through friends, but they didn't know from day to day if he was dead or alive. Meanwhile, the Nazis took over the estate and an officer commandeered the house for his headquarters."

Armand poured himself a glass of sherry from the decanter on the coffee table. Kate waited, watching him, not wanting to interrupt.

"So," Armand continued, "Maya's grandfather found himself a prisoner in his own home with no power to protect his granddaughter and her children. Stefan, you may recall, was only six at the time, but he quickly surmised that the survival of the family depended on placating the Nazis.

"Well, as it turned out, the officer who had commandeered the estate was an ardent music lover who had already heard of Stefan's talent. He immediately befriended the child, insisted that he be allowed to practice, even found teachers who could work with him. Oh yes, he was quite encouraging. In return, he asked only. . ." Armand paused and smiled bitterly, ". . . only obedience. And gratitude."

He was silent for so long that Kate finally said, "Obedience? What did Stefan have to. . . do?"

Armand stirred, and sipped his wine. "Could have been worse, I suppose. The man could have assaulted him, tortured him, killed him outright. But there are more subtle forms of torture, aren't there? He required Stefan to be his. . . *friend*. And Stefan realized that if he wanted his family to stay alive, he had better comply as best he could.

"So for five years he played recitals for this Nazi, he went riding with him, played chess with him, ate at his table, laughed at his jokes. He knew this man was an enemy, the enemy of his father, a monster who was holding prisoner those he loved. And yet he had to pretend to be the monster's friend." He shook his head sadly. "Can you imagine the ambivalence? The confusion? The conflict in a child of six, seven, eight? He had to rely on this man for everything, to appease him, flatter him. He had to. . . love him. And perhaps, after all, he *did* love him. But he would have to loathe himself, would he not, for loving his father's enemy?"

"That's horrible," Kate managed to say.

Armand sighed. "There is more. Stefan believed that his actions would keep his mother and brother safe. In his mind, he had made a pact with the devil, sold his soul if you will, to protect those he loved. It was only later, when he began to understand the things that he had seen and heard, that he realized that his mother and brother had been forced to provide sexual favors to the Nazi, probably to insure Stefan's safety."

At this, Kate's throat squeezed into a knot and for a moment she thought she would be sick.

"For Stefan, that would have been a profound failure. His acquiescence to the demands of his father's enemy had not saved his loved-ones from humiliation and dishonor. And so, he buried this revelation."

Kate stared at him. "What do you mean?"

"When we experience something that is so contradictory, so traumatic, that we cannot bear to consciously think about it, we blot it out. This is referred to as repressed memory, or more clinically, *dissociative amnesia*. Stefan couldn't bear to think that his complicity had been in vain."

"But he was just a child," Kate said. "How could a little boy understand something so twisted, so. . . perverse?"

"Ah," said Armand, "you are looking for logic. Guilt is not logical. And the next blow came in 1948 when his father died. Stefan, his mother, brother and grandfather had escaped to Switzerland, but his father stayed behind to fight against the Communists. Stefan was fourteen. He begged his father to let him stay and fight, but Martin refused. He said he would join them in Switzerland, and told Stefan to look after Janos and Maya. They never saw him again."

"So once more, Stefan was faced with being responsible for his family," said Kate.

"Precisely." Armand sighed and shook his head. "Things were difficult in Geneva. I don't know how much you know about what happened to refugees at that time, but they were not exactly welcomed with open arms. The Swiss refused to grant them work permits or access to housing and medical care.

"Stefan and his family were luckier than most. They had friends in the music world who gave them a place to stay, a tenant house on an estate. Stefan's grandfather was an accomplished horseman so he was put in charge of the stables while Stefan and Janos helped out with the chores. Maya worked in the kitchen.

"Then Stefan met François Dumond, a musician who had left France during the occupation and had stayed on in Geneva." Armand peered at Kate over his glasses. "You know, of course, about François?"

Kate nodded. "He was a great help with Stefan's career."

"Indeed he was. He was also a great friend to Stefan and his family. That became especially significant because shortly after Stefan began his studies with François, his mother suffered a heart attack that left her an invalid. With François's help they were able to get medical care for her, but it was very expensive. Suddenly the family was faced with enormous bills and no money."

"Isn't that when Stefan began playing concerts again?" said Kate.

Armand nodded. "Concerts and then more concerts. He made recordings, drove himself incessantly. But of course he couldn't make his mother well no matter how many concerts he played, no matter how good the reviews were. He had failed to protect his mother from sickness, and he could not restore her health."

"And then François was killed in a boating accident." Kate recalled.

"That's right. However, Stefan's reputation continued to grow, and he was more and more in demand. He paid the bills, put his brother through school. But it was never enough."

"And then there was Clara," Kate said.

"And then Clara," Armand agreed. "And Janos, of course. A repetitive pattern. Everyone that he loved seemed cursed by misfortune. He told me once that he could not help but believe he was to blame. He felt he was being punished. I think that it was just toward the last that he began to work his way out of the hell he'd lived through, to stop hating himself for things he couldn't control or change."

"He did seem more at ease the last time I saw him," Kate remembered. "He said he'd spent some time in a monastery in Japan."

Armand smiled and sipped his wine. "We talked about that the last time I saw Stefan. It was good to see him feeling so positive. If only he'd had a little more. . . time."

Armand lapsed into silence and for several minutes they both sat quietly looking out the window at the garden.

Kate reached to turn off the recorder, but she stopped. Then she sat back and looked at Armand. "There's one thing I don't understand," she said.

He glanced at her. "Yes?"

"You said that Stefan had repressed the memory of his mother's forced liaison with the Nazi officer."

"Yes?"

Kate frowned. "So then, how did *you* know about it?"

Armand gazed at her for a moment and then took a deep breath. "Because," he said softly, "*I* was that Nazi officer."

After a moment of stunned silence Kate managed to gasp "You? But. . . but how is that *possible*?"

Armand looked down at his hands. After a moment he said in a low voice, "My name is Werner Hoffmann. I grew up in Freiburg. In 1938 I joined the German army and became an officer. I participated in the occupation of Czechoslovakia and was put in charge of administering several army units in the Prague area. I took over the

Sedlak family residence, Maya Molnar's family estate, to use as my office and base of operations. I stayed there until March of 1945." He looked up at Kate. "How do I know? Because I was there. *I* am the monster who did those heinous things. And I have tried for twenty-five years to atone for my sins."

Kate stared at him wide-eyed, trying to process what she was hearing. She felt as though she had stepped off the edge of a precipice and was falling in slow motion with nothing to grab onto. Was she dreaming?

Armand got to his feet and began to pace, his hands behind his back. "I was not political, exactly. I didn't care much for ideology. But I came from a middle class family that had essentially bet everything they had on me, and I wanted to make them proud. After I graduated from university, I was recruited by the German army and offered a career path as an officer. At the time, I thought it was a logical decision. So, for the next seven years I did what was expected of me. I was a soldier. I dealt with the. . . enemy."

He stood still for a moment, then ran his fingers through his hair and began once more to pace back and forth. "Then, two months before the Russian offensive, I deserted. It was clear by that time that Germany would lose the war, and I decided I would take my chances and try to escape. I had gotten word that my parents and my younger brother had been killed in one of the many bombing raids on Freiburg, so there was no reason for me to try to go home. Instead, I made my way west toward Stuttgart which was by then under American control. I had a cousin in Stuttgart and thought he might help me.

"Everything was in chaos. The Germans were evacuating prisoner-of-war camps and marching the captives through the countryside. There were thousands of refugees. I lost myself in the flood of displaced people. I followed the rivers—the Elbe and then later the Danube—to have some idea where I was going. It was like. . . like wandering through hell. Everything was so. . . broken. Mine fields. Bombed out villages. . ."

Armand paused and stared straight ahead in a sightless moment of remembrance. Then he took a breath and continued. "Once in Stuttgart, I contacted my cousin. We. . ." Again he hesitated. "We searched through the ruins of a nearby village. In the basement of a house that had been bombed we discovered the bodies of a family. The man—the father—was about my size. He still had his identification papers. So I took them. At that moment I became Armand Becker.

"With my cousin's help, I had myself. . . medically altered. Even my fingerprints. My cousin helped me obtain additional documents from the Red Cross. Quite literally, I turned into a different man."

He stopped and looked at Kate. "I wanted only to begin a new life, to have a second chance. To somehow make up for what I had done." He gave a mirthless laugh. "Mr. Hyde became Dr. Jekyll."

Again he began to pace. "I wanted to run as far away as I could. So I made my way further west and managed to reach Le Harve. I found a job as a deck hand on a steamer and ended up in Barbados. I decided to stay and was offered a position teaching French at a local school.

"Not long after that I met Veronique. We fell in love and were married. Her family was very generous to me and encouraged my ambition to become a doctor. I went to medical school in Jamaica and then in France.

"After that, Verrie and I moved to Southern California to be near her family. They had sold their estate in Barbados and returned to the U.S., so we moved to Santa Barbara. I practiced there for several years, and then had the opportunity to attend the Jung Institute in Geneva, so we moved to Switzerland for four years before returning to Santa Barbara where we have lived for the past fifteen years." He stopped, sank into the lounge chair and poured another glass of sherry. "And so," he said, "now you know my story."

"My God," Kate said, her voice thick with anguish. "Who else knows about this?"

"No one."

"Not even Veronique?"

"She knows only the lies I have told her. That I was from Alsace. That I fought in the French Resistance. That I was a. . . hero."

Kate struggled to find words. "But, what about Stefan? You said you met him again in Geneva, you became his patron, his friend. Didn't he recognize you?"

"Amazing, isn't it? I thought so too at the time. You can well imagine my trepidation as I stood in line after the recital that night in Geneva, waiting to congratulate Stefan on his performance. Surely, I thought, he will recognize my eyes, my voice, something. I don't know why I felt compelled to confront him. I was terrified, but something pushed me to take the risk.

"But as I shook his hand and told him how much I enjoyed his magnificent performance of Beethoven's Sonatas, he looked directly at me and smiled in a warm, jovial way and thanked me graciously. Even later at the reception, when I invited him to have dinner with Veronique and me he was charming and friendly, but a little reserved, as one would be with a new acquaintance. My God, I thought, he really doesn't know who I am. My doctors had done their work so well that I was completely transformed. Or perhaps his mind simply refused to access the memory. I will never know which."

Again he lapsed into silence. After a moment he said, "I've asked myself again and again, *why*. Why did we do it? If we could have said 'no,' then why didn't we? Yet, no one refused. I didn't hate Jews. Or Americans. I simply did as I was told. My final question, which I will have to answer very soon now, is still 'why?'"

Armand downed the rest of the sherry in one swift gulp and sat the glass down. He gestured toward the recorder that sat on the table. "I will leave you to decide what you should put in your book because for me it is no longer relevant. But for others. . ." He looked away and sighed. "For others, it may be."

CHAPTER

10

Sacramento, California
September 1970

The tall, heavy-set man rose to his feet and waved to Kate from across the crowded patio.

"Jerry!" Kate cried, making her way through the maze of glass-topped tables and chattering diners toward the shaded alcove. "Great to see you!"

Jerry McClosky hugged her with unabashed enthusiasm. "You look terrific, Katie," he beamed. "California must agree with you."

"Always has," Kate returned. "Gosh, I was surprised to get your call."

"And why is that? You've always been one of my favorite people." He grinned at her. "Damn, you are one fine-looking woman."

"You, sir, are as full of it as ever. But thanks anyway."

He pulled out a chair for her, waited until she'd settled in, then sat down across the table from her. They ordered lunch and talked about Jerry's new house, Marian's latest art show, Stefan's death, and the latest films of Bergman and Truffaut. Over coffee, Kate said, "Correct me if I'm wrong, Jerry, but I don't really believe you drove all the way to Sacramento just to have lunch with an old friend."

"No? Not even a beautiful gal like you?"

"Not unless you have an ulterior motive."

Jerry laughed. "Okay, I'll admit it. I'm trying to seduce you."

Kate studied him thoughtfully and saw the twinkle in his small, bright eyes. "We've known each other for years, Jerry. What took you so long?"

"My sense of fair play. Never make a pass at a client's wife"

"Uh huh. Especially if the client's a gold mine?"

He shrugged. "My doctor assures me I'm not in this business for my health."

"Now we're getting somewhere."

"Okay, you got me. I have a question and you might have an answer."

"Shoot."

"It concerns Carl."

"You know we're getting divorced."

"Yeah, but you're still probably closer to him than anybody."

"So what do you want to know?"

Jerry rubbed his chin. "Rumor has it Ozawa's leaving San Francisco. I'd like to see Carl take over as music director and principal conductor of the symphony, but I don't know if he'd be interested."

"Why don't you ask him?"

"Because, Carl doesn't have much sense about this kind of thing. We both know he's made some truly lousy decisions. I was all for his move to New York, but I can't see him staying on as director of a little chamber orchestra forever. He's been there almost a year. I think it's time he moved on, and the San Francisco position is perfect."

Kate shook her head. "I don't know, Jerry. He really loves New York. He's teaching a class at Julliard, and he still has the Salzburg position."

Jerry's forehead knotted. "Don't think we could lure him back to California?"

"Maybe, but he likes the innovative atmosphere in New York."

"But there's great stuff happening out here. Have you heard about the New Music Center at Stanford? Pretty exciting. And there's a growing audience for experimental music in the Bay Area."

Kate patted Jerry's hand. "Why don't you call him?"

Jerry was quiet for a minute, pondering, tracing little circles in the ring of water left by his wine glass. "Damn," he muttered. "I'd sure like to get him back out here. At least on a part-time basis." He smiled wryly. "Too bad we don't have something like the Berkshire Music Center. He's always loved Tanglewood. If we had something comparable, I'll bet we could get him to run it."

Kate took a sip of espresso. "I've often wondered why nothing like Tanglewood happened out here. You'd think the San Francisco orchestra would love to have a summer headquarters. And the weather's so much better here than it is back east."

"Well," said Jerry, "I guess the right place just hasn't turned up. Would have to be really special, something with a sense of history. Far enough away from the City to have a unique identity, but close enough to be accessible."

Kate sat up straight.

"Should have some amenities in the area," he continued. "B&B's, restaurants, antique shops." He gave her a quizzical look. "Katie, why are you staring at me like that?"

"Jerry, I've just had the most phenomenal idea!"

"What?"

"Mockingbird!"

"Your ranch?"

"Yes!"

He sat back and gave her a puzzled look.

"Don't you see?" she cried. "It would be absolutely perfect!"

"But Mockingbird's your home, Kate," he protested. "You're not exactly an aging dowager wanting to dispose of the family estate."

"Listen to me, Jerry. There's over seven hundred acres at Mockingbird, and a bunch of buildings that could be remodeled for practice rooms, classrooms, offices. And the old barn would make a grand little recital hall. We could start off modestly—a few summer concerts and workshops. If we showcase first-rate artists, we're sure to draw a crowd. You probably think I'm crazy, but why couldn't we make this happen?"

"Hold on," Jerry laughed. "Are you serious?"

"I've never been more serious in my life. Look," Kate continued, "I've been trying to figure this out for the past year. Not the music center idea, that just hit me, but trying to figure out what to do with Mockingbird. I don't want to sell to developers. But things are changing. There are new subdivisions and shopping centers and freeways everywhere. The ranch has been losing money the last few years, and this year's harvest was marginal at best. We barely covered expenses. I'm sad to say the ranch is actually a better tax shelter than a producing farm. I've been trying to think of how to set up some kind of non-profit enterprise or something and suddenly here it is, right in front of me."

"Okay," Jerry said slowly. "How do you see this working?"

"Well, I'd have to work out the details. Maybe I could set up a foundation and then deed most of ranch to it. I'd keep fifteen or twenty acres for myself. I could maintain a life interest in the estate with Cory as beneficiary. We probably would want to stipulate that a family member would always be on the board of directors and. . ." She sat back and took a deep breath. "What do you think?"

Jerry's face broke into a broad grin. "I think you may be onto something."

"Really? You don't think I'm crazy?"

"Every great reality started out as somebody's crazy idea. Why not try?"

Kate toasted him with her espresso. "To Mockingbird."

Jerry raised his glass. "To the American River Music Festival at Mockingbird."

"I like the sound of that."

"So do I." He leaned forward and tapped on the table. "We need to put together a committee to start working on this. Why don't I make up a list of suspects and send it to you by Monday?"

"I'll call Jean Molnar and Veronique Becker and see what they have to say," Kate offered.

"You know," said Jerry, "we're going to need a really tight proposal to get funding—a renovation plan, cost estimates, solid specs on buildings and equipment. Know anybody who might help us out?"

A slow smile spread across Kate's face. "As a matter of fact," she said softly, "I think I know *exactly* the right person."

CHAPTER

11

San Francisco, California

A week later, Kate drove to San Francisco, located the address on Montgomery Street, and rode the elevator up to the twelfth floor. The receptionist, a smartly dressed woman with cropped silver hair, looked up and smiled. "May I help you?"

"I'm here to see Mr. Ashida," Kate said.

"You must be Mrs. Fitzgerald. He told me to expect you."

"That's right."

"He's stepped out for a few minutes, but he'll be right back. Please, make yourself comfortable."

She indicated one of the sleek Eames chairs next to the window. "Can I get you a cup of coffee?"

"No, thank you." Kate sat down and looked around the office. The carpet was charcoal grey, the walls white, the chairs covered in plum-colored leather. A Sam Francis print hung above the glass-topped side-table. On the opposite wall was a large charcoal drawing of Christo's "Valley Curtain," signed by the artist. Through the floor-to-ceiling windows she could see boats moving like toys across the silver surface of the Bay. A bank of fog hung lazily across the Golden Gate.

When a few minutes later the door opened and Tommy stepped into the office, Kate wondered for an instant if she would have recognized him had he passed her on the street. His face was thin and haggard, cheeks hollowed, eyes circled with shadows. A white streak, like a lightning bolt, slashed across the front of his black hair.

Then he saw her and smiled, and his face was at once familiar. He crossed the room and took her hand in both of his. "Kate," he said, "really good to see you."

"It's been a long time, hasn't it?"

"Far too long. How are you? You look wonderful."

She tried to smile. "Thanks. I'm doing okay." She hesitated, then added. "I heard about your wife. I'm so very sorry."

Tommy nodded. "So am I." For a moment their eyes met and held each other, then he said, "I want to hear all about this project of yours. How about if we talk over lunch? I made a reservation at the Fairmount."

"Super. I'm starved."

"I'll be back around three," he told the receptionist as he and Kate headed for the door.

Over Sole Meuniere Kate told Tommy about her plans for Mockingbird. He listened, his eyes never leaving her face. "And I'm hoping that you might be available to work on this," she concluded. "I want everything to be the best. And, well, that would be you."

He leaned back, studied her for a moment, then said, "I take it you've moved back to California?"

"That's right."

"And Carl?"

"He's in New York."

He waited.

She lowered her head. "We're getting divorced."

"I see." For several moments they were both silent, focusing on lunch. Then Tommy looked up and said, "That must be hard on your son."

Kate put her fork down and nodded. "Cory loves the ranch, but he misses his friends and he talks a lot about Carl. I know he misses him too."

"How old is Cory?"

"He'll be six in a couple of months."

"God," Tommy smiled and shook his head. "Has it really been that long?"

"Really has."

Kate took a sip of wine and studied her companion. Noting the perfectly tailored dark blue suit, the immaculate white shirt, the jade cufflinks, she said, "You don't look much like that dusty farm boy I used to know."

He grinned. "Believe me, I'd trade this get-up in a second for a pair of jeans and a tee shirt if I thought I could."

"What's stopping you?"

"I don't know. Habit, maybe. I've buried myself in my work for so long I don't know how to quit."

"Tired of success?" Her tone was light but guarded.

"Has its moments, but. . ." He shifted in his chair and looked away. "Everything seems so damned pointless." His voice was low and strained. "Ever since Miko died I've felt as though I'm just going through the motions, filling up the time to keep from. . . I don't know."

Kate nodded.

He glanced at her and said, "Rough year."

The darkness was there again, covering his face like a veil. She tried to think of some way to console him, but he had pulled inside himself so suddenly, so completely, that she stayed silent.

Then in an instant the darkness lifted and he smiled at her and said, "I think your project sounds wonderful. And I'm truly pleased you thought of me."

"Then you'll consider helping us?"

He hesitated. "I'd like to."

Kate blurted. "So, what do we do now? When can you start?"

Tommy laughed. "You haven't changed a bit. I was always amazed by the way you'd dive right in the minute we got to the river, and there I'd be wading in one toe at a time."

"I guess caution never has been my strongest suit," Kate agreed. "When I know what I want, I just go for it."

"And you really want this music festival? It'll take lots of work."

"I know. But I think the West Coast needs a place to rival Tanglewood and Wolftrap. And what a way to keep Mockingbird intact. I'd hate to sell the family ranch to developers."

"That sounds familiar," Tommy mused.

Kate blushed. "Yeah. That's my daddy talking."

The waiter came and took their plates away. Tommy brushed at some crumbs with his napkin, then glanced up and said, "Do you have a construction budget in mind?"

Kate set her empty wine glass down. "That's why I need you. We have to get some idea of the cost." She continued excitedly, "Do you know Verrie Becker, Armand Becker's widow?"

"Armand Becker. Let's see. The gospel according to Jung?"

Kate laughed. "That's the one."

"Let's say I know *of* him. I didn't know he'd passed away."

"A few weeks ago. He was interested in the idea of a west-coast music festival, and Verrie has agreed to be chair of our fund-raising committee. She's convinced she can bring in close to a million dollars by next summer. We can use that as a match to go after grant funding."

"Impressive."

"Does that provide additional incentive?" She tilted her head and grinned at him.

The waiter arrived with the bill and while Tomy signed the receipt Kate gathered up her purse and coat.

"Tell you what," Tommy said, getting to his feet. "Give me two weeks two finish up my current project, and I'll see what I can do."

Tommy held her coat for her and waited for her to gather up her notes, then followed her across the dining room to the elevator. Outside the hotel lobby, the afternoon was blue and brisk. A cable car rumbled past, bell clanging. "Still my favorite city," Kate said.

Tommy nodded.

At the entrance to his office building she took his hand and gave it a quick squeeze. "Take care," she said. "And call me."

"Two weeks. You can count on it." He hesitated, then said, "I'll need to make a site visit. After all, I haven't been to Mockingbird for over ten years."

"Still beautiful and peaceful. The river hasn't changed a bit," she told him. "You can come up for a visit anytime." Once more their eyes met. "I'm glad you want to do this, Tommy. I don't know what I'd have done if you'd said no."

Tommy shrugged. "You'd have found yourself another architect."

CHAPTER

12

San Francisco, California
October 1970

On a brilliant October morning three weeks later, Tommy rose early, put on an old Kyoto Institute of Technology sweatshirt and a pair of jeans, took the tarp off his new Datsun 240-Z, and headed east toward the mountains.

The Bay was magnificent—blue almost to blackness—and the hills were beginning to turn green from the first autumn rains. He sped past the little valley towns of Fairfield and Davis, then past the golden dome of the Capitol, and into the foothills of the Sierra.

A peaceful, honeyed warmth took hold of him with each passing mile. His mind became as clear as the cloudless sky. For almost a year he had lived alone, done his work, spent his evenings going over projects until, finally exhausted, numbed by fatigue, he was able to fall asleep. The darkness had stayed with him day and night.

But after his meeting with Kate, he went home early from the office. Instead of heading for his studio, he walked into the garden. Looking around, he noticed beds left untended, weeds between the rocks. He spent the weekend restoring the plot to its former pristine beauty. Then he called his cousin Ben and they went out for dinner. *So this is what food tastes like*, he thought. The world was a revelation.

He stopped the car at the crest of a hill. For fifteen minutes, he sat looking down at Mockingbird. Fresh snow glinted on the mountain peaks to the east. The trees were bare, but beneath the network of naked branches, purple vetch was beginning to spread. The air had a clean, sweet scent. He could hear the river whispering in the distance.

Kate met him at the courtyard gate. He followed her into the house and stood looking around. "You haven't changed things much," he said.

"I painted the walls and put down some new carpet," she told him. "Otherwise it's still the same old place. Would you like some tea?" she added.

"Sure." He glanced around the living room. "I see you still have the piano," he called to her.

"Cory's taking lessons," she answered from the kitchen. "He's no Mozart, but he loves playing and has a good ear. And yes, I still give Chopin a go now and then."

"Where is Cory?"

She emerged from the kitchen and handed him a cup of Orange Pekoe. "Staying at a friend's house at Lake Tahoe. He's decided he wants to learn to ski, and it's supposed to snow this weekend."

"I'd love to meet him."

"You will." She sat down on the sofa and smiled at him.

Tommy sat down and sipped the tea, watching her over the rim of his cup. She was just as he remembered her—freckles scattered across her nose, red-gold hair cascading to her waist. A milky-skinned beauty dressed like a field hand in jeans and a flannel shirt. His throat ached at the memory.

"Take a look at this," she said, leaning down and pulling a fat blue binder from under the coffee table. "Let me show you what I've put together so far."

Noon came and went and they still sat, leaning over the table, scribbling notes, making sketches.

"I think you're right about the barn," Tommy said. "It would make a wonderful recital hall, and I think I know a way to work out the seating without messing up the acoustics. Here, I'll show you." He began another sketch but felt Kate's eyes on him and looked up. "What?"

"You must be starved," she said solemnly.

He gave her a blank look and then laughed.

"It's after two, for God's sake," she said.

"And I have lunch all ready and waiting in the fridge."

They demolished cold roasted quail, tangy goat cheese, sourdough bread, golden pears, and then spent the rest of the afternoon tramping around the ranch, discussing possible sites for class rooms, administrative offices, parking lots.

Shadows lengthened and the light was turning gold when Kate finally said, "I don't know about you, but I think I've had enough for one day."

"And I've got enough notes to keep me busy for six months," Tommy declared.

"I'll start dinner," said Kate. "I hope you still like abalone."

"Some things never change." Suddenly serious, he added, "Would you mind taking these notes back to the house? I'd like to have a look at the river."

She watched him walk away, head down, hands shoved deep in his pockets, heading for the bluff.

An hour later he still hadn't returned. It was nearly dark as Kate made her way up the dirt road that wound between the shadowed groves. A half moon sat grandly in the eastern sky. She felt a rush of relief when she spotted him at the top of the hill, sitting with his back against a tree, looking down into the canyon. "I used to come up here almost every morning," he said as she drew near.

"I know." She sat down next to him.

"I'd read this story about the Indians and one of the characters went on a vision quest and saw a white buffalo. When he told the shaman, the old man said that to see a white buffalo was a very powerful vision. He said that the young man would be blessed with great happiness and that all his best dreams would come true. So every morning I'd come up here and look and look, hoping one day I'd see that buffalo."

"And did you?"

"No." He laughed softly. "I saw a white horse once, but I guess that didn't count."

"Oh, I don't know. I expect a white horse vision is pretty good too."

They were both silent for a minute, listening to the river. Then

Tommy said, "Are you planning to live here after the property is turned into a music center?"

"Yeah. I thought I'd keep fifteen or twenty acres on the bluff. Thought I might build myself a house up here." She glanced up and met his eyes. "Then every morning I can watch the sun come up. . ."

". . . from behind the Range of Light," he finished.

She caught her breath. "Yes."

Tommy looked away.

I hurt him, she thought. *I always seem to hurt him.*

He sighed softly and leaned back against the trunk of the oak tree. "So good to be here."

"To be home?"

He glanced at her. "I can't say that. I don't have the right."

"You have as much right as I do. You grew up here just like I did."

"Yeah."

"And cared for the land as much as I did."

"Yeah."

"Tommy?"

He looked up and met her eyes. She said, "Why don't you stay here? At least while you're working on this project."

She had to lean toward him to hear his reply. "Thanks for the offer, but I'm snot sure I'm. . . ready. Understand?"

"Of course." She got to her feet and held out her hand. He took it and she helped him up. Side by side, they walked down the hill toward the ranch house. "Hey Tommy," she said softly, "if ever you're ready, you're welcome to come home."

CHAPTER

13

Mockingbird Ranch
November 1970

There was something about an autumn morning—a freshness in the air, a chill settling in the low spots, tufts of mist rising from the canyon, new snow catching the first light on the peaks of the Sierra.

Kate smiled, turned away from the window and pulled her bathrobe more tightly around her. The house was still dark and quiet and smelled of candle wax and cinnamon. And just-brewed coffee. She poured a cup and sat down at the kitchen table.

The notepad from the previous evening caught her eye, and she read over the scribbled message that she'd left for herself—a to-do list to start the process that would transform Mockingbird Valley Ranch into the Mockingbird Music Center. So many notes! But the first thing was the cost estimate she needed to organize a realistic budget for the project.

"Call Tommy!" said entry number one.

It had been over two weeks since he'd visited Mockingbird and gathered the architectural specs and other information he needed for a preliminary estimate. Wouldn't hurt to give him a gentle poke. She glanced at the clock. Eight forty-five. He would surely be awake, even on a Saturday.

She got up, crossed the room, and picked up the fat blue binder with Mockingbird Music Center written in felt-tipped marker on the cover. She set the binder on the table and grabbed the phone from the counter. Okay. The number should be right here on the first page.

Yes. "Four one five . . ." she read the number aloud as she dialed, sat back and waited while the ring tone sounded.

"Hello?"

"Hi, Tommy. It's Kate."

"Hey."

His voice sounded strange. Tight and thin as though he was holding his breath. "I didn't wake you, did I?" she asked.

"No, I'm just a little. . . tired."

"I'm sorry. I wanted to ask about the estimates for the renovations, but I can call back later."

"No, it's okay. Let me just . . .get my. . . Oh, Jesus. . ."

"Tommy?" she said. "What's going on? Are you all right?" She heard something drop and a crash of broken glass. "Tommy?" There was no response. "Tommy?!"

Silence.

"Oh no. No!" she muttered. He must have fallen. Or maybe he was sick. What should she do? She should go to him, see if he was okay. But San Francisco was a two-hour drive, and she realized with sudden panic that she didn't know his home address. She banged down the receiver, then dialed the operator. "For Tommy Ashida," she said. "Do you have an address? . . . No, that's his office. Do you have a residence address?"

"I'm sorry, miss. That's all we have."

Cold panic engulfed her. *Okay, think! Who would know?* Frantically, she dialed his office number. "Hello," the machine voice said. "You have reached Ashida and Associates. Please call us back during office hours, Monday through Friday 8 a.m. to 5 p.m. If you'd like to leave a message. . ." Saturday. Of course no one was there.

What about his family in Stockton? She got the number for Ashida Produce Company and dialed. "Come on. Pick up!" she muttered.

"Ashida Produce. How can we help you?"

"This is Kate Fitz. . .I mean Kate McPhalan in Auburn. I'm a friend of Tommy's."

"Oh, sure. I remember. How nice to hear from you. This is Tommy's Aunt Pearl."

"Pearl, you've got to help me. I think Tommy's sick or hurt. I was talking to him on the phone and suddenly he... stopped. I don't know what happened."

"Oh, my goodness!"

"Do you have his address? I thought maybe I should send an ambulance or does he have a friend that could go see if he's okay?"

"My son, Ben, is in San Francisco," Pearl said. "I'll call him right away."

"Please let me know what happened!" Kate cried.

"Of course, dear. What's your number?"

Kate gave Pearl the number, then sat for an hour watching the phone, panic rising around her like a fast tide.

San Francisco Medical Center, San Francisco

Deep, translucent blue, everywhere, enveloping him like a pool of sweet water that wavered slightly. Little ripples seemed to sigh and sway, a dreamy song he couldn't quite hear.

Then Connie, his mother, was there, smiling at him, nodding her head. "That's right," she said. "Everything is okay. Just remember what I told you, 'When one door closes, another one opens.'"

He struggled to reply, but she faded back into the blue light.

"Tommy?" The voice seemed to come from far away. "Tommy?"

His eyes blinked open. Where was he? What was going on? Who was calling to him? He squinted into the hazy light, tried to focus on the face that floated above him. Was he dreaming? "Kate?" he tried to say but it was more a groan.

"Hey," she said. "I'm here."

He tried to wake up, to move, but he seemed immobilized. Little plastic tubes enveloped him. He frowned and tried to remember what had happened. He recalled that the phone rang and he answered and then everything went black. "Where..." he tried to say, but the sound was a fuzzy rasp and he realized there was a tube in his throat.

"It's okay," Kate said. He felt her fingers stroking his arm. "You're going to be all right."

"His vitals are good," someone said. "He needs to rest. You can come back in an hour."

Kate squeezed his hand. "We'll be back."

The light was turning gold and liquid. He closed his eyes and drifted.

"That was a pretty close call," the doctor said. Dr. Hill was a respected cardiovascular surgeon on the staff at the hospital. "A few more minutes and we could have lost him."

Kate glanced at Tommy's cousin, Ben Ashida. "Thank God you were home when Pearl called."

Ben nodded. He turned to Dr. Hill. "What exactly happened?"

"An aortic aneurysm," the doctor explained, "Basically, a ruptured artery. In this case, the aneurysm occurred in the chest cavity. The event triggered a myocardial infarction—a heart attack. But the surgery was successful. We were able to repair the ruptured artery. There was damage to the heart muscle, but that will heal over time. We don't see any additional complications. No neurological or renal damage."

"What caused it?" Ben asked.

Dr. Hill shrugged. "There can be several different causes—high blood pressure, injury to the artery, a congenital abnormality. I'm not sure in this case. We didn't find evidence of atherosclerotic plaque or other indications of heart disease. Sometimes severe stress can bring on the event. Was your cousin under a lot of pressure?"

Ben nodded. "He's had a hard time the past year. His wife died and he's been depressed." He glanced at Kate. "What do you think?"

"I only saw him twice over the last couple of weeks, first when I talked to him about the project at Mockingbird, and then when he came up for a site visit."

"He was really excited about the Mockingbird project," Ben said. "He called and told me all about it."

"Stress isn't only caused by something negative," the doctor noted. "Good things can be stressful as well. Any big change can put stress on the body."

"So what's the prognosis?" Ben asked.

"I'm cautiously optimistic," Dr. Hill replied with a smile. "Basically he's in good shape—not overweight or diabetic. Doesn't smoke, so that's a plus. We'll keep him in the hospital for a week or so and see how he does. If his condition continues to improve he'll be able to go home. But he'll have to take it easy and recuperate for about eight weeks."

Ben frowned. "That could be a problem. He lives alone. Maybe we could hire some help or maybe he could go stay with my mom and dad in Stockton." He looked at Kate. "Any ideas?"

Kate thought for a moment, then said, "Well, he could come stay at Mockingbird. I'm not working a day job. Now that Alex, my sister, has moved to San Francisco there's just Cory and me in the house. Jaime and Consuelo take care of the ranch. We've got plenty of room, and somebody'd always be around if he needed anything."

"I can't ask you to do that," Ben said. "It's not like he's, you know, *family*."

Kate put her hand on Ben's arm. "Come on, you know he was."

Dr. Hill glanced from one face to the other. "Well," he said, "I'll leave you two to think it over. I can recommend a good re-hab center if you like. I'll check with you both tomorrow. Good night."

"Thanks, Dr. Hill," Ben called after him. Then he looked back at Kate. "You'd really do that? Take care of him for two months?"

Kate smiled. "I'd love to."

14

Stockton, California

"They've taken him *where*?" David demanded, throwing his nephew a venemous stare.

Ben frowned and glanced uneasily at his mother, Pearl, who was standing in the doorway of David Ashida's cottage. She motioned her son to continue.

"To Mockingbird Ranch," Ben said.

David's forehead furrowed into a scowl and his lips were pressed to a thin, tight line. "And the reason for this?"

"We thought it was the best option for everyone," said Ben.

"And who is *we*?"

"Ben and your brother and the doctor and me and Kate. The idea makes sense, David-san," Pearl interjected, stepping inside and closing the door behind her.

"And no one thought to consult *me*?" David's face was livid now, eyes glittering with rage.

"You weren't *there*," Pearl said. "They were ready to discharge Tommy and we had to make a decision. I tried to call you, but there was no answer. We could have put him in a rehab center, but we talked to Kate and she said that—"

"Have all of you forgotten what *happened*? Forgotten the reason that we left Mockingbird?" David's voice was shaking. "My son brought dishonor on his family by engaging in. . . relations with Mr. McPhalan's daughter. We left in *disgrace*." He shook his head fiercely. "The stain of our humiliation has not gone away. And now you tell me that my son will be living in her house? What were you *thinking*?"

"Wait a minute, Uncle David," Ben said. "Kate is a client of

Tommy's. He's been working with her for the past month on a renovation project. Didn't he tell you?"

David sucked in his breath. "No. I've not heard about this project."

"Kate wants to establish a music festival at Mockingbird, and she hired Tommy's firm to design the buildings and oversee the renovations," Ben said. "Tommy was at Mockingbird a few weeks ago to begin the site study and cost estimates. He was so excited about the project. Kate said that being at the ranch would make it easier for him to continue the planning once he's feeling better."

David sat down on the sofa, closed his eyes and pinched the bridge of his nose. "This is not a good thing," he said tersely. "I will not permit it."

"It's a *business* deal," Ben said. "Plus he'll be getting great care. Better than he could have gotten in rehab." Ben glanced around the room. "Or here," he added.

David shook his head and said nothing. Pearl put her hand on Ben's arm and said, "Why don't you let me have a word with your uncle? Go keep Willie and your brother Francis company. I'll be along soon."

Ben threw up his hands. "Okay, Mom. He's all yours." He went out and slammed the door behind him.

Pearl sat down next to David on the sofa and was quiet for several minutes. When David continued to brood in silence, she finally said softly, "I *do* understand, David-san. I remember very well how angry you were, how upset Connie was. And poor Tommy, he—"

"Poor Tommy?" David looked up sharply. "His folly was the reason for our disgrace!"

"Hear me out," Pearl said. "We have two stories here. One of them is ten years old and one of them is right now. What happened then is gone. Mr. McPhalan is dead. The ranch now belongs to his daughter. She and Tommy are no longer star-crossed teenagers straying into forbidden territory. They're adults, able to make their own decisions."

David coughed roughly and looked away.

"Please listen," Pearl said more gently. "Your son has been through hell in the past two years—his mother's death, his wife's suicide. Almost dying himself of a broken heart. He's been living a life of desperation and loneliness. Is that what you want for him, your only child? Is your pride more important than his life?"

David lowered his head and remained mute, staring down at the floor.

"*Think*," Pearl said. "Tommy needs time to heal. He needs good care. He needs a reason to live. If Kate McPhalan can help him, then I say that is a good thing." She got up and started toward the door, then turned and looked at him. "Dinner will be ready in an hour," she said. "I hope you will join us."

After she left, David continued to sit slumped on the sofa remembering the personal humiliation his son had caused him. Ten years had passed, but David still burned with the shame of Owen McPhalan's outrage when the young lover's secret romance was revealed. The anguish of their forced separation. It was brutal, a traumatic episode that left deep wounds. For everyone.

David glanced at the photo of his wife, Connie, that sat on the end table next to the window. If she was still here, would she tell him, as Pearl had, "He needs to heal. He needs good care. He needs a reason to live."

Maybe Pearl was right. Ten years had passed and the wounds had turned to scars. They were still there but no longer open and bleeding. He loved his son and wanted what was best for him. If that now meant setting aside old grievances and providing support, then he would have to put his pride away and do what he could to make things right.

Very well, then. Slowly he got to his feet and went to wash his face and hands before going up the path to his brother's house for dinner.

CHAPTER

15

Mockingbird Ranch

R ain. Spattering against the window, drumming on the tile roof, a luxurious downpour falling on field and orchard and forest.

Tommy lay still for a while listening to the clatter of raindrops. Then slowly he sat up, wincing a little at the pinch of the sutures that had closed the four-inch incision in his chest. He took a deep, careful breath, braced his back against a pillow and looked out the window. The light was grey, but through the mist he could see the dark shapes of the pear trees climbing the slope behind the house. He was at Mockingbird. He was alive.

Kate and Ben had stayed close by during that first week in the hospital, updating the rest of the family on his progress. Kate had contacted his office in San Francisco and told his associates what had happened. She had relayed messages to Tommy about the progress of on-going projects. Since he'd set aside some time to work on the Mockingbird plans, his associates, Andy and Frank, were already handling the other contracts and obligations.

Tommy closed his eyes and lay back on the pillow. *How could this be? How could he be here in the very place he'd dreamed of, wished for? How could he possibly deserve to be here after all that had happened?* He let the idea float. He was too tired to think, but the question hung there like a small flame flickering in the dusk of his mind.

A soft knock on the door interrupted his thoughts. "Tommy? Are you awake?"

He straightened up. "Yes."

The door opened and there was Kate, smiling at him shyly. "I brought you some tea."

"Thanks."

She crossed the room and set a little tray down on the bedside table, then poured a cup from the porcelain pot. "How do you feel?"

He took a sip of tea. "Tired. Sore. Everything's still kind of. . . kind of hazy. Like a dream." He took another sip. The tea was good. The intensity of little details intrigued him—the taste of the tea, the warmth of the liquid in his throat. Everything seemed magnified.

"Speaking of dreams," he said putting the cup down on the bedside table, "I had a funny one last night."

She sat down at the foot of the bed and waited.

"I was walking along a pier. The waves were really high and they were crashing against the seawall. I thought they might destroy the wall. The water flooded over the edge of the wall, and suddenly I was waist deep and started to panic. But then I saw a bunch of sea otters swimming toward me. They surrounded me and I felt like they would keep me safe. So I wasn't afraid any more and the water started to go down. I was going to be okay." He glanced at Kate and grinned. "Pretty transparent, huh?"

She returned the grin. "Good dream."

"Mr. Sheeda?" Cory peeked around the doorway, blue eyes wide and serious.

"Hey there," Tommy said, "come on in. And remember, you can call me Tommy."

Cory sidled into the room, still looking cautious. "Mr. Tommy, do you do karate?"

Tommy nodded. "A little. But I'm better at Akido."

"What's that?" Cory asked, stopping beside Kate and leaning against her. She put an encouraging arm around her son's shoulders.

"It's a different kind of martial art. I learned it in Japan."

"Where's Japan?"

"Far away. Across the Pacific Ocean."

Cory considered this information. "Farther than Cleveland?"

Tommy nodded.

Cory looked up at Kate. "Can we go there?"

"Maybe someday. Meanwhile, why don't you go see if Consuelo has breakfast ready."

"Okay." Cory looked at Tommy. "Will you teach me to do Akido, Mr. Tommy?"

"I can do that," he looked at Kate, "if your mom approves."

"I think that would be fine," said Kate. "But first, Mr. Tommy has to get well."

"I hope you get well quick," Cory said.

"Thanks," Tommy replied with a grin. "So do I."

After Cory left, Kate opened the bedside table drawer and took out a notebook and thermometer. "Time for the morning ritual," she said. "Open wide."

"Yes, ma'am."

After she had recorded his temperature, she headed for the door. "Don't forget to weigh yourself before you come down to breakfast," she said. "And take a Tylenol."

"You're just a born nurse," he teased.

"And be careful on the stairs," she ordered as she headed out the door. "Be sure to hold onto the railing."

The daily rush of breakfast, getting Cory off to school, overseeing the list of ranch chores and anticipating up-coming activities had kept Kate fully engaged since her return to Mockingbird six months before. For the past two weeks, she had also taken care of Tommy whose recovery was still in its early stages. Twice a day she took his temperature and logged the results to track any sign of infection. He needed to be weighed morning and night to be sure he wasn't accumulating fluids. And there was a regimen of medications to organize.

The physical therapist came twice a week to monitor his progress. Kate also called his San Francisco office once a day to be sure everything was running smoothly. Tommy was patient and cooperative, but she knew he was also emotionally fragile and distressed. He was very young to have had a major heart problem.

After breakfast each morning, she helped him settle down on the sofa next to the fireplace and built a fire to keep the room warm and cozy. He told her not to bother, but she could tell how much he appreciated the warmth and the cheerfulness of the blaze.

From the sofa, he could see out the big picture window that overlooked the courtyard with its peaceful clutter of flowers and greenery, and the graceful trunks of the oak and fig that held center-court. A terra cotta fountain on the opposite wall of the courtyard provided a small gushing waterfall that made a pleasant sound even on dark winter days when a dusting of snow might frost the leaves of the azaleas and camellias. At an altitude of a little over twelve hundred feet, the winters at Mockingbird could be brisk, with occasional flurries when the snowline dipped into the Sierra foothills.

Today it was too warm for snow, but a cold rain was falling and the wind was restless, swirling the dead fig leaves around on the courtyard tiles. Kate poured a last cup of coffee from the pot in the kitchen and went back to the living room. Seated cross-legged on the sofa with a blanket draped around his shoulders, Tommy looked to her like a Buddha under the Bodhi tree. Smiling, she sat down next to him. "Want me to read the paper to you?" she asked.

He glanced at her and she thought he looked too serious. "No," he said quietly, "that's okay. I know you've got a lot to do."

"No problem," she said lightly. "I'd rather sit here with you."

That got a slight smile. "Want some coffee?" she asked.

He shook his head and half-turned away from her.

"Fran's coming at eleven for your therapy session," she said. She was prattling on, not sure what to say. "I'll bet she'll make you climb stairs today."

He said something muffled and unclear.

"What?" She leaned toward him.

He straightened up with a little shuddering sob, his eyes closed. She put her hand on his arm. "Hey," she said gently, "what's wrong?"

He hunched his shoulders. "God," he muttered brokenly, "I'm pathetic."

He rubbed his eyes angrily with the back of his wrist, pushed back his hair and took a deep breath, grimacing slightly. "Everything just seems so. . . hopeless," he said. "I don't know where I belong." He looked at Kate. "Why am I so. . . confused?"

"The doctor told me that you'd probably be depressed after the kind of event you had. So being sad and scared, I think that's only natural. Maybe you should get some counseling? That might—"

He shook his head, frowning. "No. That's not acceptable. I have to figure this out for myself." He looked at her wordlessly for a moment, then glanced out the window. The rain was coming down harder now, big drops making transparent craters on the glass. "I just feel off balance. I can't make any sense of this."

"Does it have to make sense?" Kate asked.

He looked at her quizzically. "That's my head talking, huh?"

"Yup." She grinned at him. "Let it go, Ashida. You don't have to make sense. Remember what your mom always said, 'We find the path by walking on it.'"

"One day at a time?"

"That's what we've got."

He nodded.

"So," she said, "feel up to taking a look at the renovation plans for the barn?"

"Yeah."

"Yeah?"

He gave her a genuine smile. "Bring 'em on."

When she checked on him an hour later, he was bent over the plans, tracing lines and making little notes in the margins. Kate watched him, filled with a mix of delight and trepidation. Where would this lead? What should she do? After a minute, she shook her head and went back to the kitchen to start lunch.

CHAPTER

16

New York, New York

With a groan, Carl crumpled the paper into a ball and tossed it angrily into the wastebasket. He was stuck. The fledgling theme that was nestled somewhere in his mind refused to show itself and take flight. The pieces of the puzzle just wouldn't come into focus, and it was driving him crazy.

Grimacing, he twisted his neck in slow circles, then got up and looked out the window. The Chrysler Building glowed like a scalloped Christmas tree, while seven stories below Gramercy Park seemed a quaint ceramic replica. A cold, grey mist was falling. Lights blinked like fireflies in the gloom.

The apartment was austerely furnished—he'd saved only a few choice pieces from what he was now calling "my former life." A glossy black Steinway stood next to the fireplace. A single leather-covered wing-backed chair and a rosewood coffee table set atop a Persian carpet. The Biedermeier cabinet that he'd bought years ago in San Francisco served as a bookcase.

Except for the muted drone of the city's endless traffic, it was quiet. He missed the sound of voices, of laughter. His son. His wife. But his new apartment was a good place to work, and work had filled his days—and nights —these past ten months.

The intercom buzzed. "Hey, big brother," Ali's voice sounded metallic through the call box, "you ready?"

"Be right down."

Sleet was falling by the time their cab stopped in front of Marian and Nikki's building. The foyer of the complex was freezing, but inside the third-floor loft it was warm and bright. "Get Ali and Carl a drink would you Nick?" Marian directed. "I've got to baste the turkey."

"Can I help?" Ali offered, following Marian into the kitchen.

Drink in hand, Carl prowled around the loft, pausing to study the paintings that lined the walls and stood stacked against the paint-spattered table. "Looks like you're working hard," he called to Marian.

"Every minute I can. Hey Nick, show Carl your new project."

"Where do you work?" Carl asked.

"One floor up," Nick replied. "Want to see?"

The freight elevator opened into another cavernous loft. Nick flipped on the lights and Carl stood blinking at the mass of cables and equipment. "Television?" he said, raising his eyebrows.

"I'm not sure where I'm going yet, but I've really gotten into video. Here, take a look."

Four symmetrically arranged monitors fluttered to life. On two of the screens deer grazed, anxiously raising their heads every few seconds. On another, a car careened down a darkened freeway, darting in and out of traffic, narrowly avoiding disaster. On the fourth screen an astronaut explored the moon. Murmuring voices discussed a seemingly random series of events, but certain words were repeated over and over—mask, deception, pyramid, mask, deception, pyramid. Electronic music accompanied the conversation, rising occasionally to drown out the voices. The astronaut, his voice thin and metallic through the headset, described the Sea of Venus.

Carl watched for several minutes, then glanced at Nick. "I hate to call this *interesting,* but that's the generic reaction, I suppose."

Nick laughed. "I haven't found quite the right word yet myself. I've been thinking of calling the piece 'Informed.'"

Carl nodded.

"There's got to be more to TV than *Star Trek* and game shows. I'm exploring the possibilities," Nick said.

"Technology's extending possibilities for all of us," Carl agreed. Excitedly, he described his recent work with synthesizers. "Have you heard the album *Switched-on Bach*?"

Nick shook his head.

"Fantastic recording. Came out a couple of years ago. Wendy Carlos was behind the project. She put together an eight-track recorder and assembled a selection of Bach's music done entirely on a synthesizer."

"Wow," Nick said. "I'd love to hear it."

"Drop by sometime and take a listen. But you know," he added, "I've been more involved with melodic line in the past few months. I have this idea for a piano concerto in my head, but I can't seem to get it right. Driving me nuts."

"Marian said you'd been composing again. Why'd you stop in the first place?"

Carl shrugged. "No one could understand what I was doing. *Even I* couldn't understand what I was doing."

Nick leaned against the wall, and folded his arms across his chest. "Tell me."

"When I started out," Carl said, "I thought I knew what I wanted. I experimented. Followed breadcrumbs. Then I started studying more theory, analyzing compositions, taking them apart.

"There's a kind of. . . viciousness to formal analysis. Pretty soon, you're questioning everything you thought you knew. Or loved. Beauty was banal. Truth was an illusion. Order was decoration." He threw up his hands. "Too many new restrictions. So, I went through a period of breaking every rule I could find. But that didn't help."

He gave Nick a sardonic grin. "I worked my way through serialism—Schoenberg, Stockhausen, Barraque. By extension Cage, Messiaen. Twelve tone, post-tonal, multiple serialism. Then minialism: Riley, Reich, Glass, the Hypnotic School. Non-narrative, non-teleological, non-representational. Stasis. But what happens when you start reducing everything?"

"Eventually, you end up with nothing?" said Nick.

"Right. You get to ontological reductionism. Reality is composed of a number of entities that can be reduced to a single substance. Wholes are no more than the sum of their parts, and if you push that thought far enough you come up with *nothing*. You've obliterated reality. I had descended into chaos, and there was no way out. What was it John Cage said? 'I have nothing to say, I am saying it, and that is poetry'?"

"But once you jettison abstraction and futurism and constructivism and Dada and op and pop and conceptualism, what's left?" Nick said. "What does 'nothing' look like?"

"The sound of one hand clapping?" Carl offered.

"Maybe we're all just making art for other artists these days," Nick said. "But some things need to be said with or without an audience. Even if you think you're saying nothing."

"Isn't that an exercise in futility?"

"Maybe. Or not. I'm not going to let that stop me. I'm an explorer. I keep exploring."

Carl smiled. "Maybe you have more courage than I do."

"Or less sense."

They both laughed.

Nick sat down on the sagging sofa next to the window. He rolled a joint, lit it, inhaled. Held it out to Carl.

"No, thanks."

"Don't do drugs?"

"I'm trying for clarity."

Nick grinned, took another toke and blew out a stream of smoke. "Okay. The path ran out, right?"

"Right. So I'm trying to find another path. I've been studying piano concertos—old, new, traditional, experimental. Analyzing, deconstructing, reconstructing. Chasing my tail. I have an *idea* of what I want."

"Which is?"

"I keep coming back to. . . *luminous*. But what does *that* mean?"

"The sound of light?"

Carl nodded vigorously. "But not *impressionism*."

Nick took another puff. Held it. Exhaled. "What about. . . *reflection*?"

Carl thought for a moment. Then he smiled. "Yes," he said. "When they leave the hall, I want people to take something with them that they'll remember—something that will haunt them. Something like the sound of light."

"What a groovy dinner," Ali announced. "Even my mom can't cook turkey this good."

"I can't take all the credit," Marian laughed. "Nikki made the stuffing."

"An old Italian-German-French-Canadian recipe," said Nick. "Very American."

They were all silent for a moment. Then Carl said, "Have you heard from Kate?"

Marian caught the tremor in his voice. "Got a letter last week."

"Then I guess you know she's filed for divorce."

"She told me."

"Well, then you *do* know," he said and laughed at himself. A rather forced laugh.

Nick got up and said to Ali, "Come on, sport. Help me clear and clean."

After Nick and Ali disappeared into the kitchen, Marian asked gently, "Would you like to see the letter?"

Carl nodded. She went to a nerby desk and got the ketter, then handed it to him. There were many pages. When he finished reading, there were tears in his eyes. "Thanks," he said hoarsely. "I didn't think it would be as hard on her as it's been for me."

"Not an easy decision."

"I kept hoping she'd change her mind."

For several minutes the silence was broken only by the noise of traffic and the clatter of dishes from the kitchen. Then Carl cleared his throat and said, "I heard the book she was working on was published."

"Just out," Marian said, beaming. "Want to see?" She grabbed a volume from the bookshelf and handed it to him. "A genuine, autographed first edition!"

"Songs of the Summer Sea: Poems by Julian Francis McPhalan," Carl read. "Edited by Mary Katharine McPhalan-Fitzgerald." He opened the book and read aloud,

> Just as the work of the generation of poets from the 1950s mirrored the disillusionment of the post-war era and acted as an indictment against materialism, so the work of Julian McPhalan presages the decade of the 1960s with all its romantic idealism, its mysticism, and its visionary belief in the holistic integration of all living things. It is this chord of pantheism, of animistic identification, that is the hallmark of MacPhalan's work. His recurring symbol of the sea provides a framework for his vision of an inclusive, integrated system, a world in which all living things are intertwined and mutually dependent.
>
> His is a vision of hope, of deep and abiding love. He replaces cynicism with compassion, despair with faith, rejection with tolerance, and bitterness with an almost holy acceptance of the world as a flawed but glorious expression of creative vitality. McPhalan's poems show us a place which, like the sea, is brimming with elements of mystery and beauty, and he captures with extraordinary clarity that feeling of awe and wonder that forms the core of true revelation.

After several minutes, Carl closed the book and looked at Marian. "I had no idea," he said.

"Neither did I, really."

"You hadn't seen his poetry?"

"Not much. He showed me a few early ones. But remember, he was only seventeen when I left Mockingbird and moved back east. And then only four years later he. . . he was gone."

Carl nodded and looked back at the book. "Quite an accomplishment."

"For both of them," Marian said.

"Why," Carl said after a moment, "do we always underestimate the people closest to us?"

Later that night, Carl and Ali took a cab back to their apartments. "You're awfully quiet," Ali said as the cab threaded its way through the Thanksgiving traffic toward Washington Square. "Because of Kate?"

"Kate. And Marian and Julian. They're quite a family."

"You're forgetting Alex."

Carl shook his head, smiling. "Oh, no. I could never forget Alex."

"Kate told me Alex has moved to San Francisco. She says she's doing better."

"When she starts playing again she'll be doing better," Carl said firmly.

"You think that's possible?"

"She won't stay away forever. She just needs a good reason to get back to work." After a minute he added, "and I think I may be able to give her a reason."

Just then it came to him—the whole construction, like a blueprint unrolling before him. He inhaled sharply and glanced out the window. The cab crawled past Washington Square toward Ali's apartment. He couldn't wait for the traffic to clear. He had to go— now! He grabbed his wallet and handed the driver a ten.

"What are you doing?" Ali asked in surprise.

"Sorry," he told her breathlessly. "I'm getting out here. I'll call you in a day or two."

Leaping from the cab, he headed east on Fourth Street and then turned north at Fifth Avenue. Breaking into a jog, he covered the fifteen blocks to his East Twentieth Street address in record time. Instead of waiting for the elevator, he took the stairs and arrived at his front door gasping for breath. Fumbling with the keys, he shoved the door open and dashed to the piano, flinging his coat into the corner.

D minor. That's what he was hearing in his head. Something like the second theme in the third movement of Mahler's First Symphony. Dum da dum da dum dum, dum da dum da dum. But the theme he wanted came from a Hopi Indian song he remembered from his childhood in Arizona. Lyrical but wistful, a sweet lament. Dum da dum da dum. C D F A G. The hell with theory. He wanted *sound*! He wanted *emotion*! He wanted. . . *humanity*!

He grabbed a handful of staff paper and sat down on the piano bench, played the theme, scribbled notes on the paper. He couldn't write fast enough to keep up with the construct that was running through his mind.

He hummed as he wrote, played another line. The first movement would be marked *allegro*. A rowdy procession as Kokopelli, the Hopi flute player, enters a village, transforming winter into spring. The bravado and flirtation ends with a riot of chords and arpeggios that stops abruptly.

Then a second movement, marked *andante*. Contemplative and questioning, the minor theme is introduced by the flute, then taken up by the piano and becomes a dialogue of question and response. Has Kokopelli fallen in love? The movement ends with a wandering, repetitive introspection—perhaps along a stream that murmurs (strings and woodwinds) beneath the lover's quiet conversation. The sound is hypnotic, ephemeral.

And the final movement, marked *maestoso*, considers redemption. It begins quietly, like the dawn, then builds to a finish that is triumphant. At the last, strings and horns below, the woodwinds holding everything together, and above it all the piano, dancing like Kokopelli's flute, in the sunrise above the mesas. The hunchback flute-player's spirit singing of love and death, and the soul of music itself.

Carl didn't notice when the sun came up. Only later did he realize that the living room was flooded with light and that his shoulders ached. He looked around at the scattered sheets of music paper and began to laugh. "Beauty from chaos?" he muttered. He gathered up the sheets, trying to put them in some kind of order.

He found the first page, scanned it quickly, humming, nodding. Flipping through the sheets of paper, he followed the music in his mind. Yes, the basic structure was there. There would be revisions, additions, but he had the concept firmly down on paper.

He sat back down on the piano bench and picked up his pen. At the top of the first sheet he wrote. *Kokopelli's Dream: A Piano Concerto for the Right Hand in D-Minor*, by Carlos Estevan Morales.

CHAPTER
17

San Francisco, California
December 1970

The year 1970 was one of radical extremes. Half a million people died in a cyclone in Bangladesh, but the Nuclear Non-Proliferation Treaty was ratified by forty-three nations. Mountaintop removal strip mining operations were launched in central Appalachia, but the first Earth Day celebration was held on April 22. The largest Rock Festival in history took place on the Isle of Wright with 600,000 people attending, while Paul McCartney announced that the Beatles had disbanded.

Japan became the world's fourth space power, but the Apollo 13 moon mission was canceled when two oxygen tanks exploded prompting the crew's infamous message: "Houston, we've had a problem." The Kent State Massacre had left four unarmed students dead, but the voting age was lowered to eighteen. And Bill Gates used the name "Micro-soft" for the first time in a letter to his friend, Paul Allen.

For Alexandria Archer (McPhalan), 1970 had also been a year of contrasts. It started with a move to Los Angeles following the disastrous Christmas Eve blow-up in Lenox where she had revealed Carl and Marian's long-kept secret romance and sent her sister Kate's marriage spiraling into ruin. Los Angeles was a blur of drugs and promiscuity that she only wanted to forget. Her career as a concert pianist had gone down in flames following the self-inflicted injury that rendered her left hand useless. And her life-long teacher, mentor and sometime lover, Stefan Molnar, had died.

But she was still alive. She had made peace with her sister, Kate, and even with her nemesis, Carl, and she was determined to start over. To make a new life for herself. Exactly how and where and what, she left to fate. Or instinct.

So, in September 1970, she left Mockingbird Valley Ranch for the second time in her life—the first had been in 1959 when she and her mother, Marian, had moved to Boston—and decided to settle in San Francisco, a city she had always loved but had never had the chance to fully explore.

The opportunity came with a job offer from the San Francisco Music Conservatory to teach piano master classes, and to serve as a mentor for the advanced keyboard students. Alex hadn't applied for the job. The chairman of the keyboard faculty had called her. She suspected that Jean Molnar, Stefan's widow, might have been responsible, but didn't enquire.

And now here she was, walking along Twenty-first Avenue toward the apartment on Judah Street that she had rented three months earlier. Located in the Outer Sunset district of the City just a couple of blocks south of Golden Gate Park, the neighborhood was an appealing mix of comfortable older homes and newer apartment complexes. It was an ethnically diverse section of the City with Italian, Russian and Irish roots, and a newer influx of Asian immigrants. Within one block it was possible to come across an Irish pub, a Thai noodle shop, a Russian bakery, and a Chinese laundry.

Alex enjoyed the eclectic mix. Like many of her neighbors, she felt a kind of un-belonging. Having lived in so many places, she felt disconnected to all of them. The art of being out of place.

She was also *almost* used to the imposed anonymity of no longer being "famous." Even at the Conservatory there were only a few students who recognized her, although many of the faculty knew of her past accomplishments and of the accident that had ended her career. They seemed hesitant to mention it, thinking, perhaps, that she would be offended or even worse, distraught. While friendly enough, they kept their distance. That suited her. She wanted some time to think, to reconstruct her life, to figure out her next move. She was making lots of changes: address, identity. She had even made the revolutionary move of learning to drive and buying a car: a pre-owned white Chrysler Imperial with ivory leather seats. She didn't drive the car that often, but there it was in the driveway, a symbol of her new-found independence.

This particular December day was delightful. After the cold fog of "summer," the City was enjoying a string of balmy days filled with sunshine and afternoon temperatures that inched toward the low seventies. Alex walked slowly along Judah Street. The afternoon was so pleasant that she turned north on Twenty Seventh Avenue and walked the two blocks to the park. There was a small lake just off Lincoln Way on the south side of the park that she had claimed as her "secret place" to sit and think.

The grass along the lake's edge was cool, slightly damp, and filled with clover. She settled herself and watched two honeybees collect nectar. So industrious. She wondered how they converted nectar into honey. Maybe she should become a bee keeper. A useful profession: gathering and dispensing a beautiful amber substance that would make people endlessly happy.

She lifted her left hand and studied it. The break had healed, but was known medically as an "unstable fracture" which meant that the bone fragments had shifted, leaving the wrist slightly crooked. In addition, the radial nerve had been damaged which brought about numbness in the last two fingers of her left hand.

Her doctor, a respected surgeon, had used the latest technology, an external fixator, a metal rod that was placed parallel to her forearm with long screws, or pins, that were attached to the wrist bones to hold them in place during the healing process. But the results were not completely successful. Periodically, the joint became tender and stiff. The hand was serviceable—she could tie her shoes or pick up a paperclip—but there was no possibility of playing even a simple piano composition.

If only, Alex thought, her right hand had been injured. There was a wonderful body of piano compositions written for pianists who had no function in their *right* hand. Robert Schumann was probably the best-known keyboard artist whose career had been complicated when he lost the use of his right hand. But there was also the Austrian pianist Paul Wittgenstein, whose right arm had been shot off in World War I. He'd commissioned works for the left hand from some of the greatest composers of the day—Strauss, Prokofiev, Ravel.

But there were hardly any piano works for the right hand. As the pianist Leon Fleisher, who suffered from focal dystonia, a neurological condition that affected his hand, had remarked, "When the gods go after you, they really know where to strike."

It was Alex's nephew, Cory, who opened the new path for her. During the three months she'd stayed with Kate and Cory at Mockingbird, she had truly enjoyed working with the little boy in the same living room on the same Steinway where she had begun her own career. It was a new beginning somehow, a chance to rediscover her inherent love of music. Not just piano music, not just *playing* music or performing, but the music *itself.* She needed to be surrounded by music, engulfed in it. Music was her love, her passion, her *life.* In teaching, she was able to at least be a part of the world she knew and loved.

Still, she thought, gazing at the placid water of the lake, watching the pattern of light and darkness flicker on its rippled surface, *there must be a way.* Carl was right. She had never really *tried* to make a full recovery, to regain the use of her left hand. *Maybe,* she wondered, *because she couldn't bear to fail? What if she tried everything and still there was no result?*

She remembered something Carl had told her while they were sitting in a booth at Casa Morales when his father, Jorge, was in the hospital. Carl had said there was a doctor in San Francisco. Somebody at the S.F. Medical School who was having great success working with injured musicians. What was his name? Williams? Wilson? Carl had written the name down for her at the time, but she couldn't remember where she'd put it. Had she even kept it?

Suddenly excited, she jumped up and began to walk very quickly, and then to jog, toward her apartment. She had to find that name.

———∘∘◦}◦{◦∘———

New York, New York

Although Carl left Julliard early that Friday—he met with a student at three and left the school shortly before four—darkness had already closed in by the time he reached his apartment on East Twentieth Street. Only a thin spear of sunlight sliced through the steel canyons between the tiers of skyscrapers. A single ray hit the top of the Chrysler Building like a spotlight, and Carl paused to take in the view as he slipped off his coat and unwound his muffler. He felt as though he was shedding his skin, like a serpent in springtime, even though outside the temperature was near freezing and the official start of winter was only four days away.

Maybe he felt released because it had been a year of transformations, of leaving behind and moving ahead. Behind him were old jobs—the position in Cleveland that had run its course. And then over the summer a break with his appointment in Salzburg. And of course, the old relationships—the separation and soon-to-be-divorce from Kate, and a farewell to Kristen Manz, his mistress in Austria.

On the other hand, he had re-united with his father, Jorge, had moved into a new life in New York, and a new job with Julliard and the Contemporary Chamber Orchestra, and had experienced a break-through in his composing, creating what he thought of as his first significant piece of work in twenty years.

The sun dipped suddenly behind the skyline on the west side of the Hudson River, leaving the city awash in purple shadows. Carl tossed his coat across a chair. Glancing down, he noticed that the small red light on the telephone answering machine was blinking. Probably his sister Ali with one of her endless questions, or maybe a student seeking advice. Could be Nick, who had become a friend when he and Carl discovered a mutual enthusiasm for experimental technology. They were talking about the possibility of a collaboration that would combine sounds and images. Carl opened the top button of his shirt, rolled up his sleeves and tapped the message button.

"Ummm, Carl. Hi. Alex here. I. . . uh. . . when we were at Casa Morales. . . you know when Jorge was in the hospital? Uh, you gave me the name of a doctor at the medical school in San Francisco who might be able to take a look at my hand? I can't seem to find his name anywhere. I must have lost it. Could you maybe—if you have time— give me a call? I'm here most evenings. Thanks. Oh, my number is 415-417-7172. Thanks. Bye."

Carl sat down and looked at the phone. When had he last heard Alex play? He closed his eyes and thought. London. They were rehearsing the Brahms D-Minor Piano Concerto with the London Symphony, and Alex was the soloist. He got into a terrible row with her over the tempo of the second movement, and with what Carl felt was a departure from Brahms' dynamic indications. They had stomped off opposite sides of the stage. He remembered yelling at the music director, "Nigel, if you *ever* ask me to work with her again, so help me I'll strangle you!"

We were a couple of spoiled brats, he thought and had to smile at the memory. But somehow, they had worked things out. In the concerto, who was the boss? The conductor? The soloist? The composer? It had to be a consensus of all three.

And so they had worked through the problems, and the concert was a stupendous success. He remembered the explosion of applause as they finished the final movement. Alex rose from the piano bench and he grasped her hand and together they raised their arms to celebrate their victory. In the thrill of that moment he had felt such a rush of admiration, of amazement, of. . . love? Their eyes met in a look of pure joy.

He opened his eyes and stared at the telephone. Then he replayed the message and wrote down her number.

CHAPTER

18

Mockingbird Valley Ranch

From the kitchen window, Kate watched her sister Alex coming up the walk to the courtyard gate. A year had passed since that disastrous Christmas Eve in Lenox that had sent the family spinning into a life-changing free-fall. Relationships, careers, lifestyles, all tossed into an abyss. Her life in Ohio, her life with Carl, seemed like years ago, a distant memory, a dream perhaps, disconnected from the present.

And yet, here was Alex, crossing the tiled courtyard, lifting her hand to knock on the door. Kate set down her dishtowel and headed for the foyer.

In her usual blunt fashion, Alex thrust a paper bag into Kate's hands before even saying hello. "Gift," she said. "I thought you'd like some sourdough bread from Fisherman's Wharf."

"Always a favorite," Kate replied. "Come on in." She gave Alex a quick hug and closed the door against the cold dampness of a rainy afternoon.

Alex followed Kate into the kitchen. "Where is everybody?"

"Tommy and Cory are in the living room. They're decorating the tree." Kate glanced at her sister. "You look awfully serious."

"Two hours alone on the Interstate is a great opportunity for introspection. So, guess I've been . . . introspecting."

"Well," teased Kate, "you know what they say about an unexamined life."

Alex smiled bleakly. "What the heck," she said. "Good to be here."

"Can I get you something? Coffee? Cocoa?"

"Cocoa? Really?"

"Yeah. The guys are having a cup. What do you say?"

"Why not."

Kate made a cup for each of them. In the living room, Cory and Tommy were busy hanging ornaments on the seven-foot fir tree that Kate had brought in from the woods. The room was filled with the scent of resin enhanced by the warmth coming from the fireplace. Cory dropped the sea-shell angel that he held back into the shoebox and ran to hug Alex.

"Aunt Alex," he cried, "look at our tree!" Grabbing her hand, he pulled her closer. "Mr. Tommy put on the lights," he announced. "And Mommy put the dove on the top, and now we're putting on all the animals and stars and stuff. Wanta help?"

"You're going to put me right to work, huh?" Alex said with a grin. "Hi, Mr. Tommy," she added. "How are you doing?"

"Better," he said. "Good to see you, Alex. Happy Christmas."

"Same to you." She looked around at the tree, the blaze in the hearth, the familiar furnishings, her mother's watercolors, dark beams, the piano. The *piano*. Shaking her head, she said, "I'm going to take this suitcase up to my room and then, Nephew Cory, I will be pleased to help with the decorating." *Where am I?* she thought. *Looks like a Norman Rockwell painting, for God's sake.*

Dinner was a big tureen of oyster chowder and a watercress salad with bright red cherry tomatoes sprinkled with fresh feta cheese. The bread that Alex had brought from the City was a great accompaniment. They toasted the holiday with a glass of fume blanc and nibbled Christmas cookies for dessert.

They moved into the living room to enjoy the fire and the finally-finished Christmas tree with its pile of presents. "Hey," Alex suggested, "let's read *A Christmas Carol*. Remember, Kate, how we used to do that every Christmas Eve?"

"That's right," Kate replied. "Let me see if I can find it."

A moment later she was back with a worn, leather-bound volume. "Right where it always was. Who wants to start?"

"I do!" Alex exclaimed. They all settled back, Kate and Tommy on the sofa with Cory between them, and Alex in the wing chair next to the fire. She opened the book and began, "'Marley was dead to begin with. There is no doubt whatever about that. The register of his burial was signed by the clergyman, the clerk, the undertaker, and the chief mourner. Scrooge signed it. And Scrooge's name was good for anything he chose to put his hand to. Old Marley was as dead as a doornail.'"

They took turns reading the story. Even Cory managed a couple of pages with some assistance. Kate brought out cups of eggnog for the adults and more cocoa for Cory. It was almost ten when Tommy looked at the clock and said, "Whoa. Past my bedtime." He looked at Cory. "What do you say, ace? Time for us to turn in?"

"I'll be back down in a minute," Kate told Alex.

"Take your time. I'm not going anywhere."

Kate tucked Tommy and Cory in for the night and returned to the living room where she found Alex on the sofa reading a magazine. Alex looked up as Kate came in. "Have you seen this?" she asked, waving the magazine in her sister's face.

Kate glanced at the cover. "No. Christy Malacchi gave it to me. Said there was something about Julian's book in it. Why?"

"This is a huge pile of crap!" Alex announced indignantly. "Take a look."

Kate sat down and scanned the page. Then she began to giggle.

"Not funny," Alex exclaimed. "Why can't journalists get anything straight?"

"I expect that if Julian was reading it he'd be laughing his head off," Kate said.

"Look here," Alex pointed. "It says I was a child prodigy. Well, that's news to me. Mother wouldn't even let me appear in public until I was almost twelve. And what's this crap about Mom being part of the Bay Area Figurative movement? She didn't even start painting figures until she moved to Boston. She was still doing abstractions."

"Well, they were based on figures."

"Bullshit. She just wanted an excuse to paint her instructor in the nude."

Kate laughed. "At least you guys got some press. I don't see anything about me."

"He saved you for the end. There's a big thing about you and Carl on the final page. And look at this. He says Julian was a friend of Jack Kerouac. Julian didn't even *know* Kerouac, did he?"

"He may have seen him at a poetry reading or served him a drink at the Blackhawk," Kate said. "But as far as I know Julian didn't hang out with any of the Beat writers. He said he found their work strident."

"He's being labeled a *neo-Romantic*, whatever *that's* supposed to mean." Alex shook her head. "Can you believe this stuff?"

Kate read a few paragraphs. "Well," she said, "at least it's pretty accurate about his relationship with Alan Townsend. I like what it says about the Townsend Foundation scholarship program. Julian would have been so pleased."

"The guy probably just wants a grant from them," Alex grumbled.

Kate put the magazine aside. "I suppose we could write a letter of rebuttal, but I wonder if the story isn't bound to get worse."

"Meaning?"

"I don't know. It's strange, the way people want to turn artists into legends, heroes. Next thing you know they'll be calling Julian the James Dean of the literary world."

For a moment Alex was silent. Then she said, "I guess I never thought about Julian being a hero, but he was, wasn't he? I mean it was pretty heroic just to be who he was and to go on writing beautiful poetry even after all the lousy things that happened to him—fighting with Dad, being treated like a freak, losing his partner." Alex scowled and chewed her lower lip. "All just because he was. . . different."

"You know," Kate said, "a hundred years from now, no one will remember Daddy's real estate empire and this house may not even be standing. But I'll bet they'll still be looking at Mom's paintings and reading Julian's poetry."

"Or maybe playing Carl's music," Alex said thoughtfully, her face taking on a look of grave concentration that Kate had never seen before. Suddenly, she sprang up from the sofa.

"Where are you going?" Kate asked.

"I'll be right back." She returned a few moments later with a thick manila envelope. Dropping down on the couch, she handed the envelope to Kate.

"What's this?" Kate saw the New York postmark. "Something from Mom?"

"From Carl," Alex said.

Kate looked at her expectantly.

Alex swallowed. "I'm afraid to open it."

"Why?"

"I. . . I'm afraid I know what it is."

Kate handed it back to her. "Come on," she said firmly. "It's Christmas. Open your gift."

Slowly, Alex tore open the end of the envelope and pulled out a musical score. She read from the note clipped to the first page. "This is for you, Alex. *Kokopelli's Dream: A Piano Concerto for the Right Hand in D-Minor*, Merry Christmas, from Carl."

She smiled a little, then quickly began to scan the sheets of music. Kate watched her, thinking that there was an ethereal sort of beauty to this moment. She was aware of a quiet mingling of joy and sadness.

Alex didn't say a word. But presently she got up and crossed the room to the piano. She sat down, spread the music before her and began to play.

PART II

CHAPTER

19

New York, New York
January 1971

M arian arrived home just after six. She had been at a meeting—
some of the women called it a "consciousness-raising"
although Marian was not totally comfortable with that title. Maybe
a "discussion group"? They were reading a new book by the feminist
author Germaine Greer titled *The Female Eunuch*. They argued about
the implications of whether or not women had been separated from
their libido, were hated by men, had been taught to hate themselves,
and to reject their own sexuality.

The topics covered in Greer's book made for great discussion,
but Marian was not sure that it raised her consciousness. Mostly,
it made her guiltily glad that she had left California when she did,
and had "taken as her lover a young Canadian sculptor. . ." Many of
the women Marian met were still writhing in dead-end marriages,
suffering from what one of them called "compassion fatigue" —doing
everything for everybody else while doing nothing for yourself.

When Marian arrived home the entry foyer was cold, and the
floor was wet from snowmelt tracked in from the street. As the
elevator groaned its way toward the third floor, Marian reviewed the
meeting she'd left an hour before.

Most of the women in the group were married to stock brokers or
attorneys or professors or other professionals and had children, which
made it sound as though they should have been happily fulfilled. But
they were experiencing the same feelings of entrapment and isolation
that had plagued Marian before her escape from Mockingbird.

Then there were the more radical voices—the Redstockings, the

Radical Feminists, the Separatists—those who contended that only *lesbians* were "true" feminists, those who were opposed to marriage altogether. It went on and on as antithetical opinions collided and groups split apart and re-formed. It was exciting, bewildering, amusing, irritating. A kind of self-revelation, a new form of collective therapy.

Marian had to wonder how she'd managed to break free from what she now considered to be a "socially imposed prison" in spite of her isolation and guilt and economic hardship. *Just stubborn, I guess,* she told her "sisters." It made her think about her daughters and their very different ways of coming to terms with identities and relationships—Alex's volatile, ill-fated impetuosity. Kate's more pragmatic retreat to her childhood sanctuary. Women were finding new ways to transform themselves, but it was a stormy path with plenty of causalities on all sides.

She shivered as she exited the elevator. But inside the loft she shared with Nick it was warm and bright and she was so happy to be "home."

In the last six years that they had lived together—the last two as husband and wife—they had modified the loft into a comfortable live-work space, and also leased the loft upstairs for Nick to use as a studio. Marian's work space was separated from the living quarters by a free-standing six foot high wall that gave her the floor to ceiling wall of north-facing windows, but afforded the living space a view of the street and the tops of trees. The Chelsea neighborhood was a mix of residential and industrial complexes with a rich history and a diverse ethnic population.

"I'm home," Marian called as she unbuttoned her coat and tossed it, along with her muffler, onto the sofa.

"Me too." Nick's voice came from the kitchen. She found him chopping vegetables on the square butcher block positioned next to the stove.

"Ummm," she noted. "Smells good."

"Lamb stew," he replied. "And a salad." He glanced up. "How was the meeting?"

"Perplexing. Loud. Provocative. How was your day?"

"Good. Had a long talk with Carl about what we're going to need for our project. We're thinking of calling it 'The Hudson River School: Part Two.' What do you think?"

"Too conservative," she replied with a smirk. "How 'bout 'Up the Creek Without a Paddle?'"

Nick straightened up and narrowed his eyes. "We'll talk over dinner," he said. "Meanwhile, want a drink?"

"I think I'll take a shower first," Marian said. "I want to wash off all those doubts and opinions and allegations."

Nick nodded. "Too much subversive rhetoric on an empty stomach is a recipe for trouble. Oh," he added, "Jon called. He wants you to call him back tonight after eight. Says he has a commission to discuss."

Marian raised an eyebrow. "No details?"

"Nope."

"Hmmm." She headed for the shower.

It was almost nine when she remembered to call her art dealer, Jon Fisher. She was pleasantly stuffed with Nikki's delicious lamb stew, salad, French bread, and several glasses of pinot noir. She felt as mellow as a summer afternoon despite the rain-sleet mix coming down outside the window. Jon answered on the third ring. "Hi," she said. "It's Marian. What's up?"

For the next several minutes she listened as Jon described the proposal he'd received from one of Marian's collectors, Roberto Gonzales. True to his word, Roberto had purchased two of Marian's paintings the month after she'd first met him at his estate near Valle de Bravo in Mexico. Over the past four years he had added four more of her paintings to his collection.

She'd seen him only once during that period—when she and Nick were married in Valle de Bravo in 1969. Since then, they had found it increasingly difficult to spend time in Valle, and resorted to the Lenox house as a more available getaway. But Roberto had written several times to say how much he enjoyed having Marian's work in his collection.

Now, he wanted to invite her to paint a mural on the wall of a newly constructed guesthouse. "He said," Jon added, "that your landscapes of the area around Valle are the most beautiful thing he's ever seen aside from the artist herself."

"Yikes," Marian said, remembering the not-so-subtle pass that Roberto had made the last time she was in Valle.

"Yikes?" Jon repeated. "Is that a no or a yes, sweetheart?"

"It's an 'I don't know,'" Marian replied. "When does Roberto want this mural?"

"Yesterday," said Jon. "Tomorrow at the latest."

"I'll get back to you," said Marian.

"Sorry, babe," Nick told her. "I can't take time away from my work just now. Carl and I promised to have a preliminary description of our collaboration ready by the end of the month. The folks at the Rockefeller Foundation don't make exceptions on grant deadlines."

Marian was wadding up little pieces of paper and tossing them at the poster of Leonard Nimoy that hung on the wall above the television. "And why," Nick continued, "do you always bombard Mr. Spock when you get pissed?"

"It helps me think," Marian said. "And I'm not pissed. I understand that you need to work on the grant proposal. It's just that I'm... unnerved about going down there for three or four weeks and spending time with the predatory Senor Gonzales."

"He's the one who should be unnerved," Nick said with a smirk.

She looked at him. "And why exactly is that?"

"I don't think you need a chaperone," Nick replied. "I'm pretty sure you can take care of yourself."

"I don't know," Marian countered. "I did everything I could to discourage you, cookie. And look at me now." She lobbed another spitball at Spock.

"Yeah, but I'm disarmingly charming. And gorgeous. And an artist."

"And a great cook," she added.

"Right. So see? *No problema.*"

"Still," she frowned and pulled at a lock of hair, "I'll need some help. I'll have to get materials, set up, clean up."

"Why don't you take Allison?" Nick suggested.

Carl's younger sister, Allison, had been spending time with Marian and Nick off and on for the past six months since her move to New York to attend Parsons, a renowned art and design school that had recently merged with the progressive New School for Social Research. Marian had become a mentor and friend, and Ali made herself useful as a studio assistant.

Marian thought for a moment. "I don't want her to miss classes."

"Maybe they could set up an independent study for her," Nick suggested. "You know how they like to stress alternative learning environments and international experiences, eh? Besides," he added, "she *is* half Mexican after all."

That brought back her memories of Carl's struggle to accept his Mexican heritage and the painful journey that had led him from angry denial to joyous discovery. She was so proud of his progress. *Take Ali to Mexico*, Marian thought, *what a great idea*!

CHAPTER
20

Mexico City, Mexico

The Aeronaves de Mexico DC-8 floated gently down into the blue haze that covered the Valley of Mexico and the country's capital, the Distrito Federal, DF, Mexico City, the largest metropolitan area in the western hemisphere. Rising above the smoky soup that filled the valley—once a vast lake—were the volcanic peaks, Popocatepetl and Iztaccihuatl, connected by a ridge known as the *Paso de Cortes.*

Allison Morales was just one month short of her nineteenth birthday. Twelve years younger than her brother Carl and five years younger than her brother Silvio, who had been killed in Vietnam in 1969, she was the "baby" of the family—a scrappy, brilliant little girl who had grown into a fierce, articulate activist constantly involved in causes that ranged from anti-war protests to social justice issues and political organizing.

She was also a talented designer who wanted to use her artistic abilities to advance the causes that captured her attention. For the past several months, she and Marian had been discussing women's liberation and the feminist theories that were bursting through the barriers of suppression. It was a heady time to be young, bright, and engaged in social change.

Allison downplayed her attractiveness with understated, almost careless attire and a casual bob that let her curly black hair attend to itself. She wore no makeup. Even so, with her oval face, dark brown eyes and olive complexion, she had a captivating charm that boys, and now young men, found alluring. Until they started a conversation. Allison's caustic wit and intellectual intensity frightened off all but the most determined admirers. Which suited her just fine, thank you very much.

Today, however, dressed in a black "power to the people" tee shirt, black jeans, and worn grey sneakers, she looked much younger than her almost nineteen years. She also had her nose pressed to the airplane window as she looked down at the city. "It's huge," she said to Marian. "Goes on forever."

"Almost nine million people," Marian replied. "Five years ago it was around seven million."

"Where did they come from?"

"Mostly from the rural areas, farming communities that haven't changed much in a few hundred years. In DF people can have electricity, indoor plumbing, a job. Industrial production is concentrated in the city. So is education, culture, even publishing. It's where the action is. It's also," she waved her hand toward the plane window, "where the pollution is, as you can see."

"What's causing it?" Allison asked.

"Mostly traffic congestion—cars, trucks, buses. Plus a lack of regulation—there are no emission standards, no crankcase ventilation, no catalytic converters. Geographically, the city is in a bowl. It's like a caldron surrounded by mountains. There's nowhere for the fumes to go, so they just sit there." She peered over Ali's shoulder out the window. "So, that's what you get. Muck."

Ali shook her head, her mouth tightening to a line. "That's so totally whacked."

"I believe my correct response is 'right on'?"

Ali gave her a grin. "Yep. Bitchin'." After a minute she asked, "So where's Valle de Bravo?"

"About ninety miles southwest of the city." Marian waved her hand. "Just a ways over those mountains."

"How long will it take to get there?"

"Depends,' Marian replied. "It's not a long drive, but the roads aren't great and the weather can be a factor." She gave Ali a smile. "But it's worth the price. You'll see."

Roberto Gonzalez had sent his driver to pick them up at the airport. It was getting dark as the black Mercedes wound its way through the city and south into the hills to the suburban community of San Angel, just south of Mexico City. Ali watched the grand spectacle of the architecture along *Avenida Insurgentes* roll past—modernist skyscrapers, colorful murals, crowded sidewalk cafes, charming parks, people and cars and a whirl of activity. Lights blinked on and the sky to the west glowed blood-orange behind a pile-up of purple mountains. *It is sooo big*, she thought. Allison was used to big cities—San Francisco, Boston, New York—but Mexico DF seemed unmanageably huge, even more so than Los Angeles which she had only visited twice and thought of as a sprawling, ugly mess. Mexico DF was massive.

When they pulled up to the gates of the Gonzales family home, Ali took a minute to take in the magnificence of the place—the intricate wrought iron gates, the eight-foot-high security wall topped, embedded, she noted, with shards of broken glass. The brick-paved drive was lined with Italian cypress trees. A three—tiered fountain served as a focal point in front of the house. And then the house itself: a white adobe castle with a red-tiled roof and wrought iron window grills in a fleur-de-lis pattern.

Several cars were parked along the drive. "Senor Gonzales has invited a few friends to meet you," the driver informed them. "Just a small party. Only twenty or so guests." He held the door open for them and took their luggage from the trunk. "Ernesto! Jose! Pronto!" he cried and two young men scurried up, greeted them with great enthusiasm and picked up their bags. A maid appeared from the tall blue double doors and directed the men to take the luggage to the guest suite, then said in English, "Welcome to Casa Hermosa Vista. Please, come in."

The foyer was round, with a high dome and twin staircases that wound up on either side to a balcony that overlooked the lower floor. "I know you must be tired," the maid said. "If you would like to refresh yourselves or change from your travel clothes, I'll be happy to show you to your room."

Allison thought the remark might be especially aimed at her, judging from the maid's glance at her tee shirt and jeans, but she said, "No thanks. I'm fine."

"Me too," Marian agreed. "Where's Roberto?"

"Right this way." The maid ushered them into the main living area with its massive wooden beams, white walls, gilded mirrors and numerous art works—paintings, sculptures, glassworks, ceramics. Ali immediately spotted one of Marian's landscapes prominently sited over a black leather sofa.

Voices and music came from the next room. When they went through an arch into the dining room, Allison was amazed to see an attractive blond-haired woman dressed in white Capris and a turquoise silk blouse dancing with a tall black man atop an enormous dining room table. *Ball of Confusion* by the Temptations blared from the stereo. About fifteen other people were milling around the room, some watching the dancers, others moving to the music or talking.

A tall man with a moustache and dark wavy hair wearing a paisley shirt and white bell-bottom jeans, straightened up from the hearth of the stone fireplace that dominated the end of the room and came toward them. "*Hola!*" he cried. "Marian, you're here. Welcome to Casa Hermosa." He gave Marian a hug, kissed her cheek, then turned to Allison. "And this must be Senorita Morales. *Buenas noches, mi querido.* Good evening, my dear."

"Very nice to meet you, Mr. Gonzales," Allison said, meeting his look with calculated confidence. Marian had warned her this guy could be a little . . . pushy. He shook her outstretched hand with a hint of amusement. Then he took Marian's arm and said, "Come in. Come in. What can I get you to drink? I have a big pitcher of sangria, or would you prefer white wine?"

"Wine would be good," Marian said.

"And for you, senorita?"

"I'll have a beer," Ali said.

"Of course. I would introduce you to my wife, Tatiana," he said, glancing at the couple gyrating on the tabletop, "but as you can see, she is otherwise engaged just now."

"Ah," Marian said. "Your wife."

Roberto gave her a smile. "Yes," he said. "We have reconciled."

When he left them to see about the drinks, Marian said in a low voice, "Whew. I think that means I can relax."

Allison couldn't contain a giggle.

It was after nine when dinner began to emerge from the kitchen—enchiladas with chicken and green chiles, pork tamales, squash blossom quesadillas, red hominy stew, turkey in mole sauce, fresh corn tortillas, sugared fritters, and a dish of tropical fruits in a delicious syrup. Beer, wine, rum and tequila flowed freely.

After the plane trip, the excitement of seeing Mexico City for the first time, the food and drink, and the introductions to numerous guests, Allison was feeling light-headed, and looked for someplace quiet to sit down. She had just spent fifteen minutes listening to Tatiana Gonzales tell her a long story about a Mexican artist named Frida Kahlo who had a love affair with the Communist revolutionary Leon Trotsky.

Allison had never heard of Frida Kahlo, but she did recognize the name of Kahlo's husband, artist Diego Rivera. "She is better painter than him," Tatiana proclaimed. "She is one who will be star!" Tatiana—tall, blond, voluptuous, effusive—did not request, she commanded. Did not inform, but dictated. Every sentence seemed to have an exclamation point at the end. Allison, hardly a reticent communicator herself, was overwhelmed by the tidal wave of Tatiana's words delivered with a flamboyant Russian accent.

Marian came to Ali's rescue and was soon debating with Tatiana the merits of Mexican tequila compared to Russian vodka. Allison took the opportunity to sidle away from the crowd and search for a quiet spot to relax. She headed down a dimly lit hallway.

Most of the rooms were closed, but toward the end of the hall she saw light coming from a half-open door. When she looked in she saw a library—floor-to-ceiling bookcases, a Colonial period desk, a large stone fireplace and two leather wing chairs next to the hearth. In one of the chairs sat a young man. He appeared to be in his early twenties with shoulder-length black hair pulled back into a ponytail. He had on grey slacks and a black turtleneck sweater, wore a pair of old-fashioned horn-rimmed glasses, and was immersed in reading from a leather-bound book. He glanced up as Allison came in and gave her a questioning stare.

"Oh," she said, "Sorry. I... I mean *Lo siento, por favor perdóname.*" "Sorry, please excuse me."

The young man stood and set the book down on the coffee table. "No, it's quite all right," he said in lightly-accented English. "Please," he gestured toward the empty wing chair, "come in." As she approached he held out his hand. "Francisco Gonzales," he said. "The reclusive son of our host."

Allison smiled and took his hand. "Allison Morales. Reclusive guest." His handshake was pleasantly firm, business-like but gentle.

"Ah, yes," he said, "I saw you at dinner. You are with Miss Archer, the artist, yes?"

"I'm her assistant," Allison replied. His eyes were a warm brown and very intense. The angle of his dark brows gave him a quizzical look, as though he had asked a question and was waiting for a response. He looked more Spanish than Indian, although his skin was the color of amber.

"Can I get you anything?" he asked.

Always so solicitous, she thought and was reminded of her father, Jorge. *So polite.*

"Thank you, but no. I've had plenty of everything." She sank gratefully into the chair.

He smiled and sat down. They looked at each other for a minute, then he said, "Tell me, what do you do as assistant to the artist?"

"Whatever's useful. Carry supplies, mix paint, clean up."

"Have you worked with her long?"

"No, just the past few months. Since I moved to New York."

"From where?"

"I was," she hesitated, "I was going to school at Kent State, but there was a. . . a terrible incident and I left and moved to New York to be near my brother."

"Ah, yes," he said, nodding. "The massacre."

Surprised, she said, "You know about that?"

"Of course." Noticing her look he added, "I go to school at Harvard. So I am not far away from Ohio."

"What are you studying at Harvard?"

"Law. And you, Allison Morales? Do you now go to another school?"

"Yes," she replied. "I'm studying design at Parsons."

"A part of The New School for Social Research, yes?"

"Since last year, yes."

He cocked his head and smiled slightly. "Which people would you like to see empowered?"

After a moment she realized he was looking at her tee shirt: a black tee with an iconic clenched fist and "Power to the People" written across the front in a brushy red script. *Maybe*, she thought, *not the best fashion statement at the home of a conservative Mexican family?* But he had asked, so she answered, "Any who are oppressed."

He raised an eyebrow. "You are an activist?"

"Yes, I am," she said decisively. If he didn't like it, too bad.

But he nodded and gave her a thoughtful look. "So am I," he said.

By one a.m. Marian was exhausted. To say that it had been a long day was an understatement. All but a few of the guests had left and two maids were hard at work cleaning up.

"There you are," Tatiana strode toward her, looking wide-awake. Marian tried to straighten up from her sprawl on the living room sofa. "You must be *izmuchennyy*, very tired. Is time for you to sleep. Come, I show you to your room."

"Have you seen my assistant, Allison?" Marian asked as Tatiana guided her down the hall. She realized that Ali had disappeared not long after dinner. Where could she have gone?

"*Nyet.* But I ask the maid. Here, this your door. I tell your assistant to join you, yes?"

"That would be great," Marian said. In the room, she found their suitcases setting on luggage racks, located her nightgown, robe and slippers and staggered into the adjacent bathroom. It was enormous—filled with marble and mirrors. She set out her toiletries and was just starting to brush her teeth when she heard Allison's voice from the bedroom.

"Marian? Hi. I'm here."

She poked her head out and saw Ali in the middle of the room, arms outstretched, turning in slow circles. *Good lord*, she thought, *what's she gotten into? Acapulco gold? Magic mushrooms?* "Be right out," she called.

"No hurry."

"Where *were* you?" Marian asked as she took off her robe and tossed it onto a blue velvet-covered chair next to one of the twin beds. "I haven't seen you for hours?"

"I was with Francisco," Ali replied dreamily.

"Francisco? Roberto's son?"

"That's the one."

"But where—?"

"We were in the library talking."

"For three hours?"

"Was it that long? I guess I lost track."

Allison gave Marian what she could only described as a goofy grin, half embarrassed, half blissful. *Uh oh*, Marian thought. *This looks like trouble.* She sat down on the bed. "What did you talk about?"

"Everything. God, he's amazing! He's in his second year at Harvard Law and he's been involved in student protests against the war and he knows everything, I mean *everything*, about the Mexican Revolution and about migrant workers and the Chavez movement and—"

"Whoa," Marian held up her hand. "How did you get into this conversation?"

"He was in the library reading, trying to escape from the party and all that endless small talk and socializing, and I was trying to find a quiet place to hide out, and we just ended up in the library talking. It was. . ." she paused, gazing into space in a starry-eyed way Marian hadn't seen before, "it was. . . *magical*."

"Sounds like a great discussion."

"Totally awesome." Ali started taking off her clothes, then spotted her suitcase and riffled through it, grabbed her robe, and disappeared into the bathroom. When she came out a few minutes later Marian was already in bed. "He wants me to go on a hike with him. After we get to Valle I mean. He said he wants to show me something."

I'll bet, Marian thought, but she said, "That sounds nice." She was too tired to ask for any more details before she fell asleep.

CHAPTER

21

Valle de Bravo, Mexico

"It's not far," Francisco said. "Just about twenty kilometers from here. We'll be there by around ten."

Allison looked out the window of the pickup truck. The narrow road wound through fields of stubble left from the harvest of corn and beans. Farmsteads were scattered along the road and into the hills that rose upward to the east. Adobe farmhouses, brown as mud, with tiled roofs and window boxes filled with bright red geraniums dotted the landscape. Children, goats and chickens cavorted together in a yard. In one field, she saw a farmer pushing a plow behind a pair of placid oxen.

At an elevation of slightly over six thousand feet, the village of Valle de Bravo was already in the mountains, but Allison was awed by the the neighboring ranges that rose even higher. In the distance, Ali could see the towering cone of Nevada de Toluca, an impressive volcano with an elevation of over fifteen thousand feet.

The pickup turned off the main road onto a rutted, unpaved path. "They call this the Los Saucos highway," said Francisco with a laugh.

"Some highway," Allison said. "I hope the horses don't mind being jolted around."

"They are used to it," he answered. "We tow them around all the time."

The horse trailer was hitched behind the truck. Francisco had explained that the place he wanted to show Allison was accessible only by horseback. "And even so, we'll have to hike the last quarter mile. Is too steep for the horses."

The winter day was beautiful, the sky a deep azure blue with small white puffs of clouds sailing past. The mountains to the east were topped with an icing of snow. Both she and Francisco were layered in sweaters under their coats. "We'll be up at about ten thousand feet," Francisco warned, "so it will be a little cold."

After bumping along for fifteen miles, Francisco parked the truck alongside the road. Ali helped him unload the horses. They tossed their heads and snorted and seemed pleased to be finished with the trailer ride. The horses—a bay gelding with black mane and tail, and a grey mare with the small pointed ears and the dish-shaped face of an Arabian—were already saddled, so Francisco and Ali mounted and she followed him into the forest.

A dirt trail, made barely passable by tangled roots and piles of stones, followed a meandering path up the mountainside. The horses picked their way slowly around the obstacles, bobbing their heads and whuffling as if to show their dissatisfaction with the route.

The forest was dense, filled with towering oyamel fir trees and thick vegetation. Yellow and red wildflowers dotted the sides of the path. Ali was surprised to see flowers this time of year, but Francisco explained that, despite the elevation, the mountains were still sub-tropical with the temperature rarely dipping to freezing.

After half an hour, Francisco turned and gave Ali an encouraging smile. "Not much further," he said.

She was tingling with anticipation. Although she had tried repeatedly to get him to tell her where he was taking her, Francisco remained adamant—it was a surprise. She must be patient. Patience had never been Ali's strong suit. Now she was somewhere between furious and exhilarated.

In the five days since she had met Francisco Juan Arturo Gonzales y Martinez, she had experienced a barrage of new feelings—excitement, wonder, frustration, distress, and a heady, disorienting happiness that was totally new to her. Every day seemed to bring a new revelation.

"Okay," he called as they rounded a curve in the path and entered a small open space between outcroppings of granite boulders. "This is where we leave the horses."

They dismounted and tethered the horses to sapling trees, using the lead ropes he had brought along. "They can graze while we gaze," he said cryptically, flashing her a teasing smile.

They clambered up the steep path that led to a plateau, grabbing at tree roots and slipping on gravel. He helped her up the last few yards. They were both breathless from the exertion and the altitude. They stood for a moment at the summit, gasping a little from the climb. When Ali glanced around, she saw that the plateau was still densely forested, fir trees towering into the sky.

Then, something caught her eye. A bush next to the trail was moving. And behind Francisco, another bush was covered with an orangy mass that seemed to be vibrating. "What on earth!" she exclaimed.

Francisco laughed. "Look around you, Allison Morales," he said. "You are one of the few people to see this magic."

Even as he spoke, a great swarm of orange and black butterflies detached themselves from the tree branches and soared into the sky in a great spiral, a sunburst of beating wings that sounded like the soft patter of rain.

Allison let out a squeal of delight. "My God, Francisco, what *are* they?!"

"Monarchs," he replied. "Monarch butterflies."

"But there must be millions of them," Ali cried. There were more and more of them everywhere she looked—resting on bushes, massed on tree branches, flitting into the air. Two of them lit for a moment on her shoulder before fluttering away. Amazed, overwhelmed, Allison held out her arms like a Pantokrator embracing the world, and turned her face skyward in a wordless prayer.

Francisco came to stand beside her, looking up also at the clumps of vibrating color. "Actually," he said, "scientists believe there are billions of them. But nobody really knows. So far, no one has studied them or found a reason why they come to this place every year."

"They come every year?" she repeated, looking at him.

He nodded. "Every winter. Like clockwork. Usually about the time of the *Dia de los Muertos*, the Day of the Dead. Some of the old people say they are the souls of the departed who have returned to celebrate the fiesta."

"How did you find this place?" Ali asked.

"During my childhood, we spent family holidays at our ranch in Avandaro," Francisco replied. "Some of the local kids knew about the *Bosque de los Monarcos*, the forest of the Monarchs. I used to come up here with them. It was a big deal because the Indians are very superstitious about the butterflies, so we always had to sneak up here and not tell anyone." He glanced around. "Even today, not many people know of this place."

He put his arm around her shoulders and together they stood watching the spectacle. "Where do they go when they're not here?" asked Allison.

Francisco shrugged. "I don't know. They are like the birds, you know? Like all the things that migrate—the swallows, the geese. They stay here for the winter months and then in the spring, they leave. I suppose they go north."

"It's amazing," Allison said softly. "Like Africa or like. . . like Eden. Paradise before the Fall."

"The whole of the world was like this once," Francisco said. "An unspoiled paradise. But more and more, we have defaced it. Polluted it with our hubris, our *progress*."

She heard the anger in his voice and glanced up at him. "Is that what you meant when you said that Mexico was a third-world country when it came to ecological problems?"

"Mexico is a poor country. It looks at the United States and it sees a rich neighbor lecturing about ecological concerns when it's people are struggling to find enough food to keep from starving. Our resources are already limited. Jobs, opportunities, industrialization— those are the things at the top of Mexico's agenda, not saving whales or whooping cranes. In many ways, we are still a feudal society in which the people in power think only about maintaining their position and extracting any resource that will make them more powerful." He sighed and shook his head.

"So," said Ali, "that's why you've decided to study environmental law at Harvard?"

"Is a new program. Not even a year old." Excitedly, he described the formation of a new group called the Harvard Environmental Law Society that wanted to institute classes in environmental law in order to respond more effectively to ecological problems. "We think it's time for the Law School, and laws in general, to question the exploitation of nature. We want to put morality ahead of politics and economics. But the challenge is huge, especially in the third world." He smiled ruefully. "My father, Roberto, sent me to Harvard Law so I could become a lawyer for his company. He is not so happy that I came back filled with these *subversive* ideas."

"What made you challenge your father's authority?" Allison asked.

Francisco didn't answer for a minute. Then he looked at her and said, "This place for one." He glanced around. The butterflies were still swirling among the treetops. You could hear the soft beating of their wings. "So much of the magic is being lost, destroyed. And for what?" He was silent, looking up at the trees.

"And also," he continued, looking back at her, "it was the landing on the moon."

Ali laughed. "Really?"

"Yes. Twenty months ago I was in my apartment in Cambridge with two friends, and we watched on the television the landing on the moon. It was breathtaking. I was filled with awe at our technology, our capacity for accomplishment.

"But then I saw the image of the earth—that beautiful, fragile blue sphere floating in the blackness, and I realized how vulnerable we were. How vulnerable the planet is. At the same time, I saw the limits of our world and the boundlessness of our imagination, and I thought, that planet is my home and the home of every living thing that we know of, *La Madre Universale*, the universal mother that has given us life. We must protect her. After all, if you can't drink the water or breathe the air, what difference does the rest of it matter?"

Ali put out her hand and rested it on his cheek. "That's really beautiful," she said.

He bent and kissed her gently on the mouth. "Come," he said, "we'd better go." They got back to Avandero in time for a late lunch.

Allison Morales was not a virgin. She had slept with four young men—well, boys really—but each had seemed more like a political statement, a declaration of independence, an experiment in social psychology, than a love affair. Had she "loved them?" Sort of. At the time. In a way.

But *this*, she thought as she lay next to Francisco, watching him as he slept, listening to the soft sound of his breathing, was completely different. "It means so much more when it's meant," he had whispered to her the night before as they lay in each other's arms.

She could feel his heart beating against her breast, and the feel of it filled her with joy and tenderness and a wonderful and frightening sense of being in the moment, in a small fragile sliver of time that was all you could ever possess for certain. She wanted to cry and laugh at the same time and to say again and again to him, "*Te quiero.*" "I want you. I love you."

CHAPTER

22

San Francisco, California
February 1971

"The x-rays are somewhat... inconclusive," the doctor said. "It's impossible to determine the exact cause of the impairment using the available technology." Dr. Williamson turned to his patient. "If you agree, my recommendation is to attempt a surgical procedure to reconstruct the wrist and to relieve any pressure on the nerves that may be effecting mobility. In addition, there may be indications of synovitis, an inflammation of the membrane that lines the wrist joint. We would be able to relieve the inflammation during surgery."

Alex considered her options. She could do nothing and continue her teaching career, occasionally perform the very limited right-hand repertoire. Or she could take a dramatic chance that the complex surgery suggested by Dr. Williamson might produce a successful outcome. Even if she went ahead with the operation, it would take a year of therapy and rehabilitation before she would know if the procedure was truly successful.

She looked up at Dr. Williamson who was waiting patiently for her response. "Okay," she said. "Let's get the surgery scheduled."

Dr. Williamson was an avid fan of classical music. He had heard Alex play on two occasions, once as a soloist with the San Francisco Symphony during her first West Coast tour in 1968, and again at a recital in London when he was in town for a medical convention. He also had four of her recordings, including the one made of her debut with the Cleveland Orchestra. He brought that one with him to the operating theatre on the day of Alex's surgery. "So you can hear how the Rachmaninoff Second is supposed to sound," he said with a grin.

And so, as she slipped into unconsciousness, Alex was listening to her former self performing Rachmaninoff's *Second Piano Concerto*: listening to what she had once been, and what she hoped she would once again become.

Kate slid into a booth in the inside dining room of The Firehouse Restaurant in downtown Sacramento. It had always been one of her favorite places since she had celebrated her eighteenth birthday there not long after the place opened in 1960. It was one of the first buildings to be renovated in the new Sacramento Historic District, and was later designated an historic landmark. With its dark paneling, cozy bar and spacious courtyard, the restaurant had the feel of Old Sacramento, a fragment of history left over from the Gold Rush era.

Kate took the menu from the waitress, scanned the offerings and took a sip of ice water. Everything was so good, it was always difficult to decide what to order.

She glanced up and saw Jerry McClosky, Carl's music agent, coming toward her. She waved, then got up to give him a hug. He hadn't changed—still a great, lumbering bear of a man with a hefty frame, unruly dark blond hair, and a round face that was pink from the cold outside.

"Hey, pretty lady," he greeted her, planting a kiss on her cheek. "Hope you haven't been waiting long."

"I just sat down," she assured him. "It was great to hear from you. What brings you to Sacramento?"

"Just had a very interesting meeting with Carl's father, Jorge. Do you know about this concert Carl wants to do in the Fall?"

"I know that he's planning to be in California next October. We arranged for him to visit with Cory. But he didn't mention a concert."

"Still in the planning stage. Carl gave me a call just before

Christmas and talked to me about doing a concert with the SF orchestra." Jerry grinned broadly. "Better fasten your seat belt, Katie."

Kate raised her eyebrows. "What's going on?" she asked. "What's he done now?"

Jerry's booming laugh filled the room. "He wants to do a benefit concert for the Farm Workers Union. What do you think of *that*?"

His words had the desired effect. Kate, rendered momentarily speechless, sat and stared at him. Presently, a smile began at the corners of her mouth and spread across her face. "Well," she said softly, "I'll be damned."

Eager now to divulge the details, Jerry sat forward. "When he called he said, 'Here's what I want to do, Jerry. Fix it.'"

"Sounds like him," Kate said.

"At first I thought he was nuts. I had no idea how the orchestra administration would react, let alone the patrons. But once I started checking, I was amazed at the support. The good citizens who have been boycotting grapes and lettuce were totally thrilled with the idea. And there are a lot of them out there. Quite a few are subscription ticket holders. I got together with the music director and the Symphony League and worked out the details. In fact, I'm planning to give Carl a call this evening and give him the green light."

"So you just talked to Jorge and Rose about the proposal?"

"Yep. Their Mr. Chavez just got out of jail. Seems he refused to obey a court order to stop the boycott against one of the growers."

"That's right," Kate recalled. "I saw an article in the *Bee*. Coretta King and Ethel Kennedy both visited him to show their support."

"The union membership is growing, and they now have contracts with the grape growers," Jerry said. "But they're still working on the vegetable growers. They're moving their headquarters out of Delano, so they need help setting up their new operation. Carl suggested we could raise enough money to help them out. Hey," he added, "that's a silly smile you've got on your face."

"Do you know what a breakthrough this is for Carl?" Kate said.

"I know that he's been fighting this battle a long time. Nobody knows that better than you, I expect."

"It's been tearing him apart for years, and I never knew how to help him. I guess he had to work through it himself." She shook her head.

They sat smiling at each other. Then Jerry asked, "How's Alex?"

"Much better. Last time I talked to her she said that now that the surgery is over, she's starting to work with a physical therapist to rehabilitate her hand. Meanwhile, she's been practicing to get her right hand up to par."

"Hmmm," Jerry nodded. "Good."

"Do you have some particular reason for being interested?"

"Carl wants her on the program for the October concert."

"My word," Kate exclaimed. "Another bombshell. You're certainly full of surprises this afternoon."

"She didn't mention it to you?"

"Not a word. But I know she's been putting in a lot of time practicing. I thought she was just eager to see if she could improve her condition."

"Carl's hoping that she won't back out. He wants to encourage her, but he doesn't want to scare her off. Kind of a delicate balance."

"She *can* be skittish," Kate said with a smile.

"I'll let him know that she's working on it. That should set him at ease a bit." He cocked his head. "He wouldn't tell me what he wanted on the program, only that he wanted her as soloist. Any idea what he's up to?"

"Oh yes," Kate replied. "I think I know *exactly* what he has in mind."

CHAPTER
23

Mockingbird Ranch

"Okay," Tommy said. "I think that's enough for today, Cory-chan." He bowed and Cory bowed back.

"Thank you, sensei," Cory said gravely.

"Remember what I told you. Practice stepping on the balls of your feet, not heel first. Work on your pivots and keep your hips and shoulders in harmony. Okay?"

Cory nodded. "Okay, Mr. Tommy."

Tommy watched the boy as he trotted up the path and disappeared into the house. Then he turned and scanned the orchard. The wildflowers were spectacular—yellow and purple clover, deep orange poppies and lapis-blue lupine, bright yellow mustard and magenta wild radish. The flowers painted dizzying splashes of color between the rows of pear trees, and up the hillside toward the river bluff. Seeing them made Tommy happy and sad, homesick and nostalgic. He turned his back on the display and walked up the path, and through the courtyard gate. Sitting down in one of the rustic wooden chairs under the protective canopy of the fig tree, he gazed at the worn terra cotta tiles and tried, again, to make sense of his situation.

He'd been living at Mockingbird for four months, and had made an excellent recovery from the aneurism and heart attack that had nearly ended his life. Physically, he was almost "back to normal," but he still felt anxious and confused.

He was sleeping well and Kate was almost obsessive about his exercise and diet regimen—logging his activity, feeding him supplements, reading books and articles on the best kinds of foods for "cardio health." He smiled a little, remembered teasing her about being his nanny. "I just needed a project," she countered. He remembered how she used to fuss over her brother, Julian, the same way.

But what was he to her? An old friend? A substitute sibling? And what was she to him? An ex-girlfriend? He couldn't find a name for what they shared. They had been lovers. They would always be friends. But he couldn't figure out where this was leading. Why was he here? At Mockingbird? With Kate? And what should he do next?

Over the past four months, he and Kate had talked about so many things—his professional aspirations, her struggles to find a direction for her life, her hopes for her son, their travels to other countries, their marriages, their losses. He knew that he could just continue to stay at the ranch. Kate wasn't going to kick him out. She seemed to be content to let him take his time, to heal and come to terms with what had happened to him. But he shouldn't expect that to last indefinitely.

He'd gone as far as he could with the preliminary drawings of the music center project. The cost estimates were done. He had even included affordable options for improving the structural integrity of the century-old buildings to protect them from earthquake damage. But until the financing was available and the permits and zoning issues resolved, there wasn't much more he could do, professionally, at Mockingbird.

He could go back to San Francisco. Move back into the Twin Peaks house. Pick up where he left off back in October. That seemed logical. Then why didn't it feel "right?"

He sighed and pressed his fingers together and tried to think of a solution. But the harder he thought, the fuzzier the future looked. It was so *comfortable* to be at Mockingbird, to have no responsibilities, to be surrounded by caring people and to live so quietly and peacefully in such beautiful place. But he needed some kind of test. Some way to measure his options, to re-think his life.

———◦oo◦❂◦oo◦———

"You're sure you'll be okay?" Kate asked.

He had made a great recovery, but he still needed to be careful—watch his diet, take his medications, rest when he was tired. Would he do that if he was alone? He gave Kate a reproachful look. "Hey, I'm a big boy. I can look after myself."

She cocked her head. "I don't know, Ashida," she replied. "Last time you were on your own you gave us all quite a scare."

He smiled. "I'll be more attentive to myself, okay? And Ben will be checking up on me."

"I'll update you on the project."

"You'd better."

They stood in the courtyard looking at each other. She didn't want him to leave. They both knew that. But she also knew that he needed to make the decision himself. She had to let him go. It was the only way to not lose him.

She wanted to fix this moment in her mind, to remember him standing there before her, wearing jeans and his Kyoto Institute of Technology sweatshirt, smiling a little half-smile, the arc of his black hair across his forehead, that strange white lightning bolt slashing through it, his serious, impenetrable eyes.

"So," he said suddenly, "off I go." He gave her a quick hug and a peck on the cheek. "Wish me luck."

"Always," she said.

One last smile and he turned resolutely and walked through the gate and down the path to his car. He waved as he opened the driver's door and slid in behind the wheel. She waved back. Little puffs of dust spurted from the tires of the Z-car as he drove off down the drive. The wind caught them and they disappeared into the sweet morning air. And then there was nothing to do but go back inside a house that suddenly seemed very big and very quiet. And very empty.

———∘∘o🙰∘o∘———

Sacramento, California

Kate found a parking space on Alhambra Boulevard, fed the meter and walked around the corner to the Rosemount Grill. It was dim inside the restaurant after the bright light of the spring sun and she blinked and narrowed her eyes, trying to adjust to the change. She spotted Chris Malacchi-Salinger in a booth near the back of the restaurant and made her way through the lunchtime crowd. Chris got up as Kate approached and held out her arms.

"Hey, lady," Chris cried. "Good to see you."

"You too, Chris," Kate responded as they hugged. They sat down opposite each other and Kate took a minute to study her friend. Except for the trim navy blue suit and patterned silk blouse, Chris didn't look much different from when they were roommates at Berkeley back in 1961. Her hair was still a mass of black curls, her round face with those pink cheeks and pretty brown eyes still cherubic and sweet. She had put on a few pounds but they made her look voluptuous, not stout. "You're looking great," Kate told her.

"You too. I'm so glad you called me. We haven't seen each other since. . . when was it?"

"Dad's funeral, I think," Kate said. "Summer of '69."

"God, almost two years."

"I forgive you for being so busy, counselor," Kate teased. "So, how are you and Lennie doing?"

"Malacchi and Salinger, greatest law firm in Sacramento," Chris returned. "We just took on a junior partner, which will really help with the workload."

"And how are the twins?"

"Fine. They'll be starting kindergarten in the Fall."

Kate shook her head. "They do grow up fast, don't they?"

"Super fast. But tell me, what's this big project you've gotten into and how can I be of service?"

"Let's get right to it," Kate said, pulling a sheath of papers out of her purse and spreading them out on the table. For the next hour, Kate described the music center project and the problems that had to be resolved before it could become a reality. The waitress came and went and hot turkey sandwiches were brought and devoured. Over a second cup of coffee, Kate finished by saying, "It's the permitting process that has me totally flummoxed. I had no idea it would be so complex. I've been trying to wade through it, but I'm drowning in legalese."

"And that's where I come in," Chris said. "There are a couple of ways you can go with this. Let me talk to Lennie and we can get back together. We'll give you some options. Don't worry, girl," she added, "we'll help you work through this."

"Thank goodness," Kate said with a sigh. "I was floundering around like a beached seal."

Chris shook her head, grinning. "It's all just a conspiracy to help us lawyers make a bundle."

"So it's a good thing to have a lawyer in the family. Or in this case, almost family."

"I promise to solve your problem and not charge you a cent."

"Really? I could pay at least something."

"Strictly pro bono, my dear. Makes us look less predatory."

They both laughed and decided to get dessert. Over the cheesecake with strawberry sauce, Chris said, "Last time we talked, Tommy Ashida was staying at Mockingbird. Is he still there?" She cocked her head expectantly.

Kate looked away, then back at Chris. "He's moved back to San Francisco."

Chris raised her eyebrows. "Ah. Dare I ask what that means?"

Kate shrugged. "I wish I had an answer. It was. . ." She struggled for a moment, searching for the right words. "It was wonderful having him at the ranch. Seemed so. . . right somehow. Like everything had finally, I don't know, come full circle or something. He and Cory had a great time getting acquainted. Cory really misses him. He keeps asking me when Mr. Tommy is coming back. I don't know what to tell him. Someday? Never? I have no idea."

"Have you heard from him since he left?"

"He's called a couple of times to get an update on the project.

Very businesslike. I think. . ." she paused and glanced around the dining room, then looked back at Chris, "I think he's got to work through a whole lot of feelings, and there's not much I can do to help him."

"Except be there," Chris said.

CHAPTER

24

Mexico City, Mexico

"Thanks for giving us a ride," Marian said from the back seat of the rented Renault.

Francisco's eyes glanced up to meet hers in the rear view mirror. "No problem," he said.

Allison was sitting next to Francisco in the front seat as they sped along the highway that led from Toluca to the Mexico Federal District, known as DF. Marian thought that she had never known Allison to be so quiet.

The mural that Marian was creating for the guesthouse at the Gonzales's week-end place in Avandaro was nearly completed. She was pleased with the wall-sized landscape of the lake, it's surface burnished by the setting sun, mountains with a shawl of wispy clouds around their shoulders dissolving into a purple twilight. Roberto and Tatiana were delighted. They had invited all of their neighbors over to see the "masterpiece" and Marian had enjoyed the collective admiration. There was one last thing to do—the piece needed to have a final coat of varnish to protect the surface.

Marian had forgotten to put the varnish on the list of supplies, so a trip to DF was necessary to get the special product that she insisted on using. Happily, Francisco was on his way to catch a plane back to Boston to continue his studies at Harvard, and offered to give them a ride into town. In a show of what Marian had decided was a politically motivated defiance of his father, Francisco insisted on driving himself rather than relying on the family chauffeur.

The highway descended in a long, slow curve through subtropical forests from Toluca's 8,750 foot elevation to DF's 7,943. DF was a pale ghost of skyscrapers and smaller buildings enveloped in the ever-present blue-grey haze. They drove east on *Paseo de la Reforma* and through the beautiful greenery of Chapultepec Park.

"There is the new Museum of Anthropology," Francisco said, pointing to a monumental grey building grandly situated on the north side of the thoroughfare. "You should go and see. Just opened a few years ago and the architecture is amazing. So is the collection of artifacts."

They continued on through the city—a tangled maze of narrow streets and broad avenues, Colonial Spanish buildings standing beside black glass high-rises, small shops, and huge apartment complexes. The contrasts were amazing.

And then they were at the airport. It seemed to Marian that they were still in the center of town with a sprawl of buildings and roads stretching away in all directions. Francisco stopped at a bus terminal and said, "It's probably best for you to get out here where you can catch a bus back to downtown. I must take the car to the rental return."

He got out and opened the door for Marian, then went to the passenger side to open Ali's door, but she was already getting out. She and Francisco stood looking at each other for a long minute. Then he pulled her into his arms and kissed her. Marian looked away, a lump rising in her throat.

Lunch eaten, museum enjoyed, varnish purchased, Marian and Allison took a taxi back to the bus station and got on the first class express bus to Toluca. The bus was clean and comfortable and took only about forty-five minutes to reach the city—an ancient site that had been occupied since at least the first century A.D.

As they neared Toluca, Allison could see the Nevado de Toluca, the great snowcapped volcano that stood less than twenty miles southwest of the town. The Aztec god *Tolo* supposedly lived in the crater of the volcano.

The bus station was crowded and filled with exhaust fumes from the line of buses, taxis and trucks. The passengers from the Mexico DF express trooped off—mostly well-groomed men in dark suits and a few fashionably dressed women. Marian and Ali went into the station and bought tickets to Avandaro. The only bus going in that direction was a third-class local that would be leaving in fifteen minutes—barely enough time to get a quick drink of soda and take a trip to the ladies room.

Looking around the station, Allison noticed groups of women and children sitting on the floor. Some were beggars, others appeared to be just waiting for their bus to depart. When she and Marian went to the rest room, an older woman made a point of handing them both a paper towel before they could reach for one themselves. They left a few pesos in the box on the counter and she thanked them profusely. Allison was once again struck by the extremes of poverty and affluence that she saw everywhere.

They boarded the bus, which resembled a school bus, although it was painted bright blue instead of yellow. They set out on the road south toward Avandaro. Marian was sitting next to the window and Allison on the aisle. Across the aisle sat a toothless old woman holding a caged chicken on her lap. In front of her was a man with two large jugs of what Ali decided must be *pulque*, a popular drink made from the fermented sap of the agave cactus. She caught a whiff of the sour, yeasty smell of the brew.

The bus rattled along for half an hour, then stopped abruptly. She heard a muffled expletive from the driver and several of the passengers got up and craned their necks to see what was going on.

"Can you see anything?" Ali asked Marian who was looking out the window.

"No. We're out in the middle of nowhere. Maybe there's a problem with the engine?"

There was a commotion in the front of the bus, loud voices, someone calling "¡Ándale! ¡Ándale! ¡Arriba!" The driver stood up with his arms raised. Then a swarthy complexioned man with a bristling moustache climbed into the bus. He wore a sombrero and a white shirt and white trousers. Two gun belts made an "X" across his chest. And he was carrying a rifle. Additional white-dressed armed men followed him.

The passengers were very quiet. They all sat down, looking anxiously at each other, averting their eyes from the banditos. Allison, however, stared at them with open fascination. Who *were* these guys?

They didn't seem overtly threatening. None of the passengers had been pulled from their seat or assaulted. The bandit leader made his way down the aisle, glancing from side to side, a little smile on his lips as if he was amused at the fear his entrance had provoked.

But when he got to Allison he paused and looked down at her. For a moment her heart stopped and her mouth went dry. She had read the news reports about the Poor People's Party, the small rebel force led by a former school teacher, Lucio Cabanas, and his underground war against the Mexican elite—the kidnappings, the armed attacks and bombing attempts. Did the bandit think that Allison, and perhaps the blond woman who sat next to her, would bring a profitable ransom? She held her breath and looked directly at him.

He gave a broad smile and pointed to her tee shirt. It was the same "Power to the People" shirt she had worn when she arrived at the Gonzales mansion on her first night in Mexico City. Turning to his followers he said gleefully, *"Hola, amigos. Mira aqui. Una pequena guerrilla!" Look here, guys. A little revolutionary.* The other men guffawed and nodded. Then the bandit turned back to Ali and said, *"Buena suerte, amiguita." Good luck, little friend.* He tipped his hat to her, then continued toward the back of the bus and sat down. His men did the same.

The driver closed the bus door and off they went with the passengers still warily quiet. A few of them stole a glance at Ali who was amused but perplexed. "Do you think we're all right?" she asked Marian.

Marian shrugged. "Let's hope so. At least I think he liked your politics."

After about twenty minutes, one of the bandits came up the aisle and spoke to the driver. The bus halted and the group trooped off with a chorus of *"Buenas tardes"* and *"Gracias por el paseo." Good afternoon. Thanks for the ride.*

The passengers heaved a collective sigh of relief and began at once to laugh and joke with each other, pleased to have survived their brush with the Party of the Poor.

Ten days later, Marian and Allison were back in Mexico DF preparing to leave for the flight back to New York. In a proprietary gesture of concern, Roberto had insisted on coming with them. Marian had to wonder if a chauffeured Mercedes was not a better kidnapping target than a third class bus, but accepted his offer.

Now they sat in the first class lounge at Aeropuerto Internacional de la Ciudad de Mexico, drinking margueritas and watching the jetliners roll past. Tatiana had grabbed the opportunity to go shopping with some friends. She and Roberto would meet later for dinner before driving back to Avandaro.

Roberto, dressed in a dark navy blue suit, white shirt and navy and red tie looked every inch the successful businessman. Marian wore a pale blue linen pantsuit, while Allison had on jeans, a Parsons tee shirt and a red and white hand-woven serape that she had bought at the market in Valle de Bravo.

Roberto was giving Allison a slightly dubious look. "You know, *paquita*," he said, "in Mexico it is the *men* who wear serapes."

Ali smirked at him. "Well Roberto, in America women wear whatever they like."

He sighed and shook his head. *"Qué lástima!* Pretty soon we won't be able to tell the girls from the boys. What a shame." But his eyes were twinkling.

Allison nodded gravely. "Progress, Roberto," she said.

"So it would seem." He finished his drink and got to his feet. "And so, *cariñas,* I will bid you both farewell. For this time at least."

He smiled at Marian and kissed her hand. "I am in awe of your artistic skill, Señora. Thank you very much for the beautiful mural. I will treasure it."

Then he looked at Allison. "For some reason, *pequita,*" he said with a rueful grin, "I think I will be seeing you again. Probably rather soon." He gave her a little hug. "Keep an eye on my subversive son, will you?"

"You can bet on that," Ali replied.

They watched him walk across the lounge and through the entrance to the concourse.

An hour later they were settled into their seats for the return trip to New York. Ali, from the window seat, watched as the plane banked over the white-topped hulk of Popocatepetl and headed north.

"I'm curious about something."

Marian's voice interrupted her thoughts and she turned to look at her. "What?"

"Did Francisco tell you anything about his mother? I'm pretty sure Tatiana isn't his mom."

Ali laughed. "No, she's. . . let's see, wife number four I think. Francisco says it depends on whether you count wife number three who apparently took off with a bullfighter after three weeks of marital bliss with Roberto. Francisco's mother was wife number one, Cecelia. She was some sort of social worker. I didn't get the whole story, but she died while he was quite young—five or six I think. Apparently she contracted polio while working with indigent families. Francisco thinks that's one reason his dad is so defensive about social justice issues. Helping the poor can get you killed."

Marian nodded. "Okay. That makes sense." She studied Ali for a moment, then said, "What comes next, for you and Francisco I mean."

Ali looked away. "I don't know exactly. We promised that we'd get together as much as we can once we're both back in school, but. . ."

She hesitated. "A long distance romance? I'm not sure how that's going to work."

Marian nodded sympathetically.

"One thing I do know though," Ali said. "Francisco really opened my eyes about environmental issues. I've decided, well, I think I'll finish up this next semester at Parsons, and then I'm going to look into going to law school."

"Law school?" Marian said, surprised.

"Uh huh. Environmental law. I'd like to think I could make a difference somehow."

CHAPTER

25

Auburn, California
April 1971

Kate met Chris Malacchi-Salinger on the steps of the Placer County Courthouse. Andy Curtis, a tall young man with collar-length dark blond hair wearing a grey suit and sunglasses, stood next to Chris. Andy was one of Tommy Ashida's associates and would represent the firm at the pre-development meeting with the Placer County Planning Department. Kate had hoped that Tommy would be able to attend the meeting, but he'd arranged for Andy to come instead. Keeping his distance, Kate thought with a hint of frustration.

Kate hadn't met Andy personally, although she had talked to him often on the phone during the time that Tommy was recuperating at Mockingbird. She felt like she was meeting an old friend.

"I hope we've got everything we need," Chris said. "I gathered up all the permit forms that I could think of—conditional use, variances, new development, the assessor's parcel page, access information and, of course, a history of the ownership."

Andy waved a packet of documents in the air. "And I have the design site review and the conceptual site plan ready to go."

Kate shook her head. "So many hoops to jump through. Daddy would have been tearing his hair."

"Well," Andy said easily, "the good news is that nobody can just waltz in and build a cement factory next door. The bad news is you have to pass the permit endurance test to get anything authorized. Overall, though, I think I'd vote for the regulations."

Kate nodded agreement.

The meeting lasted until past noon. Over lunch at Awful Annie's, a laid-back café not far from downtown, the thre discussed potential outcome.

"I still don't understand why they want the names and addresses of the adjacent property owners, " Kate said. "No one has to use the Mockingbird driveway unless they want to. All of the neighboring properties can be accessed off the county road." She glanced at Chris. "We've let your folks use the drive when the water was high and the county road was flooded. And Tassos Stavros has always been welcome to do the same."

"Still," Andy said, "they'll probably want to have the names to make sure there's no problem with the noise ordinance."

"I feel like I'm walking on eggs," Kate said. "One wrong move and all we'll have is an omelet."

Chris laughed. "It's a slow process, but we'll get there eventually."

They finished their Bloody Marys and launched into the justly popular California burgers. For dessert there was fresh blackberry cobbler with vanilla bean ice cream. Over coffee, Chris made a list of the information and materials they still needed to gather up to attach to the application. "And," finished Chris, "we have to post the public notification signs and—" she ruffled through her notes, "I think that's it. We should get a hearing date by let's say. . . September?"

Kate shook her head in dismay. "Maybe I should just stay with the pear ranch."

"Come on," Andy said, "after all the work you and Tommy have already put into this project? Don't give up now."

"I guess not." Kate looked at Andy. "How's he doing, by the way."

Andy hesitated for a moment, then said, "He's fine." He gave Kate a little smile. "But I think he misses you."

"Yeah," Kate said. "I miss him too."

Two weeks after the Planning Department meeting Kate got a call from Ned Warren. Ned had been business partners with Kate's father, Owen, in developing American River Estates, a subdivision that backed onto a nature preserve that had been established along the river. The proceeds from the land sales had helped fund Owen's political campaigns. Kate hadn't talked to Ned since Owen's funeral two years before. After the obligatory pleasantries, he requested a meeting.

"What's this about?" Kate asked.

Ned hesitated before saying, "I'd rather talk in person if that's okay."

"All right," she replied. "Your place or mine?"

"I'll come there," he said.

"Fine." *At least we'll be on my turf*, Kate thought.

The next afternoon, Ned's blue and white Oldsmobile Cutlass pulled up to the courtyard gate. From the kitchen window, Kate watched him get out and start toward the house. A walnut grower turned developer, Ned was a tall, rangy man in his late fifties with close-cropped grey hair and skin the color and texture of leather from years spent under the California sun. He was dressed is denim jeans, a plaid sport shirt, and snakeskin cowboy boots. Kate remembered that Ned always seemed to have a new pair of fancy boots, a sort of trademark.

"Hi Katie," he greeted her with casual affection. "How've you been?"

She offered him a beer or some iced tea. He took the tea and they settled down on the living room sofa. After a few remarks about the weather, Cory's school, and the arrest of the so-called Machete Murderer, a serial killer who had murdered a number of migrant laborers and buried them on the nearby Sullivan Ranch, Ned got down to business.

"I understand that you've applied for a land use permit to set up some kind of concert hall," Ned said.

"We've asked to have a hearing on a land use permit," Kate replied, surprised that word was out so quickly.

Ned nodded. "Takes a while to work through the process."

"Yes," Kate agreed. "It's a bureaucratic jungle out there."

Ned sipped his tea. Then he set down the glass and said, "Katie, let me be candid. I know that Mockingbird isn't profitable as a pear ranch anymore. All the growers are having problems. If it wasn't for the Williamson Act and the tax breaks it ensures, a lot of the ranchers would have given up already."

Kate knew that Ned was referring to the California Land Conservation Act, commonly known as the Williamson Act, that enabled local governments to enter into contracts with private landowners for the purpose of restricting parcels of land for agricultural use. In return, landowners received an agricultural tax rate instead of the higher rate. The usual length for the initial contract was ten years.

Ned continued, "I know that Owen put Mockingbird under contract back in '66 which means you might have problems getting that permit until the agreement expires in 1976."

"We looked into that," Kate interrupted. "My attorney thinks that—"

"Wait a minute," Ned said. "Attorney or not, it *is* a potential obstacle, right?"

"Could be," Kate acknowledged grudgingly.

"I have a proposition for you," Ned continued. Kate was aware that he was watching her carefully, looking for the right way to lead the conversation. "If you run into a blank wall, I'd be willing to buy you out, fair market value, cash." He tilted his head and pursed his lips. "Just sayin', you need to keep the possibility in mind."

"Come on, Ned. We both know that I'm not going to sell Mockingbird," Kate replied. "You know how Dad felt about the ranch."

"Of course I do. That's why I'm giving you an option here. You could keep a nice parcel—twenty or thirty acres—for yourself and your family. The kind of development I have in mind would be over the long term. I wouldn't even start until the conservation contract was up." He was studying her intently. "You could use the cash to buy another piece of land for your concert operation. Something with the right zoning already in place. I'm just asking you to think about it."

Kate frowned. There was a kind of undercurrent here, something beneath the surface that she couldn't make out. "Much as I appreciate your offer, Ned," she said calmly, "you need to know that what I'm trying to do is to keep Mockingbird intact. It's pretty clear that I don't have the resources to keep running a deficit year after year just to be sentimental, but I think I've come up with a plan that can work, and that will benefit everybody in the long run."

"I agree, it's an interesting idea," Ned replied. "I can see that it would be a beautiful place for a music center and would likely help out the local economy—hotels and restaurants and such. I'm just. . ." He paused and glanced around. "I'm just trying to offer an alternative. Just in case you. . . need one."

There was a warning behind his words that made her skin prickle. He knew something and he wasn't going to tell her what it was. But she had to ask.

"Ned, is there anything I should know? Something that you've heard maybe?"

He shifted uncomfortably and looked away. Then he looked back at her and said, "Let's just say you might come up against a few. . . impediments. If that happens, you know where to reach me." He got to his feet and gave her a perfunctory smile. "Well, I better get going. Lots of work to be done."

"Reminds me of Dad," she said. "That's what he always said."

With a more genuine smile, Ned replied, "They don't make 'em like Mac McPhalan anymore. He was the real thing." He nodded in agreement with himself. "Bye now, Katie."

He saw himself out. Puzzled, Kate sat on the sofa and stared at the fireplace.

CHAPTER
26

San Francisco, California
July 1971

Five months had passed since the surgery, and Alex was guardedly optimistic. She had been almost compulsive in following Dr. Williamson's instructions in the weeks after the operation—keeping the hand elevated, using ice to reduce swelling, gently flexing her fingers to prevent stiffness. The bone fragment that was affecting the ulnar nerve had been removed and the inflammation of the membrane had been treated. The cast—which had been changed several times—was finally removed, much to Alex's relief. Bathing with a plastic bag over her arm was cumbersome and annoying, and more than a few times she wondered irritably if the whole thing had been a mistake.

But then came the wonderful day when she pinched the end of her ring finger and felt it. Not just a tiny bit, but *fully*. She had feeling in her fingers! She began to cry with joy.

After that came week after week of therapy, motion exercises, strengthening exercises, flexibility exercises. She spent three afternoons a week in the physical therapy facility at the UC Medical School flexing her fingers, bending her wrist and squeezing a tennis ball until she was ready to scream. Why did it take so long? She felt like an athlete or a dancer being readied for a contest.

But Alex was not an athlete or a dancer. While working with physiologists who talked endlessly about how the body *worked*, she felt a sense of frustration, almost fear. If she reduced making music to a mechanical exercise, if she thought of it as "kinesthetic movement," then where was the magic? She couldn't "think" about her fingers when she was inside the music, swept away by the power and passion of the sound. It was a dilemma.

Then came the real test. A Saturday afternoon in late July. The weather had been unusually cool during the month with fog closing in day after day. The day before, July 30, a Pan Am 747 had hit a light pole on take-off and had to return to the San Francisco airport for an emergency landing. On the afternoon of July 31, almost 19,000 people were at Candlestick Park as the San Francisco Giants took on the Pittsburgh Pirates.

Alex was unaware of either the aviation accident or the baseball game. She was totally focused on her left hand as she sat down at the Steinway that took up almost half of her modest living room and rested her fingers on the keys.

She began with scales. C major, G major, D major—playing each two octaves with no pause in between. She finished the set of twelve major scales and stopped, her hands frozen in mid air above the keyboard. She sucked in her breath and let it out—very slowly. Then she covered her eyes with both her hands and sat very still for several minutes. She could hear water dripping from the eaves. Somewhere down the street a car honked. She made a little sound, somewhere between a gulp and a whine. For the first time in almost two and one half years, she had made music with her left hand. Not perfectly, not easily, but it was a start.

Highway 99, Central Valley, California

With the music center project in limbo until the hearing was set, and with the pear harvest still over a month away, Kate turned her attention to her "other project," the biography of Stefan Molnar that she had started almost two years before. To reconnect with her subject, and possibly gather additional primary source information, she decided to pay a visit to Jean Molnar Westmorland. Several times, Jean had invited her to "come and stay for a week or two and be sure to bring Cory." Now seemed like the perfect time, so Kate made the arrangements and set out for Santa Barbara.

The landscape down Highway 99 was hot, dry, and barren. South of Sacramento, the San Joaquin Valley spread out between the Coast Range to the west and the Sierra Nevada to the east, a long, flat trough of former marshland and desert that had been transformed into an agricultural factory. Nearly thirteen percent of the agricultural production of the United States came from the San Joaquin Valley, leading to its nickname, "The food basket of the world." Grapes, nuts, citrus, peaches, tomatoes, and asparagus grew in abundance in the valley along with alfalfa, cotton and other non-food crops. Cattle and sheep ranches of monumental size cover the foothills of the mountain ranges, and huge oil fields dominate the southern part of the valley.

A few months earlier, Kate had bought a sturdy little Datsun station wagon and now she zipped along the bee-line highway through the little valley towns of Galt and Lodi, Stockton, Manteca, Turlock and Merced. Cory had named the car *Sulu* after his favorite Star Trek character.

Cory loved to quote lines from movies and TV series, and as he and Kate followed highway 99 toward the south he kept up a constant soliloquy of observations and instructions: "Once in Siberia there was a meteor so great that it flattened whole forests," he intoned, noting the flat treeless, terrain." When they turned onto the road toward Paso Robles he cried, "But sir, that'll lead us directly into the Romulan Neutral Zone." Then, "Second star to the right and straight on 'til morning." As they passed a huge eighteen-wheeler he asked, "You think it's a Klingon battle cruiser?"

"Looks like it," Kate said.

"Do you think the landing party's in danger?"

"Might be," Kate said. "We'd better beam them up."

Cory made a whirring sound. "Energize!" and clapped his hands. "Yea! We made it!"

"Thank you, Mr. Sulu, Kate said. "That will be all."

"Aye aye, Captain."

They got to Santa Barbara in the late afternoon. The sun hovered above the blue humps of the Channel Islands. The ocean looked like cerulean satin with an over-glaze of powdered silver. The palm trees stood, tall and stiff, dead fronds puffed around their necks like bushy beards.

The Mediterranean-revival architecture made the town look like a movie set. They drove along the ocean past Stern's Wharf and the Zoo, then headed up into the hills to the village of Montecito. The sun was extinguishing itself in the harbor, sending out long streamers of gold and coral, as they drove through the wrought iron gates of the Westmorland estate.

Two dogs—a black poodle and a grey and white Australian shepherd—dashed down the drive to meet them. Barking and jumping, they escorted the Datsun to the front steps of the Grecian style main house.

Jean, dressed in denim bell-bottoms and a paisley shirt, shouted for the dogs to be still. They circled her, whining and smiling, as Kate and Cory got out of the car. "Welcome, welcome," Jean cried. And then, "Good lord, Cory, you must have grown a foot!" She hugged them both heartily.

An Hispanic woman dressed in a grey uniform with a white apron appeared and was introduced as "Angelina."

"If you need anything, she's the person to ask," Jean said. "*Donde esta Jose?*" she asked the maid.

"*En el granero,*" Angelina said. "In the barn."

"Always in the barn," Jean laughed. "Oh well, we can each grab a suitcase."

"Where's Janos?" Cory asked as they carried luggage into the house.

"Up in his room," Jean said. "Go on up. Second door on the left. You can just leave the bag here, honey," she added. "Jose will bring it up later."

"God," Kate said, glancing around the two-story foyer with its marble columns and intricate molding, "I'd forgotten how grand this place is."

"Nice, isn't it?" Jean agreed. "So bright. Light everywhere."

Kate remembered the Molnar's stone castle in Cleveland with its dark wood and leaded windows, a brooding stage set for Jean and Stefan's all too turbulent marriage.

"Let me show you your room," Jean said, guiding Kate down the hall and through an archway to an outdoor patio. An oval pool dominated the terrace. On the opposite side of the pool was a white clapboard guesthouse with green shutters and window boxes filled with vari-colored bougainvillea.

"Wright's in L.A. working on some business deal," Jean said as she opened the guesthouse door, "but he'll be back tomorrow. He's looking forward to seeing you."

Kate followed Jean inside, admiring the green-and-white garden theme of the cottage. "Oh," she said, "it's charming, Jean."

"Great place to hide out if you want to get some work done," Jean said with a laugh. "Gets a little hectic around here with Janos and his friends and the dogs and the servants and everything. Now," she gave Kate a hug, "I'll let you get settled in. There's a bottle of chardonnay in the fridge if you're so inclined. And some Pellegrino if you're not. I'm going to go check on dinner." She waved her arm at the patio. "Take a swim if you like. Hope you brought your suit. Dinner won't be for an hour or so and I'll keep an eye on the boys." And away she went.

So relaxed, Kate thought. *I've never seen Jean so informal I mean, denim pants?—and so at ease. She seems. . . happy.*

CHAPTER

27

Montecito, California

It didn't take long to acclimate to the constant but unhurried flow of activities at the Westmorland estate—the nanny, a French woman named Georgette who looked after the boys, the house staff, Angelina and two other maids, Jose who seemed to be a sort of general manager, two gardeners, and the chauffeur.

Wright, Jean's husband, was around at breakfast and dinner and then disappeared on business. A tall, silver-haired man with a slight stoop, grey-blue eyes, and slender, aristocratic hands, Wright still had a Louisiana accent, a carry-over from his childhood in New Orleans. The family had made a fortune in turpentine before re-inventing themselves as Southern California royalty. Westmorland Holding Company was involved in a number of enterprises including utilities, broadcasting and communications media. Combined with the substantial assets that Jean brought to the marriage, to say that the family was comfortable was to vastly underestimate their status.

Jean, Kate thought, seemed perfectly at home in the upper echelon. She was passionate about her causes—the Red Cross, the newly founded Doctors Without Borders, the United Nations Children's Fund. She was also active in local charitiesthe garden club, the zoo, the arts. She was a very busy lady.

With her host and hostess engrossed in their pursuits and Cory occupied with Janos and his friends, Kate was able to spend the majority of her time working on the biography of Stefan which so far only consisted of a large box of notes and taped interviews.

The days followed a predictably pleasant pattern. After breakfast, usually served pool-side, everyone went their separate ways. Lunch was available, but optional, and Kate sometimes grabbed some bread and cheese from the kitchen and ate at her desk, a white antique roll-down with a pretty view of the garden.

In the late afternoon, she went for a dip in the pool or took Cory and Janos for a walk along the bluff that overlooked the harbor. The air was soft and sweet with the scent of grass and dust. Now and then the tangy fragrance of kelp rose up from the beach below. The smell of sun-drenched eucalyptus brought back a flood of memories.

Dinner was more formal—a gathering at the rosewood table in the dining room for a meal that was served in courses—a vichyssoise, a watercress salad, a rack of lamb with grilled vegetables. Wright favored French Burgundies, a Grand Échezeaux perhaps or a Montrachet. Dessert and coffee were served in the living room.

While the genteel formality was grand, and the food and wine delicious, Kate couldn't help thinking that she would never want to live in such structured predictability. Was there ever room for spontaneity?

After dinner on her way through the living room, Kate noticed the Hamburg Steinway in the corner and remembered so vividly that evening almost a decade earlier—Stefan playing Mendelssohn's *Variations Serieuses*, Armand and Veronique sitting on the sofa, the moonlit terrace, ("On a night like this I should have been playing Debussy.") She'd been pregnant with Cory and was so overwhelmed about the pace of her life, the sudden dramatic changes, her marriage, the baby. Stefan. Too much sponteneity perhaps? She had to smile.

But soon she settled into the routine, and after the first week in her new surroundings, she had produced a solid outline for the book. After the second week, the quotes, the letters, the interviews were sorted, transcribed, put into chronological order, but she still agonized over what to do with the interview with Armand Becker in which he had stated:

"My name is Werner Hoffmann. I grew up in Freidburg. In 1938 I joined the German army and became an officer. I participated in the occupation of Czechoslovakia and was put in charge of administering several army units in the Prague area. I took over the Sedlak family residence, Maya Molnar's family estate, to use as my office and base of operations. I stayed there until March 1945. I am the monster who did those heinous things. And I have tried for twenty-five years to atone for my sin."

She must have read that portion of the interview with Armand at least a dozen times, but she was still at a loss. If she didn't use the information Armand had given her, if she didn't reveal the abuse that Stefan had suffered during the Nazi occupation, then how could she explain his life, his frustration and self-doubt, the guilt he harbored, the trauma that haunted him? If she wanted to portray Stefan's power as an artist, the depth of his emotions, then she couldn't leave out the most significant experience of his life, of having to somehow placate the monster who had imprisoned him and his family, the sadist who had made him responsible for their safety at the price of his own integrity.

But if she told the whole story, if she revealed Armand's secret identity, who would be harmed? Veronique, Armand's loving wife, who believed that her husband was a resistance fighter? Their children, who knew nothing of their father's early life? Other friends and family who knew Armand only as a respected and caring physician, an acclaimed scholar, a warm and loving friend? And what about Armand's patients who trusted him with their most painful secrets? Would they feel betrayed when they learned of the secret that *he* had kept? A difficult decision. She decided that she would have to talk to Verrie again.

So, on a lovely Saturday morning, Kate found herself sitting on the same pretty terrace where she and Carl and Stefan had often gathered when visiting Santa Barbara, admiring the ocean view and the colorful pots of geraniums and feeling the balmy air waft in gently from the sea.

Verrie, always so chic, was dressed in white slacks and a pale pink cotton blouse. Her silver hair always seemed to have just come from the salon and her rose-colored nails were perfectly manicured. How could she look so stunning, so flawless at eight o'clock in the morning?

They had finished a light breakfast of croissants, homemade strawberry jam and an asparagus omelette. The maid had just cleared away the dishes when Kate got out her tape recorder and notebook. They talked for a while about Stefan's career—the concerts that Verrie and Armand had attended, the amazing discography, his interpretations of Brahms, Chopin, Liszt.

"What was your favorite performance?" Kate asked.

Verrie thought for several moments, then replied, "You know, I think it was a recital that he did at the Tanglewood Festival. Armand and I were in Boston for a conference and decided to go to Lenox for the weekend. I don't remember now exactly when it was." She waved her hand "Sometime in the early sixties I think. Anyway, he played the Chopin Preludes. All twenty-four of them.

"It was an evening recital and you know the Shed, open and airy. When he started the program we could see lightning in the distance—just a flicker on the horizon. But by the time he was halfway through the program, the storm was upon us." She laughed. "When he started on number fifteen, you know, the *Raindrop Prelude*? Oh my, the sky was lighting up and the thunder was rumbling. As if all of nature was listening to him play and responding to the music."

She paused, lost for a moment in the memory. Then she looked back at Kate. "That was, well, a phenomenal experience."

"Sounds magical," Kate said, thinking of Stefan's music, the effect it had on people.

"Yes," Verrie agreed. "Magical."

"Just a few more questions," Kate said. She paused and studied her notes, wondering how to phrase what she wanted to ask. Finally she said, "I'm still curious about how Stefan and Armand met. Armand said it was in Geneva. You went to a concert and afterward invited Stefan to join you for dinner, something like that. But then, he and Armand became good friends. How did that happen exactly?"

Verrie looked out at the ocean, then glanced at Kate. "There is... another story here, isn't there?" she said softly.

"You tell me?" Kate replied.

"Do I know what happened before that night in Geneva? Do

I know why Armand was so determined to practically *adopt* this
young musician? Granted, a wonderful, talented musician. But we
had heard other great pianists. So why Stefan Molnar?"

She rested her chin on her hand, paused, then said, "To tell you
the truth, Kate, I don't know the whole story. But I think I gleaned
bits and pieces over the years. I know that Armand had met Stefan
before, although he wouldn't admit it. I also know that Armand's
past was rather. . . uncertain. You should understand, it was wartime.
Things were different. Sometimes, the details didn't matter so much.
Only that you were alive and that you had a chance to have a future.
So, we looked ahead, not back."

Kate waited as Verrie seemed to struggle with her thoughts, her
eyes searching the horizon. Then Verrie turned once more to Kate.
"There were. . . contradictions. Anomalies. But whatever else might
have happened, I think that you need to remember that Armand did
a lot of good in this world. In his life. All of us have made mistakes.
Some more than others. If we're lucky, we get a second chance. We
get to try to make amends. To replace something bad with something
good."

She sat up straighter and lifted her chin. "I'm proud of my
husband. Proud of his accomplishments and his generosity of spirit
and his dedication to his work and his family. He was, ultimately, a
good man, Kate. Do what you must, but I hope you remember that."

Kate set her notes aside. After a minute she said, "Thank you,
Verrie. I think I know what I need to do."

A few days later as she drove along Highway 1, heading north toward
home, Kate once more reviewed her options. Cory was asleep in the
back seat. The radio played softly—a Schubert *lieder*. What should
she do? The question kept biting at her. After so many years, what
good would it do to tarnish Armand's memory?

And yet, shouldn't the truth be told? She struggled as she drove along the shore. The ocean was silver, partially obscured by a light fog. Kate felt that, like the sea, the truth was blurred, shadowy.

Then, from the radio, came the sound of the *Prayer* from Wagner's opera, *Rienzi, der Letzte der Tribunen,* a favorite of Aldolph Hitler. "*Almighty Father, look down,*' sang the hero, "*The power that your authority gave to me, let it not yet perish. My God, who gave me great power, grant my profoundly ardent prayer!*"

The sun hung in the sky, a pale white orb thinly veiled by the fog. The veil had to be stripped away. She would tell the truth.

CHAPTER

28

Cambridge, Massachusetts

Allison loved to watch Francisco when he was reading. She was reminded of that first moment when she saw him sitting by the fire in his father's library, deeply engrossed in a leather-bound volume. He looked, she thought, like some wild creature intently focused on its prey, devouring words, pages rushing by. He ingested information like a hungry wolf gobbling down a meal.

In the six months since returning from the trip to Mexico, Allison had made some significant changes in her life. She'd finished up the spring semester at Parsons, then had applied for, and gotten, admission to Boston University's environmental science program. Allison wondered what would happen to her relationship with Francisco after they were both back from Mexico. Would the magic still be there? Would the distance between Boston and New York prove to be an insurmountable obstacle? Did he think it was just a fling?

But as it turned out, the relationship not only persisted, but actually blossomed after their return to the States. They managed to get together almost every weekend, and she ended up moving in with him over the summer.

And so here she was in his apartment in Cambridge overlooking the Charles River. The apartment was a townhouse, a two-story brick with white trim. The views of the river from the living room and upstairs master bedroom were lovely—silver water, skiffs and sailboats skimming past, distant skyline, glimpse of the Boston University Bridge.

There was only one problem. Francisco had been recruited to join a group called the Sierra Club Legal Defense Fund headquartered in San Francisco, and he wasn't going to turn down the opportunity. He was planning to leave Boston at the end of the Fall term and Allison had to decide what to do next: stay in Boston and finish her undergraduate degree at Boston University? She still needed two full semesters to graduate, and her course work was all over the map from design and art courses to political science and philosophy, to literature and botany. Or should she follow Francisco to California? Okay, her parents were nearby and it would be great to be back in California, but where would she go to school? She got dizzy thinking about it.

"Go to Berkeley," Francisco advised.

"I don't know if I can get in," Alison replied. "I haven't always been a stellar student."

"Then finish up at San Francisco State," he said. "You'll only have two semesters of undergraduate work to finish. That would work, yes?"

She frowned and rubbed her nose. "Maybe."

He studied her carefully for a moment, then sat down next to her on the floor and took her hand in his. "Whatever you decide, *mi vida*, I will honor your decision. I want to be with you, but you must do what is best for you, yes?"

He was so beautiful, she thought, with his dark hair falling across his forehead and his warm brown eyes so intense behind his glasses. She looked at him and felt that she was somehow looking at her self, her other half, some other part of her that she hadn't realized was even there until she met Francisco. And strangely, it was a sweeter, more tender, more nurturing half—the perfect compliment to her strident, aggressive, impatient self. He was gentle, she was fierce. He calmed her, she energized him. They were so good together.

"Maybe," she said, giving him a little smile. "I'll send out a few applications and see what happens?"

He nodded. "*Deje destino decide*," he said. "Let fate decide."

—∘∘○❘◎❘○∘∘—

"How can they say it's incomplete?" Kate asked. "I don't know what they're talking about."

Chris Malacchi-Salinger frowned and scanned the letter a second time. "Something to do with getting written consent from the adjacent property owners on the private road access issue. I know that Dad wrote a letter of consent. The only other owner affected is Stavros, so it must be him." She put the letter down and looked at Kate. "Why would Tassos Stavros object? He doesn't even use that access road unless there's high water at the bridge."

"Beats me," Kate replied. "I haven't seen him since Dad's funeral and he was cordial enough then."

"Do you want to give him a call?" Chris asked. "Or do you want me to do it?"

"Your family probably knows him better than I do," Kate said.

Chris nodded. "Okay," she said. "I'll follow up and see what I can find out."

A week later, Chris dropped by the ranch. It was a Friday afternoon and the light was honey-colored from the heat and dust of late summer. The winter rains had yet to make an appearance. Cory was upstairs doing his homework and Kate was going over the harvest figures that Jaime had brought to her. Not a bad harvest considering all the problems they'd had. And there was still a week or ten days to go before the final figures were in. The workers were still busy in the orchard and the packinghouse had been a hive of activity for almost a month.

But, once again, they would be lucky to break even. When all the bills had been paid for the workers, the irrigation, the utilities, the fertilizer, the fungicide, the distribution fees, the taxes, Jaime and Consuelo's salary, there wasn't much left. What was she supposed to live on? She hadn't demanded anything but a small monthly child support stipend from Carl. The divorce was a mutual decision after all, more her idea than his. She had a little income from Owen's real estate holdings, although most of that had gone toward his political campaign costs. She had been "unemployed" since leaving her job at Kent State eighteen months before.

She was trying to puzzle through her options when she heard a knock on the door. Chris was still dressed in her "work clothes"—a conservative knee-length skirt and matching blazer, beige silk blouse and knee-high brown leather boots. "Pleasantly professional" she explained. "Sharp but not intimidating."

"Greetings, counselor," Kate said. "Want a drink?"

"Do fish swim?" Chris responded.

"White or red?" Kate asked as she headed for the kitchen.

Chris followed her. "White. I need it cold and I need it now."

"Uh-oh," said Kate. "This sounds bad." She poured them each a glass of chardonnay and they sat down on the sofa.

"Not *too* bad," Chris said after taking a drink. "But it's confusing to say the least." She then told Kate about a rather bewildering conversation that she'd had with Kate's neighbor, Tassos Stavros. Initially he claimed that he didn't know anything about responding to any permit application questions. But then he admitted that he had voiced concerns about "traffic and noise and stuff" and that he'd also gotten a call from "someone" (he couldn't remember the name) who'd asked him a bunch of questions about how he and the other neighbors felt about having a "three ring circus" in their neighborhood. Chris reported that Tassos had ended the conversation by saying, "I don't have nothing against the idea really, but when some guy says 'You don't want all that dust in your face, do you now?' what the hell are ya gonna say? Ya say 'Of course not.'"

"Curiouser and curiouser," Kate said. She got up and poured them each another glass of wine. "Sounds like someone *is* out to get us. But who? And why?"

Chris agreed. "Doesn't sound like anyone from the neighborhood. It's got to be coming from somewhere else."

"I've got an idea," Kate said. "Dad told me that Danny Papadakis was really miffed when he replaced him as campaign manager. But who was the guy that replaced him?" She thought for a moment. "Ed something."

"Ed Collins?" Chris said.

"That's it. Do you know him?"

"Sort of. I haven't seen him for quite a while, but he used to be on the Auburn City Commission and he certainly knows everybody in the area. At least anyone with political ties." Chris took out a small pad and made some notes. "Let me do some more digging and I'll see what I find."

Another two weeks passed before Chris called to say that she had some interesting information and could Kate meet her for lunch at the Firehouse in Sacramento. The air outside the restaurant smelled scorched and the sky had a brassy patina. Farmers were burning the stubble in the rice fields on the west side of the river, so Kate and Chris decided to eat inside despite the balmy late September temperatures.

They took a table in the back of the main dining room and ordered steak burgers and a glass of zin. "My Mom knows Cosima Stavros, Tasso's wife, pretty well," Chris said. "She had a chat with Cosi about how she felt about the music center. Turns out she's all for it and said Tasso was sorry he'd been talked into objecting. But the most interesting thing I found out has to do with something else entirely.

"Cosima is the treasurer of a church group that's part of the Greek Orthodox community and she knew Dan and Helen Papadakis through the church. Even though Helen and Dan aren't together any longer, Cosima praised Dan's generosity and told me that he sent money on a regular basis to her to write checks to a charity. He wanted the money to go through the church group fund instead of sending it directly, 'to set a good example,' she said."

"Okay, so Dan sends Cosima a check and she puts it in the fund, and then writes a check to a charity? Which charity?"

"Good question," Chris replied. "Cosima wasn't sure. She said the checks go to a numbered account in Reno that she thinks is for a children's hospital, but she wasn't specific. She shut up at that point and my mom let it go, but it sounds to me like there's something going on. That's a weird setup."

"Certainly sounds convoluted. Any way we can get more information?" Kate asked.

"Lennie has a friend with a law firm in Reno, so I'm sure he can find out something for us."

Kate sat back and gave Chris a wide-eyed look. "God, this is starting to sound like a spy novel or a detective story. Where's the Maltese Falcon?"

Chris took a sip of wine and said with a smirk, "Well, if someone's trying to flip us the bird, we'll just have to flip it right back at them."

CHAPTER

29

San Francisco, California
October 1971

"Mrs. Fitzgerald." Robert Ashford, best friend of the late Alan Townsend, executor of his estate and President of the Townsend Charitable Foundation, rose to greet Kate. "How very good to see you, my dear," he said as he shook her hand. "Please," he gestured to the leather-upholstered wing chair in front of the dark mahogany desk, "have a seat. Can I offer you something? Tea perhaps?"

"That would be lovely," Kate said.

Robert pressed the intercom button. "Stephanie, could you bring us a pot of tea and two cups? Thank you, dear." He came around from behind the desk and sat down facing her across the round marble coffee table. He hadn't changed much, she thought. His cloud of white hair was a bit thinner and a few more creases lined his high forehead, but he was still meticulously dressed in a tailored charcoal grey suit, white shirt, maroon and silver silk tie. His blue eyes sparkled as he peered at her over his spectacles. "Now then, please tell me more about this project of yours. I must say it sounds quite intriguing."

Kate went over the basics of the music center project. Robert listened attentively, interrupting only when Stephanie, a briskly efficient young woman dressed in a straight blue wool skirt and black turtleneck sweater, came in with the tea. He poured them each a cup, sat back and said, "Go on."

"The preliminary plans are finished and I have the cost estimates for renovations and construction. So, once we get the final permits, it's on to the question of financing."

"Who's your architect?" Robert asked.

"Tommy Ashida. Ashida and Associates," she said.

Robert raised his eyebrows. "Oh, they're quite good I hear. Making a name for themselves here in the Bay Area."

"Tommy's an old friend," Kate said.

"Hmmm." Robert studied her thoughtfully. "What's the estimated cost?"

"About three million."

Robert nodded and sipped his tea. "So, how can I help?" he asked, setting his cup down and leaning forward.

"I thought I might apply for a grant from the Townsend Foundation. I'm hoping you can suggest a strategy."

"Of course." He got to his feet and smiled at her. "Please excuse me for a minute. I'll go and fetch some information on our programs and we can take a look at what would fit your needs. I won't be a moment."

While he was gone, Kate took the opportunity to study the office interior. Two beautiful floor-to-ceiling fanlight windows that overlooked a small park dominated the wall behind the desk. Glass-door bookcases lined the paneled walls displaying leather-bound volumes as well as several small sculptures—a marble Buddha head, a bronze Siva Nataraja, a pre-Columbian Mayan jaguar. The polished wooden floors were accented with Persian carpets. Several Indian miniatures, beautifully framed, hung on the wall above the fireplace. So opulent, yet comfortable.

"Here we are," Robert said, crossing the room and setting a large binder down on the table. "This is a directory of our current programs. But before we begin our search, let me say that we all loved the book that you did on Julian's poetry. An elegant tribute to say the least."

Kate smiled. "Thank you so much."

"You might also be pleased to learn that we just awarded this year's Julian McPhalan Scholarship to a very talented young lady who is studying literature at Mills College."

"That's fantastic!" Kate exclaimed.

Robert laughed lightly. "Doing our best to keep the Muses alive and well. But now," he sat down and opened the binder, "let's see which of these programs would work best for you."

They spent an hour discussing the various grant options available through the Townsend Foundation, and settled on a cultural facilities program that provided matching funds for renovation, construction or acquisition of facilities. "The amount of the match depends on how much you can raise up to two million dollars. It's a one-to-one match for every dollar you raise, and there's also a twenty-five percent in-kind allowance that counts toward the total."

"So we could count volunteer and pro-bono services toward the in-kind amount?"

"Yes. Plus the appraised value of donated property."

Kate nodded. "I think this would work."

Robert smiled. "Excellent. Once I have an application from you, I can take it to our board for approval." He gave her a conspiratorial wink. "I think it's safe to say that I have some influence with our board members."

As Kate left the office and stepped out into sunlight, she was smiling. Yes! This was going to work. Despite the obstacles, she felt sure that the Mockingbird Music Festival was actually going to happen!

Kate had invited Tommy to meet her for lunch at the Fairmount just a couple of blocks away from Robert's office on California Street. He was waiting for her at one of the tables in the dining room which had multiple sky-lit domes and marble columns. He put the menu down and stood up when she approached, gave her a quick kiss on the cheek, held her chair for her. He was wearing a grey suede jacket, dark slacks, a white shirt, no tie. Business casual.

"How'd the meeting go?" he asked after they had settled in and each ordered a glass of Pinot Gris.

"It was great," she said, and told him about her conversation with Robert Ashford. She then launched into a description of the permitting problems. Tommy studied her, listening quietly, until she finished.

"So," he said. "You've encountered some. . . issues?"

"Right. And I don't know where to go from here."

They ordered lunch—Dungeness crab cakes for him, a Salade Nicoise for her. He was quiet for several minutes, thinking, then looked up and said, "I have an idea that might solve the zoning problem."

"Let's hear it."

He smiled at her instant enthusiasm. "You might be able to do the music center without re-zoning the property, or even putting it in a trust."

Kate frowned. "How?"

"If the festival was part of *ranch* operations. That way you wouldn't have to worry about getting out of the Wilkerson Act contract. You could remain an agricultural enterprise, and still host a music festival."

She cocked her head. "How would we do that?"

Tommy leaned forward. "Two years ago the Mondavi Winery started a summer concert series. They focus on jazz and pop music, but it could be a prototype for the American River Music Festival. They advertise it as an evening in the vineyard with wine, food and music."

"Okay, but an evening in the pear orchard? Doesn't have quite the same appeal."

"Vineyard, Kate."

"Vineyard?"

He held up his hands. "You have one."

"One what?"

He laughed. "A vineyard, dummy." He sat forward excitedly. "You've never developed it, but there are close to twenty acres of old vines at Mockingbird. I used to think it was a shame that your family used the grapes for making jelly or left them to feed the birds. Didn't you tell me that your great-grandfather mentioned in a letter that he was experimenting with making wine like his Italian neighbors?"

"You're right," she said. "There was even an old wine cellar someplace. I can't quite remember—maybe under the barn? I remember Dad showing me a trap door and making me promise not to open it. Something about falling in or getting lost."

"Before Prohibition, the Mother Lode area had a lot of wineries," Tommy said. "I remember that from my fourth grade history class."

"You know," Kate said, "This could be a fantastic marketing angle."

"You think?"

She sat back and grinned at him. "All right, Ashida. I'll get together with Chris Malacchi and see what's possible."

"And I'm going to do some more research about making wine in the Gold Country," Tommy said.

In the hotel lobby, Tommy gave Kate a little hug and set out for his office. The afternoon was warm and the sun was bright. October was one of the least foggy months in the City and the temperature was a balmy seventy-eight degrees. He took off his jacket and slung it over his shoulder.

It was only a few blocks to his office on Montgomery Street. The elevator whisked him up to the twelfth floor. He went straight to his private office and closed the door, pausing only to ask his receptionist to hold his calls.

The afternoon light slanted across the City, turning the buildings golden, deepening the contrast between blue water and dun-colored hills. The Golden Gate, burnished to a fiery crimson by the light, seemed magnified against the landscape.

He sat down in one of the chairs next to the window and stared at the Christo drawing of "Valley Curtain." What an ambitious project—stretching a "curtain" of cloth across Rifle Gap in the Rocky Mountains. The project was still in the planning stage, and Tommy had bought one of the preparatory drawings that would help raise cash to make the vision a reality. He loved the brashness of Christo's ideas, the sense of adventure. The very outrageousness of the concept gave him a heady sense of freedom.

Since leaving Mockingbird six months before to return to San Francisco, he'd examined his priorities. He liked his work, his associates were loyal and talented, his clients were, for the most part, gracious and easy to work with. But he was not *happy*. His work was his life, but that wasn't enough to sustain him.

After work each day, he went home to his beautiful empty house filled with sad memories. The occasional visits to his family in Stockton, the outings with his cousin Ben, the now-and-then dinners at his associates homes were no substitute for what he needed—to love, to be loved, to find a true home, not an empty castle haunted by ghosts. He felt frozen, locked into a crypt of his own making. He wanted badly to break out. But how? He covered his eyes with his hands and pressed them against his temples. How?

He knew what thawed his heart, what made him happy, what and *who*. But it seemed unfair to burden Kate with his still-fragile physical and mental state. He worried that she might begin to think of him as a problem instead of a partner.

And she had rejected him before. He could well remember the anguish of reading those words that she had written to him almost ten years ago: "So many things have happened in the last four months. Please tell me you understand." He understood all right. He'd have to be crazy to set himself up for another rejection like that one. He'd never survive.

Opening his eyes, he looked once more at the Christo drawing— that huge rocky gap spanned by an ephemeral curtain, a crazy risk that might fail.

He knew at that instant that he had to try. He jumped to his feet, then sat back down. What should he do? He would call her. He got up and started toward his desk, but stopped, frozen with indecision. She must still be driving. She'd only left a half hour before.

Maybe he should write? What would he say? I love you, I want to be with you, I *have* to be with you, I can't live without you? It would take a letter two days to reach her, and another two for her response to arrive. If she responded.

No, he decided, there was only one thing to do. He had to go to Mockingbird and talk to her. Now!

CHAPTER

30

Tommy saw the accident happen. Just before the exit from the Bay Bridge to Yerba Buena, a car in the far left lane swerved suddenly, sideswiping the pickup truck in the center lane. The truck fishtailed, then spun three hundred and sixty degrees while horns blared and other cars swerved and crashed. He heard the crunch of metal, the squeal of tires, and then silence with little puffs of smoke from burning rubber.

He missed the pileup by inches. No damage to him or his Z-car, but in front of him was a mountain of mangled steel and broken glass. People began to emerge from their wrecked vehicles, moving slowly, dazed. Most of them appeared to be all right, a few limped, held hands to their heads, or sat down quickly on the asphalt.

Tommy jumped out of his Datsun and ran to the nearest cars, peering into broken windows, asking, "Are you all right?" Most of the people managed to mumble a response—"I'm okay. Just shook up." "I don't know. I think maybe my leg's broken." "My little boy hit his head on the dashboard. He's bleeding."

Others joined Tommy in going from car to car. Only a few people seemed seriously injured. One woman who said she was a nurse, began a sort of impromptu triage, instructing volunteers to hold a folded cloth across a wound to stop the bleeding, telling other people not to move in case their back or neck was injured.

Tommy ended up sitting on the asphalt next to the open door of a Pontiac sedan, holding a whimpering toddler in his lap while the child's mother lay on the front seat holding a makeshift bandage to her bleeding shoulder.

It seemed to take forever for the ambulances to arrive. Of course, trying to get emergency vehicles through the jammed up traffic on the bridge in the afternoon rush was a major problem. The five eastbound lanes were on the lower level of the Bay Bridge; the upper level held the five westbound lanes. The police called in ambulances from Oakland since the lanes on the east side of the carnage were fairly clear.

When the last of the ambulance sirens died away, the tow trucks began to clear away the disabled cars, while workers swept up broken glass and police officers talked to the witnesses. It was five hours before traffic once more began to move.

Kate had left the City right after her lunch with Tommy and drove straight back to Mockingbird. Traffic was fairly light on the Interstate, and she turned into the ranch's long driveway well before dusk. As she got out of the car she noticed storm clouds piling up over the mountains to the east. An early-season thunderstorm would be a welcome relief from the summer's last blaze of heat.

Consuelo had made lasagna and Kate and Cory enjoyed an early dinner at the kitchen table. Cory went off to his room upstairs to "do some homework." (*Did first graders really have "homework,"* she wondered?) Kate settled down on the living room sofa to go over the notes from her meeting with Robert Ashford. She tried to concentrate on the grant information and budget figures that sat before her, but her thoughts kept wandering to the lunch with Tommy and his idea of building a winery at the ranch.

He was so enthusiastic. She loved the way his eyes—so often somber and distant—glowed when he got excited about something. He would suddenly come to life, full of animation and energy, and then later retreat again into that shell of his. *After all this time*, she thought, *he's still such a mystery to me.*

How long had they been friends? They were both five years old, younger than Cory was now, when the Ashidas had arrived at Mockingbird. Kate and Tommy became instant pals, roaming the unspoiled wilderness of the river canyon, riding their horses on the trails that wound along the bluff. Playing cowboys and Indians between the boulders that littered the flood plain. Going to Saturday afternoon movies at the theater in Auburn—Roy Rogers and the Sons of the Pioneers. And then later. . . Well. The bitter sweetness of their love affair hung in her mind like a distant star, glittering and beautiful and very far away, surrounded by the velvet black of empty space. She sighed and tried to concentrate on grant deadlines.

But she couldn't stop thinking about him. She was delighted to have him back in her life. It seemed such a natural thing to have him here at Mockingbird. Where he belonged. Or not. She cherished the memory of taking care of him during the months of his recovery—his quiet patience, her tenacious determination. He was so familiar to her. Yet so unfathomable. She felt as though she knew him better than anyone, and that she didn't know him at all. She shook her head, got up, poured herself a glass of zinfandel, and went to the door.

The tiles of the patio were still warm, but there was a touch of chill in the breeze that drifted down from the mountains. She could almost smell the rain even though it was still far off. Lightning blinked along the eastern horizon, not close enough for her to hear the thunder. She sat down on the bench beneath the fig tree. The evening air was full of the scent of late-blooming jasmine. The wine had gotten even better after two hours of air, the flavors deepening, filled with that mix of blackberries and chocolate and something dark and rich like the earth itself. She held the glass up and looked at the deep red-violet color of the wine.

Dark already, and Tommy was only now passing the little town of Davis, still fifteen miles west of Sacramento. He sped across the Yolo Causeway, an elevated stretch of highway that spanned the marshy rice fields and irrigation ditches that bordered the west side of the Sacramento River. The lights of the city glittered before him, and the upraised arms of the Tower Bridge welcomed him to the Capitol. But he was only passing through, intent on another destination. He would be in Auburn in an hour, and from there it was only a short drive to Mockingbird. What would he say when he got there? He had no idea.

As he left the city behind and headed into the foothills, he saw a flicker of lightning ahead. He remembered the excitement that everyone felt when the first rains arrived in the fall. The long, dry, hot summer was finally quenched with a plentiful, soothing drink of cool water, and the land came alive again after its seasonal hibernation. It made your pulse quicken and your body rejoice. Or maybe it was something else that was causing this sensation of excitement mixed with apprehension. He smiled at himself, chuckled softly. "You crazy bastard," he said aloud. "What the hell are you doing?"

Kate finished her wine and took the empty glass into the kitchen. She washed the dishes, dried them and put everything away, then went upstairs and told Cory it was time for bed. For a bedtime story, Cory requested Jack London's *Call of the Wild*. "I asked the librarian at school and she said it's really, really good. There's this dog named Buck and he gets stolen and they take him to Alaska and he gets sold to these really bad people and—"

"I remember the story," Kate said. "I read it too back in the day."

"Really, Mom?"

"Yes, really. Now, it's getting late, so let's read a chapter and then it's time to go to sleep, okay?"

Cory nestled down and Kate began, "'Buck didn't read newspapers, or he would have known that trouble was brewing, not alone for himself, but for every tide-water dog, strong of muscle and with warm, long hair, from Puget Sound to San Diego.'"

When she had finished the chapter and put the book aside, Cory said, "Mom, can we get a dog?"

Kate thought for a moment, then said, "Sure. That would be great." She remembered Joey, the German Shepherd who had been her friend and companion for years. Cory should have a dog too.

"Yipee!" Cory cried. "I want to get a husky, like Buck."

"We'll see. Now, time for bed."

She tucked him in and went back downstairs. It was almost ten, but she didn't feel sleepy. She could look at more grant applications. Or maybe watch something mindless on TV. Nothing sounded inviting. She was so restless. Maybe it was the weather.

The storm was closer now. She could hear the thunder ricocheting off the mountainsides, the sound magnified by the echoes. She went back out into the courtyard and stood there for a while, watching the glints of lightning. When big drops of rain began to splash onto the tiles and spatter into her hair, she finally went back inside. She lay down on the sofa and looked up at the dark stripes of the beams.

Tommy had passed Auburn and started down the narrow winding road that followed the river canyon when the car mysteriously coughed, sputtered and came to a halt. "What the. . ." He tried to start it, but the engine growled a rebuttal and refused. Then he noticed the fuel guage. Empty. "God," he exclaimed, slapping a hand to his forehead. "I am an idiot!" How had he not noticed that he was low on gas? "Of all the stupid, ridiculous. . ." He put his head down on the steering wheel and laughed. *Ashida*, he told himself, *you are a total dork.*

Then the rain arrived—enormous drops the size of quarters spattering the windshield. He sat up and looked at them, heard them battering the roof. Lightning flared, illuminating the canyon, fir trees bent and swayed in a stately dance. How far was he from the ranch? Probably at least two or three miles. He shook his head, at once amused and flummoxed. "Well," he said aloud, "what else can I do?" He took the keys from the ignition and opened the door.

31

Mockingbird Ranch

Kate must have drifted off to sleep because the next thing she knew someone was banging on the front door. She blinked and sat up, feeling woozy and disconnected. Who on earth would be knocking on the door at this time of night? She made her way to the foyer and turned on the porch light. "Who's there?" she called, trying to sound at least slightly intimidating.

"It's me," came the reply. "Tommy."

She opened the door and there he was, standing in front of her, water dripping off his jacket and running down his face. "Hey, Kate," he said with a crooked grin.

"Hey, Tommy," she replied, blinking, still feeling only half awake. Was this a dream?

"I thought I should. . . That is. . . Um. . ." He stared at her for a minute, then said, "Kate, I want to marry you."

For a moment she was too stunned to say anything. Then she gasped and ran to him and hugged him so hard that she nearly knocked him over and cried, "I want to marry you too!"

They became lovers again that night. Holding, touching, whispering in the darkness with the rain falling gently and the river singing in the distance. They flowed together and became one, tears mingling, bodies intertwining. Near dawn they finally fell asleep. The rain continued to patter softly on the roof and the river hummed, and a mockingbird lit on a branch outside the window and sang as sweetly as a nightingale.

When Kate woke, the sun was shining and the room seemed very bright. She turned over, sleepy and deliciously contented, and reached for him.

But he wasn't there.

Her heart lurched and she sat up. She was alone. Had it all been a dream? She jumped up, threw a robe on, and dashed to the door. The hall was dark. At the top of the stairs, she froze and listened.

Voices. They were coming from the kitchen along with the scent of brewing coffee and frying bacon. She sat down on the top step to catch her breath, then went down the stairs and through the living room.

Tommy, barefoot, wearing a tee shirt and slacks, was standing at the stove turning strips of bacon while Cory, still in his pajamas, sat watching. When Cory saw her, he jumped off the stool and ran to her. "Mommy!" he cried gleefully, "Guess what? Mr. Tommy's back! He's making us breakfast!"

Tommy looked over his shoulder at her and grinned. "Coffee's ready," he said.

They took their time lingering over breakfast, enjoying the strong, hot coffee. Then they moved on to the bacon and French toast with maple syrup and fresh-squeezed orange juice. It seemed, Kate thought, so *right*. As though life was *meant* to be this way: simple and calm and uncomplicated.

After a while, Consuelo came to clean up and Cory ran off to play with Teresa, Consuelo and Jaime's daughter. Jaime gave Tommy a ride to get gas and pick up the Z-car.

They were back in an hour and the morning was still young. The sun was warm, the breeze was cool, the orchard sparkled from the rain, and the day—a Saturday—stretched out before them like a meadow full of wildflowers.

"What do you want to do?" Kate asked.

"I don't know. What do *you* want to do?"

"You decide."

"No, *you* decide."

They both started laughing. "I know," Kate said. "Let's go visit the river."

"You're on," Tommy agreed.

They saddled up two horses—a strawberry roan named Daisy and Kate's Buckskin mare, Frosty, who was growing into her name, her coat now sprinkled with grey. She was going on eighteen, but was still full of energy and ready for any adventure.

"Cory wants a dog," she told Tommy as they headed for the bluff. "We've been reading *Call of the Wild*, so of course he wants a Husky."

"I hear they're great dogs," Tommy said.

Kate pictured the four of them—Tommy, Kate, Cory and a large, frolicking dog. Just like a real *family*. She shook her head and smiled.

They rode along the ridge, then followed the steep trail that led to the flood plain. An oak hammock stood at the base of the bluff. Tangled blackberry vines and dense thickets of wild grapes bordered the path. The horses picked their way through the underbrush, pausing now and then to bite off a mouthful of milkweed. The air was heavy with the smell of damp leaves and decaying vegetation.

The river was low after the summer dry season, but the water still ran swiftly over the gravel shoals. They paused at the water's edge to let the horses drink. Then Tommy stood up in his stirrups and cried excitedly, "Look, Katie. A salmon run!"

It was true. The center of the river was filled with the silver bodies of hundreds of Chinook salmon. The water seemed to boil as they raced against the current, trying to find their way home.

Kate watched the fish struggle and thought of all of the obstacles that lay ahead of them—fishermen, otters, eagles and bears, their natural predators. And then the man-made barriers: the dams and hydroelectric plants, the concrete stairs called fish ladders that they would have to ascend, leaping up from one tiny pool to the next.

And even if they passed these hurdles there were other natural impediments—waterfalls, rapids. If they managed to reach their natal waters, there would be still more problems. The fish would battle each other, females against females for places to nest, males against males for access to females.

Every kind of obstruction was placed in their way, yet they stubbornly persisted, did whatever they had to do to get home, to fulfill their destiny, to start a new cycle of rebirth and life and death, the ancient endless cycle that was the world.

Whatever it takes, she thought, *we'll do anything to get back home.*

CHAPTER

32

San Francisco, California

"Quite a rehearsal," Carl said. He and Alex were walking north on Van Ness past the Civic Center. The afternoon had been warm, but then the fog rolled in and the streets were already damp. A few streetlights had winked on.

"Good to be back," Alex replied without looking at him. She walked along, head bent, eyes cast down.

"Are you frightened?" Carl asked.

"Petrified. How 'bout you?"

They both stopped and faced each other. For a moment they were absolutely still, and in the rose-tinted gloom of a foggy twilight Carl thought she was almost unbearably beautiful. "Totally panic-stricken," he said, not at all sure that he was thinking only of the music.

"Know what?" said Alex. The mist had settled in her hair and tiny drops glittered among the honey-colored curls.

"What?"

"I'm starving."

Gravely, he replied, "So am I." He glanced around. "Where are we, anyway?"

"Bush," Alex said, pointing to the street sign.

"Good Lord," Carl exclaimed, "we're almost to North Beach. What a hike."

"Felt good though, didn't it?"

"Very good." He knew he was staring at her and quickly looked away. "Tell you what, we can catch the cable car about two blocks from here. There's a great little restaurant on Green Street called New Pisa. Do you know it?"

"No."

"I used to eat there when I was a student at the Conservatory. It's the sort of place that gives new meaning to the word 'unpretentious,' but the food was always good. What do you say?"

"I say let's eat."

They got to the restaurant and settled into a booth. Over the pasta marinara they invented a musical buffet—turnips Toscanini, oysters Oistrakh, doughnuts Debussy. "How about Frijoles Fitzgerald?" Alex suggested.

Carl rolled his eyes. "Hey," he said, "maybe we should give up the music business and start a restaurant. I can see it now—Concerto in Flakey Pastry for Mandolyn and Truffles."

"Fantacie Impromptu aux Flagellot. You'd look dashing in a toque."

"And I can picture you behind the bar dishing up daiquiris," Carl said.

"Please," Alex sniffed, "I'd be at the piano pounding out goodies from Gershwin."

"We could call the place Casa Contralto," Carl suggested.

They both laughed. "Let's go find a bar," Alex said. "I feel like getting drunk."

"What else can you do," Carl said, "on the eve of your execution?"

A sliver of glare seeped past the edge of the curtains and stabbed Carl in the eyes. "What time is it?" he muttered, raising his head a fraction of an inch from the pillow. *And where the hell am I, anyway?*

"Nearly noon." Alex's voice sounded very awake.

He opened his eyes and tried to remember how he had gotten to Alex's apartment. He sank back with a groan. "Oh, God," he murmured, "it's only an hour 'til rehearsal. We'll have to cancel the concert. Tell everyone we were abducted by aliens. Kidnapped by the Mafia. Defected to Paraguay."

"Ha," she snorted, "I'm the one who has to do all the work. All you do is stand on your soapbox and wave your magic wand."

She sat at the dressing table, wrapped in a sheet, combing her hair. "Alex," he said plaintively, "how the hell did I get here?"

She smiled into the mirror. "Three sweet young men from Tokyo helped me haul you into a cab. One of them lent me his Nikon so I could record the event for posterity."

"You didn't!"

"Wanta bet?" She turned and smiled at him demurely. "What a hit you'll be back in Japan—'American conductor rescued from tavern by honorable engineering students.'"

"Lord," he mumbled, covering his eyes.

"Actually," she bounded up and dashed to the window, clutching the sheet around her, "you'd better hurry and get decent, sweetie pie. I ordered breakfast from the bakery around the corner, and you're the very image of debauchery." She flung open the curtains, flooding the room with a burst of light.

"Aagh." Carl pulled the blanket over his head. "Where are my castle, my dungeon, my casket now that I need them?"

"Vampire-wise," she remarked, "you're not half as convincing as Maestro Molnar was."

Carl uncovered his head and looked at her. "No?"

"No."

"Maybe you have to be Hungarian." He lay back and stared at the ceiling.

She crossed the room and sat down on the foot of the bed. "I'll never stop missing him, you know."

"I know," he replied. "Neither will I." He got up and headed for the bathroom.

The shower helped. By the time he came back to the bedroom, breakfast had arrived. Alex had it arranged on a table next to the window.

Over coffee he was thoughtful, eying her guardedly. "Alex," he said, "about last night. I'm afraid I really can't. . . recall much. Uh, did I. . ."

"Relax," she said with a laugh. "You were asleep within two minutes after we got here."

"Oh."

"You snored."

"Ouch." He rubbed his fingers over the stubble of beard that had collected on his chin. "How. . . romantic of me."

Sunlight sparkled on the glasses, glinted off the silver flatware, flashed from the china coffee cups. He took a sip of coffee. His eyes followed her as she got up and walked to the window. *Who else,* he wondered, *could look quite so elegant dressed in a knotted bed sheet?*

"I did a lot of thinking last night," she said. "About you and Stefan and Kate. I had to ask myself why it was that I spent so many years trying to hurt you."

He was silent, watching her.

"And I also thought about the way you looked that day in the hospital when you were trying to explain about chaging your name from Morales to Fitzgerald, snd your mother called you a bigoted fool." She glanced at him. "I don't think I've ever seen such pain on any human face. When I saw that, I understood for the first time that other people could hurt as much as I can. Quite a revelation for a brat like me." She gave a little smile. "I owe you for that one."

"You don't owe me anything," he said quietly.

"Yes, I do. I'm not much good at saying thank you—haven't had much practice—but I want you to know I'm grateful to you."

"For what?"

"For not giving up on me." Her blue eyes studied him intently, and he felt a kind of rush that wasn't sexual as much as a kind of dizzying joy that made him suddenly warm all over. She frowned as though she was struggling with a perplexing problem, then said slowly, "I think I'm in love with you, Carl. I think I've been in love with you for years."

———◦◦◦❧◦◦◦———

As the final notes of *Kokopelli's Dream: A Piano Concerto for the Right Hand in D-Minor* died away there was an intense silence in the concert hall, then an avalanche of applause. Alex rose from the piano bench and bowed to the audience, then turned to acknowledge the conductor. Carl bent and kissed her hand. Then beaming, he joined the orchestra and the audience in an ovation that seemed to last forever.

Cheeks flushed, eyes gleaming, Alex bowed again and again. A small, dark-haired boy ran down the aisle to the edge of stage and held out a bouquet of yellow roses. She accepted the tribute, then turned and pulling a single blossom from the spray, held it out to the figure on the podium. His words, as he took the flower, were lost in the roar of applause, but she read the meaning of his lips. "I love you too," she whispered, and they stood gazing at each other in the midst of the wave of adulation.

From the air, Manhattan didn't look that big—a blunt-nosed fish surrounded by water on three sides with a tail that stretched northward between the Hudson and the East River. Two clumps of skyscrapers— one uptown and one downtown—secured the body, and the dark rectangle of Central Park marked the start of the gills like a green label. Hard to believe that concentrated in that one beast was the most powerful center of art, culture, finance, and wealth on the planet.

Carl had only been gone two weeks, but it seemed as though an eternity had passed since he'd left for California. A week of rehearsals with the orchestra, the debut performance of *Kokopelli's Dream*, the extra week he'd stayed on in San Francisco immersing himself in a passion that had started how many years ago? In a strange way, he felt that he had known Alex forever, as though they had been together even when they were so totally estranged, so openly hostile. The connection, the attraction, had always been there, but warped by circumstance and misunderstanding, thwarted by choice and chance. It had mostly been an open sore—painful, inoperable, and endlessly frustrating. "We share a bizarre history," she had said last night.

He agreed. In fact, the past week had been a revelation. He was obsessed with her, wanting to know *everything* about her, to devour her completely. Where had she been all those years? What had she been doing and with whom? As he sat gazing out the airplane's window at the city he thought was his home, he felt a a desperate need to catch the next plane back to San Francisco. Having finally connected, how could they now exist apart?

They'd talked it over, adult to adult, being reasonable and sensible and understanding. Of *course* he had to go back to New York. Of *course* she had to stay in San Francisco. They both had obligations, responsibilities, they had *contracts* for God's sake. They would see each other again soon. Maybe at Christmas? (*God, two months? Might as well be forever.*)

He suddenly realized that he was so upset about being away from her that he'd forgotten to be afraid of the plane landing. The wheels were already touching down on the runway at La Guardia, and he hadn't even bothered to grip the arms of the chair or close his eyes and count to fifty. He had to laugh. Too crazed with love to be terrified of flying!

On the taxi ride into Manhattan he thought about last night— the sweet scent of her hair, the soft curve of her neck, the delicate lines of her body, the exquisite softness of her skin. He held her damaged hand and kissed it, and told her to keep working. "I get so discouraged," she said, her luminous sapphire eyes gazing at the still slightly misshapen wrist. "It takes so long to see any progress. Scares me. What if—?"

"Shhh," he soothed. "I know how hard it must be, but keep going." Then he grinned. "I talked to Jorge about a follow-up benefit concert for the FWU next year. I want to be sure that you're ready by next October. And so, my love, you have one year."

She gave him a sardonic smile. "Is that so, maestro?"

"Same time next year?" he said, nuzzling her hair. "We'll do the Rachmaninoff Second. You'll get to start over." Then he kissed her and all other thoughts bolted from his mind.

CHAPTER

33

San Francisco, California
November 1971

A lex dreamed about him. Not every night, but at least every other night. Sometimes he was very real—almost a physical presence that she could see and feel and touch—the tousled dark curls of his hair, the splendid line of his neck, that sensuous lower lip. In other dreams he was remote, cloud like, floating like an incomplete thought just out of reach.

When she turned on the radio to KDFC, the Bay Area's classical music station, and heard Beethoven or Brahms or a violin concerto, she closed her eyes and pretended that he was conducting the orchestra or was the soloist. She could see him so clearly, that look of passion and devotion, the elegant position of his arm, the way he closed his eyes when he played, became completely one with the music. God, she wanted him.

She felt feverish and restless, as though she was suffering from some tropical disease. Everything was slightly out of focus. She couldn't concentrate on anything for very long. Before she knew it, her thoughts wandered to him like a butterfly to a blossom.

Classes and doctor visits and therapy sessions went past in a blur. Squeeze and release. Squeeze and release. Flex and straighten. Flex and straighten. But she still wasn't seeing the progress she hoped for. Dr. Williamson, although pleased that she continued to work hard, said when they met in his office on a Friday afternoon in mid-November, "I'm starting to wonder if we might not be dealing with dystonia."

"With what?"

"It's a neurological condition," the doctor explained. "You said that you were having trouble with 'coordination,' a loss of control."

"Yes," Alex said. "It's like there's a glitch in my timing. The fingers of my left hand just don't move when I want them to. They're. . . sluggish."

"Hmmm." Doctor Williamson thought for a minute, then said, "Dystonia is a strange condition. Robert Schumann was probably an early example. He was having trouble controlling the fourth finger of his right hand, so he contrived a mechanical exercise machine to solve the problem. Unfortunately, his fanatical practice only made the problem worse.

"But it's difficult to connect the condition to a specific injury. You see, when a person suffers a physical trauma, such as your wrist fracture, there is often a slowing of the rate for transmission of electrical impulses along the nerve. The body then tries to compensate for the changes and a new pattern is established. However, once the altered movement has become normalized and the brain has been re-programmed to accept the new pattern, it becomes increasingly difficult to override it and return to the former pattern. As far as the brain is concerned, the problem has been solved. But that doesn't mean that everything is as it was before the injury."

"So, what can we do?" Alex asked.

Dr. Williamson sat back in his chair and met Alex's look. "I'm not sure," he said.

"There are lots of potential culprits for dystonia. Genetics, physical injury, overuse, nutritional issues. And psychological problems, which are my specialty." Dr. Falina Diaz said. Her warm hazel eyes surveyed the new patient.

"Is there a name for this. . . condition?" Alex asked.

"Psychogenic dystonia. The symptoms can closely resemble your earlier diagnosis of focal dystonia, but whereas focal dystonia has an organic—that is to say a non-psychogenic origin such as a physical injury—psychogenic dystonia is a *psychological* disorder, a psychiatric dysfunction that causes physical symptoms." Dr. Diaz picked up the clipboard from her desk and adjusted her glasses. She scanned the Patient Information form again, then set the clipboard and glasses aside and looked at Alex.

"There are several ways to proceed. I'd like to suggest a possible course of action, and then we can discuss the options. I think that you should continue your physical therapy under Dr. Willianson's guidance. That will ensure that that the organic physical cause of the problem is adequately addressed.

"Second, I'm going to recommend a nutrition specialist who can work with you to make certain that you are following a beneficial diet that meets your needs. You mention in your patient history that there were times when your diet has been. . . less than optimal."

Alex smiled. "Yeah, well I guess champagne and ice cream is sort of iffy."

Dr. Diaz nodded. "Very *iffy*. Also, you mention several personal losses that were quite traumatic. Your brother, your father, your teacher. I think we should explore your feelings about what happened, and how these incidents affected you."

"All right."

"Tell me," Dr. Diaz continued, "do you keep a record of your dreams?"

"Not really. I remember them if they're. . . compelling."

"I'd like you to begin writing down what you remember from your dreams. Try to think back and see if your current dreams have any similarity to those you had in the past. We'll be able to use your dreams as a starting point to discuss your current mind-state."

"I suppose I can do that."

They talked for another fifteen minutes about the proposed course of treatment, about when and how often to meet, about Alex's teaching schedule and her physical therapy appointments.

After her new patient had left, Dr. Diaz spent an hour looking over the patient's history and making notes based on her observations during the first session. Pausing, she looked out the window and thought, *This is going to be a challenge.*

On the way home from the doctor's office, Alex stopped at a bookstore and purchased a small notebook with blank pages. The red cover had a Chinese character written in black. The little card tucked inside the book identified the calligraphic inscription as the Mandarin character for "Feelings."

That night before she went to bed, Alex opened the notebook and wrote, "Dr. Diaz wants me to get in touch with my feelings. What an assignment. I've spent years trying to get *rid* of my feelings because they cause me endless pain and suffering, and do nothing but get me into trouble. My feelings have a face—a grotesque, charred, monstrous face. My feelings are the black-hole girl, the one who throws chairs through windows and slices her arms with razor blades. She is so full of hate and so powerful, and yet so pathetic and so full of pain. How can I possibly deal with her?"

That night, she dreamed that she was playing Liszt. The B-Minor Sonata, a tirade of raging emotions, a spiral of frenzied near-chaos that Liszt had dedicated to his friend Robert Schumann who at the time had already entered the sanatorium at Endenich where two years later he would die. Clara Schumann, Robert's talented wife, didn't like Liszt's sonata, contending that it was "merely a blind noise."

In her dream, Alex broke off after the first thematic statement and sat frozen, too terrified to continue. This composition was madness. Or worse. Faustian. Satanic. She couldn't play this.

Then she realized that there was someone sitting next to her on the piano bench. When she glanced around she saw it was Stefan. He was smiling at her—that little half-smile of his. "Don't be afraid, *draga*," he said softly. "You can do this. Continue, please."

She began to play once more and realized that the theme that had begun with such menacing violence had been transformed into a lyrical melody of delicate beauty and serenity. *So*, she thought, *you take your pain and turn it into art.* She woke up smiling and reached for her notebook. Here was a dream worth remembering.

CHAPTER

34

Auburn, California

"Do you know a Clarissa Whittington?" Chris said.

Kate thought for a moment, then replied, "Sounds vaguely familiar. How would I know her?"

"She's on the planning council for Placer County."

"Ah. She was at the most recent planning meetings, wasn't she?"

"She's the reason for all the delays."

"Really?" The surprise was audible in Kate's response. "Any idea why?"

"No. But when I went through all of the notes, at every council meeting that reviewed your application she voiced concerns and asked for more information. And it's never the same concern. One time it's access. The next it's noise. The next it's land use. She's been pulling up one excuse after another almost at random—anything that might delay the process or bring up a potential violation, no matter how absurd."

"Just stalling for its own sake?" Kate said incredulously. "I don't understand."

"Then you don't know her? You haven't had any problems with her before?"

"No."

"What about your father?" Chris asked. "Did he possibly have a run-in with her when he was in office? I'm asking because this seems almost like a personal matter. A vendetta of some kind."

"I don't know. But of course I was in Cleveland most of that time so I wouldn't have heard about his day-to-day problems."

"Who would know?"

"What about Ed Collins," Kate said. "He was Dad's campaign manager after Danny left the team."

"Let's talk to him," Chris said.

The next Wednesday, Kate met Chris and Ed Collins at Tosh's in Folsom. Perched on a bluff above the American River, Tosh's was a long-time favorite of the locals, a sprawling bunkhouse of a place with dark wood, a worn plank floor, and windows that overlooked the Rainbow Bridge, Lake Natoma, and the historic village of Folsom. Ed ordered a draft beer while Chris and Kate decided to indulge in strawberry daiquiris.

Chris had already had two conversations with Ed about Danny and Owen's rift, so he was aware of the issues that had come up and the delays with the land use permits. "Does the name Clarissa Whittington mean anything to you, Ed?" Kate asked.

Collins frowned and shook his head. "She's on the planning council. That's all I know."

"Apparently, she's been consistently opposed to the music center project, but I can't figure out why," said Kate. "She seems determined to block the permit, but it doesn't make sense. It's like it's. . . random or something."

Ed took a sip of beer. "I haven't paid her much attention," he said. "Kind of a mousey little lady. Never heard anything about her obstructing much of anything. I think she and her husband live in Rocklin. I believe he's retired from the Southern Pacific railroad." He took another sip.

"How could we get more information?" Chris asked. "We need to know what her motive is."

"You could ask her?" Ed suggested, grinning.

Kate and Chris exchanged looks. "That seems a little. . . awkward," Chris said.

"You know," Ed said, "come to think of it, my sister Nancy might be of help."

"How so?" Kate asked.

"She works in the library in Rocklin. Funny how much gossip you hear in a library. People must have this idea that the library's safe ground or something. Like talking to your hair dresser." He nodded. "I'll see if Nancy knows Clarissa Whittington."

The next week, however, was Thanksgiving and Kate put Clarissa Whittington, the Planning Council, Danny, Ed and land use permits out of her thoughts, determined to have a good holiday. She and Cory had been invited to go to Stockton for the Ashida's Thanksgiving dinner. "You'll get to meet the whole tribe," Tommy said with a smirk.

Kate rolled her eyes. "Yikes."

He gave her a peck on the cheek. "Relax. There's only going to be about fifteen or twenty rowdy Nips roaming around drinking and telling stories. How bad could that be?"

She shook her head. "Serves me right, Ashida. That's what I get for sleeping with the help."

They both burst out laughing. "If things get too ugly, I promise to rescue you," Tommy said.

"I'll hold you to that."

Stockton, California

Eighteen members of the Ashida family, including Tommy, had gathered for Thanksgiving dinner at Pearl and Willie's house behind the produce store in Stockton. Kate and Cory made twenty for the family feast.

Kate was delighted that several traditional Japanese dishes were included in the Thanksgiving dinner including pickled daikon and inari sushi. As she offered a tray of tempting morsels, Tommy's

Aunt Pearl told Kate that the sushi was named after the Shinto god of fertility and agriculture which seemed very appropriate for a Thanksgiving meal.

The food was delicious, but Kate wondered about the fact that of the eighteen family members present, two—David and Tommy—were one line, while the other sixteen were Willie and Pearl's brood—Francis and his wife Hanuko and their three little ones, Alan and his wife Lucille and their twin daughters, Mary and her husband Greg with their three boys, and Ben who was still a confirmed bachelor. Most Japanese families were small, yet this house was packed with three generations of adults and kids and the friendly lumbering presence of Chibi, the family's oversized Golden Retriever. Tommy's cousin Francis was recording everything on his Super 8 film camera to document the occasion.

The cold rain outside kept everyone in. The children raised a ruckus while the men tried to watch football. The women congregated in the kitchen to help Pearl with the cooking. Everyone chattered and laughed in a mix of English and Japanese. Chibi, determined to join in, let out an occasional bark.

Cory had immediately gotten acquainted with Greg and Mary's boys and was off in one of the bedrooms playing Monopoly. Tommy was talking to his father and glanced now and then at the Detroit Lions beating up on the Kansas City Chiefs.

Ben sat down on the sofa next to Kate and gave her a weary smile. "What a circus, huh?" he said as though offering an apology.

"I think it's great," Kate replied. "Do they celebrate Thanksgiving in Japan?"

Ben hesitated, then said, "I don't think so. My folks always said it was the great American holiday and they wanted to be sure they got it right."

"Well, this sure tastes right to me," Kate said, taking a bite of sushi.

Ben looked around. "It's always a great excuse to get the clan together."

"I love family get-togethers," Kate replied. "Especially when I can be a fly on the wall."

"Ah," Ben said, "a Watcher. That's usually my game."

Kate set down her plate. "What's it like," she asked, "seeing the world through the camera's lens?"

He looked at her for a moment, then glanced away. "Intriguing. Scary. Humbling. Detatched. All of the above." He looked back at her and she read a kind of sadness in his face. "Makes me feel like a voyeur sometimes. An observer. I watch. I record. I don't. . . comment."

"You must have seen some remarkable things."

"Remarkable and terrible. Makes me wonder why people are so eager to watch the news. Maybe seeing how fucked up things are makes them feel better somehow. Safer. At least it's happening somewhere else. To somebody else."

Then he gave a little laugh and said, "Hey. Where'd all that come from? We're supposed to be having a party here."

"Giving thanks," Kate said with some irony.

"Yeah. That *is* the name of the game, right?"

After a minute, Kate said, "I guess I should go see if I can help out in the kitchen."

"Naw," Ben said. "Mom's got things under control. Just enjoy yourself." He got up. "I'm gonna check out the big game."

Kate watched him cross the room to join the knot of men gathered before the TV. Then she saw David Ashida glance in her direction. He got up and walked across the room and stood before her. "Hello, Kate," he said gruffly.

"Hello, Mr. Ashida."

"David."

"Okay, David."

They looked at each other warily, then he cleared his throat and said. "We need to talk." He jerked his head in the direction of the door. "Please."

Kate got up and followed him. She glanced at Tommy but he appeared to be engrossed in the game. *Odd, he didn't usually watch football.* They went out the back door. The rain had stopped, but the sky was the color of slate and the wind was cold. Bare trees rattled their branches and made a creaking sound.

But inside David's cottage it was warm and cozy. He switched on the lamp and motioned for her to sit on the upholstered sofa. "I will make some tea," he announced and disappeared into the kitchen.

Uneasy, filled with trepedation, Kate wondered what would come next. What exactly did David want to talk about? She took a deep breath and looked around. The apartment was simply furnished—a sofa, two arm chairs, a dresser with framed photos on top. She recognized a picture of Connie, David's late wife, and one of David and Connie with little Tommy between them. And one of Tommy dressed as a cowboy sitting on a pinto pony.

There was also a black and white photo of Connie holding a baby. She was standing on a dirt street in front of a row of barracks. Dark clouds piled up in the sky. A ridge of mountains could be seen in the distance. *The internment camp*, Kate thought, and a shiver of cold made her neck prickle.

But David was coming through the doorway with a teapot and two cups. He poured them both a cup and sat down opposite her in one of the armchairs. "I want to thank you," he said gravely, "for taking care of my son when he was ill."

Kate swallowed and met his eyes. "My pleasure," she said, "and an honor."

He pursed his thin lips and took a drink of tea. The he set the cup down and leaned back in the chair. She waited as he sat staring thoughtfully at the ceiling. "Sometimes," he said slowly, his eyes returning to her, "the river has dreadful currents, powerful forces that can disrupt our course and send us headlong into dangerous waters. It is not the fault of the river that these currents exist. It is not our fault that we are caught in them. But we are not helpless in the face of danger. We are not simply the victims of our fate. We have reached a precarious moment and we must make a choice. What action can we take?"

He paused again and studied her carefully. "I have come to believe," he continued, "that harboring old grievances, recalling old wounds, is not a prudent course. It has taken me many years to reach this point. When I learned of your. . . relationship with my son, my pride was wounded, my family's honor was at stake. I was angry, and I took refuge in my anger. But anger," he paused and looked at Kate intently, "anger is a poor refuge. It feeds on itself like a fire on wood. It must constantly be fed. And when it finally burns itself out there is nothing left but ashes."

Kate waited, almost afraid to breathe.

David picked up his cup and drank, then looked at her once more and said, "My son has told me that he wishes to marry you. He has asked for my blessing." His eyes wandered to the photos on the dresser. Kate followed his gaze and saw that there was another picture that she hadn't seen before—a little black and white snapshot of Kate and Tommy with their arms around each other's shoulders grinning at the camera. They were standing in front of the barn at Mockingbird and looked to be around ten years old. They were skinny and ragged in their play clothes and looked blissfully happy.

David glanced back at Kate. "There are some things," he said, "that even the strongest current cannot disrupt. You and he," he pointed at the photo, "are meant to be together. I will not be the one to stand in your way."

Kate closed her eyes and bit her lip to keep back the tears. When she opened her eyes he was looking at her with the same impenetrable gaze that reminded her of Tommy. She took a deep breath. "Thank you, David," she said.

He nodded, then got to his feet and set the teacup on the side table. "Come," he said. "I expect that the feast is nearly ready. We mustn't keep them waiting."

As Kate followed David up the path to the house, she felt a growing warmth despite the cold rain that buffeted her face. *Oh my God*, she thought, *it's going to be okay.*

She stopped for a moment inside the living room doorway. Tommy turned away from the television and gave her a questioning look. She smiled and nodded. He grinned and gave her a thumbs up.

"Come on everyone," Pearl called from the kitchen doorway. "Time to eat!"

An hour later they had finished dinner, but everyone was still gathered at the table. The turkey and stuffing were demolished, the kami salad and yams with Ginko nuts gone were gone, the sliced mangoes and pumpkin pie nearly consumed. Tommy stood up and tapped with a spoon on his water glass and said, "Hey, everyone. Quiet down. I have an announcement."

Heads turned, the children fell silent, eyes looked up expectantly. Tommy looked at Kate and she met his eyes and returned his smile. "I'm glad that we could be here with all of you tonight," Tommy said, "because I want you to share our happiness. Kate and I have decided to get married. So," he seemed suddenly at a loss for words, "there it is."

He sat down, as a chorus of gleeful congratulations and applause filled the room. Pearl, who was sitting next to Kate, enveloped her in a smothering hug. "Oh, honey, that's wonderful! I'm so glad for both of you!" she exclaimed. Cory, who was across the table next to Tommy, jumped up and down and clapped his hands. From the end of the table, David looked around at the jubilant crowd and shook his head. And smiled.

———∘∘∘❖∘∘∘———

Mockingbird Ranch

It was a very simple wedding. They went down to the courthouse in Auburn, filled out the paperwork, paid the fee, and the judge went through the brief ceremony. Chris was Kate's witness and Ben was Tommy's. Cory watched solemnly from the sidelines.

After the ceremony, they all went back to Mockingbird and enjoyed a dinner that Consuelo prepared to celebrate the occasion— corn pudding, Red Snapper Vera Cruz with tomatoes and olives, chiles in walnut sauce, fresh tortillas, fruit salad and coconut ice cream. And champagne.

The wedding party walked up to the bluff and watched the sunset—not just a time of day, but a phenomena that began with the sun inching toward the horizon, the Coast Range changing from a vaporous blue line to a solid purple wall, the valley awash with lavender light that grew darker as the sun's fire was quenched, until all that was left was a crescent of gold where the sky met the hills. Alpine glow still brushed the tops of the Sierras to the east, a delicate pink light reflecting off fresh snow. The river whispered, singing to itself, laughing in hushed tones, and a ghostly mist began to rise from the canyon.

Back at the house, the fire felt good and the group enjoyed one last glass of champagne before Ben and Chris said goodnight and Tommy carried Cory up to bed.

Elsewhere that night, the world was not as quiet—a record-setting snowstorm dumped two feet of snow over the Mid-Atlantic and Northeast including nearly 23 inches in New York City; India and Pakistan were at war; the Soviet spacecraft Mars II orbiter crash landed on the Red Planet, making it the first man-made object to reach the surface of Mars; a 6.3 earthquake shook the Kamchatka Peninsula and rattled windows in Japan's northern provinces; volcanoes were erupting in Chile, New Guinea, the Canary Islands, and St. Vincent, West Indies.

But at Mockingbird Valley Ranch on the American River near Auburn California, the night was peaceful. The stars hung like early Christmas ornaments in the black dome of the sky, a waxing crescent moon rose over the peaks of the snow-capped Sierra, and the river sang a joyful song of celebration for the two lives that had finally been joined.

CHAPTER
35

Mockingbird Ranch
December 1971

"Where is Mineral King?" Kate asked. "The name doesn't ring a bell."

"Right next to Sequoia National Park," Allison replied. "There were silver mines there in the late 1800s. That's when a permanent road was built. It goes right through two of the most important groves of giant sequoias, the Redwood Creek Grove and the Atwell Grove."

Kate looked at Cory who was sitting on the raised hearth next to the fireplace sipping hot chocolate. "Remember the giant trees we took you to see last summer, honey?"

Cory nodded. "They were really *big!*"

The family had gathered after dinner in the living room at Mockingbird. The fire was a cozy counterpoint to the cold drizzle outside, and the Christmas tree was dressed in all its seasonal glory.

Allison and Francisco had arrived the day before. They were in the midst of moving to San Francisco where Francisco would be working with the Legal Defense Fund and Ali had been accepted at San Francisco State to finish her undergraduate degree. Jorge and Rose Morales, Allison's parents, would be arriving the next day to spend the Christmas weekend, and Alex was coming from the City as well. Kate had asked Alex if Carl was going to be coming with her but no, Carl was stuck in New York rehearsing for a New Year's concert. Marian and Nick had gone to Mexico for the holidays.

Everyone wanted to meet Francisco. ("Harvard Law? No kidding?" Alex had exclaimed. "Way to go, Allison!") Kate thought it would be grand to have a Christmas gathering, and just hoped there would never be a replay of the disaster in Lenox two years before when Alex's revelation of Carl and Marian's affair had sent the family spinning into turmoil.

"So Walt Disney wanted to build a huge ski resort right next door to the sequoia groves?" Kate said, putting down her wine glass and nibbling a Christmas cookie.

"Still wants to," Francisco said. "They've been working on the project since 1965 and they went ahead with it even after Mr. Disney passed away. They had all the permits in place by 1968 and planned to build a new road through the groves to accommodate the estimated 14,000 visitors per day that they anticipated would visit the park. They planned to have fourteen high-capacity ski lifts, two huge hotels, an ice skating rink, ten restaurants."

"Good Lord," Tommy exclaimed, "that's practically a whole city. Just imagine the traffic, the infrastructure, the air pollution, the garbage."

"Exactly," Francisco agreed. "That's when the Sierra Club got involved. A group of attorneys who were working with the Sierra Club established the Legal Defense Fund to try to fight the Disney Corporation and preserve the wilderness. The LDF is independent of the Sierra Club, but it shares the goal of keeping environmentally sensitive wilderness areas free of development. The idea is to use existing laws that give citizens the right to go to court to enforce environmental laws when the government can't."

"Or won't," added Allison.

"So what happened to the project?" Kate asked.

"Right now, it's tied up in the courts," Francisco said. "We won the first round, but lost on appeal, and then took the case to the California Supreme Court. We lost there as well, but we're appealing the decision."

"Meanwhile," Ali chimed in, "the NEPA, the National Environment Policy Act, was passed by Congress. It requires that corporations provide an environmental impact report before they can proceed with development."

"So," finished Francisco, "that's where it stands now. It will take a couple of years for Disney's people to complete the impact report, so we've bought some time. A stall tactic."

Kate and Tommy exchanged glances. "Sound familiar?" he asked. "Uh huh."

Allison tilted her head. "What sounds familiar?"

"We've been dealing with some stall tactics of our own on the music center project," Tommy explained. "Lots of foot dragging and nit picking."

"We think there's something fishy going on," said Kate. "It's possible that one of the county commissioners is on the take, but we haven't got any proof. All very. . . " she waved her hand "shadowy."

"What makes you think there is corruption?" Francisco asked.

Kate explained about the peculiar negative votes from Clarissa Whittington, the odd banking practices, the numbered accounts and imaginary charities. "My friend Chris, who is an attorney, is looking into it, but so far she can't find any solid evidence of wrongdoing."

"Perhaps I could meet with Chris," Francisco offered. "As an outsider, I might be able to see some connections. After all," he smiled ruefully, "as a Mexican, I am, you might say, well-versed in the behind-the-scenes methods of corrupt officials."

"That might be really helpful," Kate said. "Thanks, Francisco. I'll give Chris a call and maybe we can set up a meeting before you guys leave for the City."

But first, there was Christmas to celebrate. Alex drove up from San Francisco on Christmas Eve and Rose and Jorge arrived just at dusk to share a simple holiday dinner. Afterwards they all piled into Alex's roomy Chrysler and drove into town to look at the Christmas lights. Then it was on to St. Joseph's for Midnight Mass—swags of greenery, candles everywhere, angelic children's choir. Back at Mockingbird they each opened one present from the pile under the Christmas tree, had another glass of Cold Duck, and finally got to bed well after two.

Cory, of course, was up bright and early on a fine sunny Christmas morning and set about tearing into his presents while the blurry-eyed adults sat around drinking coffee and grilling Ali and Francisco on their plans.

"Berkeley law?" exclaimed Rose. "My goodness, Allison, that's quite a switch."

"I got inspired," Ali replied, giving Francisco's hand a squeeze, "by the Cisco Kid here."

"Cisco Kid?" said Jorge. "What is this?"

Francisco tried to scowl at Ali but he was laughing. "My nickname at Harvard," he admitted.

"So, does that make me Pancho?" Allison asked.

"I don't think you quite fit the profile, *chiqita*." For a moment they were lost, gazing at each other. Jorge and Rose exchanged bemused glances.

"Look everybody," Cory cried, "my dad sent me a book. *White Fang* by Jack London! See the picture on the cover? It's Buck! Just like in *Call of the Wild!*"

"Let me see," said Alex. She opened the cover, "Wow, Cory. This is a first edition!"

"Cool," Cory said. "That's good, right?"

"That's special," Tommy said. "Makes it even more valuable."

"Some day I'll have a dog just like Buck!" Cory exclaimed.

Francisco and Ali wanted to get back to the City and settle into their new apartment on Russian Hill before the semester started, but they stayed at Mockingbird long enough for Francisco to meet with Chris Malacchi-Salinger and her husband Lennie at their Sacramento office. Back at Mockingbird, he reported the results to Tommy and Kate. Ali listened attentively.

"Here's what Len found out from his friends in Reno," Francisco said. "That numbered account that Danny's been sending checks to is a front. There is no charity. The account shows withdrawals that then have shown up in Clarissa Whittington's bank account, so he's actually paying *her*."

"Jeez," Kate said, "she didn't sound like a crook."

"Well, Chris also found out from Ed Collins that Clarissa has money problems. Her husband has cancer, and the medical bills have about wiped them out. So she certainly has a motive for playing on the fringe. I expect Danny told her that no one could possibly find out."

"Wow," said Tommy. "Kind of a moral dilemma, isn't it? I mean, it is *bribery* and she is guilty of accepting a bribe, but I'd hate to get her into trouble under the circumstances. Sounds like she has enough problems."

"Here's a thought," said Francisco. "Chris and I feel like we have enough evidence to go to Danny and let him know that we're on to him and that we could shut him down if we decided to bring charges. I wouldn't be surprised if he might decide to settle out of court. Agree to stop the pay-offs, maybe make a nice up-front contribution to the Whittington family, and then stay out of our way."

"I still can't figure out why he's been doing this," Kate said, shaking her head. "Why try to get in the way of the music center project?"

Francisco shrugged. "Some guys, you know, they're just. . ."

"Rotten," Ali said. "My dad, Jorge, has run into that kind of thing with the restaurant—people trying to shut him down, lying about health and safety conditions, harassing him for no reason."

"So you and Chris are going to meet with Danny?" Kate said.

"If you approve," Francisco replied.

"What do you think?" Kate asked Tommy.

"Well, since we've shifted the focus to starting a winery that will have an affiliated concert series, and since that means we don't need new zoning or a land-use change or an early release from the agricultural contract, we should be able to get the permits for access and the public event clearance without much trouble. It takes the issue off the table, so that even if Danny won't back off he's dead in the water. So," he grinned, "sure. Go for it. Tell the s.o.b. to get lost."

PART III

CHAPTER

36

January 1972

With Cory back in school, Tommy in San Francisco for a series of meetings, and the holidays over for another year, the house seemed empty and quiet. Kate was still at the breakfast table having a third cup of coffee and reading (just one more chapter) of Herman Wouk's *Winds of War*. She felt a little guilty that she couldn't seem to put the novel aside and get on with all the other things she should be doing—finishing Stefan's biography (how *was* she going to tell the story of Armand Becker?), going over the plans for the winery, (was there an existing building that could be renovated or would they have to build a whole new facility for the wine-making operation?), writing a press release on the new construction that would soon begin at Mockingbird. But the novel had grabbed her. The Germans were beginning their invasion of Poland when the phone rang.

It was Chris. "Danny caved," she said gleefully. "Totally caved."

"Really?" Kate said in surprise.

"Francisco was amazing. He was so calm and sincere, but he had Danny squirming like a worm on a hook. It was a beautiful sight."

"Tell, tell!" Kate exclaimed.

"We met in Danny's office in Sacramento and he had his attorney there with him. It was obviously set up to be intimidating as hell, but Francisco just kept nibbling away at Danny's story and getting him to contradict himself. I tell you, it was priceless. I'd love to see him in action in a courtroom sometime."

"So, Danny agreed to back off and not interfere any more?"

"Yes, and even better, he agreed to give Clarissa and her husband a nice 'humanitarian aid' check, as Francisco put it, to help her family get back on their feet."

Kate let out her breath in a sigh of relief. "That's great news, Chris. Now we can really get to work."

"Full steam ahead."

"Thanks for all your help."

As she hung up the phone, Kate couldn't help glancing at the photo of Owen that sat on the fireplace mantle. She toasted the photograph with her coffee mug. "This one was for you, Daddy. We finally got him."

Motivated by Chris's news, she put World War II aside and got busy getting specs for the furnishings they would need for the new recital hall. She was so absorbed with the project that she was surprised when Consuelo appeared and began to make lunch. Consuelo's round, tan face broke into a wide grin when she heard about the results of the meeting with Dan. "That Francisco," she crowed, "*es un hombre muy listo*! What a clever guy."

After lunch, Kate went to the barn to do some measurements and when she got back she noticed the answering machine was blinking. "Good afternoon, Kate." She recognized Robert Ashford's pleasantly civil voice. "Please give me a call, my dear, at your earliest convenience. I have a bit of news for you."

"Why does everything happen all at once?" Kate asked aloud as she dialed the number for the Townsend Foundation. "Hi, Stephanie. I'm returning Mr. Ashford's call?"

Robert picked up a moment later. "Thank you so much for getting back to me. I have some news for you about the grant application. I took the proposal to the Board, and they were unanimous in their support. They only had a very few questions that I'm sure we can clarify in the contract."

"Oh, my goodness! That's wonderful, Mr. Ashford. What was the amount that they agreed to fund?"

"The entire request. Seven hundred and fifty thousand."

"That's *amazing!*" *Tommy was going to be thrilled. So was Alex. And Carl. Everyone!*

Robert chuckled. "Now all you have to do is raise the additional two and a quarter million."

She laughed breathlessly. "Yes. Right. There is that."

"I'll be sending you the grant papers next week. Meanwhile, congratulations, my dear. I'll look forward to attending the festival."

After she hung up the phone, Kate took a few minutes to gather her thoughts and quiet her thumping heart. Then she picked up the phone once more and dialed Jean Molnar Westmorland's number.

San Francisco, California

"Tell me about your family." Dr. Diaz was seated in an upholstered armchair next to the window. Alex had taken her usual place across the coffee table from the doctor. After nearly four months of bi-weekly sessions, Alex felt more and more at home. In Falina Diaz's office, cozy neutral-colored furniture sat on a beige carpet. Lots of houseplants surrounded a big bay window that looked out on Sacramento Street. Dr. Diaz's office was not far from Alex's apartment. On nice days she liked to walk to her appointments. The route took her through the eastern edge of Golden Gate Park and past the University of San Francisco campus.

But today it was cold and somber, and the fog-rain mix was chilling, so she had driven to the doctor's office. Despite the low grey clouds and drizzle, the office was bright and the small collection of Indian Mandalas on the walls was a colorful addition.

"My family?" Alex repeated. "Which one?"

"There is more than one?"

"It's confusing, though I guess in the beginning we were pretty... conventional."

"How so?"

Alex kicked off her shoes and sat back. "Mother, father, one sister, one brother. Maternal grandparents back east. My mom's aunt who was always sort of... around. We lived on a ranch—a *working* ranch.

Pears and cattle and such. I went to school. I took piano lessons." She frowned. "What am I supposed to be saying? Why does this matter?"

"What did you like to do after school?"

"I don't know. I practiced. Any spare time I had, I practiced."

"The piano?"

"Yes. I had to practice at least three hours a day even on school days. I went for lessons twice a week. It was a long drive to my teacher's house, but Mom was serious about finding a good teacher, so if that meant driving forty-five miles round trip rain or shine, that's what we did."

"Tell me about your teacher."

"Teachers. There was Mrs. Caponis. She had great credentials — Mom always interviewed prospective teachers—but she taught out of her home, and she had two little kids. Sometimes they got in the way. So then I took lessons with Dr. Chatman at Sierra College. And then he got me into a conservatory program for gifted children and after that ther were others. One of them was German. Fritz Kroener. He was an orchestra conductor as well as a pianist, and I was always sure that if I didn't perform up to his standards he was going to pull out a Lugar and shoot me."

"So you felt. . . anxious about your performance?"

"Petrified. No mistakes allowed. I had to be perfect. Anything else was a disaster. I remember one time I had a recital and right in the middle I blanked. I had to stop and I couldn't go on. When I got home I hid in the barn for hours." Alex looked down at her arms and gave a rueful smile. "Sliced myself up pretty good that time."

"You felt you should be punished for making a mistake?"

"Of course."

"Did your mother punish you?"

Alex sighed. "No. She was always so damned cheerful. 'That's okay, honey. We all make mistakes. You'll do better next time.' Only. . ."

"Yes?"

"Only she never *meant* it. I *knew* she didn't. I could tell that she was disappointed in me." Alex shot the doctor a hostile look. "People lie, you know that? They lie all the time. You can't trust them!"

"What makes you think so?"

"They just cover everything up. A bunch of hypocrites!" Alex realized her voice had edged up to a shrill cry and she made an effort to control herself, but she was blazing mad.

"Does that make you angry?"

"Are you kidding me?" Alex jumped up and began to pace back and forth in front of the window. "I could. . . I could spit nails I'm so pissed off."

She began a tirade about her perceived rebuffs—her mother's favoritism of her brother Julian, her father's preference for her sister Kate. Marian's flight from Mockingbird on what Alex termed "a pretext," Marian's affair with Carl, the family break-up, Julian's death. Her own affair with Stefan. The disastrous liaison with Marty.

At length, her anger partly exhausted and suddenly replaced by a desperate sadness, she sank down in the chair and began to sob. "And now, see, it's really awful because I've finally gotten into a relationship that makes me feel *right*. Only it *isn't* because Carl was married to my sister and. . . God, it's too damned *confusing*." She waved her hands in the air. "How the hell am I supposed to *play* when all these *issues* are hitting me?! All the time, hitting me!"

Dr. Diaz leaned forward and handed Alex a Kleenex. "Exactly what we're going to try to figure out," she said.

After Alex left, Dr. Diaz sat down at her desk and contemplated the session. *So pretty*, she thought picturing Alex's oval face, her golden hair and azure eyes, *but so layered, like an onion. Layer over layer*. Picking up her pen, she wrote, "Patient presents with several specific symptoms including marked sensitivity to rejection, fear of abandonment, impulsive behavior including substance abuse, self injury, and severe dissociation. Early sexual abuse? Possible Bipolar Disorder? Or perhaps Borderline Personality Disorder? Will continue to explore the possibilities."

CHAPTER

37

Mockingbird Ranch
February 1972

Kate and Tommy stood in front of the barn on a beautiful bright February morning. "I wish I could remember where that trap door was." A light frost still clung to the edges of the grass, and the hills stood out sharply defined against the crisp, blue sky. Kate looked around frowning as though the landscape was suddenly going to reveal an answer.

"So if it wasn't in the barn, then where?" Tommy said.

She looked at him. He waited patiently, leaning against the corral fence. Dressed in jeans and an old plaid wool shirt that had once belonged to Kate's father, Owen, he looked very much like a rancher. Well, a Japanese rancher. She had to smile.

"What?" he asked, brushing the wing of black hair back from his forehead.

"I like you better this way."

"What way?"

"Cowboy. Rancher. Non-city person."

"Ah, shucks, Miss Kate," he drawled. "I'm just a poor country boy."

She ran to him and gave him a hug and whispered, "I love you, Tommy Ashida."

"Me you too," he whispered back, nuzzling her hair. They held each other for a minute, then he said, "Maybe the packing shed?"

"Actually," Kate said slowly, "I'm thinking it was up this way." She started up the drive toward the house, but stopped in front of the spring house. "Maybe. . . here!"

The door creaked as it swung open. Inside the shed was dark

and damp, the old stones covered here and there with moss. "I'll get a flashlight," Tommy said.

Kate looked around. The shed was small—only about ten feet square, with the remnants of a well in the center. The well had long since been replaced by the modern water system and irrigation wells needed for the ranch operations. Sometime over the years, someone had put pieces of linoleum on the floor. They were rotting away at the edges, tattered and uneven.

Tommy came back with the flashlight and they examined the interior. "I don't see anything," Kate said.

Tommy scuffed at the linoleum with his foot and a piece broke off. He pushed it aside. "Okay," he said, "look at this. Hold the light."

She took the flashlight and he peeled back the section of flooring and there was the trap door. "Bingo!" Kate said.

They managed to pull the door up on its crumbling hinges and prop it back against the wall. Kate angled the light into the opening. "There's a ladder," she exclaimed. "Must be some kind of cellar."

"I'll take a look," Tommy said, taking the flashlight from her and testing his weight on the first rung.

"Be careful!"

"Sure." He worked his way down the ladder, then called up to her, "It *is* a cellar. A big one!"

Unable to restrain her curiosity, Kate followed him down the ladder. "Wow!" she said, looking around. They were standing in a cavern that looked to be about thirty feet long and ten feet wide, with a ceiling high enough to allow them to easily stand upright. The air in the cavern was dry and cool—warmer than outside. Maybe around sixty degrees, Kate guessed.

They made their way carefully to the end of the chamber and found an opening supported by thick wooden pillars. Kate shone the light into the shaft. The tunnel was level and appeared to have been carved right into the bedrock. "Mine shaft?" she wondered aloud.

"Could be," Tommy replied. "Lots of old gold mines around here from back in the day."

Kate glanced back at Tommy. "Should we have a look?"

He grinned. "Be my guest."

Carefully, they advanced along the shaft that followed a straight path before curving to the left and becoming smaller, although it was still possible to stand upright as they inched along.

They reached another pillared opening and went through into a small rectangular room and down another shaft that opened suddenly into a large cave.

"Whoa!" Tommy exclaimed. They both stood looking around the chamber. The "room" was at least sixty feet long, about thirty feet wide. A domed ceiling rose twenty feet above them.

"God, Tommy, look at this!" cried Kate. She scanned the light along the wall revealing a scattering of petroglyphs—concentric circles and spirals, strange stick figures and geometric markings, unidentifiable critters that looked like birds or insects.

"Jeez," Tommy exclaimed, "Indian rock carvings. This is amazing!"

"How could we have missed finding this all those years?" Kate asked. "We explored all over Mockingbird, riding from one end to the other, but we never found this. . . this *treasure*?"

They stood for several minutes gazing at the ancient markings. Then Kate glanced at the far wall and said, "I think there's light coming from over there."

"I think you're right," Tommy said.

They both walked to the far end of the cave where a curving shaft led slightly upward. There was definitely daylight coming from the end of the shaft. They scrambled up the loose gravel and found themselves in a deep overhang at tree-top level. The cave opening was about forty feet up the side of a bluff and hidden from view by a dense stand of fir trees.

"Wow," Kate said. "Where are we?"

Just then they heard a motor and Tommy pointed. "Look, there's the highway. We must have come out on the frontage road just before the bridge."

"So we're still on Mockingbird land?"

"Yeah. The eastern line of the property."

They looked at each other. "Are you thinking what I'm thinking?" Kate asked.

"Wine cellar with highway frontage?"

Kate nodded. "Uh huh."

Wednesday was Cory's seventh birthday and everyone seemed to have forgotten about it. Mom hadn't mentioned it at breakfast and neither had Consuelo, although she and her daughter Teresa seemed to be giving him funny looks and giggling and whispering together in the pantry.

Even Mr. Tommy seemed preoccupied, hiding behind the newspaper and gulping down coffee and scrambled eggs, then leaving quickly without any of his usual jokes or admonitions: "Hey, Cory-chan, listen to this one: Why did the farmer name his two dogs Rolex and Timex?"

"I don't know."

"Because they were watch dogs."

Or, "Okay, sport, don't forget to practice your Mozart. Aunt Alex will want to hear it next time she's in town."

But this morning Tommy just got up from the table, set the paper aside and said, "See you later," and out the door he went.

So now it was after four and Cory had just gotten off the school bus and it was a long walk up the driveway to the house. His backpack was heavy with homework and everyone had forgotten his birthday.

Cory stopped and looked unhappily at the landscape. The pastures were green from the winter rains and the pear trees were in bloom—great round puffs like fat white clouds decorating the hillsides. It would be fun to go for a ride on Daisy or one of the other horses. Watch the river. Skip some stones.

He would love to go take another look at those Indian pictures— *what had Mom called them? Peterglyphs? Something like that. Mr. Tommy had taken him to see them, but told him never to go into the cave by himself. Too dangerous, he said. But what if he took his pocketknife and a flashlight? Still, Mom and Mr. Tommy would be really mad if they found out. And there were chores to do. Chickens to feed. Eggs to gather.* Disgruntled, he kicked a stone along the drive as he trudged toward the house.

He paused when he noticed Chris Malacchi's car parked outside the courtyard gate. *Probably she had another meeting with Mom. They had been meeting a lot and talking about serious stuff—permits and land use and somebody named Clarissa something. Funny name, Clarissa. So Mom was busy and he would have to go change his clothes and get to work on his chores before it started getting dark. Then he could do his homework. Great birthday.*

But just as he reached the front door, he heard Teresa shriek, "He's here!" She threw open the front door and yelled, "Surprise!" at the top of her voice and he nearly jumped out of his skin. Then he just stood there staring through the open door at a crowd of smiling faces—Teresa and Consuelo and her husband Jaime. Mom and Mr. Tommy and Aunt Alex. Chris Malacchi and her two boys, and they were all shouting, "Surprise!" and "Happy Birthday, Cory!"

He was so amazed he didn't know what to say. But Teresa grabbed his hand and pulled him into the foyer. Mr. Tommy picked him up and hugged him and carried him into the dining room while everyone crowded around, talking and laughing. Tommy set him down and there on the table was a big three-layered cake with caramel icing (his favorite) and strawberries and other great-looking food and a pile of presents—just like Christmas.

"Wow," he managed to say.

And then Mom hugged him and said, "Happy birthday, honey." And Aunt Alex ruffled his hair and winked at him. He didn't know whether to cry or laugh.

But the best part came *after* the party—after dinner and cake and presents and blowing out candles and singing happy birthday. And then the surprise telephone call from his dad, Carl, who was in some place called Munich. All that was great, but then Tommy disappeared for a minute and came back with something wrapped up in a grey and white horse blanket. "What is it?" Cory asked as Tommy handed the bundle to him

"Happy Birthday," Tommy said with a grin.

The horse blanket wiggled. Cory set it down on the floor and out crawled a grey and white puppy with a pink tongue and bright black eyes and a little fringed tail that whipped back and forth. "Oh!" cried Cory, "It's *Buck*!"

"Who?" Chris Malacchi said.

"Jack London," Kate said. "The dog from the *Call of the Wild*."

The puppy scrambled into Cory's outstretched arms and licked his face and whined while Cory laughed and laughed. *Best birthday ever!*

CHAPTER

38

April 1972

The holidays were over, the late winter pruning completed, the permits finally in place, construction projects moving forward. Kate decided she could finally take some time to work on Stefan's biography. She had completed about two thirds of the writing, but she still had to complete the chapter on Armand Becker.

She remembered his words so clearly. "My name is Werner Hoffmann. I am the monster who did those heinous things. And I have tried for twenty-five years to atone for my sin."

How do you recognize evil? What does it look like? Certainly not like the vibrant, attractive man with the bright blue eyes and the white thatch of hair that she had known as "Armand Becker."

Certainly not the patron of the arts, the respected psychiatrist, the music-loving, courteous gentleman who had offered her the hospitality of his gracious comfortable home. Evil would be ugly, wouldn't it? Recognizable as something twisted and grotesque?

Or not.

Perhaps, she thought, *that was the secret of evil—-that it could appear so normal, so wholesome, so admirable.*

She couldn't help thinking of the Rolling Stones song that had recently become so popular:

Please allow me to introduce myself
I'm a man of wealth and taste ...

Was Evil rooted in Good? Some kind of mirror reflection? Was it "contagious?" Could you "catch it" from others the way fear could ignite a stampede? Had Stefan been "infected" because of the time he spent with Armand?

The more she wrestled with these problems, the more confusing they became. And the problems became even more monumental because of the example she had inadvertently chosen: the role of the Nazis in the history of the modern world.

The systematic extermination of the European Jews by the Nazi regime had become the one unequivocal example of Radical Evil, something that *had* to be prevented from ever happening again. *The* unique, unrivalled example of pure Evil, whose very name had become synonymous with "Nazi," an absolute form of Iniquity.

"I can't do it," she told Tommy that evening as they sat together in the living room after dinner. Cory had gone upstairs to do his homework. Consuelo had finished cleaning up, and the April night was just cool enough to enjoy a fire. However, the hiss and crackle of the embers did nothing to soothe her. She felt beaten, overwhelmed. They had been discussing Kate's indecision about what to do with Armand's revelations, his false identity and all that implied in terms of relationships.

Tommy watched her as she toyed with her wine glass, his expression unreadable while she fidgeted. "I should never have tried to write this book," she exclaimed angrily. "It's way outside my comfort zone."

"I didn't think you figured it would be a comfortable book to write."

She shot him an exasperated glance. "You know that's not what I meant."

"So what *did* you mean?"

"Aagh." She set the wine glass aside and stared at the fire. "I feel like the proverbial Connecticut Yankee in King Arthur's court. I'm an *American*, for god's sake. A naïf. How am I supposed to comprehend European decadence or Nazis or Old Evil? I've never experienced any of that. Nothing that bad ever happened *here*—at least not on purpose!"

"Really?"

His tone surprised her and she looked at him. His face was calm, unreadable as ever, but there was something about his voice.

"What do you mean?" she asked.

"What about the Native American genocide—European invaders looting and raping and infecting millions of innocent people with their insidious diseases?"

She stared at him wordlessly.

"What about the slaves?" he continued in the same blunt, emotionless voice. "The brutal oppression of black people, the tyranny of their masters, the KKK's reign of terror?"

"I hadn't—"

He gave her a hard look that seemed to break through the opaque mask. "What about *me*, Kate? What about Tule Lake and Manzanar? Don't tell *me* that America doesn't have its share of Radical Evil!"

"But you can't compare the—"

"I'm not saying incarceration is equal to extermination. We weren't summarily executed or stuffed into ovens. We were only stigmatized, beaten up, had our property confiscated, our families divided, our rights taken away." He took a deep breath. "No, it wasn't the same. But it *was* Evil. And it came from the same place."

"What place?"

"Fear."

"Of what?"

He shrugged. "Mortality. Non-being. Death." His voice was calm once more, his gaze level. "If you can find someone to blame for your own terror, then you can feel that you have authority over the real enemy—non-existence. If you can identify a scapegoat, you can take out your fear on it, and hope that you escape its fate."

For another moment, they sat looking at each other. Then Kate nodded. "You're right. Evil *is* here. All around us. All the time. We don't see it even when it's right in front of us because we don't want to. It's too scary. I just didn't want to. . . to believe that I had seen it."

He got up and came to sit next to her on the sofa. "We're all saints and sinners," he said. "Depending on the circumstances, we're all capable of doing something horrible or something heroic. Even a good person is capable of becoming a monster. Remember Camus's *L'Entranger*? Sometimes. . ." his voice broke a little, ". . . sometimes we're doing something horrible even when we *think* we're doing something good."

She knew he was remembering Emiko, but she didn't say so. After a minute she said, "I guess that's what I'm afraid of."

"What?"

"That by trying to tell Stefan's story truthfully, I'll end up hurting people."

"Telling the truth isn't easy," Tommy said. "Takes a lot of courage."

This time, she knew that he meant Carl and Marian and the untold truth that had eventually surfaced and wreaked havoc on their lives.

"I think," Kate said carefully, "that maybe there *is* a way to tell the story."

He glanced at her. "Really?"

"I think that besides being a story of incarnate evil, this is also a story about remorse and atonement."

"Ah," he said. "Is it possible to forgive the sinner?"

"And," she added, "is it possible for the sinner to forgive himself?"

A piece of wood cracked softly in the fireplace, sending up a burst of embers.

Yes, thought Kate, with a little smile. *I can write the story as a metaphor of crime and punishment, sin and redemption. But when the book is published, that's when the sparks will start to fly.*

CHAPTER

39

New York, New York
May 1972

"Six months is just too damned long," Carl said.

"I know, luv. We have to work something out." Alex's voice sounded hollow and thin over the phone.

"I need to see you." Carl figeted with the phone cord, wrapping it around his fingers, tugging at it—anything to relieve the frustration and irritation of feeling trapped, and not knowing how to resolve the problem.

"I know. I need to see you too," Alex said. "I need to be with you."

"I'm sorry about Christmas. I wanted so much to be there with you, but things got. . . complicated. I'd promised to do the New Years concert and—"

"It's okay. I understand."

"Classes will be over in two more weeks," he said. "And I turned down the offer to do the series at the Edinburgh Festival. So, as of May twenty-fifth I'm free. At least for the summer."

"Then come to San Francisco," Alex coaxed.

"And do what—move into the Fairmount? That would cost a fortune."

"Then move in with me."

Startled, he dropped the phone cord and sat down on the edge of the sofa. "Really?"

"Really."

"You think that would work?"

"Let's give it a try."

He looked out the window. The Chrysler Building was aglow

with lights. He could feel the city's presence—the energy, the power, the excitement. The best of everything was right there outside the window—restaurants, museums, theatre, music, a cultural smorgasbord of tempting delicacies all available at any time of the day or night.

But in the midst of plenty, he was starving. It wasn't a lack of opportunities—women had always been attracted to him. His students trailed after him, coyly or shyly indicating their admiration, their *availability*. Colleagues pursued him. Journalists attached themselves to him. The very attractive brunette who lived across the hall, a librarian at Columbia, was always "running into him" in the elevator, the laundry room, the lobby.

So, what was it that had him so thoroughly caught, pinned like an insect specimen, immobilized, enthralled? Like some irresistible force, some unconscious instinct. He HAD to be with her. HER. Alexandria Archer McPhalan. "I'll see you May 26th," he said, and hung up the phone. Did he even have a choice?

Mockingbird Ranch

"This is going to initiate a Renaissance for the entire region," Robert Ashford said, looking around at the milling crowd inside the large blue and white striped tent.

Erected in the middle of what had once been a horse pasture, the tent now overlooked the vineyards on one side and the renovated stone barn on the other. New gravel paths led through gardens of wildflowers toward the amphitheater that was still in the early stages of construction.

Robert turned to Kate and Tommy and saluted them with his wine glass. "I am thrilled to be a part of this extraordinary enterprise."

"And we are thrilled to have you and the other members of the Townsend Foundation here with us," Tommy replied.

"You're making it all possible," Kate chimed in. "You and

the other host committee members." She glanced at Jean Molnar Westmorland who was chatting with the Mayor of Auburn and a prominent Chamber of Commerce member. Verrie Becker was a few feet away engaged in conversation with a State Senator and his wife. Verrie and Jean had flown up from Santa Barbara the day before in the Westmorland corporate jet. A small entourage of friends came with them—business people, a couple of film industry moguls, art patrons eager to help launch a new venue.

"Brilliant idea to get the wineries involved," Robert said.

"Well," Tommy replied, "since we're going to be launching our own label in a few years, we wanted to make wine a part of the mix from the start. The folks in Napa have been buying grapes from this region since 1968 when Darrell Corti, an old friend of ours and a wine merchant in Sacramento, turned Bob Trinchero on to the potential of zinfandel grapes from the Mother Lode. Really got people around here thinking about getting back in the wine business. Greg Boeger just broke ground for a new winery over in Placerville."

"He bought the Lombardi-Fossati ranch," Kate added. "And he has his degrees in viticulture from UC Davis. We're all looking at this as a long-term commitment."

"As well you should," Robert agreed.

"Oh," Kate exclaimed, "look who's arrived." She hurried to the tent entrance to greet Alex and Carl. *They look so perfect together*, she thought, trying to ignore the little catch in her throat. *So perfect.* Alex was wearing a crisp white linen pantsuit with a deep blue silk blouse and her blond hair was swept up in a chignon. The lapis and gold earrings and necklace added a touch of elegant opulence. Carl, in a light grey sports coat and charcoal slacks, his pale blue shirt open at the collar, looked relaxed and happy. He gave Kate a little hug and brushed her cheek with a kiss. "How have you been?"

"Good. You?"

"Good." He smiled at Alex and took her hand, then glanced back at Kate. "Looks like a great party."

"Jean has assured me that we'll make a ton of money for the building fund," said Kate. She looked around. "She's here somewhere.

Verrie Becker too. I know they'll both want to say hi." She waved her arm toward the decorated tables that lined the sides of the tent. "Help yourself. There's plenty of great wine or lemonade if you must. And canapés from four different restaurants."

Two hours later the event began to wind down. The Sacramento Suzuki Children's Orchestra had performed. The Sierra Vista High School chorus had sung. And a string quartet from San Francisco provided an on-going medley of favorites from Bach to the Beatles.

Chris Malacchi-Salinger and her husband Len had arrived with Allison and Francisco. Jorge and Rose also put in an appearance. The silent auction was over, and Jean and Verrie were counting up the proceeds as the last of the guests drifted away carrying their auction prizes of wine and their gift baskets and tickets for tours and cruises. Two of Marian's early watercolors had brought in a nice sum. Robert Ashford and the Townsend delegation had left in their limo, and the stars were starting to appear in the evening sky.

Alex and Carl were among the last to say goodnight to Tommy and Kate who stood at the tent entrance to thank the guests for coming to support the project. Kate was intrigued when Carl shook Tommy's hand, gave him that dazzling smile and said, "Thanks for the tour. Remember, I want the first case of the '72 vintage."

"You got it," Tommy replied.

"Tour?" Kate said after Carl and Alex left.

"Yeah." Tommy looked slightly flummoxed. "He was really interested in the winery, so I showed him the cellar. Alex too. They were really excited about the idea."

"Interesting," Kate mused. "He always did appreciate good wine."

"So," Tommy said with a sly look, "our first customer?"

"Perfect," said Kate.

San Francisco, California
June 1972

"I never thought I'd be back in San Francisco," Carl said. "When I went to Cleveland in 1965, I thought it would be for keeps. Or that maybe I'd go from there to Europe—London, Berlin. I could imagine myself in those places, conducting great orchestras in grand concert halls, or maybe moving into opera like Jimmy did. Milan. Bayreuth." He paused and shook his head. "But here I am, seven years later, back in San Francisco, more or less unemployed and totally clueless about what to do next."

Alex laughed. "Come on, luv. You have all sorts of options."

"Such as?"

"Give Jerry McClosky a call. He'll line you up for a dozen guest appearances. He'd love to have you back here, you know."

"I just really feel. . . I don't know, *confused*. Do I stay here? Do I go back to New York?" He stopped and looked at her, then took both her hands in his. "What do *you* want me to do?"

They were walking through Golden Gate Park. It was a beautiful afternoon in mid-June, the kind of day that gave rise to the term "paradise climate" when talking about San Francisco. A light breeze wafted in from the Pacific, but the fog bank was well out to sea. The lawn was a deep verdant green and calla lilies bloomed in the beds that bordered the path around Stowe Lake.

Alex was uncharacteristically quiet, even solemn. She looked up at him, her expression serious, blue eyes guarded. "I can't tell you what to do, dear heart," she said. "You've got to figure it out for yourself."

"Blast!" he muttered. Still holding her hand, he started walking again, head down, frowning. "I could go back to New York in August. I haven't worn out my welcome at Julliard, and the Chamber Orchestra is still coming along. We have some good gigs lined up in the Fall—Carnegie Hall, St. Johns. Good venues."

Alex was silent.

"Please, say something."

"Something."

He stopped, pulled her close. "Don't joke. I'm desperate here."

She hugged him, nuzzled his chest. "Me too, but it's not my decision."

After a moment they continued walking. They stopped at the gate of the Japanese tea garden. "Think a cup of tea would help?" he said.

"Can't hurt."

Shaded by tall fir trees, the little patio was secluded and quiet. They sat down at a small table next to a stream. Water gurgled softly. "River music," Carl said with a little smile.

"Isn't that the piece that you and Nick are working on?"

"Yeah. We got a nice grant from the Rockefeller folks. We're hoping to premiere the work this season—maybe at the Carnegie concert. Or not." He sighed in exasperation. "You see? That's why I'm so conflicted! I can't be here and there at the same time."

"I get it."

"What are we going to do?" he said hopelessly.

"I think," she said, "that we're just going to have to play this piece one note at a time."

CHAPTER

40

New York, New York

With her close-cropped hennaed hair, huge eyes, and attenuated figure, Judith Devorah suggested a misplaced transplant from the early sixties, a black-leather-clad Twiggy, a heroin-chic Edie Sedgwick straight out of a Warhol film. She exaggerated the effect by using Kohl eyeliner and always wearing black as though she was forever in mourning. And she was, she said, in mourning—for the state of the world, for the suppression of the Goddess, the ascendancy of the Patriarchy, the marginalizing and oppression of women.

As a "graduate," as she liked to say, of the Students for a Democratic Society (Port Huron, 1962), the Civil Rights Movement (March on Washington, 1963), the Free Speech Movement (Berkeley, 1964) and the Women's Liberation Movement (Chicago, 1967), Judith had traversed an evolutionary labyrinth that had begun with the well-intentioned liberal idealism of her New Jersey upbringing. This journey was severely impacted by her parent's divorce and her mother's subsequent suicide. Then it morphed into a more political focus within the context of the Civil Rights and the Free Speech Movements, and culminated with her brief (six weeks) but significant stay at the Gay Liberation House in Washington D.C. in late 1971, where she embraced the concept of lesbian separatism: "Sexism is the root of all other oppressions, and Lesbian and women's oppression will not end by smashing capitalism, racism, and imperialism. Lesbianism is not a matter of sexual preference, but rather one of political choice which every woman must make if she is to become woman-identified and thereby end male supremacy."

Marian met Judith at the opening of the Alma Thomas exhibition at the Whitney Museum in April 1972. They were both standing in front of a large, brightly-colored canvas depicting a circular mandala-like form, wine glasses in hand, and Marian said, "Looks like a mosaic, doesn't it?"

"Make a great tabletop." Judith tilted her head and perused the painting. "Love the title."

Marian leaned forward a little and read the label: "*Lunar Rendezvous—Circle of Flowers*. Yeah, great title."

Judith glanced around the gallery. "A lot of her paintings have to do with flowers. Why do so many women paint flowers? Georgia O'Keeffe, Modersohn-Becker, Berthe Morisot."

"Victorian botanical illustrators."

"Porcelain painters." Judith held out her hand. "Hi. I'm Judith Devorah."

"Marian Archer," said Marian, giving Judith's hand a firm squeeze.

Judith's mouth opened as if frozen, then she gasped, "Oh, my God, *the* Marian Archer?"

"I guess so," Marian responded with a tight laugh.

"The artist? OhmyGod, I am *so* in awe of your work!"

"Oh, that's. . . great." Never very good at accepting compliments, Marian felt her face going red.

"Wow." Judith stared at her with dazed reverence. "I saw your last show at the Fisher Gallery. It was amazing! The colors were just so. . . so. . ." Judith waved her hands in the air. "Just so *amazing!*"

"Um, thank you," Marian said and took a gulp of wine.

"A friend of mine told me that you lived in Mexico and that you knew Frida Kahlo," Judith hurried on. "What was she like? Did you know Diego Rivera too?"

"Good heavens!" Marian exclaimed. "Where did your friend hear that? I never even *met* Frida Kahlo. She'd been dead for years before I ever went to Mexico. I was living in California until 1959 when I cut bait and moved back to Boston. Yes, I've been to Mexico and I *love* Kahlo's paintings, but I certainly never met her."

Judith rolled her eyes. "Sorry. My bad. I've just heard all these fantastic stories about you. About how you left your husband and struck out on your own and managed to claw your way into the art world and get a major gallery. It's just so. . . *inspiring!*" She was still gazing at Marian with the look of a star-struck fan. "You're a. . . a legend!"

"Good grief," Marian muttered, half amused, half irritated. "I'm an artist. I make art. What's the big deal?"

"You're a *woman* artist," Judith replied. "A *successful* woman artist. *That's* a big deal."

Marian studied the younger woman with wary interest, wondering who she was, why she was dressed like that, and whether it was worthwhile to continue the conversation.

"Come have a drink with me?" Judith said. "I have about three million questions to ask you!"

Marian hesitated for a moment, then said, "Okay." As she followed Judith out of the gallery she was thinking, *now what have I gotten myself into?*

They went around the corner on East Seventy-sixth to the Carlyle Café. Bobby Short was holding forth at the piano with a Cole Porter song, and the Marcel Vertes murals on the wall gave the place a sort of shadowy, dreamy feel, a Bacchanalian fantasy: Picasso meets Chagall in Boticelli's *Primavera*.

They each ordered a glass of wine. Marian hadn't realized that she was hungry, but the mellow surroundings and the tempting menu caught her attention. She ordered lobster bisque and a salad.

"I'll have what she's having," Judith said.

They talked for an hour after they finished dinner. Judith wanted to hear about how Marian had decided to leave her home and family, move three thousand miles, and get a job to support herself. She wanted to hear about how Marian would paint after work, how she landed a contract with a prestigious New York gallery, had three solo exhibitions in six years as well as a batch of commissions. "How the hell did you do it?" Judith asked.

"Hard choices," Marian said. "Selfishness." She looked away, watched the pianist sway to his own rendition of *Smoke Gets in Your Eyes*. She looked back at Judith's rapt face. "Putting myself first."

Judith nodded. "Necessary."

"Yeah, well. I ended up with one child dead and another in therapy. I wasn't. . . much of a mother."

"You had other things to do with your life."

"Doesn't mean I don't have some regrets, some residual guilt. There's a price to be paid."

"Every battle demands sacrifice, and we're fighting a guerilla action against an entrenched establishment. Your story is an inspiration to your sisters. But we've got to do more than just succeed in a 'man's world.' The whole structure has to be changed."

Marian frowned. "That's a big order."

"Yes. But every day women are letting go of their illusions about marriage and careers and how to live their lives, what it will take to change the system. It's not enough just to integrate women into male-defined roles. We've got to take the next step. Men aren't going to liberate women. We have to take responsibility for ourselves."

"I get it," Marian said, "but I just have trouble envisioning how it would work. In a practical way, I mean." She gave a brittle laugh. "I think we'd need a different planet. Or at least a different continent."

"We can't go on acting like we don't know what's going on," Judith said. "Our culture is dominated by the values of white males. Everybody else is relegated to an underclass, no matter how smart or talented or ambitious they are. Women are taught from childhood to be subservient, passive, weak. Otherwise we're not 'feminine.' God forbid we should be strong and aggressive and competent."

Marian sat back and rested her palms on the table. "Well," she said, "we may not have all the answers, but at least we're asking the right questions." She got to her feet. "It's been a great evening, but I've got to get going."

Judith jumped up. "I'll walk out with you."

As Marian glanced around for a cab, Judith took a card from her pocket and pressed it into Marian's hand. "Give me a call," she said.

"I'd really like to see you again." With a grin and a wave, she stalked off down the street.

Marian looked after her, a peculiar cloud of conflicting thoughts circling in her head. *Lots of energy and enthusiasm. Kind of reminds me of Ali. Now that Ali's in Boston, I sure could use a new studio assistant. But God, she's such a zealot. Wonder how she'd get along with Nikki?*

She looked down at the card. It was black with white letters. In the middle was a palm tree enclosed by a triangle. Judith's name, address and phone number ran along the bottom. Marian stared at the card for a moment, then tucked it into her bag and raised her hand to hail a cab.

San Francisco, California

"So just like that, problem solved?" Ben gave his cousin Tommy a doubtful look.

Tommy laughed. "Well, the problem of the permits and land use has been solved, but we're just getting started on the actual construction, the programming, all those *little* details."

Ben caught the intended sarcasm. "Little details, right. So what's your timeline?"

They were sitting in Tommy's San Francisco office of Ashida and Associates on the twelfth floor of the office building on Montgomery Street. The view of the Bay and the Golden Gate were usually spectacular, but today the fog had rolled in early, and the windows framed a fuzzy white blur.

"We've got quite a line-up," Tommy replied. "The plans are finished for the music center renovations and new construction, and the bids have gone out. Now that we finally have the land-use issues cleared up, we can start construction any time. We didn't have to change the agricultural use contract since we're simply changing the focus from a pear ranch to a winery. Once we got the go-ahead from the county agencies—fire department, zoning administration, utilities connection—we went right to work. I've been lining up some help to get the operation up and running. We'll start our first serious harvest at the end of the month."

Ben sat back and shook his head. "Jeez," he said, "a winery. I never thought of the Mother Lode area as a wine-producing region."

"Goes all the way back to the early settlers," Tommy explained. "A lot of the French and Italian immigrants settled in the area during the Gold Rush. When they didn't find their big claim, they decided to go into farming. The area was perfect for vineyards—Mediterranean climate, the soil was granite rich and volcanic—similar to what they had back home—so they started growing grapes. They brought over cuttings from Italy, France, set up cellars in their basements, and they were off and running. By the late eighteen-hundreds the Mother Lode was third in wine production in the state after Sonoma and Napa."

"Who would have thought," Ben said. Then he looked puzzled. "So what happened?"

"The Volstead Act. Prohibition. After 1920, most of the wineries went out of business."

"Right," said Ben. "I'd forgotten about that."

"Most of the locals kept at least a small vineyard to make wine for their own use, but the larger tracts were replaced by pear orchards.

"Kate's great-grandfather, Cormac McPhalan, put in a vineyard at Mockingbird. He got the cuttings from his Italian neighbors, but he never really got into the wine business. Maybe because he was Irish. From the start, he concentrated on fruit orchards and cattle, but the old vineyard is still there. Twenty acres of zinfandel with some Muscat vines around the edges to keep the deer away."

Tommy was silent for a moment, then said, "So, cousin, looks like I'm finally back in the farming business!"

CHAPTER
41

Avandaro, Mexico

A llison Morales glanced around the living room of the Gonzales "weekend home" in Avandaro, Mexico, and wondered if she would ever feel truly comfortable in such regal surroundings. It wasn't just the high ceilings with their massive dark wooden beams, or the softly illuminated adobe walls that seemed to glow with a mysterious inner light. Or even the burgundy-red velvet curtains that framed a view of the patio with its tiered fountain and the formal gardens beyond.

The problem, she decided, was the whole *idea* of having so much space for a family that consisted essentially of a man and his wife. Was it really necessary for a middle-aged couple to have two huge houses, several hundred acres, four cars, at least twenty servants, a stable full of pedigreed horses, original art works, priceless antiques, and more shoes than anyone could possibly ever wear?

Granted, the excess provided a reasonable living for twenty families who might otherwise be working in factories or trying to coax crops from a few acres of reluctant soil. But *madre*, as her father Jorge would say, was such consumption really *justifiable*?

Her fiancé, Francisco Gonzales, seemed very much at home in his father's spacious hacienda. But of course Francisco had grown up in luxury even though he now worked for a not-for-profit environmental agency and supported liberal causes. Allison thought she would always feel a little intimidated—as well as morally irritated—by such a display of wealth and privilege.

But tonight, she would put away these censorious thoughts and try not to make anyone uncomfortable. She had even deigned to wear a dress—well, a skirt and blouse—since a bevy of guests were coming to dinner, ostensibly to enjoy Roberto's infamous hospitality, but also to meet Francisco's American fiancée.

It was after eight when the guests began arriving. That was another thing—did everything have to begin so late? Dinner never appeared until after nine and Allison had been starving since six.

Stop grousing, she told herself sharply. She knew that her bad mood was due at least in part to feeling like she was on display in difficult surroundings. And she would have to play nice.

Francisco was suddenly beside her, holding out a glass of white wine, his warm brown eyes twinkling mischievously. "You need a drink," he said.

"No shit, Sherlock," she replied, taking the glass. She noticed the little flinch that her remark provoked. "I'll be good," she promised, and took a sip.

"*Gracias, corazón,*" he returned, giving her a conspiratorial smile. "Come," he said, holding out his hand, "let me show you off."

I'm not one of your horses, she thought to herself, and then felt guilty. He couldn't help it if he was rich.

They made the rounds of introductions to elegantly dressed people she didn't know and likely wouldn't meet again, and she smiled until her jaws ached. She was relieved when she saw Marian's friends from Valle de Bravo, Colt and Faye, come sweeping into the room—Colt wearing an incongruous disco outfit with his ever-present sunglasses, and Faye decked out in flamboyant black velvet pants and a low-cut red and gold blouse that emphasized her ample cleavage.

"*Hola,* Ali!" Faye cried, waving from across the room "Welcome back!"

Ali gave Faye a double kiss and Colt lifted her off the floor in a giant bear hug. "You guys look great," Ali said breathlessly as Colt deposited her back on the ground.

"Likewise, sweetie," Faye returned. "Francisco must be hittin' all the right buttons."

Ali blushed at that comment, but she laughed and replied, "Right on."

"How are Marian and Nikki?" Colt asked.

"We haven't seen them for a while," Faye added.

"They're doing great and working hard," Ali said. "Lots of projects keeping them busy, but they said they might get to Valle later this summer for a visit."

"Great!" Faye said, beaming. "We'll have the beer and the ganja ready!"

Jeez, the older generation, Ali thought.

The party went on until after midnight. Even though Ali and Francisco officially had separate suites, when they said good night to the guests and told Roberto and Tatiana they'd see them at breakfast, they went to Francisco's room and collapsed onto the bed.

"I *hate* parties," Allison declared, then glanced at Francisco hoping she hadn't offended him.

But he grinned ruefully and said, "I don't care much for them either, *corazón*, but my parents were keen on making the big announcement that their wayward son is finally ready to settle down."

She propped herself up on her elbows. "Is that what we're doing?" she asked, giving him a hard look. "Settling down?"

He returned her look. "No," he said, "we're just getting started at causing trouble."

She flopped back on the pillow. "Good." After a minute she said, "Must be kind of hard being part of a big, rich, powerful family. I expect they have lots of expectations for you."

Francisco, who had taken off his coat and tie and unbuttoned his white shirt, sat down next to her. "Sometimes it's like trying to swim through a wave," he said. "But I've had twenty-six years of practice. I'm getting pretty good at it."

She looked up at him. "I don't really know much about your family," she said.

He grabbed a pillow and lay down beside her. "What would you like to know?"

"Where'd the money come from?"

"Ah," he said, "good question." He hesitated for a moment, then continued, "Let's start at the beginning."

He told her about the origins of his family name, Gonzales, that was first found in Castile with connections to the Visagoths who had conquered the region in the fifth century. Variants of the name "Gonzales" later showed up in records in Spain, and were recorded in Mexico by the end of the sixteenth century.

"Alternately," he said, "some believe that the name is of Jewish origin, starting with the Jews who were banished from Palestine by the Romans and took refuge in Spain. Many of them converted to Catholicism when faced with deportation from Spain during the reign of Ferdinand and Isabella in the late fifteenth century. Perhaps," he said, glancing at her, "that's how we ended up in Mexico."

Allison smirked. "Where you lived happily ever after and got rich?"

"Oh," he said with a laugh. "That's right. You asked about my family's finances. Well, I think there were many things that contributed to our good fortune. Land grants, cattle, silver mines, political connections, banking. You name it and I expect my ancestors tried it. Because their interests were so diversified, they also managed to get through the Mexican Revolution without losing everything, though I understand that they did resort to some interesting. . . *maneuvers* to stay afloat."

Allison laughed and he turned to her and took her hand in his. "Is that enough history for tonight, *corazón*?"

"So basically," she said, "your dad is a liquor distributor with a bunch of inherited money that came from God knows where?"

"That is correct."

She nestled down next to him and he put his arm around her. "So maybe you're not too royal for a little peasant like me after all," she said.

"But what if you are not a peasant?"

She twisted around to look at him. "Meaning?"

"What do you know about the *Morales* family, hmmm?"

She turned away and shut her eyes. "Good night, sweet prince," she told him.

"Not so fast, *mia encanta*," he murmured against her hair. She smiled as his hand gently made its way down her back and circled forward to cup her breast. She turned toward him and kissed him deeply and let the conversation fade from her mind.

But later, lying beside him, her body still tingling from their encounter, she thought: *What do I know about my family?* She decided to find out.

Coyoacan-Mexico City, Mexico

"Civil registration records in Mexico are government-required records of births (*nacimientos*), deaths (*defunciones*) and marriages (*matrimonios*). Known as *Registro Civil*, these civil records are an excellent source of names, dates and vital events for a large percentage of the population living in Mexico since 1859," Ali read.

Ali and Francisco were in the library of the National Autonomous University in Coyoacan, just south of Mexico City. The day after the party at his parent's house in Avandaro, they had driven into DF to see some friends and do some research on the history of the Morales family. "I'm not even sure where to start," Ali said. "Look at all these records. It would take a year to go through them!"

"Let's start with what we know," Francisco suggested. "Your papa came to California from Arizona, yes? But he was born in Mexico. He was a farm worker until he met your mother, and after that he also worked in the oil fields and was in the army in World War Two."

"The Marines," Ali corrected.

"Right. So, anything else that you know? Who were his parents?"

Ali hesitated. "I don't know. I never met them."

"I don't think we have enough to work with," said Francisco. "But here's an idea. Why don't we go back to the house and you can call your papa. Maybe he can tell you some things that will help us."

The next day, they returned to the library with the notes that Allison had taken during a lengthy telephone call to Jorge. She and Francisco spread the notes out on the table and began to create a timeline that moved from the present to the past where they hoped to find the answers to their questions.

"All right," Ali said, "it was my *grandmother* whose name was Morales, not my grandfather." She scanned the notebook pages. "So, here's the story. Papa's mother was an educated woman from a good family. At fifteen she married a wealthy and prominent older man whose name was Ramon Ramirez. She had a lovely home, servants, etc. but no children.

"After ten years her husband died and she married her gardener, a full-blood Mayan Indian named Ikal. She was, of course, ostracized and ended up losing her home and her inheritance. She and her husband, Ikal, had five children. Papa—Jorge—was the youngest. When he was five, his father died and his mother went to work as a domestic servant." Ali scanned her notes. "Papa said that his mother used to take him past a big beautiful house and she would tell him, 'This is where I used to live. Someday, you will live in a house like that.'"

Francisco nodded, smiling sadly.

Ali continued reading. "He said that his mother couldn't support the children on her income. Then she got ill and died, and the family was split up between several relatives. Jorge was sent to live with a cousin in Juarez, near the Texas border. He ran away when he was thirteen and got across the border. For the next ten years, he worked in the fields, migrating from Texas to California and back."

She paused for a moment, then continued. "Here's what he told me about that time. 'Every payday, I would go to a used bookstore and buy a paperback book—before I bought food or clothes or anything else. Everyone laughed at me and called me *loco*, but my mother always told me that learning was more important then anything else, so I bought books while everyone else bought beer.'"

Alison grinned and Francisco smiled back. "Then he met Rose, my mother. Oh, he also said 'Rosita showed me the way out of my little life. She inspired me, and helped me to be brave.'" She stopped for a moment and looked at Francisco.

"Did he say any more about his father?" Francisco asked.

Ali scanned the notes. "Just that Jorge's original name was Jorge Ikal y Morales, but he was listed as 'Jorge Morales' on his visa card, so that's what he took as his official name. Oh, and also he remembered that his father was very tall with beautiful dark eyes and a wonderful smile. Listen to what he told me. 'He was so strong, but very gentle. He used to pick me up and lift me into the air and I would yell and then we would laugh. And he played the flute. I used to sit in the doorway and listen to him play. It was so beautiful.'" She looked at Francisco again. "God, I wonder if my brother Carl knows that Jorge's father was a musician?"

"Then *both* grandfathers were musicians, yes?" Francisco said.

"Looks that way. Wow. That's a surprise."

They read through the rest of the notes and then started trying to follow a path backwards through time.

After three more days in the library, Allison had a stack of pages that outlined the family's history. There were gaps and dead-ends and missing names, but she had a basic structure that led her to a surprising conclusion.

"Originally, we were from *California!*" she said. "From the area east of Sacramento. The Morales family owned a ranch on the American River. Holy shit, Francisco, we were *Californios!*"

CHAPTER

42

San Francisco, California
July 1972

"Hi honey, I'm home," Alex called from the base of the stairs. "Up here," Carl's voice came back.

She hung her coat on the Victorian hall tree in the entry foyer and went up the curved staircase to the second floor living room. Carl was sprawled on the red leather contemporary sofa, book in hand. Muted sunlight streamed through the bay window, creating geometric patterns on the polished hardwood floor. The stereo was playing something that sounded to Alex like squeaks, bleats and whizzes—not exactly music.

"What," she said, "is *that*?"

He looked up. "What?"

"That. . . *sound*."

He tossed the book aside and sat up. "It's called *Turenas*. It's a new composition by John Chowning. You know," he added, noticing her puzzled expression, "the guy at Stanford that I told you about?"

"Oh, right. The frequency modulation guy."

"Yeah, he does use frequency modulation," Carl said. "And lots of other stuff. I've been spending time at the Computer Research Center at Stanford. It's fascinating. He also loaned me this book on electronic music by a guy named Allen Strange."

Alex listened for a minute to the recording. "Yeah, it's strange all right. Sounds like little robot insects buzzing around a light bulb."

"Don't be too hasty," Carl admonished. "Sit down here with me and listen."

She sat down next to him and he looped an arm around her shoulder. After a minute she said, "A percussionist on LSD?"

"Shhh."

"A cat chasing mice on an organ keyboard?"

"Hey!"

"All right." She crossed her arms and listened to the sounds. What seemed to be deep organ chords alternated with high bleeps that scampered from one place to another or popped out at the listener. "How does he do that?" she asked.

"He's using a Doppler shift, a change in frequency that happens when a sound source is moving toward you or away from you. Like when a train goes by and the whistle's sound changes. The sound increases in frequency as it comes toward you and decreases as it moves away."

"Hmmm." After a minute she said, "Oh, oh. Here come those robotsects again."

"Alex!"

"I do like the way the sounds sort of drift around, like they're changing position in space. Sort of like that three-D movie where objects seem to spring out at you. What was it called? Fort Ticonderoga? I remember cannons shooting into the audience."

"Okay, that's more accurate. He *is* using space in the composition. The computer program that Chowning wrote incorporated distance, angle and velocity so the composer can use them gesturally. You can specify geometric sound paths in a two or three dimensional space."

Alex sighed and rested her head on Carl's shoulder. "God, I loved the nineteenth century."

Carl chuckled. "Yeah, but we live in the twentieth."

"You're a braver man than I am, Charlie Brown."

The sounds ended, fading away like a drifting bit of mist. Alex sat up and looked at him expectantly. "So, what should we do for dinner?"

"What?" he responded with mock surprise. "Here we are having this advanced musical discussion and all you can think about is your stomach?"

"I'm hungry."

"Hedonist."

"You bet," she cried, pelting him with a sofa pillow.

"Watch it, missy. I'll spank you."

"Promise?"

They decided to go to a little Mom-and-Pop Thai restaurant for dinner, a few blocks from Alex's apartment. The décor was travel posters and plastic flowers, but the food was exceptional—satays with luxurious peanut sauce, steamed dumplings, roasted duck with crackling brown skin, rich curries with layers of delicious flavors—and they could bring their own wine. For dessert they had the owner's homemade mango ice cream served with delicate almond cookies.

Over dinner, Carl told Alex about his meeting at Stanford and the plans for a summer institute at Mockingbird that would attract students who wanted to live and work with musicians and composers who were on the cutting edge of contemporary electronic music.

"We'll be able to offer a series of workshops with people from the Stanford faculty," Carl said. "Now that polyphonic synthesizers are small enough to be practical, we won't have to come up with a fortune to outfit the studios. And," he paused to spear another dumpling, "I want to bring in some experts in Ethnomusicology, do some seminars on ethnic music."

Alex had seen him like this before—glowing with plans, ideas spinning out like golden threads. He reminded her of Marian—great bursts of creative energy, a sort of dynamic explosion. When artists got inspired, they believed they could do *anything*. Sometimes they succeeded. Right now, she'd be happy to settle for doing *something*.

But between the surgery and the talk therapy, Alex believed she *was* making progress. She could now play relatively complex pieces without her left hand freezing up. She was beginning to think that Dr. Diaz might have a point in asking if Alex was trying to punish herself, to deal with her guilt and anxiety by taking away the very thing she loved most—her music.

But now she loved something else, *someone* else, with that same degree of passion. Would her desire to please Carl overcome her desire to punish herself? October wasn't far away. She needed to answer the question.

CHAPTER

43

Mockingbird Ranch

"What a setting!" Nick exclaimed.

Marian had parked the rented Pontiac sedan at the end of the long drive that led from the county road to Mockingbird Ranch. The pastures had long since faded from green to washed-out beige, but bright orange poppies and blue lupine were scattered among the tattered wild oats. The pear groves were a dark contrast to the fields, their branches bending under the ripening fruit. Beyond the green and golden hillsides, the rugged granite peaks of the Sierras were only lightly capped with snow.

"It *is* beautiful," Marian agreed, "but I couldn't deal with the isolation."

"How long did you live here?" Nick asked.

"Not quite twenty years." She thought back for a moment on two decades worth of memories—some wonderful, some agonizing. Her life with Owen, her children, the daily cycle of work—cooking, cleaning, canning, the endless chores.

But there were good times as well—family gatherings, holidays, the little blessings of first words, first steps, first teeth. Her beautiful babies. She swallowed hard and snapped the book of remembrance shut. Smiled at Nick. "So, here we are." She headed up the drive.

They were met at the courtyard gate by Cory and a prancing half-grown husky. Boy and dog rushed to the car, Cory waving his arms and the pup romping in circles and whining with delight. "Grandmary, Grandmary!" Cory shouted.

Marian got out and scooped Cory up in her arms. She gave him a big kiss and said, "Wow! You're getting heavy, young man."

"I'm seven," he announced importantly.

"Well then, of course you're heavy."

"Hi, Uncle Nikki," Cory called, waving at Nick across the top of the car.

At that moment, Kate emerged from the house and came toward them, beaming, arms wide. "Hi, you guys. Welcome to Mockingbird." She gave Marian and Nick a hug. "Come on in."

They trooped into the house with Buck bringing up the rear. The living room was dark and cool. Even without air conditioning, the thick adobe walls and the tile roof kept out the fierce summer heat and made the interior a pleasant refuge.

"Where's Tommy?" Marian asked.

"He's been in the City for the past week taking care of some business," Kate said. "But he should be home by dinnertime."

Jaime arrived to help bring in the luggage and soon everyone was settled in the living room. Consuelo brought in a tray of glasses and a pitcher of lemonade. Cory and Buck went back outside to play.

Kate, breathless with excitement, told Marian and Nick about the plans for the winery and the other recent developments that had put the music center on track for a summer 1973 debut.

"It's going to be spectacular," she said. "Carl and Alex are working on the program for the summer concert series. Carl has been working with some of the musicians and composers at Stanford who are using computers, synthesizers, all that ultra contemporary techno-stuff that he loves. He's decided to set up a summer institute for contemporary music here at Mockingbird."

"He told me that was in the works," Nick exclaimed. "Can't wait to hear more."

Kate bubbled with excitement. "Also, the renovations have already started on the barn and the amphitheater. And, we have the equipment to start the winery—I'll show you the operation. Everything's really moving along!"

"So," Nick said, "how can we help?"

"Well, like I said on the phone, Tommy's thinking about an art gallery. He and one of his associates got the idea of incorporating a gallery into the visitor's center. Tommy's collection could be on view, and we could also do some changing exhibitions." She turned to Marian. "But we'd like to get your take on how to structure that part of the business. Tommy's gotten information on the structural and climate control needs. That sort of thing. But we'd like to know what kind of exhibitions we should organize. What kind of art should we display."

"Oh," Marian said, "I'd love to help set that up for you!" She glanced at Nick. "What do you think?"

"Sounds great," Nick said, nodding.

"Also," Kate said. She hesitated for a moment. "Well, I'd really love for you to do some kind of art event or exhibit or something for the opening celebration. I know you're busy," she added quickly, "so if you can't, that's okay. But it would be wonderful if you could." She smiled hopefully.

Marian and Nick exchanged a glance, then Marian said, "Let me give that some thought. I'd love to do something different. Maybe something site-specific that would really fit the occasion."

Nick nodded. "Maybe an installation?"

"That sounds great!" Kate exclaimed.

Then the phone rang and Kate got up to answer it. After a few minutes she came back and announced, "That was Tommy. He's had a change of plans and won't be coming home until tomorrow, so we'll have to get along without him for dinner."

"Nothing serious, I hope," said Marian.

"Nope. Said he's meeting an old friend for dinner. Spur of the moment thing." Kate looked at them expectantly. "Want to see how the barn's coming along? It's going to be a wonderful recital hall!"

San Francisco, California

"Thank you, Ashida-san, for meeting me on such short notice." Namura Kyoshi got to his feet and bowed formally.

Tommy returned the bow, then shook Kyoshi's outstretched hand. "My pleasure to see you again, Namura-san." He met the older man's eyes with polite deference.

"Please, sit down," Kyoshi gestured to the chair across from his. They were in the dining room of the Fairmount Hotel, a beautifully decorated space with marble Ionic columns, domed ceiling, white linen, vases of flowers, gilded mirrors. Tommy had been there many times and he suspected that his former father-in-law was also familiar with the surroundings. Tommy studied Kyoshi silently, waiting for him to speak. Kyoshi, he thought, looked tired. He was thinner than Tommy remembered, and the perpetual golf-player tan had faded.

The phone call from Kyoshi had been quite unexpected. Tommy hadn't seen anyone from his former wife's family for several years. In fact, they'd gotten together just once since Emiko's funeral, and that was a rather quick, awkward pilgrimage to view the little shrine where Emiko's ashes were buried. The trauma of her suicide, the aftermath of despair and confusion, had made communication difficult. He hadn't really expected to see Kyoshi again.

But then this afternoon the old man had called Tommy's office and asked if they could meet for dinner before he left for Tokyo. He'd been in San Francisco for a week on business, he explained, and was getting ready to go back to Japan, but he had something he wanted to discuss. Intrigued, but slightly wary, Tommy agreed.

Now, Tommy sat trying very hard not to fidget while Kyoshi stared moodily into space, seemingly intent on gathering his thoughts. It was impolite to interrupt the older man's reverie, so Tommy waited with what he hoped looked like dignified patience.

Finally, Kyoshi turned to Tommy and cleared his throat. "I saw an article in the San Francisco paper this morning. About the music center that you are building at the Mockingbird ranch."

"Yes," Tommy said, a bit too quickly. "I saw it too."

"Sounds like a very grand project."

"Yes. Quite a project." *Where was this going? Why would Kyoshi be interested in the music center?* He waited impatiently for Kyoshi to continue.

"There was mention in the article about a possible art gallery. Is that in your plan?"

Tommy nodded. "We're hoping to have a gallery at the visitor's center. Right now, we're trying to estimate what the extra cost would be and what staff we'd need. We have enough funding to do the renovations and build the winery and the new amphitheater, but we don't want to go over budget. So we're trying to be realistic."

Kyoshi nodded. After another long silence, during which Tommy managed to stay calm, he said abruptly, "I am not well. I am in the process of making arrangements to place my art collection in various museums. My son, Juri, is not interested in having to deal with the collection. He's only interested in the painting's monetary worth, and has no place to display them anyway. My wife is planning to move to Paris to be near Juri after I'm. . . gone. I've arranged for a major portion of the collection to go to the contemporary museum in Tokyo, but I have a small collection of Impressionist works that were Emiko's favorites that I would like to keep together in one place. About fifteen small paintings—a couple of Seurats, a Monet poppy field, three Degas depicting musicians." Kyoshi paused and pursed his lips. "My question to you, Ashida-san, is this: would you be interested in providing a home for these paintings?"

Tommy's mouth opened and closed like a fish gasping for air. "Me? You mean at Mockingbird?" he stammered.

"Here is what I'm proposing," Kyoshi continued. "I will provide funding for a small gallery space to house the collection. The gallery would be in Emiko's name as a memorial to her. Even though her time in America was not what we hoped it would be, it was her decision to come to California and it was here that she died. I would like to think that visitors to the gallery might be reminded of her, and of her love for these Western style paintings."

Tommy was still trying to recover his bearings, but he said, as evenly as he could, "Your proposal is extremely generous, sir. I'm honored that you thought of this extraordinary gesture. I, uh, beyond that I think I. . . uh." He was trying to process the significance of the proposal. *What would be the consequences? Insurance? Security?*

What would Kate think about having Emiko's name on a gallery at Mockingbird? "I'm overwhelmed," he said simply.

Kyoshi offered a little smile. "I understand this is a surprise. So please, take your time and consider how this would fit into your plans. I wish to honor Emiko's memory with something more than a shrine in a Tokyo suburb, and this is the best plan I have devised. Otherwise, I could follow my son's advice and donate the paintings to a museum in Paris, but I wanted something... special. Something as unique as Emiko herself."

The waiter had been hovering at a distance, waiting for a break in what seemed to be an intense discussion. Now, Kyoshi nodded in his direction and the man was instantly at the table to take their orders.

Tommy relaxed enough to enjoy his dinner of Chicken Kiev served with vegetables and a crisp salad. He responded to Kyoshi's questions about the winery and the rest of the Mockingbird project.

The waiter brought the check and Kyoshi insisted on paying. "This meeting was my idea, after all," he said.

While they finished their coffee, they returned briefly to the proposed gallery. Tommy expressed concern for Kyoshi's health. "A kidney problem," Kyoshi said rather indifferently. "It will get worse, but slowly I'm told." He smiled woodenly. "Better to have time to make necessary arrangements than to just drop dead with everything undecided."

Tommy, not sure of what to say, simply nodded.

"And so," Kyoshi stood, holding out his hand, "Thank you again for meeting with me. Please let me know your decision." A fleeting little smile and a bow. "Just don't wait too long."

CHAPTER

44

Mockingbird Ranch
September 1972

In early September Tommy assembled a crew of helpers to get the first wine harvest underway. Jaime enlisted reliable workers to help. Chris Malacchi's older brother, Tony, who had been making wine from the grapes on his family's ranch for years, was an eager consultant. They also enlisted the help of Tony's uncle, Leo Malacchi, who had been a wine chemist with a prominent winery before taking a job in the Viticulture and Enolgy department at U.C. Davis, one of the oldest and most respected winemaking institutions in the country.

Tony and Leo helped Kate and Tommy assemble the required equipment—a rushing machine, stainless steel vats for the preliminary fermentation, test kits for acid, pH, SO2, a refractometer for measuring the Brix or sweetness of the fruit, supplies of sugars, Montrachet yeast, wine tannin, thermometers, hydrometers, siphon tubing, corks, bottles, corking machine. The list seemed endless. Tony also helped locate the oak casks that would be used to age the wine for at least two years prior to the first launch of Mockingbird Valley Old Vine Zinfandel.

Tommy and Tony spent hours in the vineyard testing the Brix, or sugar content, of the grapes before starting the harvest. The balance of sugar, acid and pH had to be just right or the resulting wine would be less than optimal.

When the harvest began, everyone was called in to assist, including Cory. Buck, the Husky pup, followed the proceedings with interest, flapping his tail, woofing quietly and chasing the occasional rabbit with territorial ferocity. Even Alex showed up to "help out." The grapes had to be harvested quickly so that they didn't over-ripen.

The weather was perfect—balmy and bright with daytime temperatures in the high eighties and nights in the mid fifties, with no chance of rain to spoil the crop.

For Tommy, the experience was filled with sweetness, present and past. Memories of the years he had spent caring for the pear orchards at the ranch—cultivating, pruning, harvesting—flooded back. The magpies and quail chattering, the monkey flowers and star thistle, blackberry tangles, and the scent of dry leaves and dust. It all came rushing back as he walked through the vineyard—the sun burning down, a full moon floating above the western mountains like a silver mirror reflecting the ghost of the sun, cloud shadows climbing the hills, fresh deer tracks in the damp sand beneath the willows.

The land had been there through all those days of searching and discovery, of loneliness and anguish, and the darkness of despair. This place, this bit of land, had been there, unchanging—the sun, the earth, the mountains, the orchards, the river singing softly in the distance. Everything that had happened since he had left Mockingbird that summer day over a decade ago seemed to have been squeezed into a tight little knot, a compressed file that had been put away. It was *here,* in these fields and orchards and woods, that he felt *real.* Everything else was an illusion, a fantasy. It seemed as though he had awakened from a bad dream that was already dissolving into shadows.

But the still livid scar on his chest, the flicker of residual pain, the way that darkness could suddenly engulf him—these things reminded him that the dream was in fact real.

"I have a question," Tommy said.

"I might have an answer," Kate replied, giving him a sassy grin.

"No, seriously."

She put down her glass of iced tea and looked at him expectantly.

They sat on the courtyard patio, taking a break from the hectic work schedule. It was nearly lunchtime and the air was brittle with midday heat. The oak and fig branches above provided a welcome canopy from the blistering summer sun.

"Okay, here's the deal." How was he going to broach the subject of an art gallery dedicated to his former wife, and a collection of fabulously expensive paintings from his former father-in-law's estate? What reaction would she have? His mouth went dry with anxiety. He took a deep breath and met her questioning gaze. "Um, you know how we talked about having an art gallery as part of the visitor's center?"

Kate nodded.

"Well, uh, while I was in San Francisco last month I got a call from Kyoshi Namura. You know, Emiko's father? We had dinner."

"Oh, so that's who you were meeting for dinner. Why didn't you tell me?"

"I. . . uh."

She cocked her head. "Go on."

"Yeah, well, he, uh, made me an offer. It's kind of a. . . big deal." When she didn't answer, just sat looking at him, he almost panicked. He should have just told Kyoshi no. How could he have been so dumb?

Finally, Kate prompted, "What? Like a job offer or something?"

"No. No, nothing like that. Not a job."

"Then what? Come on Ashida, spill it." Her voice had that light, teasing quality that she always seemed to use when he got up-tight.

"He wants to fund the Mockingbird art gallery for us," Tommy blurted. "He's offered to donate a very valuable collection of French paintings—Impressionist works. Seurats, Monets, the real thing. They'd be part of a permanent collection here at Mockingbird."

Kate gaped at him. "You're kidding."

"Nope."

"My God, Tommy, that's incredible!"

"But there's a catch," he added quickly.

She waited, staring at him.

"He wants to have, uh, Emiko's name on the gallery. He, uh, wants it to be a sort of memorial to her."

He waited for a reaction, but she just sat there looking at him. "So, what do you think?" he finally said, his voice tight with apprehension.

"How do you feel about that?" she asked.

"I. . . I don't know exactly," he said. He got up and went into the kitchen and poured himself another glass of tea. Then he returned to the courtyard and sat down next to her. For several minutes they were both silent. He could hear the voices of the workers from the vineyard, the fast chatter of Spanish. A mockingbird lit on a branch of the oak tree and began a complicated soliloquy.

Then Kate reached over and took his hand and looked at him. "I think it's a beautiful idea."

"Really?"

Their eyes met and she smiled. "Yeah. Really. I think we should do it."

He let out his breath. "I didn't know how you'd react."

"I understand. But it's just such a healing sort of gesture. A really meaningful way to honor her memory, you know?"

He shut his eyes for a moment. Listened to birdsong. Distant voices. A dog barked. Cicadas buzzed faintly. He glanced at Kate. She was still looking at him with a wistful, tender gaze. "I loved her so much," he said. "And I. . . I tried so hard to make it work. But she was so out of reach, so lost, and I couldn't. . ."

She nodded. They were both silent, lost in thought.

"So," he said, getting up abruptly, "back to work."

"Drink water," she called after him. "Take breaks. Don't get too tired."

He shook his head and smiled.

CHAPTER

45

San Francisco, California
September 1972

Alex and Dr. Diaz sat in the doctor's office. Alex had taken off her shoes and tucked her feet up under her like a teenager. She was feeling relaxed. Maybe even *happy*. It felt odd. But nice.

"How are you and Carl getting along?" Dr. Diaz asked.

Alex felt her face grow warm and knew she was blushing. "We, uh, we're still in a kind of a discovery stage I guess. I've known him for years, but mostly it was a hostile relationship. Or not. I don't know." She frowned and looked out the window at the sunny September afternoon. No fog today. Just a robin-egg sky and fuzzy golden light.

"Where did you meet him?"

Alex swung her gaze back to the doctor's gently intense face. So Spanish, Alex thought, with that café-au-lait skin and the dark hair drawn back into a bun. "At Tanglewood," she said in response to the question. "He was a student there. Summer 1959, I think. I was living in Boston with my great-aunt Gwen. Mom was staying in Lenox at my grand parent's old summer house. Somehow—I never did get the story quite straight—she met Carl and he was helping her build a studio. I remember that I went up for the weekend and Mom had some errands to do, so she left me with Carl for the afternoon. God. . ." she paused, smiled. "We had such a great time. I had a huge crush on him, but then of course. . ." She stopped, looked away.

"Then?" the doctor prompted.

"I found out he was having an affair with my mother."

Dr. Diaz nodded. "And how did that make you feel?"

Alex sat up. "How the hell do you think I felt? I was totally furious. I could have killed them both!"

"Why were you so mad?" said doctor Diaz.

"Because! She. . . I. . ." Alex got to her feet and roamed around the office like a trapped cat. "She shouldn't have done that. It was *perverse.* He was so much younger than she was. Hardly more than a child, and to think that she. . ." She stopped and glared at the doctor. "She was acting like a whore! And I was so jealous! Oh, God." She stopped pacing and sank down in the chair. "That doesn't make any sense."

"It's called 'dichotomous thinking,'" said Dr. Diaz. "Black and white thinking. I've noticed that you seem to see things as 'all good' or 'all bad.' Like when you tell me that if you weren't perfect, then you had failed."

"But she was supposed to be my *mother*, for God's sake. She was supposed to take care of *me*, not run off with some some *teenager*! It wasn't fair. I. . . hated it when she did improper things. I wanted her to be. . ." she stopped, closed her eyes and shook her head. "Damn! I wanted *her* to be perfect, didn't I?"

"And when you found out that she wasn't perfect?"

"Then I wanted her punished."

"Hmmm."

The room was silent for several minutes. Finally Alex said, "I was always so afraid that she'd leave. That I'd be left alone. I couldn't stand to be alone. Made me feel like I didn't exist. Then I'd have to cut myself. 'I bleed, therefore I am.'" She choked to a stop and hugged herself. "Why am I such a mess?" she said through clenched teeth.

"That's what we're here to find out," said Dr. Diaz.

After a few more minutes, during which Alex stared stonily out the window, Dr. Diaz said quietly, "Let's talk about something else. I want you to tell me if you can remember anything really bad happening to you when you were little."

Alex glanced at the doctor. "What, like getting hit by a train or falling off a bridge or something?"

"Anything that you remember that really upset you."

Alex sat up and thought for a moment. "I really hated it when people fought. Dad and Mom didn't get along very well. They were always trying not to argue in front of us, but we knew they were angry."

"You and your brother and sister?"

"Right. And Dad used to yell at my brother Julian all the time. Seemed like Pooh could never do anything right."

"Pooh?"

Alex smiled. "That's what my sister Kate called him. And he called her Roo. You know, like in *Winnie the Pooh*?"

"Ah, yes. So your father didn't get along with Julian?"

"He was always just. . . mad at him."

"What about you? Was he mad at you?"

"No. I don't think he knew what to do with me. But he and my sister Kate, they were always on the same wave-length, you know? I just wanted to play my piano and be left alone. 'I have to practice.' That was my 'get out of jail free' card."

"What else upset you? Was there anything that you were afraid to talk about perhaps? A secret of some kind?"

Alex looked at the doctor with narrowed eyes, then looked away. "I don't know. There was this one time. . . " She stopped.

"Yes?"

"Well, I was staying at a friend's house. Sally Bolten. I must have been around seven or eight. She lived in Sacramento and sometimes Mom would drop me off there after my piano lesson so Sally and I could play. Sally had a little sister, Carrie, who had Downs syndrome. She was a pathetic little thing, but sweet. For some reason she liked me. I was always rescuing her. She tended to wander away and I'd have to go find her.

"Anyway, I can't remember what happened that day, but I had some kind of panic attack and started crying and couldn't stop. When Mom came to pick me up I was still crying, but I couldn't tell anyone *why*. Mrs. Bolten, Sally's mom, kept asking me why I was crying, but I couldn't tell her. It was a secret."

"How do you know it was a secret?"

Alex shrugged. "I don't know. I just remember that there was something that I was supposed to keep secret. I wasn't supposed to tell anyone. But I don't have a clue what it was."

"Was Sally's father there?"

"Yes, I think so. I don't remember actually. He had an office down in the basement. He was a college professor, an economist I think. We weren't supposed to go down there, to the basement that is. He was always working. But Carrie used to wander down there sometimes and I'd go down to get her."

"Do you remember if you went to the basement the day you had the panic attack?"

Alex shook her head. "I don't know. I don't remember." After a minute she added, "I don't have to remember, do I? I don't want to."

"Did you ever go to Sally's house again after that?"

"I don't think so. Her father, the professor, took a job at a university in Panama, and I never saw them again." After a minute she added, "I do remember that Mom told Mrs. Malacchi, our next door neighbor, that she heard that Professor Bolten had died. He committed suicide."

"How did that make you feel?"

Alex chewed her lip and stared at the doctor. "Relieved," she said.

46

New York, New York

Marian had had a busy summer. Besides the trip to California to visit Kate, Tommy, and her grandson, Cory, she and Nick had made time for a trip to Valle de Bravo for two relaxing weeks in their lakeside villa. They had no sooner gotten back when they headed for Lenox to take in the last week of the Tanglewood Festival season. With all the traveling there was little time to work on her art, although she had done a lot of sketching and taken bunches of photos to use for landscape paintings.

But the idea of doing something radically different had been planted when Kate asked her to do "a piece" for the opening celebration of the Mockingbird Music Center. Throughout the summer she gnawed on the idea of an installation of some kind, though how this would translate into reality was still a total mystery. For some reason, however, she thought that it should have something to do with the new ideas that were sparked by her participation in the women's movement.

Marian was still perplexed by the competing ideologies and fiery rhetoric that had emerged from the second wave of feminism which began in the early sixties and gained momentum throughout the decade. While Marian firmly agreed with the basic concept that women were an oppressed group that had been economically, socially and psychologically marginalized by the patriarchal structure of society, she was not convinced by the more radical splinter groups who called for a complete annihilation of patriarchal influence. She was more inclined to agree with liberal feminists like Betty Friedan who held that radical feminism could potentially undermine the gains of the women's movement by inviting a backlash against political and economic reform.

It was, therefore, with some misgivings that she decided to hire Judith Devorah as her new studio assistant. While she admired Judith's energy, her knowledge of the art world and her skill-set, she found Judith's radical politics daunting. *But*, she reasoned, *maybe as we get to know each other and work together we can influence each other in positive ways.*

For starters, Judith and Marian shared an interest in the ideas that Linda Nochlin had presented in an *ArtNews* article titled "Why Have There Been No Great Women Artists?"

On a rainy afternoon in mid-September, Marian and Judith were taking a break from stretching and priming a half-dozen large canvases that Marian planned to use for a new series of portraits. Judith was sitting on the sofa next to the window reading a copy of *ArtNews*, while Marian sat nearby at a wooden table, drinking coffee and making notes on a small pad.

"Listen to this," Judith said.

Marian looked up. "Ummm?"

"This Nochlin article says that in order for women to fully enter the art world mainstream, organizational and institutional changes would need to take place." Judith glanced at Marian. "Do you think that's even *possible*?"

"Well, Lucy Lippard wrote a piece and said that specific tasks would have to be accomplished before women artists could gain the recognition they deserved."

"Tasks? Like what?"

Marian thought for a moment. "Okay. Lippard thinks that works by women artists from the past must be located and exhibited, a new language would have to be developed in order to effectively write about women's art, and new critical theories would have to emerge to address the content of women's art and its history."

"Hmmm. That's a big order."

"For sure. But organizations like A.I.R. Gallery and Women Artists in Revolution are already providing greater opportunities for women to exhibit their art. Did you know that in 1970 there was a twenty-three percent increase in the number of women artists included in the annual exhibition at the Whitney Museum? Now, that's progress!"

"About time," grumbled Judith, turning back to the article.

Marian smiled and sipped her coffee.

Marian and Judith were also both excited about the publication of a new periodical, *Ms. Magazine*, that had just hit the newsstands. They poured over the first issue and wrote the editor, Gloria Steinem, a note of congratulations. "A voice of our own!" Judith exclaimed.

"Sure ain't *Ladies Home Journal*," Marian agreed.

They spent many hours talking to their women friends about what kind of projects might be appropriate to the new discourse and what would be representative of the ideas that motivated the women's movement. How was art going to reflect these changes? What subjects, materials, techniques, and styles would address women's issues?

A whole body of women's creative production—quilting, weaving, embroidery—had been systematically relegated to the category of "handicrafts," not appropriate for inclusion in the body of "fine art." But what difference was there, women asked, between the geometric designs of a Mondrian canvas and those of a Shaker quilt? Why was he a *genius* while the woman who designed the quilt was a *hausfrau*?

It was Judith who introduced Marian to Anna Mendieta's work and especially the "earth-body" sculptures that would become her best-known creations. Other artists were also exploring the "non-commercial" possibilities of land art and performance art.

Something about the land/art connection tugged at Marian's consciousness. "The ranch is all about the land," she told Judith as they sat in Marian's studio one autumn afternoon drinking coffee and brain-storming ideas for the Mockingbird project.

"So, a land-art installation. What do you remember most about the land?" Judith asked.

Marian toyed with her half-empty cup. "It was red," she said slowly. "Rust red. And in the summer, it was dry. So dry it was like. . . like a moonscape."

"Blood on the moon," Judith mused. "That's got some power."

"But it sounds so, I don't know, negative. This is supposed to be a celebration."

"Doesn't mean you can't make a powerful statement, right? I mean women, blood, the moon, all connected. Menses, childbirth. Think about it."

"I will."

"Hey there," Nick said as he walked into the loft, tossing his leather jacket on the kitchen chair and striding over to give Marian a quick kiss on the cheek. "Coffee break? Hi, Judith," he added.

"Hi," she returned cooly.

"Yeah," Marian said. "We finished up the inventory for the Boston show, so we decided to take a break. Oh," she added, "Carl called. He's got some tapes for the river-music project finished and he's going to send them to you tomorrow, so we need to keep an eye out for the UPS guy."

"Great. I can get to work on the video. Did you pick up the batteries for the camera?"

"Nope. Forgot. I'll get them next time I'm out."

"Thanks, babe. I'll be upstairs if you need me." He paused at the door. "Bye, Judith."

"Bye." Judith gave Marian a disapproving look as the door closed behind Nick. "Babe? Really?"

"Come on, Judith. It's a term of endearment after all."

"It's demeaning. Like you're a little kid and he's the grown-up."

"Arrgh," Marian groaned, covering her eyes with her hands. "Get over it, will you?"

"You gotta admit it's sexist."

Marian gave her assistant a withering look. "No more politics, okay?" She got to her feet. "It's getting late. How about if I walk you home? I've got to stop and pick up some dinner."

"Yeah," Judith muttered, "you can get those batteries while you're out."

———◦◦◦∘◉∘◦◦◦———

On the walk that evening Marian noticed something that would plant a small seed of doubt in her mind, a seed that she would subsequently try to smother. Without success.

She and Judith were heading down Eighth Avenue toward Judith's apartment when Marian spotted a convenience store and decided to get the batteries for Nick's camera. While they were in the store, Judith bought a pack of cigarettes and when she opened her purse, Marian spotted something that surprised her: a pistol.

"What?" Judith said, noticing Marian's startled look. "Never seen a gun before?"

"Sure. But I'm just sort of taken-aback I guess. Do you have a license for that thing?"

Judith tossed her head. "Of course. If you live in this city, you need to be ready for anything. I have a right to defend myself."

"Still," Marian said, "isn't it kind of, I don't know, *dangerous*?"

"This is a dandy little gun," said Judith. "A Smith and Wesson 642. Durable, reliable and absolutely lethal." She grinned at Marian. "You should get one."

Marian made a face. "I hate guns."

"And I hate thugs," Judith replied.

Neither of them brought up the subject again, but Marian had to wonder if the world was really so dangerous that carrying a gun had become essential. What a dismal thought.

CHAPTER
47

San Francisco, California

With the Second Farm Worker's Union Benefit Concert only six weeks away, Alex was bouncing between anguish and exaltation. Her playing had improved steadily, but she was still suffering panic attacks when she thought about actually walking out onto that stage and proclaiming herself "cured." What if something went wrong? What if her hand froze up? What if? What if?

In her sessions with Dr. Diaz she tried to be positive, but felt like she was bluffing. She supposed the doctor could see through her act. But she went home from the appointments and dove into her practice schedule with obsessive determination.

She had been going over and over the score of the Rachmaninoff *Second Piano Concerto*, marking every passage that still challenged her capacity for technical brilliance and emotional depth. As she studied the piece, she discovered, and re-discovered, the history of the composition that now seemed especially poignant in light of her own struggles.

The 1897 premiere of Rachmaninoff's *First Symphony* had been derided by the critics of the day, and the composer fell into a paralyzing depression that lasted for several years. The *Second Piano Concerto* marked his recovery from both the depression and the psychological block that accompanied it. To overcome his illness, Rachmanioff had worked with Nikolai Dahl, a music-loving physician who was investigating psychological therapy through hypnosis. The Second Concerto was dedicated to Dr. Dahl.

The connection with her problems of depression and psychogenic dystonia inspired Alex to interpret the music in light of her own recovery. It seemed to be the perfect vehicle to herald her re-emergence as an outstanding performer.

She felt relatively confident about the first two movements—the darkly turbulent first movement with its undercurrent of tension and its climatic intensity, and the more romantic and contemplative second movement. But then came the third movement—marked *allegro scherzando*—a flurry of notes alternating between the orchestra and the piano that stayed barely inside the boundaries of do-able virtuosity right up to the explosive, triumphant ending.

What the hell, she thought, glaring at the score. If Rachmaninoff could do it, so can I.

She also noticed that her sessions with Dr. Diaz seemed more comfortable. How lovely to have someone to talk to without having to be on guard all the time. She wasn't going to shock Dr. Diaz no matter what she said, so she felt at ease. She had never felt at ease talking to anyone. She was beginning to see that issues and people were not just black and white, for you or against you. And not everyone was a liar. The world was a beautifully complex place. She'd always known that when she interpreted a piece of music. Now she could apply that interpretation to the rest of her experiences.

"His name was Ikal," Allison said. "He was a Mayan Indian, and apparently he had only one name."

"And he was my *grandfather*?" Carl stared at his sister in amazement. "You're certain of that?"

"That's what Papa said," Ali replied. "He remembered him quite well."

"Plus we did a lot of research at the library in Mexico City," Francisco added. "It's an amazing story."

Carl and Alex exchanged looks, then Carl looked back at Allison. "I'm really. . . stunned," he said slowly.

They sat around the table in the kitchen at Ali and Francisco's apartment on Russian Hill. The bay window overlooked the serpentine descent of Lombard Street, and further away the lights of the East Bay twinkled and gleamed. They had just finished dinner—a red snapper Veracruz, corn tortillas and a big green salad. Since meeting Francisco, Allison had periodically been overcome by an urgent need to do something "domestic," a side of her that no one had previously witnessed.

"You should ask Papa yourself," Allison said to Carl. "He can tell you the whole story."

"You said this Ikal played the flute?" Alex said.

"Not just played the flute, but also *made* them," Francisco said. "Jorge told us that he remembers listening to his father play. He said the melodies were wonderful."

"And the Morales family used to have a ranch on the American River?" Carl was still wide-eyed with wonder.

"Rancho Las Posas. Not far from Folsom. You remember Folsom, don't you Carl?" said Ali.

Carl nodded. "Sure. It's just down the river from Mockingbird." He sat back and stared out the window. "I'll be damned," he said softly.

New York, New York
October 1972

"Luna?" Nick gave Marian his best quizzical 'what are you talking about?' look.

"You know," Marian responded, "The *moon*." She was standing in the door of the bathroom with a towel wrapped around her in a kind of *Birth of Venus* pose—only with a towel—and Nick was trying not to think about how much he would like to take away the towel. She had just washed her hair and it streamed down around her shoulders while little rivulets of water ran down her arms. She looked. . . delectable.

He shook his head. "Okay. Luna. The moon. How do you plan to turn the moon into installation/performance art?"

She made a little impatient gesture with her hand. "I'm getting dressed," she announced, "and then we'll talk."

"My loss," he muttered.

"Could you get me a glass of wine?" she called from the bathroom.

She was so excited. He could see the sparkle in her eyes, the heightened tone of her voice as she explained her idea over the chicken stir-fry he'd made for dinner. "The moon is just so *significant* right now," she said, waving her chopsticks in the air. "Ever since the moon landing four years ago there's been this wonderful fascination with all things lunar. It's so *auspicious.* I mean the timing couldn't be better. The moon landing, the women's movement, the Jungian archetypes—it just all comes together. So I got this idea for a very marvelous multi-media piece for the opening of the Mockingbird Festival that will zoom in on a mix of symbolism and science, and explore the attributes of the moon as goddess." She paused and looked at Nick. "What do you think?"

"You're spectacular," Nick said softly.

Marian grimaced and shook her head. "No really, what do you think of the *idea*?"

He tried to imagine what sort of multi-media performance-natur e-goddess-mythological-psycho-drama would emerge from this amorphous concept, but his head was spinning. "Do you have an idea about how to organize this this gargantuan beast?"

Marian laughed and munched an egg roll. "As a matter of fact," she said, "I do. I found a prototype that would be perfect."

He leaned back against the wall and studied her. The energy and excitement were palpable. She was glowing. "So tell me already," he said.

"Okay. The whole Luna project will be based on the *Carmen Saeculare*, the *Song of the Ages*. It's a choral hymn commissioned by the Emperor Augustus and written in Sapphic meter by the poet Horace. In 17 B.C. it was performed as a festival hymn at the opening ceremony of the *ludi saeculares*, the secular games, by a choir of twenty-seven boys and twenty-seven girls. It was the earliest lyric poem whose performance was documented in detail. *But,*" here

Marian sat up straighter and waved her hand, "whereas Horace's song was a hymn to both gods and goddesses for the fertility of the land and for protection for the child-bearing mothers of the city and the sanctity of their marriages, I want to modify it to concentrate on the power of the moon and of women.

"First, I want to create a Mandala garden on that south-facing hill across from the amphitheatre so it will be visible from the auditorium. Maybe it will be more of a *labyrinth* so that people can use it as a meditation exercise. But each part of it will relate to phases of the moon. The plants too—like moonflower, evening primrose, night phlox, angel's trumpet—you know, flowers that bloom at night? Oh," she hugged herself, eyes gleaming, "it's going to be so beautiful, Nikki!"

Nick, who was staring at her with an expression that registered his confusion, said slowly, "Sounds amazing, but how the hell are you going to pull this off? I mean, it will take a *huge* amount of work, eh?"

Marian laughed. "Volunteers, cookie. I'll have lots of help!"

"Volunteers?"

"Of course. I'm going to select twenty-seven women to assist me. A collective experiment. Everybody working together. No patriarchal hierarchy. We'll develop it over the next year using the *Saeculare* as a guide. I've been talking to some of the women in my CR group and they're really excited. I think we can pull this off, Nick."

"Wow." He was quiet for a moment, then said, "How can I help? Or should I just get the hell out of Dodge?"

"It's going to be an all-woman production, but I also want documentation. That's where you come in. I want you to videotape the whole process—start to finish." She gave him a huge grin. "What do you say?"

Nick wadded up his napkin and tossed it at her. "I love you," he said.

But putting together twenty-seven "initiates" who were able to work together was, Marian soon discovered, a huge challenge. Within the scope of "women's liberation" there were dozens of different opinions and interpretations of exactly what women needed to be liberated from and how they should go about their liberation. Marian counted at least ten different groups including Radical Feminists, the Redstocking group, Politicos, Liberal Feminists, and Political Lesbians, who were separated by ideology and sometimes even by class thus perpetuating the very institutions that they claimed were oppressing them. A bewildering map of warring factions.

Marian decided early in the process that she wanted to be inclusive in her selection of "volunteers." She was hopeful that members of several different groups could be persuaded to work together. But she also wanted to set up collectively determined "rules" so that the group effort was not undermined by political bickering. Each "initiate" would be required to sign an "oath of agreement" to follow the regulations outlined in the manifesto that was collectively accepted.

Marian included her assistant, Judith Devorah, and two of Judith's lesbian separatist friends on her team because she felt strongly that *all* of the various feminist points of view should be represented in the collective endeavor. Judith and her two friends, Ellen and Bette, had grudgingly agreed to follow the principles of the *thiasos*, the sacred band, and its inclusive philosophy. Surely, Marian thought, they'd be able to work out their differences.

CHAPTER

48

San Francisco, California

Koe's Auberge was a small restaurant—white linen tablecloths, pleasantly dim lighting, quiet but cozy. Tucked into one of the twelve blocks that separated Nob Hill from North Beach, it captured the best of both world, an elegant eccentric.

Kate studied the menu, a hand-printed sheet that listed the classic bistro fare that one might find in one of those family-owned Parisian cafés—roast chicken, steak frites, coq au vin, cassoulet, boeuf bourguignon. She glanced around the table at the other members of the pre-concert dinner party.

Marian and Nick had flown out the day before and were staying at Mockingbird. Along with Kate and Tommy they had stopped in Sacramento to pick up Rose and Jorge. Cory had begged to come along, but was placated by an invitation to spend the night at the Malacchis. Allison and Francisco met them at the restaurant. Ben Ashida and his new partner, Jose, were also there, along with Jerry McClosky, Carl and Alex's west coast agent. They had invited Robert Ashford from the Townsend Foundation to join them, but he declined saying that he had to be in Los Angeles on business.

The party was grouped around a large round table in a corner of the dining area. Two waiters, dressed smartly in black trousers and white shirts, were taking good care of them.

"The owner's from Saigon," Jerry confided to Francisco. "Learned his French cooking there from a Parisian chef."

"Owen and I used to come here back in the day," Marian said. She and Nick exchanged smiles. "Great place for a celebration."

"I don't know what to order," Allison said, pouring over the menu. "It all looks so good."

Everyone got something different—Kate decided on the beouf bourguignon, while Marian chose the coq au vin and Nick went with the braised lamb shank. Rabbit and wild mushroom pie was passed around to sample. And everyone got a taste of Francisco's deliciously rich cassoulet.

Jorge insisted on splurging on several bottles of Grands Echezeaux, a legendary Pinot Noir from the Côte de Nuits region. "Too bad Carl isn't here to enjoy it with us," he remarked.

When the dessert menu was offered, everyone groaned and proclaimed they were "way too full." But they decided they *had* to taste the pear tarte Tatin and the delicate crème brulee.

The waiters kept them on schedule through the soups and salads and entrees and desserts, and there was plenty of time to get to the War Memorial Opera House located not far away on Van Ness. The large banner that hung at the entrance of the hall displayed the new UFW symbol—a black eagle on a field of red, but now with the words: Farm Workers, AFL-CIO.

"We are now an independent affiliate of the AFL-CIO," Jorge said proudly. "The United Farm Workers of America."

"Clearly something to celebrate," Tommy said.

"Yeah," Jorge agreed, "but there is still a lot to be done. Cesar is great at getting attention for *La Causa*, but now it will be a question of actually doing the administrative work to issue contracts and monitor compliance. That sort of stuff is not his strong point. He likes to make the big statement, you know? Not run the day- to-day details."

Kate nodded. "And the devil is in the details."

"But tonight," Jorge said, linking her arm with his, "tonight, we celebrate. Let's go and listen to the music!"

The lobby of the opera house with its solemn Doric columns and gilded corbelled ceiling, its gold and glass chandeliers and marble floors, was awash with people. The usual crowd of tailored gentlemen and silver-haired matrons contrasted with the younger set of sophisticated forty-somethings in their country-club best. Groups of students slouched about in their counter-culture regalia. A large contingent of Latinos, dressed in their Sunday finest mingled with with businessmen in grey suits and rep ties. An eclectic mix.

Kate and Tommy, along with the rest of their party, took their seats in the center orchestra section reserved for family members, long-time patrons, and special guests. The orchestra members were trooping onto the stage, the magnificent glossy black Steinway grand occupied a central position, lights glowed on its polished surface. There was a hum of chatter and a rustle of programs as the audience settled in.

The concertmaster entered to applause, bowed, sounded the A and the instruments found common ground. The lights went down. Then Carl strode briskly to the podium, turned, acknowledged the applause. Seeing him there, on stage, in his element, still made Kate catch her breath. He was so gorgeous. Usually, there was no introduction before the concert began, but tonight Carl raised his hand and stepped forward to address the audience.

"*Buenas noches amigos y gracias por estar aqui.*" "Good evening everybody, and thanks very much for being here," he said. Even through the microphone, his voice was warm. "It's gratifying to see such great support for the United Farm Workers of America and *La Huelga*, the cause, and to see you here to celebrate their accomplishments. I also want to thank the members of the orchestra and the Symphony League, and the rest of our generous sponsors for helping us prepare for this very special occasion."

There was a burst of applause. When the audience quieted, Carl continued. "We have a wonderful program for you and we'll get to that in just a moment. But first I want to introduce someone who has been my inspiration, someone who has honored the principles of justice and tolerance that we celebrate here tonight. Someone who taught me to embrace the belief that this country can still be a refuge for all those who seek a better life." He gestured toward the audience. "Papa, would you stand please?"

Jorge got slowly to his feet. Carl smiled that dazzling smile of his and said, "My father, Jorge Morales, started his career harvesting lettuce in the Arizona fields. He came to America with nothing but the clothes on his back and his willingness to work hard to achieve his dreams. His success was earned by blood, sweat and tears. I just want to acknowledge my debt to him as a mentor and a friend, and as a model for whatever modest success I've enjoyed in my own career. *Papa, tu eres mi héroe.* Dad, you are my hero."

The applause was deafening. Jorge looked around in a daze, smiling uncertainly, gave a little wave, then sat down. When the hall fell silent, Carl said, "And now, we hope you enjoy the concert." He mounted the podium, raised his arms and began.

The first half of the concert featured three works by Mexican composers. First, Blas Galindo's *Overtura Mexicana*, a vigorous composition based, as were most of his works, on indigenous Mexican themes. Next, Carlos Chavez's *Sinfonia India* focused on three Indian melodies using indigenous Mexican instruments. The third piece was a work by Pablo Moncayo titled *Huapango* inspired by the popular music of Veracruz, one of the places, according to Moncayo, "where folkloric music is preserved in its most pure form." The program mentioned that all three of the composers had studied under Aaron Copeland at the Berkshire Music Center at Tanglewood where Carl had been a student twenty years later.

The audience was enchanted by the performance. During intermission, Jorge was surrounded by enthusiastic admirers showering him with questions about his past, his family, his connection with the U.F.W.

Kate found herself caught up in the swirl of activity that also included Tommy, Rose, Allison, Francisco, and a stream of dignitaries and supporters. Photographers snapped their pictures for the society columns. There was hardly time to enjoy the Sangria, Margaritas, and dark beer that poured from the lobby's bar.

But soon the lights signaled the end of intermission. The crowd dispersed and trailed back into the auditorium to enjoy the second half of the program, the *Piano Concerto 2 in C minor* by Sergei Rachmaninoff. The soloist was Alexandria Archer.

The program notes told the story of the concerto, of Rachmaninoff's depression, his struggle to overcome his fears, the triumph of his resurrection as a composer with the success of the concerto. Plagued by self-doubt, he had abandoned his music. But when inspired to compose again, he wrote the music that would make him immortal.

The parallel of Alex's story was not lost on the audience. This was all about perseverance in the face of extreme conditions, about continuing the struggle even when the obstacles seemed overwhelming, about overcoming adversity and fighting back no matter how slim the hope or how daunting the odds. The comparison with Cesar Chavez's story was obvious as well.

From the moment she walked on stage, you could tell that Alex was *back*. Kate felt a great surge of emotion—love? Pride? Empathy? She was thrilled to see Alex in the spotlight, looking invincible once more. From the elegance of her slender figure, in a turquoise gown, to the triumphant gleam in her sapphire eyes as she bowed and settled herself at the piano, Alex was fully in command.

Carl turned toward the soloist and for a long moment they shared an intense look. Then Alex nodded and Carl pivoted and faced the orchestra.

Kate's heart skipped a beat. *This is so right*, she thought. *They truly belong together.* At that moment, she relinquished him completely.

Then the first movement began with that slow, ominous series of chords, like the tolling of bells. A somber *momento mori* that set the musical scene for all that followed.

Throughout the weeks of rehearsal, Alex had reviewed in her mind the uncanny connection that she had with the Rachmaninoff Second. She remembered the conert at Tanglewood over twelve years before when she'd heard Stefan Molnar perform the concerto, and how that evening had changed her life.

Then, she had insisted on playing it for her professional debut in 1964 with the Cleveland Symphony, despite Stefan's admonishment that she should play somethig "different and daring." No, she told him, it *had* to be the Second. In the end, he had agreed. That was the performance that launched her career.

Now, she felt once more that ineffible connection to a work of art that had framed her life. "He wouldn't have been able to compose it without Nikolai Dahl," Alex told her therapist, Dr. Diaz, a week before the concert. "It was Dahl's course of hypnotherapy that gave Rachmaninoff the courage to resume composing after being panned so badly by the critics." She smiled at Dr. Diaz. "The Second was his comeback. And now it will be mine."

By the time Alex had finished the second movement—that languid flowing stream filled with yearning—she knew the "comeback" was real. Like a lark on the wing, she sailed through the tempestuous third movement, building the momentum, all grace and power, provocative and intricate. Carl himself seemed mesmerized as he brought the final passage to its explosive conslusion and pivoted to stare at Alexandria with a look of amazement.

The next day, the review in the *Chronicle* called the performance "Pure magic. What a remarkable and triumphant resurrection of a profoundly talented artist. The combination of Ms. Archer's poignant interpretation coupled with Maestro Fitzgerald's (or is that now Maestro Morales?) elegant but powerful guidance made this an evening to remember. Whereas too many pianists and conductors have over-sentimentalized Rachmaninoff's sublime concerto, Fitzgerald and Archer hit exactly the right combination of passion and structure. Archer's command of the keyboard was effortless and deeply moving, with a clear articulation of the notes. Together, the conductor and the soloist created a masterpiece of their own. We've missed you, Alexandria. Welcome back."

"What have we got so far?" Carl asked.

Nick held up a binder and a box. "Stuff."

"How do we make music out of stuff?" Carl asked.

"Let's take inventory," said Nick.

For the next six hours, they sat on the leather sofa in Alex and Carl's living room and argued, wrangled, cajoled, drank green tea (Carl), smoked a joint (Nikki), and finally ended up abandoning the "stuff" and going out into an unusually warm San Francisco October evening to a small French bistro that served down-home favorites: cassoulet, coq au vin, soupe l'oignon. They shared a bottle of Clos Veugot.

"The Greeks had forms," Nick said. "But they were argued out of existence in the Middle Ages when those metaphysical guys determined that their purpose was to give meaning to the meaningless. Maybe that's the answer. We're back in the Dark Ages."

"Darker Ages," Carl corrected. "Now we've got nukes."

"So what do we do?" Nick said. "Eighty-six it?"

Carl sat back in his chair and poured himself another glass of wine. "Let's laugh at it," he said.

"'Sound is the vocabulary of nature.' Thus saith Saint Pierre," Carl intoned.

"The apostle?"

"The Schaeffer. Musique concrete. Take natural sounds and abstract them into a composition. You should hear what he could do with a locomotive."

Nick hit his head with his palm. "Right. The original tape loop guy. From France."

"Exactly. Sound collage."

They had descended into the basement of the apartment complex where they had, with the landlord's blessing, they'd set up an improvised sound studio and brought in equipment: a Moog synthesizer with an 8-track tape recorder, two four channel reel-to-reel tape machines, a Bose speaker system, two television monitors, camera equipment, and mixing, splicing and editing devices.

Carl had spent hours recording random water sounds—rain

pattering, toilets flushing, sprinklers sprinkling, waterfalls, lapping waves, roaring rapids. A huge collection of "water music" ripe for splicing.

Nick had been with Carl on a number of his "explorations," videotaping the sources of the sounds, suggesting ways to gather additional "music." Carl's plan was to intersperse "nature's symphony" with a variety of traditional musical instruments using sampling practices pioneered by Pierre Schaeffer. The sounds would be synced with Nick's images. The entire production would be a collaboration between humans and nature, a co-produced Happening.

"I think we can divide the composition into three movements," Carl said. "I loved your idea of *reflections*, so there's a whole group of sounds that I want to combine somehow with light. You know, sound and light are similar with regards to *reflection*. The difference is that light travels at a hundred and eighty-six thousand miles per second and sound travels at one-thousand one-hundreed- sixteen feet per second, about seven-hundred and sixty-eight miles per hour. So, they use the same laws of reflection, but sound is much slower. Both sound waves and light waves bounce off of objects. Reflection of sound waves off surfaces leads to echo or reverberation. I think we can use the synthesizer to simulate these phenomena."

"Let's look at how we can combine the water-light images with the sound," Nick said.

The video projector whirred to life and the screen was covered with scintillating patterns of reflected light. Carl played the sound of lapping water through the synthesizer, adjusting the dials to modify the sounds, setting up a reverberation that danced in concert with the fluctuating ripples of light.

"Goddamn," Nick said softly. "This is going to work."

By mid-December, when Nick went back to New York, they had a rough draft of *WaterLight*.

CHAPTER

49

New York, New York

"Look at this, Nick. It says that Apollo Seventeen will be the final manned mission to the moon." Marian was propped up in bed, drinking coffee and reading the *New York Times*. They were planning to go out for some breakfast, but the morning seemed to be getting away somehow.

Nick had just gotten out the shower. He was wandering around the room, barefoot, wrapped in a towel, looking for his glasses. "Gotta be here somewhere," he muttered.

"Nikki, are you listening?"

"Sure," he replied. "You said 'moon.' But then you're always saying 'moon.'"

She scowled at him over the rim of the paper. "Final manned mission to the moon," she repeated.

He stopped to stare at her. "Really? Let me see that!"

She relinquished the *Times* and he scanned the article. "Damn!" he said, "How the hell am I going to get to the moon if they're not even sending astronauts?" He tossed the paper down and sprawled on the bed next to her. "This isn't fair, Maryanne."

She picked up the paper and continued reading. "Well, cheer up, cookie," she said. "It says the Russians are planning to keep working on their space program. Maybe they'll give you a ride."

Nick propped himself up on his elbow and said, "*Govorite li vy po angliyskiy?*"

Marian put the paper aside. "What?"

"Means 'Do you speak English?' I think."

"How'd you know that?"

He shrugged. "*Ya, nemeogo govoryu po-russki.*"

"What?"

"I speak Russian, a little."

"Why? How?"

"I had a friend in high school, a Russian Jew whose family had refused repatriation after the war and ended up in Canada." Nick smiled, remembering. "Isak Brodsky. That guy was outta sight. Totally wacked. God, could he drink."

"*Dasvidaniya,*" Marian said.

Nikki blinked at her. "You want me to go?"

"No," she said. "That's just the only Russian I know. What does it mean, anyway?"

"Means 'Goodbye.'"

"Oh." She squinted at him. "Where were we going with this?"

"I was going to the moon."

"Right! The moon. Nineteen seventy-three is going to be very big moon-wise. Not only will we have had the final moon landing, but also on June thirtieth there's going to be a very long solar eclipse, more than seven minutes. Unfortunately, we won't be able to see it in California, but I still think it's an important idea to incorporate that into *Luna*. Maybe a "'seven minutes of silence' or something."

She glanced at him. "What do you think?"

He tilted his head and smirked. "I think you're looney, but I love ya anyway. Come here, babe." He caught her hand and pulled her to him.

"Nikki," she said, struggling, laughing, "let me go. You are *such* a bad influence!"

"Fly me to the moon and let me play among the stars," he sang in a woozy imitation of Sinatra. "Let me see what spring is like on Jupiter and Mars. You are all I long for, all I worship and adore."

"I think you left out a line," she said, nuzzling his chest.

"Right," he said, "In other words, I love you."

"That's it."

They totally forgot about breakfast.

—∘∘o⟩●⟨o∘∘—

San Francisco, California

The day after Christmas, Carl and Alex drove back to San Francisco from Mockingbird after a long Christmas weekend. As they turned on to Judah Street and parked in front of Alex's apartment, Carl thought that despite all his misgivings about leaving New York, it was wonderful to be near family, to spend time with his son, Cory, to see Ali and Francisco and Jorge and Rose. How could he have been so blind all those years? *I was a dope*, he thought as he got out of the car.

He was part-way up the front steps when a maroon Pontiac drove up and stopped. Carl recognized Jerry McClosky's car and said to Alex, "Hey, look who's here."

Alex, who was unlocking the front door, paused and glanced at the car. "He usually calls," she said, "before he drops by."

Jerry parked the car and curbed the wheels. He waved as he got out and came toward them. He was carrying a cardboard box under his arm.

"Hello, you two," he greeted them. "Merry Christmas."

"Same to you," Carl said. "We just got back from Mockingbird, but come on in and have a glass of holiday cheer."

"Don't mind if I do," Jerry said as he followed them into the foyer. He greeted Alex with a hug and a peck on the cheek.

Upstairs in the living room, they shed overcoats and settled down next to the fireplace. Alex's only nod to Christmas decorations was a flock of greeting cards from friends and fans that covered the mantle.

"What brings you to our little abode?" Carl asked as he handed Jerry a glass of cab and sat down on the sofa.

"Just playing Santa," Jerry replied with a grin.

Carl raised his eyebrows. "Really?"

"Yup. I'll get right to it." He bent down and carefully opened the cardboard box. Carl and Alex exchanged a bemused look. Jerry straightened up and held out a violin case.

"What's this?" Carl asked.

"Take a look," said Jerry.

Carl took the case and put it down beside him on the sofa. He snapped open the fasteners and raised the cover. Then he sat staring down, his expression morphing from curiosity to awe. "Oh. My. God," he said faintly.

"What is it?" Alex said, leaning forward for a look.

Jerry was beaming. "Merry Christmas," he said.

Carl looked at him in amazement. "What. . .? How. . . ?" He looked back at the violin that lay in the velvet-lined case. "Jerry," he said, "this is Anya's Del Gesu! What is it doing here?"

"Anya passed away," Jerry replied. "A few weeks ago. It was very sudden—a stroke. She was in Vienna with her family at the time."

"I didn't know," Carl said.

"The official announcement isn't out yet. I wouldn't have known except I was in Vienna to see my sister and her family. Shelly knew Anya and she heard from friends about her passing. Then I got a call from the Wilhelm family attorney wanting to know how to reach you."

Carl shook his head. "Why?"

"Because," Jerry said, "Anya left you the Del Gesu."

"Wow," Alex said. "That's incredible!"

Carl just stared at Jerry. Finally he said, "Me? Why would she leave it to me?"

"The attorney said that Anya told him you deserved it. That you were meant to have it, and she had just been taking care of it for you."

Carl looked back down at the violin. "I don't know what to say."

"Why don't we ask the violin to do the talking?" Alex suggested, getting up and heading toward the Steinway. "What say we give it a trial run?" She turned and gave Carl and impish grin. "Let's do the Schubert Fantasy in C. That should give your Del Gesu a workout!"

Carl looked down at the beautiful instrument in its blue velvet bed. He remembered the summer he'd spent with Anya in Vienna. He was sixteen and full of hopes and dreams and raw ambition. Anya was in her mid forties—worldly, a renowned musician, still attractive in a reserved, slightly condescending way. He was her pupil, but he was also full of fun and youthful enthusiasm, and he charmed her relentlessly. When she finally succumbed, he had been almost frightened by the intensity of her desire. She took control of him, instructed him with the same demanding rigor that she applied to teaching him music.

And, she let him play her beautiful Guarneri del Gesu violin, an extraordinary instrument that had been made in the mid-seventeen hundreds by a master violin maker. Bartolomeo Giuseppe Guarneri's workmanship was considered second in quality only to those of Stradivari. Indeed, some of the world's most famous violinists— Niccolo Paganini, Jascha Heifetz, Yehudi Menuhin—*preferred* Guarneris to Stradavaris.

Carl had gotten his Schuster and Company Markneukirchen violin when he was in high school. It had cost almost two thousand dollars which, at the time, seemed like a fortune. All he could afford. It was a fine violin—bright, resonate, well-balanced—and had served him well over the years. But what violinist wouldn't dream of owning a legendary masterpiece like a Strad or a del Gesu?

"Well?" Alex prompted.

Carl looked at her and back at the violin. Then carefully he took the instrument from its case and walked to the piano. She played an A. He tuned the fiddle. She sat down and put her hands on the keys and began to play the wistful, tender opening of Schubert's Fantasy in C.

Composed in 1827, just one year before Schubert died at the age of thirty-one, the C Major Fantasy was written to display the excellence of two performers. A demanding work, the piece begins with a series of soft piano figurations that serve as counterpoint to the lyrical clarity of the violin. The seven continuous sections of the piece move from delicate to exuberant before culminating in a jubilant finish. The right mix of skillful technique and passionate energy results in a true *tour de force* for the performers.

Jerry watched the two young musicians as their music interacted, flowing back and forth with infinite skill, first sweetly singing, then racing toward consumation. How alike they were, and yet so different—Alex completely focused, intent on the sound, while Carl closed his eyes and appeared to become one with the melody.

As the final triumphant notes died away, Jerry pulled out a handkerchief and daubed at his eyes before saying thickly, "Now I understand why she left the Del Gesu to you."

PART IV

CHAPTER

50

Sacramento, California
January 1973

First they ignore you, then they laugh at you, then they fight you, then you win.—Mahatma Ghandi

J orge Morales kept a poster with Ghandi's quote on the wall above his desk. His daughter Allison had made the poster in 1965, almost eight years ago. She was only thirteen that summer, but already she had embraced social justice as an obsession that would shape her future. Now, at age twenty-one, she was studying environmental law and living with a Mexican activist. Jorge shook his head with amazement. Life was certainly full of surprises.

Despite the bombing incident that had nearly ended his life three years ago, Jorge had continued to work with the United Farm Workers as a community organizer and activist to help raise support for the farm workers union. As a former migrant worker himself, he well knew the plight of the field help—the unsafe working conditions, the pitifully low pay, the lack of basic necessities such as toilets and clean drinking water. And the endless fear of being fired any time for any reason. Or no reason at all.

Recently, the wife of one of the workers had told Jorge, "It's better now that we have the union. The wages are better and we have a medical plan. There are toilets in the fields and we get twenty minutes to rest morning and afternoon!" Jorge nearly wept as he listened to her story.

Yes, there had been a few victories. The previous fall, Proposition Twenty-two, a state initiative sponsored by California agribusiness that tried to curtail the right of farm workers to organize or to encourage consumer boycotts, had been soundly defeated. Jorge had spent a great deal of time working to bring down Prop. 22.

But the next test would come when the contracts that had been signed with growers as a result of the successful grape boycott of 1970 came up for renewal. Since then, the Teamsters had gained strength, and Jorge could see that there would again be a struggle for power. April fifteenth was the signing deadline. The cold dread that he felt in his heart was barely concealed by stern resolve.

San Francisco, California

"Something awful happened when I was seven years old," Alex said. "I think I was raped." Her voice was as raw as her words.

Carl stared at her. He didn't move or speak, just let the words sink into his mind, and settle slowly into his consciousness. He had to will himself to remain calm. For God's sake—how and who and where? Who would do such a thing? He didn't want the image, but there it was before him—a beautiful blond child, small and defenseless, wailing in anguish.

She turned away from the window and glowered at him. "Aren't you going to say anything?"

He was still too stunned to speak. He just looked at her and thought that somehow this outrage, this incident, somehow explained so many things. But how could one traumatic, terrible event shape an entire life?

She tossed her head with that characteristic arrogance, blond hair catching the light that flooded in through the bay window. Outside, the sky was a cold, deep blue without a shred of clouds to dim the sun's intensity. For a moment, she seemed to be part of the light, something angelic or insubstantial. But then she stared at him with her sapphire eyes and said coldly, "It's not too late, you know."

"What?" he said, nearly choking on the word.

"To change your mind."

Now he *was* confused. "Change my mind?" he echoed feebly.

She shrugged, crossing her arms, and turned once again to the window. "You don't have to stay, you know. You can still go back to New York."

"But. . ." It started to dawn on him what she was saying, feeling. The way she always reacted with anger when she felt threatened, like a cornered animal.

She had come home from her doctor's appointment in a bad mood, but he knew Alex well enough to know that she likely wouldn't brood for long. Her moods came and went like sunbeams on a day when puffy clouds alternately coveredd and revealed the light. Mood swings were just a part of. . . being Alex.

But this seemed different. Darker. So he hadn't pressed her for an explanation. He would wait it out. Let her calm down. They could talk later.

But her sudden revelation had caught him completely by surprise. And then the immediate assumption that he might use her revelation as an excuse to leave? What was she thinking?!

But, of course, if he knew the answer to *that*, he would know what to say. "Can I get you something?" he said and immediately regretted it.

She spun around. "What?" she barked. "Like an aspirin maybe? A little something for the pain?"

He went to her and tried to hug her, but she pushed him away. "Don't touch me!" she cried, her face crumpling. When he tried to take her arm, she jerked it away and fled down the hall. He heard the bedroom door slam.

He felt paralyzed. Should he try to calm her down? Call her doctor? Call an ambulance? This was no time to miscalculate. This was a *crisis*. What should he do? Slowly, deliberately, he walked down the hall and tapped on the bedroom door. "Alex?"

"Go away!" Her voice was muffled, ragged.

He tried the door. Thank goodness it wasn't locked. Maybe she *wanted* him to follow her. He looked around the room. She wasn't on the bed or in the recliner next to the window. Puzzled, he stood in the middle of the room, frozen.

Then he heard whimpering coming from the closet. He found her huddled on the floor behind the coats and dresses. He sank down on his knees and gathered her to him. Gently, he stroked her hair. Kissed her damp temple. She cried and cried.

Finally, she stirred and rubbed her eyes with the back of her wrist. "I'm so sorry," she managed to whisper.

"I love you, Alex," he said softly.

That brought on another onslaught of tears, but presently she hugged him. "Help me up?"

"Sure." He helped her to her feet and guided her into the bedroom. She sank down in the chair and covered her eyes with her hands.

He went to the bathroom and brought back a damp washcloth, watched as she pressed it to her face. After a few minutes she put the cloth aside and leaned her head back against the chair, her eyes still closed.

Carl sat down on the foot of the bed. "Want to talk?"

She shook her head. "Maybe later."

"Okay."

He started to get up, but her eyes flew open and she started up. "Don't leave me!" she cried. The terror in her voice shocked him.

He sat back down. "I'm not going to leave," he said. "Not now. Not ever. Okay?"

She gave him a guarded look, then lowered her head.

It was later that evening that they settled down next to each other on the sofa. Carl had made a little fire and the small flames danced and darted above the glowing embers.

"The things is," Alex said, "I still don't *really* know what happened. I mean, it's not like I suddenly had a *vision* or some kind of flashback. It's just that based on all the. . . evidence, I had to believe that *something* happened that day, something that changed everything. How I thought. How I felt about other people. How I felt about *me*. And when Doctor Diaz and I made a comprehensive list—the symptoms, the episodes, the depression, the panic attacks, substance abuse, eating disorders, abandonment fears, inappropriate anger, the list goes on and on—it all *fit*." She gave a little laugh. "In fact, I'm pretty much a classic case. Maybe somebody should do a book about me—you know like *Sybil*?"

"Haven't read it," Carl said.

"Neither have I. I heard about it on a radio show. It's about a girl with multiple personalities."

"So," Carl said, "does Dr. Diaz think that's what you have? Multiple personalities?"

"No. See, I'm *aware* of my different states of mind. People with multiple personalities often don't even know they have these other selves." Alex paused for a moment, then said, "She calls it *borderline disorder*."

Carl waited.

Alex glanced at him. "Get me a glass of wine and I'll tell you all about it."

He brought them both a glass and settled back down beside her. "Okay, shoot."

"I told you some of the symptoms—abandonment issues, panic attacks. But there's also dichotomous thinking, black and white thinking, fear of being alone, self-injury, not feeling real. Man, I'm a casebook study." She looked up at him. "Didn't know you were going steady with a basket case, did you?"

"You're kidding, right?"

She laughed. "All right. So you've always known." She looked away. "I thought it was just the obsessions—you know, music, performance, all the stress. I never tried to find a starting point, a *cause*. But apparently people with my illness often have a history of childhood abuse or trauma. Something that sets them on a path to self-destruction. Even though it's terrible to think that I had this *trauma* when I was little, at least that helps to explain all the stuff that came afterwards, the twisted relationships and irrational outbursts."

Carl took Alex's hand—her left hand—and drew it to his lips. He looked at her intently. "What happens next?"

"It's a bit like rehab on my hand," she said. "Lots of work and hope for the best."

Carl smiled. "We'll work on it together, okay?"

She looked at him suspiciously for a moment. Then she sighed and snuggled against him. "Okay."

CHAPTER
51

Mockingbird Ranch
March 1973

March was always a difficult month for Tommy. Seven years had passed since his mother, Connie, had died, but every March he found too many reasons to remember her.

Maybe it was the weather. Northern California was in the full throes of Spring. The air grew soft and sweet. The annual outburst of golden poppies began to carpet the hills. Red and white ranunculus sprouted in fields and gardens. Red spiraea and blue bells were everywhere. And the wild mustard was starting to spread its golden mantle across the orchard. A few miles away, in the little town of Volcano, one of the ranches devoted a whole hillside to thousands of daffodils. And the pear trees, God bless them, were covered with a froth of white blossoms. Joy and beauty everywhere.

But for Tommy, March was the cruelest month. The month when he first lost Kate to Carl Fitzgerald. The month, years later, when he first told Emiko that he was in love with her. March had too many sad memories. And sometimes they all came back at once.

He walked through the vineyard at Mockingbird, vines that had been planted almost a century ago. The gnarled trunks and knobby branches looked grotesque, like arthritic elders or ravaged gnomes hobbling slowly through the bright green field. Yet new shoots were already beginning to burst from their winter shells, pushing outward toward the light. You could barely see the beginnings of the buds that were forming. Six months from now, the vines would be heavy with clusters of purple fruit, and the second harvest of Mockingbird Old Vine Zin would be underway.

Tommy loved the ranch. Loved the land, the fields, the orchards, the vineyard. Loved them with the deep, heart-aching passion that had consumed him for most of his life. But that passion could also become a chasm, a bottomless pit of despair. And when he started to fall into that abyss, he found it very hard to find anything to break his decent.

He could feel the darkness coming. Sometimes he dreamed that he was driving across a bridge, an arched span that traversed a body of water. He would start up one side of the bridge, but he couldn't see past the crest. The road appeared to run out at the top of the span, and he knew that if he kept going he would plunge off the edge and the dark cold water would swallow him. Those were the dreams that he woke from and said to himself, "I can't see a future for myself. Not here. Not anywhere."

He stood shivering in the sunlight, listening to the dove's muted discussion, the urgent calls of the quail. The light was blinding, but the darkness was eating the sky one bite at a time. He sank down on his knees and put his arms around the rough furrowed trunk of one of the vines and squeezed his eyes shut and held on. Soon, he was certain, this terror would pass.

Sacramento, California
March 1973

Rose Morales was sitting at the table in the dining room of the pleasant white brick house that she shared with her husband Jorge. Outside the window on this pretty day in early March, she could see the garden with its thirty-three varieties of rose bushes that Jorge had planted over the years—one bush for each year of their marriage. An hour earlier, Rose had gotten a phone call and was delighted to hear that her daughter Allison and Ali's Mexican boyfriend, Francisco, had decided to drive up from the Bay Area for the weekend.

Strange, the way things worked out. Even though her son Silvio was gone (was it really almost four years since she had gotten the news of his death in Vietnam?), Rose's youngest child, Allison, had recently returned to California after four years back east, and now Carl, her eldest, was also back and once again living in the City. With Alex McPhalan, of all things! Rose was not quite comfortable with the fact that Carl had managed to work his way through relationships with both of the McPhalan sisters, let alone their *mother*(!), but *that*, she decided, was not her business. The important thing was, Carl had come home.

Rose had spent many hours over the past four years working with *Another Mother for Peace*—organizing boycotts, writing letters, sending out pamphlets—so it was with enormous satisfaction that she heard the news on January twenty-seventh that the Paris Peace Accords had been signed by the United States, North Vietnam, South Vietnam and the Viet Cong. The U.S. had halted all military activity in Vietnam.

In just a few weeks, the last remaining American troops were to be withdrawn from the region. The longest war in American history was finally officially over. During the fifteen years of military involvement, over two million Americans served in Vietnam with 500,000 seeing actual combat. A total of 40,934 were killed in action, Silvio Morales among them. There were 10,446 non-combat deaths. Another 153,329 were seriously wounded, including 10,000 amputees. Over 2400 American POWs/MIAs were still unaccounted for.

The world was moving on, but new conflicts were brewing, as Rose could clearly see from the dinner table discussion that took place that evening.

"So, just what you were afraid would happen," Allison was saying to Jorge. "The growers signed contracts with the Teamsters instead of signing with the U.F.W. *Now* what?"

"We thought we had the issue resolved," Jorge said, his forehead furrowing. "After the strikes three years ago when Cesar was arrested, we thought we had an agreement affirming the UFW's right to organize the field workers. But now, the Teamsters have been at work again to undermine the UFW. There have been many disruptions—mass picketing, mass arrests." He shook his head. "There will be more violence for sure."

Francisco was quiet, listening carefully. Now he looked at Jorge and asked, "Isn't there some way to consider legal reform as a solution?"

"There are a number of us who would like to see that," Jorge said. "But Cesar has argued against it. He believes that a truly successful union movement must be built from the grassroots, bottom to top. Not top down."

"Still," Francisco mused, "if this Jerry Brown should get the nomination for governor, maybe things would be different, no? He seems much more liberal than Governor Reagan."

Jorge nodded, but before he could speak, Allison jumped in. "Brown's amazing," she declared. "Did you know, Papa, that he was going to be a Jesuit priest but was released from his vows by the Pope? Also, he worked as an organizer for both the farm workers and the anti-war activists before he became Secretary of State. He helped bring lawsuits against Standard Oil. And he supports campaign finance reform."

Jorge and Francisco both looked at Allison. "Ay, *carino*," Jorge said with a laugh, "you could be his campaign manager!"

"I plan to work for him," Allison replied.

Jorge and Francisco exchanged a bemused look.

"And I'll help you out," Rose said. "I think he's definitely the best candidate."

"It is clear," said Francisco, "that the opposition doesn't stand a chance."

The following Monday, Rose was in the kitchen getting dinner. Jorge, who had just returned from his office in Stockton, sat at the kitchen table reading the *Bee*. The phone rang and Rose picked it up. "Hello?" For a few moments, she was silent, listening, then she said, "That is a cruel joke. Shame on you!" Her voice, usually so sweet and lyrical, was hard as steel. Angrily she slammed the receiver down.

Jorge looked up in dismay. "What is it, *paloma*?"

"Nothing!" She turned abruptly and went back to peeling potatoes.

When the phone rang again, Jorge got to his feet. "I'll get it," he said. Rose stared at him.

"Yes? Who is this?" He stood for a moment and his forehead knotted. "Are—. How—," he stammered and sat back down. "Yes, I know, but—" He was shaking his head. "That's right, but—" He was quiet, looking at the floor. Then said, "Yes. I'm still here." He glanced at Rose and her hands flew to her mouth.

"When?" Jorge said. "Can we talk to him? Yes. All right. I understand. Of course. Tomorrow will be fine." He hung up and for a moment sat absolutely still. Then he looked at Rose. "*Madre de Dios*," he whispered. "Silvio is alive."

The next morning at 8:30 a.m. a car pulled up and parked in front of the house. Two uniformed men got out and came to the door. Jorge let them in. They said they were from the U. S. Army Family Assistance unit: Captain Harold McIver and Lieutenant Donald Hearst. The Captain did most of the talking.

"A terrible mistake," he said, shaking his head. "But I'm sorry to say, it has happened before. Please consider the circumstances. There were fifteen men involved in a firefight during a search and recovery operation. Your son, Specialist Morales, came in on a chopper to help evacuate the wounded, but another firefight started and all fifteen of the men were presumed dead including the pilot. The identifications were. . . difficult.

"The recovery unit that went in to retrieve the remains tried to account for all of the casualties. They verified eleven bodies, but were uncertain about the other four. They found your son's dog tags about two feet from a badly burned body. It was assumed his identification was accurate."

"But what happened?" Jorge asked.

"Apparently," the Lieutenant said, "four of the men were taken prisoner by the VC, but we didn't know which ones. It wasn't until we got the list from Hanoi this past January that we were able to verify the identities of the POWs. We were shocked to find Silvio Morales' name on the list. We've spent the past month verifying the information. We're now certain that Silvio Morales is alive."

"So, for the past three and a half years my son has been a prisoner of the North Vietnamese?" Rose exclaimed.

"Yes, ma'am," said the Captain. "That is correct."

Rose buried her face in her hands and burst into tears.

CHAPTER

52

Travis Air Force Base,
Fairfield, California

Perhaps Historian Andrew H. Lipps captured the intangibility of the moment when he later wrote:

> *Imagine you're imprisoned in a cage; imagine the cage surrounded by the smell of feces; imagine the rotted food you eat is so infested with insects that to eat only a few is a blessing; imagine knowing your life could be taken by one of your captors on a whim at any moment; imagine you are subjected to mental and physical torture designed to break not bones but instead spirit on a daily basis. That was being a prisoner of North Vietnam. Then imagine one day, after seemingly endless disappointment, you are given a change of clothes and lined up to watch an American plane land to return you home. That was Operation Homecoming."*

A C-141 transport plane took Silvio, along with fourteen additional prisoners, from Hanoi to Clark Air Force Base in the Philippines. There, he and the other prisoners spent six days being debriefed, checked by doctors and psychiatrists, having their injuries treated. Then Silvio was flown to the Army Hospital at Travis Air Force Base in Fairfield, California. And today, after another week of treatment, his family would finally be allowed to visit him.

Silvio wondered if they would recognize him. He hadn't seen his family—father, mother, sister, brother—since September 1967, five and a half years before. He had just spent three and a half years in a prison camp in North Vietnam. He was not the same person who had left California in the fall of 1967.

Part of the change was physical: his left ear was gone, and that side of his face was a marbled, shiny scar from the burns he'd suffered when the helicopter blew up. Only part of his hair had grown back. There was damage to his left eye as well. If he closed his right eye, the world became a strangely distorted surreal landscape, fuzzy and grey and wobbly. The two months he had spent in solitary confinement in a black-washed room in a camp forty miles north of Hanoi had not improved his vision. He sometimes played a little game, closing first one eye and then the other, and wondering which eye was telling him the truth.

During the time in the prison camp, he'd also lost almost fifty pounds and now weighed less than he had at age fourteen. And he walked with a limp from the chronically infected left knee that had been injured in an especially nasty "interrogation" and had never healed properly. When he looked in a mirror, he thought he was seeing a ghost.

Then there were the nightmares, the panic attacks, the disorienting spasms of paranoia. His mind was unpredictable. Some days were better than others. The medication helped. Some. But there was an unsettling feeing of disconnection, of emotional numbness that refused to go away. He kept taking deep gulps of air, trying to relax, to think clearly. But the fog refused to lift.

The nurse, a short, plump brunette with a snub nose and a loud giggle, wheeled him out to the sunny reception room and fussed with the blanket that covered his legs. A few other vets in the room talked with visitors. "Your folks will be here any minute," she told him. "Can I get you anything, hon? Water? A coke?"

He shook his head. "Nothing. Thanks."

She turned on her heel and headed down the corridor.

Ali was the first through the door. She spotted him immediately and ran to hug him. He lifted his arms, slowly, to embrace her. Rose and Jorge were right behind her and then Carl, a little hesitant. Rose was crying, tears streaming down her face as she hugged him. "They told us you were dead," she cried. "Oh, Silvio. Silvio! I can't believe it!"

"Hey, little brother," Carl said softly.

Silvio looked up and met his gaze. "Hey, big brother," he said. Carl closed his eyes, opened them. Let out a sigh. "God, it's good to see you."

Jorge just stood there shaking his head, a look of wonder on his face.

Silvio sat down on the bed and looked around. He was mildly surprised to find that nothing had changed. The room was exactly the same as the last time he been there sixty-six months before. *They believed I was dead,* he thought, *and still they didn't change anything? What is this, a shrine?* The idea made him a little angry. He didn't know why. Did they really think nothing had changed?

He had been "home" for three days. He felt guilty that he was not "happy." Rose and Jorge were so thrilled, overwhelmed with joy, doting on him, telling him over and over how wonderful it was that he'd come back to them alive. How fortunate. How lucky. He had trouble remembering how to do the right things—smile, nod, make eye contact. He wanted to tell them to shut the fuck up.

He looked around at his childhood—at the blue and white striped curtains, the pale blue walls (blue was for boys), the dark blue desk that Jorge had built for him in a little alcove. Silvio had spent hours and hours at that desk, reading, studying, doing his homework. Writing out long lists of baseball stats, trying to figure out which teams would win their league title. What did it all mean? Why did he think it mattered?

A memory flashed back to him. He was sitting in a dark room, no windows, no lights. He thought he'd been sitting there for a long time. Maybe forever. To keep from thinking about where he was, he began making lists in his head of all of the baseball teams he could remember, which league they were in, and how many games they would need to win to capture the league title. He went through every possible combination: If Kansas City won twelve games, they could win their division and go on to the playoffs. If they won ten games they might get in if the White Sox lost three games. He played out whole World Series contests in his head.

When he ran out of baseball combinations, he did atomic numbers, charts of chemical elements, listed elements by atomic numbers. Lists were very helpful. He went on to lists of bones, muscles, organs, systems, cellular structures, constellations.

Silvio got up and limped across the room to the dresser. His knee still hurt fiercely. The VA had offered to get him a wheelchair, but he didn't want a fucking wheelchair. He could manage with a cane. He didn't tell them that the pain was actually welcomed. It was a distraction. Something to focus on.

One of Ali's anti-war protest posters was taped on the wall above the dresser. He looked at it and thought about his sister. She'd been a kid when he left—fifteen, rebellious, full of adolescent zeal. And now here she was, all grown up. A woman. Going to law school, *law school*, living with a really nice Mexican guy (he had met Francisco the night before when Ali brought him along for dinner), still full of conviction and idealism but in a more convincingly serious *adult* way. She was sort of the same person he had known. But not exactly. An older sister maybe.

On the dresser was a collection of framed photographs—Jorge holding little Silvio on his knee. They were dressed up. Might have been Easter. There was another photo—Carl and Silvio opening presents under the Christmas tree. Piles of wrapping paper strewn around, light glinting on the tinsel. Carl must have been about ten or eleven, thin with a mop of dark hair. Silvio was a chubby four-year-old, laughing, holding up a toy truck.

He turned and made his way to the easy chair next to the bed. He was exhausted, but afraid to fall asleep. The nightmares would come, and he would start shouting and wake everyone up. Then he'd have to explain, answer their concerned questions, say "nothing's wrong." But that would be a lie. There was a whole lot wrong. He just couldn't explain what it was.

At breakfast the next morning, only Jorge and Rose were there at the table. Ali and Francisco had gone back to San Francisco. Carl went with them. Silvio tried to picture Carl living with Alex, but that didn't seem possible, so he put the image aside. Nothing was the same. Everything had changed.

Jorge was reading the morning paper and asked Silvio if he wanted the sports page. Silvio accepted in an effort to be polite and pretended to read. Rose poured coffee, brought plates of eggs and bacon. Asked what kind of toast he wanted: white or whole wheat? He couldn't answer the question. What *difference* did it make?

There was a kind of dull fury building inside. He clenched his hands and tried to will away the rising tide of anger. Then Jorge set the paper down and said, "So, *amigo*, do you have any plans to share with us? Any way we can help?"

Silvio stared at his father's smiling face. Glanced at his mother. Rose tilted her head and looked encouraging. Silvio looked down at his plate. Then, very calmly, he stood up, put his hands under the edge of the table and turned it over on its side. Dishes clattered and crashed. Bacon, eggs, coffee, strawberry jam slammed together on the linoleum floor. Slivio stared at the mess. Wasn't that the Army term for food: mess? He tried to remember.

Jorge jumped to his feet, staring down in dismay. Rose let out a little shriek that turned into a sob. Silvio looked at them calmly. Then he walked out of the kitchen and went up the stairs to his room.

CHAPTER
53

San Francisco, California
March 1973

"What's this?" Kate held up a small bundle of white silk tied with a knotted gold cord.

Tommy, who was wrapping dishes in pieces of old newspaper and putting them into a cardboard box, looked up. "It's. . ." He hesitated. "I don't know exactly. Something Mom gave me before I went to Japan for the first time. I wanted to find out more about it, but never had the chance to ask her."

They were in San Francisco in the redwood house that Tommy had built in the Twin Peaks neighborhood, the house that he and his first wife, Emiko, had called home.

After almost two years of living at Mockingbird and leasing the Twin Peaks house to one of his associates, Tommy had decided to make a permanent break and sell the property. THis was a hard decision—he had put so many hopes and dreams into that piece of architecture—but it was clear that chapter of his life was behind him. Time to move on. So on this pretty March day, he and Kate were boxing up the leftovers of his former life, and making the house ready for a new incarnation.

"Can I untie it?" Kate asked.

"Go ahead."

He watched as she unrolled the scroll, recalling that Emiko had done exactly the same thing when she first spotted the bundle lying on the bedside table in Tommy's Kyoto apartment back when he was a student at Kyoto Tech. Seemed so long ago—almost ten years.

After finding out that the scroll contained the *mon*, or insignia, of the Tokugawa family who had ruled Japan off and on for centuries, Tommy had intended to follow up with some research. He wanted to find out how the scroll ended up in his mother's closet. But the chance had never presented itself.

Now, here was Kate, inspecting the scroll with sober intensity. A small spark of interest nipped at him.

"So what's the design mean?" she asked, looking up.

Tommy shrugged. "I wanted to know the same thing, so I asked one of the history professors at a university in Kyoto. He said it was the logo of the Tokugawa family."

"Weren't they like—royalty or something?" Kate asked.

"Sort of. The Tokugawa clan ruled Japan for over two hundred years until the Meiji restoration in eighteen sixty-eight. The shoguns were the heads of the government, and they were all from the Tokugawa family. They were part of the class structure, along with the samurai."

"What about the emperor?"

"The shoguns controlled the military," Tommy said, "so they were actually stronger than the emperor. Sort of like the European monarchy where the aristocratic families controlled the land and the military, while the king provided the impression of unity."

Kate looked back at the scroll. "Is it old?"

Tommy crossed the room and stood next to her, looking down at the scroll. "The professor thought so. Apparently, the design is sort of. . ." he struggled for the correct word, "like copyrighted? Only members of the family are supposed to own or display this design."

Kate looked up at him. "So, how do we find out more?"

"I don't know. Ask somebody, I guess." He went back to packing dishes.

With her biography of Stefan Molnar at the publisher and the opening of the music center still over two months away, Kate decided to see what she could find about the history of the white silk scroll with the elegant wild-ginger flower design.

She started at the California State Library in Sacramento which had wonderful historical resources. Eventually she came across information on the Yoshinobu Photography Studio that had been located in Sacramento Nihonmachi in the early twentieth century.

The proprietor was listed as Frank Yoshinobu, Tommy's grandfather, but there was very little additional information, and the records stopped abruptly in 1942 when the Japanese were sent to internment camps and their businesses were confiscated. She found nothing about where Frank had come from or who his family was.

Next, she discovered the Japanese American Citizens League and the role the League played in preserving Japanese history. She visited the archives at Sacramento State University, and found information about the Wakamatsu Tea and Silk Colony.

One afternoon a week later, she dashed into the kitchen. "Tommy," she cried. "Guess what?"

Tommy, who was sitting at the kitchen table with Cory, deep in a discussion about multiplication tables, looked up. "What?"

"There's a marker for the Wakamatsu Tea and Silk Colony over on Cold Springs Road!"

"Really?" Tommy looked startled.

"What's a wamtu colony?" Cory asked.

"Wakamatsu," Kate corrected. "Come on guys. We've gotta go see!"

They drove south on Route 49, the Old Coloma Road, crossed the South Fork of the American River, and turned onto Cold Springs Road. The road wound through pastures and groves of oak trees, and past a small lake. Kate slowed the car to a crawl.

"There!" Tommy said, pointing.

Kate pulled off the road and they all got out to take a look at the small plaque that identified the site as "California Registered Historical Landmark Number 815."

"'First agricultural settlement of pioneer Japanese immigrants who arrived at Gold Hill on June eighth, eighteen sixty-nine,'" Tommy read aloud.

Looking up at Tommy, Cory asked, "Were they related to you?"

"I don't know, Cory," Tommy replied, still looking at the plaque.

"I think they were," Kate said firmly. "When the colony disbanded in eighteen seventy-two, at least a couple of the families moved into Sacramento. I'll bet Frank Yoshinobu was with them."

"Maybe we should ask Dad," Tommy said, glancing at Kate.

"Let's do it," she said.

The next day was a Saturday, and Tommy, Kate and Cory headed for Stockton after giving Tommy's Aunt Pearl a call to tell her they were paying a visit. "Tell Dad I want to talk to him about Sacramento Nihonmachi," Tommy said, giving Kate a conspiratorial grin.

"That ought to get his attention," Kate said with a laugh.

They pulled into the parking lot of the Ashida Produce Company just before noon. Chibi, the lumbering Golden Retriever, gave them a loud welcome, and Aunt Pearl came out of the store to greet them.

"So, what's this all about?" she asked after giving everyone a hug.

"Just a little genealogical project," Tommy said. "I thought Dad might be able to help me out."

"Well," she said, glancing toward David's cottage, "he's expecting you."

David greeted them at the door, gave Cory a hug, and ushered them into the living room. "I will make some tea," he announced in his gruff way and disappeared into the kitchen.

Tommy took the small white silk bundle from his coat pocket, untied it, and spread it out on the coffee table.

A few minutes later, David came back carrying the teapot and small cups on a wood tray. He paused when he saw the scroll, then carefully set the tray down. "Ah," he said, "now I understand why you are here."

"Do you know what this is?" Tommy asked.

David poured four cups of tea and handed them around before speaking. "I will tell you what I know," he said, sitting down in the armchair next to the window.

He was silent for a moment, gathering his thoughts. "Frank Yoshinobu was your mother's father, your grandfather. You probably also know that he owned a successful photographic shop in Sacramento Nihonmachi before the. . . the war."

He paused again, lost in thought, then looked at Tommy and continued. "I met your mother in nineteen thirty-four. She had just graduated high school and was working in her father's photo shop. I worked at McKinley Park and I liked to take pictures of the gardens that I tended. Then I would take the film to Mr. Yoshinobu's shop to get it developed." He smiled, remembering. "Your mother was so sweet and so helpful. Pretty soon, I couldn't stop thinking about her. The next year, we got married. We were so happy those first few years. We had a nice house and all we wanted was to stay in Sacramento Nihonmachi and raise our family." The smile faded. "But then came the war. . ."

He glanced at the scroll. "Anyway, I never found out much about your mother's family, but Mr. Yoshinobu did tell me that he had been born in Japan, in Kyoto, and that his father had been a military man." David looked up intently. "He did not use the term 'samurai,' but he referred to him as a 'warrior.' And he also hinted at some secret. Some kind of family intrigue that forced his mother to flee the country with her small son. His father had been killed, or perhaps executed. I don't know. But in any event, Frank and his mother ended up in Sacramento."

David sat up and took a drink of tea. "That's really all I know," he said.

"Then you don't know where this scroll came from?" Tommy asked.

David picked the piece of white silk up and examined it closely. "I know," he said, "that this belonged to Mr. Yoshinobu, and that it was very important to him. I know that he gave it to your mother just before he died, and told her to keep it safe and to pass it along to her children." He put the scroll back down on the table. "But that is all I can tell you."

"I think we can fill in the gaps," Kate said.

On the way back from Stockton, they once again drove past the site of the Wakamatsu Colony and stopped to re-read the plaque. Tommy looked around at the peaceful countryside with its ancient oak trees and gently rolling pastures that were already beginning to turn from springtime green to summer gold. "I guess maybe my grandfather and your great-grandfather were both living here at about the same time."

"Within twenty-five miles of each other," Kate replied.

"You think they knew each other?" Cory asked.

Tommy smiled and ruffled the boy's hair. "Probably not." He looked once more at the landscape that was becoming uncannily familiar. "But the river knew both of them."

CHAPTER

54

Sacramento, California
April 1973

When he started to remember, Silvio remembered too much. He lay on his back in the blue room and stared out the window between the blue and white striped curtains at the bright blue sky. He thought about what had happened the day he was captured.

His team got a call to go into a hot Landing Zone to pick up casualties. The gunships were still circling as their Huey landed, but the firing had stopped and the ships flew off toward the north where you could hear the sound of small arms fire.

Silvio jumped out and ran to the nearest body. Turned it over. No way to help this one. He went to the next. The guy was alive, though badly wounded. Silvio yelled for the gunner to give him a hand. He turned back to the wounded soldier, but then he heard an explosion. The gunner went airborne and landed on top of Silvio, crushing him into the wounded man and probably saving his life. When he crawled out from under the gunner, he saw that the man's back was a bloody crater. And that he had no head. He was so fixated on the headless gunner that Silvio scarcely felt the burns on the left side of his own head

Then he realized that he was trapped. He glanced around and saw movement along the tree line. Shit, he thought. Should he try to play dead? He glimpsed two Viet Cong soldiers going from body to body. Once, they stopped and fired point blank. The body twitched. Silvio closed his eyes and waited.

He didn't have to open his eyes when the soldiers got to him. He felt them. Just do it, he thought. Get it over with. But one of them grabbed his arms and dragged him to his feet and yelled at him. The soldier yanked off Silvio's dogtags and threw them down next to the charred corpse of the gunner. Silvio stood there swaying until the soldier gave him a push and walloped him in the back with the rifle butt. He put his hands in the air and started walking.

But now, Silvio couldn't sleep. He sometimes went three or four days at a time without recalling sleeping at all, at least it felt that way. He lived in a perpetual fog bank, unable to control the phantom thoughts that circled endlessly in the thick soup of his brain. When he tried to make the circling stop, his mind seemed to turn into froth, like snow on a TV screen. Static on a radio. He wanted to howl. But he was just too tired.

At the newly opened VA hospital near Sacramento, Silvio was evaluated. His sleep problems were attributed to stress and depression. They gave him a prescription for Valium and sent him home. After the second time he overdosed and had to be taken to the hospital, Rose threw the pills away. They tried a private doctor.

Silvio sat in the doctor's waiting room. Everything was brown. The rug was dark brown and shaggy. The chairs were a lighter shade of brown plastic. The walls were painted beige. Even the lampshades were brown. Was brown supposed to be soothing? Earthy? Wholesome?

Brown was shit, Silvio thought. Or mud. Mud crawling with maggots. He was crawling through the mud trying to drag a wounded soldier to the chopper. The mud was slick as shit. The soldier's face was covered with mud. Silvio tried to wipe some of the mud off, but the face came off with it. He saw movement out of the corner of his eye. A sniper! He ducked. Someone started screaming.

A nurse was beside him. "Hey," she was saying. "Hey. Take it easy."

Silvio blinked up at her. He was sitting on the floor holding on to the chair and panting like he'd just run a marathon. He was sweating, terrified and gulping for air. After a few minutes he let go of the chair.

"Breathe," the nurse said and handed him a paper bag. "Blow into it."

He blew. Slowly, his heart stopped racing and he could breathe normally. "Thanks," he muttered. He looked around and saw several people staring at him. Embarrassed, he looked away. Breathe. Smile. Nod. Don't even try to make eye contact.

Combat neurosis, the new doctor, a short, stout man with dark hair and round wire-rimmed glasses, said. He wrote out a prescription for Valium. "It's as old as warfare," he said as he handed Silvio the slip of paper. "Described as far back as Mesopotamia."

Then why the hell do we keep having wars, Silvio thought? It always turns out the same way: the many pay the price for the monstrous ambition of the few. But to the doctor, he said, "Thanks."

However, after another three weeks, he was still experiencing a host of symptoms—insomnia, nightmares, flashbacks, hallucinations. Was he losing his mind?

Then Rose heard about a doctor who specialized in working with veterans. She urged Silvio to visit him. "I'll drive you there," she offered.

What the hell, he thought. "All right," he said aloud.

"If I go to sleep, I'll dream," Silvio explained to Dr. Colin MacKenzie. They were sitting in Dr. Mac's office on K Street a few blocks from the Capitol. Outside the window, a bright April sun burned down on the sidewalks, bleaching them to a pale grey, while the sky was an unblemished blue.

"What about?" the doctor asked.

Silvio looked out the window, then back to the doctor's tan young face. "You don't want to know," he said.

Dr. Mac sat back and pursed his lips. "Try me."

Silvio spread his hands and stared down at them. "Sometimes they were still alive when I got there, but there was nothing I could do. I remember one guy had been torn in half by a land mine. Somehow, he was still trying to talk. He said 'I'll be all right, won't I, doc?' And I said 'Sure.' I dream about that a lot. Every time I hear about 'talking heads' on TV, I want to puke. I get to meet talking heads whenever I go to sleep." He glanced up at the doctor, then back down at his hands. "In the dream, I try to put band aids on the wounds, but there's too much blood."

Suddenly, Silvio lurched to his feet. "I've gotta go," he said.

"Why?"

"I'm gonna puke."

Dr. Mac got up and handed Silvio a wastebasket. "Go ahead," he said.

Silvio gagged and retched into the basket. He finally stopped and wiped his mouth on his sleeve and slumped back down in the chair.

"Better?' asked the doctor.

Silvio nodded. For several minutes they were both silent. Then Silvio said, "I feel like I'm dead." He looked at the doctor. "You know?"

Doctor Mac shook his head. "I wasn't there. You were. So were a lot of other guys. Every story they tell me is different, but the endings are the same."

"Meaning?"

"How did you feel when you first got home?"

Silvio let out his breath in a long sigh. "I don't know." He shrugged. "Numb, I guess. I couldn't. . . I mean I didn't want to. . . remember anything. I just wanted everything to go away. I wanted everything, everyone to shut the fuck up. But it wouldn't. . . go away."

"What wouldn't go away?"

Silvio buried his face in his hands. "IT. The pictures in my head." He rubbed his face fiercely and glared at Doctor Mac. "I was supposed to be a *medic*, for God's sake, and I couldn't save them. They were already dead or almost dead. I see them over and over. I see them lying there bleeding out, and I can't do a fucking thing to stop it!" He closed his eyes and hugged himself, moaning softly. "Not a fucking thing."

After a few minutes, Silvio said, "And to think, I wanted to be a doctor." He gave a strangled laugh. "Pretty funny, huh?"

"Why do you think it's funny?"

"I'm a failure before I even start. I've already lost all my patients."

"You feel responsible for what happened to them?"

Silvio threw the doctor a furious look. "Don't you get it? I'm fucked up! I can't sleep and I can't think and I can't get rid of the fucking pictures in my head. I'm. . . over!"

CHAPTER

55

Mockingbird Ranch

M arian was feeling especially confident that morning in late
April as she finished breakfast and went down the path to the
Visiting Artists building. The spring sun was warm and the sky was
a grand blue bowl inverted over the forest. In the distance, she could
hear the river, voluptuous with snow-melt, singing a boisterous song
as it cascaded over the boulders.

In just two months the Music Festival was due to open, and
there was still a lot to do on the Luna project that had consumed her
attention for the past year.

Alex and Carl were in San Francisco working on the Festival's
opening program with the Symphony. Tommy was at his SF office
going over the final details of the renovations with his associates.
Work was almost finished on the small "state-of-the-art" gallery that
sat in its own pristine Japanese-style garden with a simple sign over
the entry gate: In Memory of Emiko Namura Ashida, 1943-1969.
Marian had helped design the gallery and acted as consultant on the
plans for the building.

Allison and Francisco were both now living in San Francisco
while Ali finished her law degree at Berkeley and Francisco continued
his work with the Sierra Club Legal Defense Fund. Amazing how
everything seemed to have circled back to where it started. Kate and
Tommy together. Carl and Alex together. Who would have guessed?
She shook her head in awe at the ways of fate.

Kate had left the ranch early that morning to take Cory to school
and was having lunch with Chris Malacchi to go over some contracts.

Kate then had an interview lined up with a Sacramento TV station to promote the festival. Such a flurry of activity!

In the Visiting Artists dining hall, Marian found her twenty-seven "initiates" in various states of undress, finishing their breakfast and chattering exuberantly. She got a chorus of "Good morning," and "Hey, Marian." She called out, "Are we ready for the morning meet?" and was met with a positive chorus.

The women trailed into the adjacent "hearth room," a large space that could be used as an assembly hall, gallery space, or informal living room. They sat down in a circle on the floor and made themselves comfortable, some holding coffee cups or still munching on muffins.

Marian started the conversation by reminding the group that there was a full moon this evening, and that the Festival would begin "two moons from now" on the fifteenth of June. As they went around the circle, each of the women shared their thoughts about the evolution of the project and what still needed to be finished. They all agreed that by afternoon they should have completed work on the wildflower garden, the centerpiece of the "lunar Mandala." They finished the meeting with a prayer to the Goddess to bless their efforts.

It was after lunch, after more work on the Mandala, after a swim in the river, and at the end of a rehearsal of the opening performance and a long discussion about the lyrics of the hymn to Luna that Nick made an appearance. He wanted to ask some questions about the video equipment that he and his assistant, Angie, would be using to tape the performance. A group of about twelve women gathered in the main house courtyard to discuss the options.

Just the night before, Judith, Marian's studio assistant, had gotten into an argument with one of the other vols about whether women who had long-term relationships with men could actually claim to be feminists. Judith voiced the opinion that only women who totally cut their ties with men were *true* feminists. "As long as women continue to serve the patriarchy and receive benefits from it, they will never be truly liberated," she proclaimed.

Marian later took Judith aside and told her *again* that as a member of the Luna team she was expected to put aside her radical feminist agenda and do her part as a member of the collective.

"We've talked about this before, Judith," Marian said. "You agreed to the requirements for participation in Luna, so I really must insist that you comply with the agreement. Otherwise—" She paused.

"Otherwise what?" Judith demanded, thrusting her chin forward defiantly.

"I don't want to have to ask you to leave, but don't push me too far," Marian replied.

"You really don't get it, do you?" Judith said caustically. "You are such as disappointment, Marian. You keep pretending to be a leader, a model, but in fact you're nothing but Nick Vecchio's bitch."

Marian squeezed her eyes shut and counted slowly. She got to five. Then she opened her eyes, glared at Judith and said coldly, "This is your last chance, Judith. Do your job and shut up or get the fuck out of here." And with that, she stomped up the drive to the main house, so angry that she could scarcely breathe.

Just before four that afternoon, chaos once again changed Marian's life. She had avoided Judith all day and didn't notice her standing at the edge of the group as Nick began explaining that he wanted to get some overhead shots so that the video would take advantage of the Mandala shape of the garden.

"But then, won't you have to use a scaffold or something?" one young woman said. "Wouldn't that compromise the naturalism of the setting?"

Just as they began to discuss alternatives, Marian saw a quick movement out of the corner of her eye. She was standing next to Nick and saw that Judith had worked her way around the back of the courtyard and was now standing next to the wall fountain. She looked. . . strange. Not listening as much as *calculating*. Glancing around, eyes narrowed, she looked like a predator waiting patiently for the right opportunity to strike.

I need to talk to her, Marian thought and started to take a step toward Judith, but at that moment Judith made a sudden flinching motion and brought out a handgun from under her jacket.

"You can stop right there, pig," she said in a rasping guttural voice. "We've all heard enough from you, *Mister* Vecchio."

It's a familiar phenomena, that frozen moment just before a disaster. Something happens to time, an odd extension, so that events appear to be unwinding in slow motion—the hood of the car crumples like a piece of aluminum foil, the ball is heading right for your face but you can't move fast enough to get out of the way, the glass falls off the edge of the table and seems to take several minutes to reach the floor.

On a pleasantly warm day in mid-April with a blue sky above and water splashing sweetly in the fountain and the scent of wisteria drifting across the patio, Judith Devorah stood stiffly next to the garden wall pointing a handgun at Nick Vecchio.

There was a collective gasp from the onlookers. No one moved or spoke or could quite believe what they were seeing. Nick gazed at his assailant calmly, then said, "What's the problem, Judith?"

"You bastard," she said with vicious coldness, "you shouldn't be here. There is no place for you here. You have to leave. If she won't get rid of you," she jerked her head in Marian's direction, "I'll do it for her."

"What if I want to stay?"

"Then I'll fucking kill you."

"Why would you do that, Judith?"

"Because you deserve it! You and every other pig. We have to decontaminate the Earth or we won't survive. Men ruin everything. They don't deserve to live. We have to get rid of you. All of you!" She raised the gun a notch and took aim.

Nick took a half step toward her and held out his hand. "Don't do this, Judith. It's not worth it. There are other ways to solve problems. Let's talk this through."

"Stay back, you bastard!" she said through clenched teeth.

"Come on Judith." Nick's voice was very calm and soft, as though he was talking to a frightened animal. "Give me the gun. You don't want this. No one wants this."

Marian held her breath and stared at Judith's face. It was pale and hard, like a mask. But then she saw Judith's eyes change, just a little, a slight narrowing. And she knew.

"No!" Marian lunged in front of Nick, her hand outstretched toward Judith, a pleading defense.

At the same time she heard a sharp crack. Suddenly she was lying on the ground. And people were screaming.

"Judith, don't!" she heard someone shout and then the gun fired again. "Oh, God," Marian thought from somewhere inside the haze. "She's shot Nikki!"

But no, she could hear Nick's voice, broken and desperate, saying, "Marian, stay with me, babe. Please, Marian!"

She tried to swim against the current, to hold onto his voice, to keep from going under. But the darkness was all around her, pulling her down, and she couldn't answer him.

CHAPTER

56

"Look, Mom. Look at all the cars. What's going on?"

Cory pointed toward the house. Kate had already spotted the cluster of vehicles—an ambulance and two police cars, warning lights blinking and spinning—in the drive in front of the courtyard.

"I don't know, Hon," Kate said. She pulled up behind an ambulance and stopped the car. "Somebody must be sick. Wait here," she told Cory. She got out and headed for the knot of people who were standing around the gate.

"What's going on?" she asked Sandy, a thin, blond-haired girl who was one of the volunteers.

"Oh, God," the girl returned, hugging Kate fiercely. "You're back!"

Kate put her hands on Sandy's shoulders. "Calm down and tell me what's up."

"Judith. . . she had a gun and she shot your mother and then. . . and then she shot herself and I don't know how—" Sandy was crying, "—how did this happen?"

Another volunteer quickly came over and put her arm around Sandy's shoulders. She looked at Kate, who was staring, wide-eyed and incredulous, at Sandy. "What—" Kate managed to say, "—what the hell is she talking about?"

"I don't know exactly," the second girl said. "It just. . . it just all. . ."

Kate pushed past the crowd of hovering figures. She saw a gurney and the backs of two paramedics. Nick was standing beside them while two uniformed policemen and another paramedic were gathered on the opposite side of the courtyard beside the fountain.

Nick glanced up and saw Kate. He immediately came to her and put his arms around her.

"What happened?" Kate cried, the question muffled against his chest.

"Judith," he said. He was breathing hard. "She shot Marian. But we think she'll be okay."

"Oh, my God," Kate gasped. "Oh, no!"

She struggled to break away, but he held her fast. "Easy, Kate," he said softly. "We need to let the medics do their work." She stopped struggling. He gave her a quick squeeze and released her. "Come on," he said.

He led her past the gurney and she could see over the kneeling paramedics. Marian was lying on the tile pavers, covered with a blanket. One of the medics held an oxygen mask over her face. The other held a pad against her shoulder. There was a pool of blood under her left arm and along her neck. Kate stared in shocked disbelief. She glanced at Nick. He was also looking at Marian.

Kate suddenly remembered Cory. Glancing around, she saw Consuelo standing in the doorway, tears glistening in her frightened dark-brown eyes. Kate went to her and they hugged each other. "I left Cory out front in the car," Kate said. "Please, Consuelo, can you take care of him for a while? I don't want him to see this."

Consuelo nodded. "Of course, señora." She moved quickly toward the gate.

"She's stabilized," she heard one of the paramedics say. "Let's get her on the gurney."

Kate's eyes met Nick's. "I'll go with her," he said. "Meet me at the hospital?"

She nodded. Then she noticed that the two policemen and the paramedic who had been kneeling next to the fountain were standing up and she could see a body dressed in black lying on the ground. Even from across the patio she could see the blood. A lot of blood.

One of the policemen, a heavy-set county sheriff with sandy hair and freckles, was an old friend of the McPhalan family. He turned and looked at Kate. She went to him. "What on earth happened, Ron?" she said, glancing down at the still form.

"Near as we can figure," the policeman said, "this gal here," he gestured toward the figure in black, "tried to shoot Mr. Vecchio and hit your mother instead. Then she shot herself. We got the same story from several witnesses. They said she was. . . well, kinda crazy I guess." He shook his head and looked down at the corpse. "Damned kids these days. Got no sense at all."

Kate heard an ambulance siren and saw the vehicle pulling away from the gate and heading down the drive. She looked back at the sheriff. "Do I need to do anything here? My mother. . ."

The sheriff waved away the question. "Go on to the hospital. We can handle things here."

Kate headed for the car. Cory was about a hundred feet down the drive, but he pulled away from Consuelo and came running toward her. "What happened, Mommy?" he cried. "Consuelo said there was an accident!"

Kate pulled him to her. "It's okay, honey," she said, trying her best to sound convincing. "Grandmary got hurt, but she's going to be fine. I'm going to go to the hospital to see how she's doing. I want you to stay here with Consuelo, okay?"

"No! I want to go with you!" he cried.

"I know you do, but it's better if you stay here until we see. . . umm, how everything is," she said lamely. "I'll call just as soon as I know what the doctor says."

Cory snuffed back tears. "Promise?" he said.

"Absolutely."

Consuelo hurried up and took Cory's hand. "You'll be better off here, *chico*," she said. "Hospitals are no fun. Teresa and me, we're gonna make cookies and we need your help."

Cory gave Kate a rueful look. "You'll call me really soon?"

"Of course." She knelt down and embraced him and kissed his hair. "Just as soon as I can."

Four hours later, Nick and Kate sat in the waiting room of the Auburn Faith Hospital, on the north side of town. The sofa was green and the fluorescent lights cast a grey-green phosphorescence that made everything look sickly.

They had read through most of the magazines and drunk too much coffee and the back of Nick's head was throbbing from the tension in his neck. He tried twisting it in slow circles but that didn't seem to help.

Kate gave him a tired smile. "Want a neck rub?" she asked.

"Naw. It'll be okay. I just need to stretch." He got up. "Maybe I'll go have a smoke, eh?"

"I'll come get you if there's anything to report."

He went out through the glass doors beyond the nurse's station. The night air was cold and smelled of wet asphalt and something pungent, pine resin maybe. The wind had brought a few clouds in from the east. They were playing hide and seek with a full moon in the sky above the trees. He took a cigarette from the pack of Lucky Strikes and lit it, inhaled sharply, wishing that it was something besides tobacco. Despite the recommendations for decriminalization advocated by the Nixon-appointed Shafer Commission, Nick didn't smoke dope in public. Seemed like asking for trouble.

But what was he faced with now but huge trouble? He sat down on a concrete bench and tried to reconstruct the past five hours—Judith's wild accusations and rambling diatribe, his own ineffectual efforts to defuse the situation, Marian's heroic action that had saved him from being the one undergoing surgery. He felt panic, pain and anguish at the thought of losing her.

He took another deep drag and squinted up at the sky. What could he have done differently? Stayed in New York? Gone to the police when Judith threatened him? Insisted that Marian not include Judith in the group of volunteers? Right, like he could tell Marian what to do.

So, what was he to make of the disaster? Was it a warning? Did it summon up some unexpected negativity because of the connection to Sappho, to Lesbos? To Judith? The killer of Holofernes? The man-killer?

Nick realized with a visceral jolt that he and Marian had been together for almost ten years, ever since the opening of her first exhibition at Fisher Gallery in New York. He had loved her work immediately—the lush color, the expressive brushwork, the intensely personal depictions of her family, her friends. She had a sort of radiance, he thought, an aura of energy that grabbed him like a magnetic force. He *had* to be with her. She was his idol, mentor, heroine, inspiration. Muse.

Nick sighed and took a last drag on the cigarette. Dropped it on the ground. Crushed it. The orange glow went dark and he felt a great rush of fear. What if? What. . . if?

But as he got to his feet and started toward the door, Kate emerged. He stopped short, frozen, trying to interpret the expression on her face as she came to him.

Kate put her arms around him. "She's out of surgery. The doctor says she's going to be fine."

He couldn't respond except to hug her hard and close his eyes as he felt his terror evaporate.

"I hate hospitals," Alex said. "I hate being around sick people."

Kate and Alex were sitting in the waiting room. Carl and Alex had arrived at the ranch that morning, and Tommy was back from the City too. Tommy had brought Cory to the hospital, but Marian was still sedated and asleep. At least Cory was able to see her and be reassured that "Grandmary's going to be fine." Carl talked Nick into going back to the ranch with him for "some lunch and a nap," and Tommy and Cory had gone with them.

So now Kate and her sister, Alex, sat on the shabby green sofa in the waiting room under the buzz of the fluorescent light. It was a kind of vigil. Making sure that some family members were there to keep track of any developments.

"Yeah," Kate said, glancing around. "Hospitals are pretty depressing. But," she looked at Alex, "I'm glad this one's here. At least we were able to get Mom over here quickly."

Alex stared out the window. "Remember when that little boy at our school, what was his name? Larry Walters I think. He had a brain tumor and Mom made us go visit him? I hated that. Poor little thing with his head all shaved and his eyes sort of crossed. I wasn't even sure he knew we were there. But Mom insisted it was the 'right thing to do.' Scared me to death. I kept thinking 'That could be me. That could be *me!*' God," she shook her head, "I really hated that."

"I remember that he had a baseball that was signed by all the members of the Solons ball club," Kate said. "I thought that was cool."

"Really? I guess I don't remember. I just wanted to get the heck out of there." Alex's eyes wandered around the waiting room, then settled on Kate. "Mom came to see me, didn't she? When I was in the hospital after I broke my wrist? I think I told her to go away."

"You were. . . distraught," Kate said.

Alex frowned. "Don't make apologies for me. I was a dope. A monster. I just couldn't stand her. . . her *sympathy*. Maybe, I don't know. Maybe I didn't feel I deserved it." She sighed. "I hated myself so much. Felt so guilty. Oh hell," she muttered. "There I go again. Me, me, me."

For several minutes neither of them spoke. Then Kate said, "How's the rehearsal coming along?"

Alex's eyes lit up. "Great! I think it's going to be an extraordinary opening program. I'm doing a recital of piano music built on the theme of the moon—you know, Beethoven's *Moonlight Sonata*, of course, and Debussy's *Au Claire de Lune*. Maybe also the Chopin *F-minor Fantasy*. Haven't quite decided."

Kate smiled. So good to see Alex brimming with enthusiasm, color flooding her cheeks, eyes sparkling.

"Sounds terrific," Kate said, wishing she could say more, communicate somehow the joy she felt at her sister's re-born love affair with music.

"Oh, my god," Alex suddenly exclaimed, "do you think Mom will still be able to do the Luna performance?"

"I don't know," Kate said, "but I don't think her team will let her down. They know what she wants, so if she can't actually participate, they'll make it happen for her.

CHAPTER

57

Carl brought a bouquet of flowers with him to the hospital—deep pink flowering quince mixed with purple and white lilacs. Now he stood in Marian's room wondering what he should do with them. He felt like a schoolboy bringing flowers to the teacher.

Marian appeared to be asleep. The room had a soft blue glow, and there was a continuous hum from some piece of equipment. The nurse had told him not to stay too long. He wondered if he should just find a vase for the flowers and leave.

But at that moment, Marian shifted position and groaned softly. Carl crossed the room and stood next to her. She opened her eyes and gazed up at him. "Carl?" she said.

"Hi."

She looked puzzled. "Where. . .?" She blinked rapidly and glanced around. "Wow. I'm a little foggy."

He put the flowers down on the foot of the bed. "You're in the hospital," he told her.

She nodded and then grimaced. "Ouch! I'm sore all over."

"It'll get better soon," he said. He pulled a chair up next to the bed and sat down.

She frowned. "Is Nikki. . .?"

"Don't worry. He's fine."

"I thought I heard him talking to me. It seemed like a dream. And I thought that Kate and Alex were here too."

"They were. I chased them off and told them to get some rest."

Marian smiled. She caught sight of the flowers lying on the foot of the bed. "Oh," she said. "Quince flowers and lilacs. I guess it's spring."

"I'll find a vase for them before I leave," he said.

"Spring was always so beautiful at Mockingbird," she said.

"Still is."

Suddenly, she seemed to come fully awake. "Good heavens," she said, struggling to lift her head. "What month is it?"

Carl laughed and patted her hand. "Relax," he told her, "it's still April. There's plenty of time to get everything ready for the grand opening."

She looked relieved. "Thank goodness!"

They were both silent for a few moments. Somewhere outside the hospital a car honked. Carl could hear muted voices from down the hall. He smiled at Marian and she smiled back.

"We've kind of come full circle, haven't we?" he said.

"You mean coming back to California?"

He nodded. "When I came to Tanglewood that summer, I thought I'd left home for good. But I guess things don't always work out the way you think they will."

"No," she replied. "Sometimes they're better."

He got up and gently kissed her forehead. "Get well soon," he said softly. "We need you."

Then he went to look for a vase.

The next afternoon Marian had two more visitors. The nurse helped her sit up and wash her face and comb her hair. She felt at least half human for the first time in a week. The feeling had returned to her left hand which, the doctor said, was a good thing. And she didn't have any fever. Her shoulder itched under the bulky cast. She decided maybe that meant the wound was healing.

She looked out the window at the fat, blue-grey cumulous clouds that had gathered and wondered if it was going to rain. Just then, Ellen and Bette, Judith's friends from New York, came in and stood huddled next to the door like shy children.

"Hi there," Marian said. "Come on in."

The two young women came slowly to the foot of the bed and stood there awkwardly. They were both blond, but Ellen had curly hair that almost reached her shoulders, while Bette's was cropped close to her head.

"Hi," Ellen said shyly. "We wanted to come by and see how you were. I mean are." She looked flummoxed.

"I'm better," Marian said. "Pull up a chair and tell me how things are going back at the ranch."

That seemed to put them at ease and they followed her suggestion.

"Are we still on track?" Marian asked as they settled themselves next to the bed.

Bette nodded. "We've been working really hard and everybody's doing everything they can to get ready."

They took turns outlining the progress that had been made on the Luna project while Marian listened and asked an occasional question. Finally, she nodded approvingly and said, "Sounds like everything's under control."

"Yes, ma'am," Ellen replied, unable to shed her Mississippi-bred manners completely. "We'll have everything ready for you."

"Good. I plan to be out of here any day." *I hope*, she thought. "Thanks for the up-date."

They got up and she expected them to leave, but then Ellen said, "We want you to know we think Judith was just so wrong about. . . *everything*. We're awfully sorry about what happened."

"So am I," Marian said.

"We never thought that she'd go that far," Bette said. "I mean, we knew she was fucked up, but we never thought. . ."

Marian shook her head. "Neither did I."

"You knew about what happened to her, right?" said Ellen.

"What do you mean?" Marian asked.

"Her family and all that."

"What about her family?"

Bette and Ellen exchanged looks. "Gosh," Ellen said, "we figured you knew about her. . . issues. She talked about you like you were her mother or sister or something, so we thought you knew about her past."

"Tell me." Marian looked from one tense face to the other. "Please."

Ellen sighed and sat back down next to the bed. Bette perched on the foot. "She had a really terrible time when she was a kid," Ellen said. "First her stepfather molested her and when her mom found out she threw him out. But then later Jude's mom killed herself, and she always thought somehow she was to blame, even though she obviously wasn't."

"And then she went into foster care," Bette chimed in. "That was nothing but shit."

Ellen nodded. "Yeah, she got passed around from one place to another and had some really bad experiences."

"One of her foster brothers used to burn her with cigarettes," Bette offered.

"Good god," Marian said. "I had no idea."

"She really hated men," Ellen said. "I mean really *hated* them."

"Not that that's any excuse for, you know, what she did," said Bette.

Bette and Ellen exchanged looks. Then Bette shrugged and looked back at Marian. "I mean, we know that Nick's one of the good guys, but Judith just didn't see it that way. She said she needed to, well, *protect* you. At least that's what she told us."

"From Nick?" Marian said in surprise.

"Yeah," said Ellen. "She said, 'I've gotta protect Marian from that man. And from herself.'"

"She thought you were wasting your time being with him," Bette said. "That he was just using you."

Marian was silent. She suddenly remembered Alex telling her "He's just after your money." Why did people want to sabotage her relationship with Nick? How could they be so cruel? Didn't they understand how much she needed him? Suddenly, she began to cry, great wracking sobs.

"Oh, jeez," Bette said. "I'm sorry, Marian. We probably shouldn't have said anything, but-"

Marian waved her hand. "No. I'll be okay. I just. . ." She took a breath and tried to stop crying. "I just don't understand why people are so. . . hateful."

Ellen stood up and patted Marian's arm awkwardly. "Sorry we upset you, ma'am."

Marian caught hold of the young woman's hand. "Judith never told me about her past," she said, still shaking with emotion. "Maybe if she had, I could have found a way to help her."

"She really loved you," Ellen said. "And admired you. And she loved working with you."

"I think you *did* help her," said Bette. "But she couldn't let go of her demons."

Marian nodded. "Thank you for telling me," she said. "At least it explains why she. . . even though it was desperate and terrible and. . . sad. So very sad."

A nurse came in at that moment and announced cheerfully, "Visiting hours are over, girls. Tell Mrs. Vecchio goodbye. She needs her beauty sleep."

Ellen looked down at Marian for a minute, then bent and quickly kissed her on the cheek. "Hope you get better real quick," she said.

"Thanks for coming," Marian replied. "You are my friends and I love you."

"We know," Bette said.

CHAPTER

58

Sacramento, California
May 1973

Silvio was sitting in Dr. MacKenzie's waiting room feeling slightly fuzzy from the Valium, but calm. After a month of treatment—medication, discussion, support from his family—he felt a little stronger, less vulnerable. He hadn't had a panic attack for two weeks.

He had brought a book with him to the doctor's office: *Last Reflections on the War* by the journalist Bernard Fall, and was re-reading the section on Fall's last report. "We've been walking now for two and a half days in a virtual desert. Now we're with Able Company on the road and Able has found a mine. Charlie Company already exploded a mine with a trip wire and. . ."

Then somebody said, "Silvio?"

He looked up and saw a young woman behind the receptionist counter staring at him. She looked familiar. He stared back at her for a minute. "Lani?" he said.

She came out from behind the counter and crossed the room. "I thought it was you," she said, smiling. Her name was Mahilani, but everyone at Sacramento High had called her Lani.

Lani and her sister Anela had moved to Sacramento from Hawaii. They knew Hawaiian dances and were always being asked to perform at parties or for the school talent show. Usually, they agreed.

Silvio remembered having a crush on Mahilani, but he'd never gotten up the nerve to ask her out. She was very pretty with golden skin, big brown eyes, and a generous mouth. He thought she was exotic and fascinating. But she was two years older than he was. He figured he wouldn't stand a chance.

Then, when he started college at UC Davis, there she was in his physical anthropology class. She wanted to be a nurse. He wanted to be a doctor. He had a fantasy that somehow they would end up working in the same hospital. Then he got drafted, and his life was put on hold indefinitely.

Now, he just sat looking at her wordlessly.

"Good to see you," she said and sat down next to him.

He caught the scent of her perfume, a mysterious, exotic fragrance that jarred his memory. He gazed at her for a moment, grateful that she didn't say, "What happened to you?" Then he smiled and said, "I guess you made it through school?"

She nodded.

After a moment he added, "You work here?"

"Good guess,' she replied with a laugh.

He smiled ruefully. "Right."

She sat quietly, smiling a little. She didn't ask him how he lost his ear or what had happened to his hair or even how he was doing. Finally, he said, "What is it you do here?"

"I'm a pediatric psychologist," she replied. "I work with kids who have learning disabilities or trouble at school. Kids who've been abused or lost a parent or a sibling."

"I don't think I've ever heard of that field," said Silvio.

"It's new," said Lani. "After I finished my Masters in psychology at Davis, I went to the University of Iowa for my doctorate. The pediatric psychology program there was the first in the U.S. But I missed California. So after I finished my residency, I was lucky enough to find a job back here in Sacramento."

Silvio nodded and tried to think of something to say.

"How's your family?" Lani asked.

"Umm. . . Good. All fine."

She looked at him quietly.

He swallowed hard and said, "Dad and Mom are great. My sister's all grown up. My brother Carl is living in San Francisco."

"Good to have family close by."

"Yeah."

A nurse practitioner appeared in the doorway. "Mr. Morales? Dr. MacKenzie will see you now."

Silvio stood up. He looked at Lani. "Good talking to you," he said. "Maybe I'll. . . see you again?"

"I'd like that," Lani replied.

As he walked toward Dr. MacKenzie's office, Silvio was surprised to find that he suddenly felt calmer, as though a little seed had opened in his heart and sent out a small green tendril of hope.

The box arrived on a Friday afternoon in the third week of May—a large cardboard box delivered to Mockingbird by the UPS driver. He sat honking in the driveway until Kate went out to meet him. "Where do you want it?" he asked.

"The living room."

She opened the courtyard gate and the front door for him, and he deposited the box on the coffee table. She started to thank him, but he was already out the door.

She didn't open the box for a few minutes. She was unleashing a potential maelstrom. A sort of Pandora's box. "Too late now," she told herself and went to fetch a box cutter.

The publisher had sent sixty books that would be available for sale at the opening of the music festival. Publicity had been sent out with the tickets, and flyers had been dispersed to the publisher's mailing list. There would be ads as well. She picked up a book and read, *Tragedy and Redemption: The Life of Stefan Molnar* by Mary Katharine McPhalan. The publisher's graphics department had created a beautiful image for the jacket cover: a ghostly grand piano on a charcoal ground with Stefan's face superimposed on the image.

Kate sat down on the sofa and held the book for a moment. Opened it. Thumbed through the pages. Then she picked up a pen, opened to the title page and wrote: "To Veronique Becker, with love and friendship, Kate McPhalan."

She then signed a second book with: "To my friend, Jean Molnar, with love."

Santa Barbara, California

The ocean was a flat, blue wedge sitting on the horizon. The late afternoon sky was cloudless, and the sun, although low in the sky, was still hot.

But in the shade of the large pepper tree that arched over Veronique Becker's flagstone patio, the air was mild and smelled faintly of rosemary.

Verrie and Jean Molnar sat next to each other in identical grey canvas chairs. On the small white table between them sat a copy of *Tragedy and Redemption*, two half-filled wine glasses, and an open bottle of German Reisling.

"At first," Verrie said, "I was angry." She waved a perfectly manicured hand distractedly. "Not just angry, *devastated*. And *furious*! I asked myself, 'How *could* she? After all we've done for her. And for her sister.' But then. . ." Verrie fell silent.

Jean lit a cigarette, inhaled, blew a stream of smoke. "I was shocked," she said.

Verrie picked up the wine bottle, looked at Jean and raised her eyebrows.

"Sure," Jean said. "Why not." And held out her glass.

Verrie poured the wine and they each took a sip. Then Jean said, "Did you. . . know?"

Verrie smoothed the front of her pale, blue silk blouse. The gold bangles on her wrist made a soft metallic clang. She ran her fingers through her stylishly-coiffed platinum hair. "I. . . *suspected*," she said.

She took another sip of wine. "There were *clues*, but, of course, I didn't want to see them. Armand and I made a sort of pact early in our marriage that some topics were off the table, and the war was one

of them. No questions. No revelations. We both wanted a fresh start."
She smiled. "Our lives began in Barbados when we found each other."

"But," Jean said, "Barbados was safe, wasn't it?"

Verrie shrugged. "No place was *safe*, dear. The U-boats were
everywhere. At least one of them was torpedoed just off the coast
of Florida."

"But you weren't personally involved, right?"

"Actually," Verrie brushed a strand of hair from her face, "I was
in Paris when the war began. My mother thought that the cultural
and educational resources of Barbados were primitive, at best. So she
sent my sister and me to live with our grandmother in Paris. I went to
Collège, middle school, and Lycée, high school, in Paris. I graduated
in spring of 1939. I wanted to stay and go to the Sorbonne, but my
father believed that the Nazis were moving toward war, and insisted
that my sister and I leave France. He tried to coax my grandmother
into coming with us, but she refused. We never saw her again."

Both women were silent for several minutes. Then Jean said,
"I was so *sheltered*. I hardly knew that the world was at war. I was
only three when Germany invaded France. World War Two was
something I read about in my high school history book. When I met
Stefan, I felt for the first time that history was *real*. Real, actual people
had been there, had seen what happened with their own eyes. Had
the scars—physical and psychological—to prove it."

She paused for a moment. "But, although I knew what Stefan had
been through, or thought I did, I found it impossible to grasp the
entirety, the *extent*. The whole thing still feels like a horror movie,
like something staged. How could people do such unspeakable things
to each other?"

The wind was coming up, bringing with it the scent of kelp,
setting the leaves of the pepper tree swaying.

"A strange thing, fate," Verrie said. "I was fascinated by the
revelations in Kate's book. And of course repelled. But I had such a
feeling of *detachment*. I found it nearly impossible to reconcile the
man in the book with my husband. I had to keep reminding myself
that she was writing about *Armand. My Armand.* This Werner

Hoffman. Who *was* he? What did he have to do with my wonderful, smart, gracious, kind husband?" She shook her head. "I can't find a way to see them as one person. I *can't!*"

Tears welled up in her eyes. Jean leaned forward and put her hand on Verrie's arm. Verrie smiled weakly, and daubed at her eyes with a crumpled cocktail napkin. "How could he have done those horrible things? I remember my life with Armand as a wonderful adventure. There's no reasonable *connection* between Armand and Werner Hoffman."

"You said that fate is strange," Jean said. "What did you mean?"

"When we first met Stefan in Geneva in 1954, he was a teenager. He'd been playing concerts for twelve years, but basically he was still a *kid*. Armand was immediately taken with him, and I thought it was because. . ." Verrie looked toward the sea and then glanced back at Jean. "We had lost a child, a little boy. Our first baby. I thought that was why Armand was so eager to help Stefan, to befriend him. All those years, that's what I believed. And now. . ." Once again, she began to cry.

After a moment, Jean said, "Maybe fate *did* play a part. Perhaps the chance to atone for past wrongs helped Armand to heal from the wound of losing a child. A chance to set things right."

Verrie nodded and wiped her eyes. "In a strange way," she said, "finding out the truth is *comforting*. Actually, I feel a sense of. . . relief." She gave Jean a blurry smile. "So, I can't be angry with Kate. The book is wonderful. A remarkable story about a very special man, and the people who loved him. Armand Becker was one of those people."

Mockingbird Ranch

Kayoko Muramoto was the curator of the Namura art collection. She arrived at Mockingbird with her installation crew the same day that three wooden crates were delivered. She was to oversee the unpacking of the fifteen Impressionist works donated by the Namura family in honor of their daughter, Emiko.

A small, thin woman with high cheekbones and black hair pulled back severely into a bun, Ms. Muramoto wore a grey suit with the Namura logo embroidered on the lapel of her jacket. She spoke perfect English and after a few formalities, got down to business.

"May I see the facility, please?" she asked.

She followed Tommy and Kate to the remodeled storage shed that was now a charming art gallery. A Japanese-style torii gate announced the entrance to a small garden, an elegantly simple "first impression." Kayoko paused to read the bronze plaque above the gallery door: Mockingbird Art Center Gallery. In Memory of Emiko Namura Ashida, 1943-1969.

Inside, the rectangular space was divided into three rooms separated by freestanding walls. The floors were light hardwood. Track lights glinted from the twelve-foot ceiling.

"The rooms are all about the same size," Tommy said. "The collection would fit into any of them, so why don't you decide about placement."

Kayoko nodded. She prowled through the rooms, stopping here and there to look around, checking every detail.

"You have a monitoring system for temperature and humidity?" she asked.

"Of course." Tommy led her to a panel on the back wall that housed the system. "Latest technology," he said.

Kayoko inspected the device. "Good," she said shortly, then turned her gaze toward the lights. "Rheostat?" she said.

"Right here." Tommy showed her the panel of dials that controlled the intensity of the light. She experimented, turning the lights up and down in different combinations. Then, apparently satisfied, she inspected the walls.

"I used a vapor barrier between the stone and the interior walls," Tommy offered quickly. "The surface is plywood covered with drywall. I used plaster veneer instead of regular hard coat because it's moisture resistant. Plus, it's more attractive."

"I like it," Kayoko said. Tommy was visibly relieved.

"Fire protection?" she asked.

"We installed an automatic system that disperses a non-toxic fire extinguishant." Tommy pointed to the pipes that ran the length of the ceiling. "It's electrically non-conductive, non-corrosive, and free of residue. We also have portable extinguishers located in each room."

"Very good," said Kayoko.

The back room of the building had two vertical windows on the north wall that provided a glimpse of the garden outside. After she had circled the room twice, Kayoko looked at Kate and Tommy and smiled. "This is the one," she said. "Visitors can begin with other exhibits, then end up here to relax and enjoy. There should be two benches," she gestured, "one on each side, so they can view the gallery and also the garden. We can hang two of the paintings in the first gallery near the entrance as an inducement to see more." She glanced around and nodded. "Yes, this is very nice."

Kate and Tommy watched with growing excitement as Kayoko's helpers unpacked the crates and, under her meticulous direction, placed the paintings around the room. Kayoko had the installers move the paintings again and again before she decided on the perfect design for the exhibit. "All done now," she finally said.

A dramatic Monet landscape of tall poplars and flower-splashed fields, the largest of the paintings in the collection, was given a prominent position on the back wall of the gallery, while the smaller works were distributed throughout the room. Two choice Seurats, painted on the tops of cigar boxes, framed an orange and sage Degas dance scene. Three Pisarro cityscapes were interspersed with two charming Renoir portraits.

Kayoko glanced around. "My guys will hang the paintings and adjust the lights. Then we can have a final look. Should take maybe two hours." She gave Kate and Tommy a big smile. "Let's have lunch!"

59

Fair Oaks, California
June 1973

D anny Papadakis wanted to be certain that he didn't leave a
trail, so he had a colleague's handyman purchase the supplies
from two different stores—a pair of hiking boots, binoculars, a small
broom with a short handle, and a detailed map of El Dorado County.

On a bright, sunny afternoon in early June, he got into the pickup
truck that he'd borrowed from his next-door neighbor. Danny told
the neighbor that his car had a flat tire, the spare was no good, and
he had some errands to run. Could he borrow the truck for a couple
of hours? Of course he could. Dan carefully removed the license plate
and substituted an old tag that he'd found in a junkyard. Then he
packed his equipment in the cab and set off.

Outside Folsom, he picked up Route 49, the historic Gold Rush
Trail, then took the Old Foresthill Road along the Middle Fork of the
American River. Turning onto a logging road, he drove a few miles
further toward French Meadows Reservoir and parked the truck in
a small grove of brush well off the road. He was now in a wilderness
area that lay between the North and South forks of the river, and some
distance from the small towns of Gold Run, Foresthill, and Colfax.

Mockingbird Valley Ranch was directly down the canyon from
his position on the opposite side of the North Fork of the river. With
any luck, he thought, a fire would swoop southwestward through the
dry forest of yellow pine, live oaks and chaparral, directly toward
Mockingbird.

Danny scouted the area carefully, looking for the best location to
initiate his plan. The sun was beginning to settle behind the canyon

ridge when he found exactly what he was looking for—a loose pile of dead pine trees surrounded by thickets of manzanita. A west-facing slope made a long, lazy curve downhill toward an arroyo.

Danny had brought his "improvised incendiary device" with him—a plastic milk jug filled with gasoline and a wad of cloth that would serve as a wick. He removed the cap from the jug and pushed the cloth into the opening. The wick would burn the plastic for at least fifteen minutes before the fire consumed the container and the gas fumes caught fire. He had plenty of time to set the fire and return to his truck. By the time the fire was discovered, he would be back in Fair Oaks.

He placed the jug among the dry branches, lit the plug, then retraced his steps using the small broom to cover his tracks. Even if he missed a few footprints, he planned to get rid of the hiking boots. There would be no trail for investigators to follow, nor would there be a way to trace the pickup truck since he had removed the license plate. No loose ends, he thought.

Looking back, he saw a thin wisp of smoke rising above the bushes. He smiled broadly and felt a warm tingling in his crotch. Who would have thought that starting a fire could be so much fun?

Wednesday evening, June 6, 1973 was a spectacularly beautiful night at the new American River Music Center, and Marian, eight weeks after the "incident," was holding up better than she had expected. Her left shoulder was still in a brace and she was taking pain medication four times a day, but her energy was coming back, and every day she felt stronger.

It could have been so much worse. The bullet from Judith's pistol had broken the humerus just below the shoulder bone. The bullet had exited cleanly, leaving only shattered bone fragments to remove, and requiring only two surgeries to pin the humerus back together. The shoulder was healing nicely and her doctor, a specialist called in from Sacramento, predicted a complete recovery.

Despite everything, her "team" had stayed together. In fact, in some strange way, they seemed to have been strengthened by the disaster of Judith's attack and the subsequent chaos. Even Ellen and Bette, Judith's zealous friends, had thrown themselves into making sure that *Luna: A Celebration of Life* was a grand success.

Everything had come together and the opening weekend, now less than two weeks away, had been sold out for several months.

As Marian sat at the dinner table surrounded by her family, she thought of everyone who had gone—Julian and Owen, the ancestors who rested in the family plot. And those who had left and returned, like the salmon, to their native home—Kate and Alex, Tommy, Carl. And Marian herself.

She looked around the table. Tommy sat at the head of the table where Owen had once presided. The idea made her smile. Dear Owen, if only he hadn't been blinded by the prejudice he harbored. But he, like everyone, was a product of a time and a place and a people who felt entitled to their opinions. Everyone had his own set of blinders.

Kate sat next to Tommy, holding Cory on her lap. She still looked so young. Hard to believe she had turned thirty last February. And Cory was almost nine. Where had the time gone?

Nick sat next to Carl. They talked a mile a minute, still going over the technical details for the *WaterLight* performance. She realized how similar they were—passionate, creative, full of enthusiasm—and yet how different: Carl the polished Classicist and Nikki the space-age hippy. She loved them both dearly.

Alex was busy talking to Francisco and Allison. How Alex had changed! No more spoiled brat, but a warm, outgoing woman with huge talent and intense discipline. She actually *listened* to people! Where had this maturity and grace come from? Then Marian saw Alex glance at Carl, and he looked at her. The moment sizzled between them. *Ah*, Marian thought, *I get it.*

She looked around once more at her family. *I am so damned lucky*, she thought. *So lucky.*

But Kate was tapping her spoon on her wine glass and the

conversations dwindled to silence as eyes turned toward her. "I think we have a few announcements," she said. "Who wants to go first?"

Eyes darted this way and that. Then Francisco stood and said, "Allow me that honor." He looked down at Allison, then back at the tribe. "I have asked this lovely woman to be my wife, and she has consented. And you, my friends, are the first to know. Except, of course," he winked at Ali, "for her father."

An outburst of congratulations followed Francisco's words. Glasses were raised. Toasts made.

When the ebullience subsided, Carl got to his feet and cleared his throat and glanced around. He ran his hands through his hair, and grinned sheepishly. "Ummm," he looked desperately at Alex who was trying to choke back a laugh, "maybe, you should tell them, hon," he said.

"Wuss," she returned affectionately. She stood up and went to him and he put his arm around her shoulders. "We're married," she said bluntly. "Two weeks tomorrow."

There was a collective gasp followed by a chorus of "How?" "Where?" "Why didn't you tell us?"

"Hey," Carl said, holding up his hand. "We didn't want any big deal, so we sort of. . . eloped. Went to Reno. Found a chapel."

"One of those tacky quicko drive-throughs," Alex interjected.

"It wasn't *that* tacky," Carl exclaimed, giving her a hug.

"For heaven's sake!" Marian exclaimed. She wanted to add, "What took you so long?" but thought she should keep that to herself.

Allison jumped to her feet and hugged both of them. Francisco pumped Carl's hand. Nikki slapped him on the back. Cory ran to them and said excitedly, "Will you still be my Aunt Alex?"

Alex ruffled his hair. "Of course I will."

Carl looked at Kate. She looked back at him and smiled.

Then Kate stood up and raised her hand and said, "Just one more." The room quieted. Kate looked at Tommy and he nodded. She turned to the waiting company. "Tommy and I are going to have a baby," she announced.

"I knew that," Cory cried. "You already told me."

More laughter, cheers, toasts, happy chatter. More wine was poured. Glasses clinked.

Then a siren wailed. And another. Shouts and a horn blaring came from outside, beyond the courtyard.

Tommy jumped up and started for the door, but at that moment Jaime burst in. "Fire," he gasped. "About twelve miles away on the opposite side of the river. The wind is picking up and pushing the fire in this direction!"

"Holy shit!" Alex cried.

Everyone began to talk at once until Nick raised his arms and shouted, "Shut up, everybody! We need to figure out what to do."

"My team!" Marian cried. "I need to warn them!"

"Tell them to be ready to evacuate if we need to," Nick called after her. He looked at Francisco. "I think you ought to get out of here, Cisco."

"We could stay and try to help," Ali said.

Nick shook his head. "Go back to Sacramento. Out of harm's way."

Francisco nodded. "Come on, Ali."

"But we—" Ali started to object.

"We'd be in the way," Francisco said firmly. "Let's go."

Someone was banging on the door. Kate ran to open it. Tony Malacchi and Tassos Stavros, both neighbors, were standing in the courtyard.

"Evacuation orders?" Kate asked.

"Not so far," Tony replied.

"A bunch of trucks went past about ten minutes ago," Tassos said. "Looked like they were heading toward the Foresthill Bridge."

They all looked up as a helicopter droned past.

Tommy came to the the door and stood beside Kate. "What are you guys going to do?" Kate asked.

"Grace took the girls into town to stay with her mother," Tony said. "I'm going to try to hang on here and do what I can."

"Me too," said Tassos.,

Jaime and Consuelo arrived breathless, carrying Teresa. "I'll take care of the children," Consuelo said.

"Cory's inside,' Kate said. "Tell him to keep Buck in the house."

"I'm going to call the fire hotline," Tommy said.

Even as he spoke, a Highway Patrol car came up the driveway and bounced to a stop outside the courtyard gate. Kate and the three men hurried to the car.

"Evening, folks," said the officer. "Wanted to let you know there is a precautionary evacuation in effect for this area. It's not mandatory, but we want to alert you to the situation. The fire is currently headed down the canyon in this direction, but of course these fires are unpredictable."

"What can we do to help?" Tommy said.

"Turn on some sprinklers." The officer glanced up. "I see you have a tile roof, so that's good news."

Another helicopter buzzed past above the tree line, its searchlight strafing the orchard.

"We have a group of women staying here at the ranch," Kate said. "Should we get them out?"

"We can send a bus," the officer said.

Tommy nodded. "That would be great."

"It'll be here within an hour," said the officer. He looked at Tassos and Tony. "You guys live here?"

"Next door," Tony said.

"Down the road," Tassos offered.

"Stay alert," the officer told them. "We're broadcasting updates on the FRS at four sixty-two Mhz if you've got Family Radio Service."

"I do," said Tassos. "I'll keep you guys posted," he said to Tommy, Tony and Kate.

"Do they know what caused the fire?" Kate asked. "There was no lightning. Maybe a campfire?"

The officer shook his head. "We're investigating. We think it could be arson, but we don't have any evidence."

"Look at that," Tassos said, pointing. The sky was the color of an eerie sunset. To the east, above the tree line, they could see a red-grey glow reflected by the clouds.

"Oh, Christ," said Tommy.

CHAPTER

60

The next twenty-four hours were a blur. Kate thought later that everyone somehow came together, assuming roles as if by instinct.

Marian herded her helpers onto the school bus that the county sent to transport them to a shelter. Then she and Bette, one of Marian's team who had insisted on staying behind, headed to the new art gallery where they packed up the paintings from Kiyoshi's collection in case they had to be moved out of harm's way.

Tommy, Carl, Nick and Jaime formed an impromptu emergency team and went to secure the animals, turn on sprinkler systems, and clear away brush from the buildings. Kate, Alex and Consuelo began assembling emergency supplies and important documents in case a mandatory evacuation order was issued.

A team of firefighters arrived a little after midnight and established a control center in the building that had been occupied by Marian's performance team. Tommy, Nick and the other men joined them to see if they could help.

A while later, Kate looked in dismay at the scene outside the window: the bluff above the orchard was engulfed in flames. She rushed outside with Alex and Consuelo following, but spotted Jaime running toward them.

"What's happened?" Kate cried. "The fire can't have gotten here already!"

"Don't worry," Jaime said. "The fire team set a backfire. The plan is to burn the brush, anything that could be fuel for the fire, from the top of the bluff down to the river. If we can keep the fire from jumping the river, it will go past us on the other side of the canyon."

"Where's Carl?" Alex asked.

Jaime jerked his head toward the bluff. "Up there."

"Sonofabitch," she said softly.

With Cory and Teresa asleep, and the emergency supplies and evacuation gear stacked in the foyer, Consuelo, Alex and Kate sat at the kitchen table listening to the NOAA Weather Radio. Marian and Bette soon joined them. The station was on emergency alert status to broadcast information about the swiftly moving fire.

So far, the fire had burned about two hundred acres but, because it was in a lightly populated wilderness area, no lives or structures had been lost. The wind had died down a bit and the fire was burning more slowly. A crew of four hundred firefighters battled the blaze which was now forty percent contained. An additional four hundred households had been put on alert for possible evacuation.

Then, just before dawn, the announcement came that the fire had suddenly bolted, and was now burning almost due west along the North Fork of the American River, heading directly toward Mockingbird. The women ran outside and looked up the hill toward the bluff.

The smoke was so thick that Alex began to cough. "We'd best go back inside," Kate said.

"Do you think we should leave?" Consuelo asked, her voice thin with fear.

"Let's see if there are any new evacuation orders," Kate advised.

Through the gloom they saw headlights approaching. The car stopped and Tassos Stavros jumped out.

"Are you leaving?" Kate called.

"Yeah."

Kate could see Tassos's wife and their two girls in the car. "What about Tony?"

"He's going to stay."

Kate glanced toward the bluff. "Then we'll stay too. Tommy and Carl and Nikki are up there with the fire team." She looked back at Tassos. "Can we do anything to help you?"

"Just be safe," he said.

She watched him drive away. *What would Daddy do?* she wondered, and knew the answer at once. Resolutely, she turned and followed the other women back to the house.

Later that morning the radio reported that the wind had died down again and the blaze had leveled off. It had now reached the Foresthill Bridge, but was still on the south side of the river. Eight hundred acres had burned, but only one structure had been lost—an abandoned cabin deep in the woods. A huge plume of smoke that resembled a gigantic cumulus cloud rose above the canyon. The cloud was rust-colored, as though the iron-rich earth had thrown a sandstorm into the sky. The sun was a pink disc floating in the cloud.

The five women roamed about restlessly, drank too much coffee, and listened to the radio. Cory and Teresa came downstairs and requested breakfast. Consuelo and Bette cooked, but Alex, Marian and Kate were too tense and exhausted to eat.

Then the announcer read the latest report: the fire was eighty percent contained, still burning, but moving much more slowly along the south edge of the river. It would likely burn itself out before reaching any populated areas.

The whoop of joy was so loud that Teresa began to cry, and Buck, who had been prowling between the table and his mat by the door, let out a howl.

"The horsemen passed by!" Kate cried, and gave Cory a bear hug.

"High topper mountain won't be all hot cockalorum after all!" Alex shouted.

"Won't be *what*?" Consuelo asked, tilting her head.

"Ashes," Marian said, laughing. "Toast!"

She and Kate fell into each other's arms.

A half hour later, they heard voices outside and rushed out the door. Tommy, Carl and Nick staggered, arm in arm, toward the house.

"Oh, my God," said Alex. "It's the Three Musketeers!"

"Daddy!" Cory cried, running to meet them. "Mr. Tommy! Uncle Nikki! Where have you been?"

Carl picked Cory up and hugged him, then set him down. He took one of the boy's hands and Tommy took the other.

"Where's Jaime?" Consuelo asked in alarm.

"Home," Tommy said. "I know he'd be delighted to see you."

Consuelo ran to fetch Teresa, then hurried toward the caretaker's cabin.

"Where's Marian?" Nick asked, looking around.

"She went to the shelter to check on her flock," Kate replied. "I expect they'll be back pretty soon."

"God," Carl moaned, "I sure could use a drink."

"Water?" suggested Alex.

Carl nodded. "That sounds great."

In the kitchen of his Fair Oaks home, a little more than twenty miles away from Mockingbird, Dan Papadakis sat in front of his television set and listened to the morning news. It was all about the terrible wildfire and the 900 acres of forest that had been destroyed.

But the good news was that the fire had been contained, and had remained on the south side of the American River away from populated areas. Dan stopped eating his scrambled eggs and stared at the TV.

The local announcer, a pretty blond, chirped happily that no homes had been damaged, although the fire had burned right down to the bank of the river. "The firefighters, with the help of local residents, managed to stop the blaze before it jumped the river. If those efforts had not been successful, we'd have a much sadder story to bring you this morning."

Dan took a drink of coffee. "Fucking river," he muttered as he got up to turn off the TV.

One week after the fire, Tommy and Kate caught up with Carl and Alex as they were about to leave to meet Carl's parents for dinner at Casa Morales.

"Have you got a minute?" Kate said. "We have a question for you."

Carl glanced at Alex. She shrugged. "Sure," he said.

"We thought if you're going to be directing the music program at Mockingbird, it's kind of inconvenient to have to commute back and forth to the City," Tommy said.

"Or to always have to stay in one of the guest houses," Kate added.

"So, we thought that you might be interested in having a permanent residence in the area."

"O-kay," Carl said slowly. "What do you have in mind?"

Tommy looked at Kate. "This isn't going well, is it?" he said.

Kate shook her head. She looked at Alex. "Maybe it would be better if we show you."

"Why not?" Alex said.

They all piled into Alex's white Chrysler sedan. From the back seat, Kate gave directions. After a twenty-minute drive, they turned on to a narrow road that wound its way through a grove of oak trees. At the end of the road, a rustic wooden sign read: American River Estates.

"Isn't this the property Daddy developed back in the mid-sixties?" Alex asked.

"That's right," Kate said. "Let's take a look, shall we?"

They drove slowly past several sprawling ranch-style homes that were set back from the road among groves of trees. The community had a rural feeling despite the upscale architecture. At the end of the street was a cul-de-sac with a sign that said: Lot for Sale. Two Century oak trees guarded the entrance to the property.

They all got out of the car and stood looking at the overgrown parcel. Carl looked at Kate. "All right," he said. "What's this about?"

Kate and Tommy exchanged looks. Then Kate said, "We'd like to give this property to you as a wedding present."

"What?" Alex gasped. "Really?"

"And a house to go with it," Tommy added. "Tell me what you want and I'll draw it up. Your only cost would be the materials."

Carl looked completely flummoxed. "Jeez," he mumbled, "that's an incredible offer, but I—"

"Don't turn it down until you've had a look," Kate interrupted.

Alex grabbed Carl's hand and they walked down a path and past a little meadow. "The property's a little over twelve acres," Kate explained. "There's a greenway at the bottom of the hill that runs along the river. Great for biking or walking. This is the last lot in the development."

"What's next door?" Alex asked, looking toward the south.

"A park and a nature center," Tommy said.

Carl stood still for a moment, then said, "Is that the river I'm hearing?"

Kate grinned. "Water music."

"Beautiful," Carl murmured. "So peaceful."

"Hey," said Alex, "we can retire here full-time when we're old and grey."

Carl was gazing around. "Seems like a piece of history," he said. "Ancient."

"Oh," said Kate, "that reminds me. This property was once part of a Spanish land grant. It was called Rancho Las Posas del Sierra. And, here's the best part, it was owned by a rancher named Juan Morales."

"No way," Alex exclaimed. She and Carl stared at each other.

"I can't believe this," Carl said. For a moment, he looked as if he might cry.

Kate and Tommy glanced at each other. Tommy shrugged. They looked back at Carl and Alex.

"You've come home, luv," Alex said to Carl.

Later that evening, after Carl and Alex had left and Cory had fallen asleep, Tommy and Kate decided to walk up the hill to the site of their new home. On the way, they talked about the news that Carl's great-grandfather, Juan Morales, had once owned a ranch where American River Estates was now located. "It's almost scary," Tommy said with a laugh. "I mean, all three of the families were right here a hundred years ago."

"Salmon people," Kate said. "We all ended up coming home. Even Silvio," she added.

"Did Carl tell you how he's doing?"

Kate nodded. "Jorge and Rose have gotten him into a treatment program. The VA wasn't a lot of help. There's a long waiting list, so he's working with a private psychotherapist. Rose told Carl that she thought recovery would take time. I guess the best news is that no one is trying to say everything's normal."

"Yeah," Tommy said, a fleeting image of watchtowers and barbed wire suddenly appearing. "Yeah. It'll take some time."

The new house was still a shell, but the basic design was evident—the two-story foyer and double staircase that led up to the living area and down to the lower-level garage and family room. On the back of the house was a spacious porch that had views of the mountains and the river canyon.

They stood hand in hand next to the house and watched the moon rise, nearly full, over the peaks of the Sierra. "And every day," Kate said, "we'll watch the sun come up. . ."

". . . out of the Range of Light," Tommy finished.

Moonlight spread shimmering bands across the landscape. Across the river they could see the charred remains left behind by the fire. "By next spring, everything will be green again," Kate said. She nestled against him and he put his arm around her shoulder. "I think I know what we should name the baby," she said.

He looked down at her. "Do you?"

"Yes. I think we should call her River."

CODA

American River Music Center at Mockingbird Valley Ranch

Everyone was there for the opening of the American River Music Festival at Mockingbird. Jean Molnar Westmorland, her husband Wright, and Verrie Becker flew up on Wright's company jet. Robert Ashford was there along with five Board members from the Townsend Foundation. Local politicians and Chamber members abounded. Jerry McClosky arrived with a striking brunette on his arm. Kiyoshi came too, accompanied by a uniformed attendant and his curator, Kayoko. He was thin and pale, and used a walker to get around, but he was all smiles as Tommy and Kate gave him a tour of the gallery. The paintings had been re-installed under Marian's watchful eye, and Kayoko found no fault with the arrangement.

Then there were the family members: three generations of McPhalans and Morales, and Ashidas. Jorge and Rose arrived with Allison and Francisco. Silvio sent his congratulations and vowed to attend next summer's festival. The whole Ashida clan was there, including David, looking stiff and uncomfortable in his dark blue suit. Ben was there with his partner, Jose. "We brought everyone but Chibi, our dog," Pearl said with a laugh.

And musicians by the score: Alex's former students, Carl's friends from as far away as New York. The first crop of fellows from the Mockingbird Contemporary Music Center. Members of the San Francisco Symphony.

The place glittered with French fashions and diamonds, sensuous fragrances and exotic fabrics. Three hundred metal laterns lined the drive. In the blue and white-striped tent, the crowd gathered to feast on Pacific oysters and smoked local trout, roasted squab and Basque goat-cheese, homemade tortillas and barbecued brisket from Mockingbird's herd of Angus cattle. And bottles of California wine from a dozen different vintners. Kate was installed at a table just inside the entryway, signing copies of *Tragedy and Redemption: The Life of Stefan Molnar.*

Since the near-disaster of the fire, the Festival team had worked feverishly to finish everything in time for the opening celebration. The Mandala garden was a geometric masterpiece clearly visible from the reception tent and the curved amphitheater. Intricate rows of pale flowers radiated outward like moonbeams on a summer lake.

Prior to the opening ceremonies, visitors were invited to explore the garden. Or to attend a wine tasting in the new Mockingbird Valley Cellars. They could also visit the Emiko Ashida Gallery with its superb collection of French Impressionist paintings. An impressive display of the architectural drawings and models from Ashida and Associates that had been used to renovate the ranch buildings and create the new amphitheatre.

As the sun began to sink behind the ridge, a bell tolled, signaling the beginning of the festival program. The chorus, the twenty-six young women who comprised Marian's "sacred band," gathered on the hillside behind the Mandala Garden. They were dressed in white and silver robes, colors sacred to Selene, the Greek Goddess of the Moon.

They began the opening "hymn to the moon," based on a Homeric poem. Marian led them in a series of intricate dance-like movements as they wove their way through the labyrinth of the garden and onto the stage of the amphitheatre. A full moon rose above the mountains and flooded the hillside with a silver glow.

"From her immortal head a radiance is shown from heaven and embraces earth; and great is the beauty that ariseth from her shining light. So she is a sure token and a sign to mortal men," they sang. "Mother of months, you sail silently across the sky, casting soft rays on the sleeping earth. You whom no man may possess, you who roam free, protecting your wild lands and dancing with the Muses on Olympus, I will remember you."

Kate then read a brief statement welcoming the guests and dedicating the festival to the memory of "All those who cherish music and the land."

Next came a recital of piano music that revolved around the theme of the moon—Debussy's *Au Claire de Lune*, Beethoven's *Moonlight Sonata,* and several of Franz Schubert's *Lieder,* poems with lunar subjects. Alex was the soloist. The music was a perfect complement to the moon-bathed landscape—pure enchantment.

The following morning, some of the visitors attended the rehearsal for the Sunday program, Dvorak's opera *Rusalka.* A guest conductor from Austria made a last-minute cancellation due to a death in the family, so the San Francisco Symphony's music director, Seiji Ozawa, stepped in at the last moment. He was delighted to use the opportunity to introduce the newly formed San Francisco Symphony Chorus to the audience. That afternoon, a young visiting conductor from France led a concert of three works that focused on the three families whose lives and destinies were tied to Mockingbird: Ashida, Morales, and McPhalan.

The program began with Kan Ishii's *Sinfonia Ainu,* that utilized the musical heritage of the Ainu people of Northern Japan; *Sones de Mariachi* by the Mexican composer Blas Galindo. Then came *Sunlight and Shadow* by the Irish composer Frederick May to complete the program. The Sacramento Youth Orchestra was joined by members of the Sacramento Symphony.

Saturday's evening program featured Carl conducting the San Francisco Symphony in the première of Nick and Carl's *WaterLight,* a work that combined overlapping natural and synthesized sounds with instrumental exploration and wide-screen imagery. The students from Carl's Center for the Study of Contemporary Music had helped set up the necessary equipment. Kate held her breath, hoping that the mass of technology would work, but the piece was a spectacular success, sound and image interacting with mesmerizing effects. The audience applauded wildly and Carl and Nick took multiple bows.

On Sunday night of the opening weekend, Kate sat in the back of the dish-shaped outdoor concert hall and listened to the last tragic moments of what at least one writer described as ". . . twelve of the most glorious minutes in all opera in their almost hymnic solemnity." As the Prince and his mermaid lover kiss for the final time, Rusalka thanks the Prince for allowing her to experience human love. Yes, Kate thought, perhaps human love *is* the most profound experience we can have.

Kate thought about all the hopes and dreams, the tragedies and triumphs, the possibilities for failure, the obstacles and personalities, and huge amounts of work that had been poured into this unlikely labor of love: the American River Music Festival at Mockingbird. There were four more weekends scheduled for the first summer series, and discussions were already underway for the festival's second season.

Her mind wandered with the waning song. *Music and art, and the land beside the river, these have been the soul of our universe,* she thought. *I know now that we are all bound together by this place—the magical link between our destinies.*

Because no matter how far we strayed, how high we reached or how low we fell, we have always been drawn back to the river. And to this place called Mockingbird.

When the music was at last finished and the sounds died away, in that space between the last note and the applause, she could hear the river singing.

End Book III

PLAY LIST FOR CONFLUENCE

Chapter 16
Switched-on Bach
Mahler, First Symphony
Carlos Morales, *Kokopelli's Dream: A Piano Concerto for the Right
Hand in D-Minor*

Chapter 17
Brahms, Piano Concerto No. 2 in D-Minor

Chapter 20
The Temptations, "Ball of Confusion"

Chapter 22
Rachmaninoff, Piano Concerto No. 2

Chapter 27
Mendelssohn, *Variations Serieuses*
Chopin, *The Preludes*
Schubert, *Lieder*
Wagner, The Prayer from *Rienzi, der Letzte der Tribunen*

Chapter 28
Liszt, Piano Sonata in B-Minor

Chapter 38
The Rolling Stones, "Sympathy for the Devil"

Chapter 42
John Chowning, *Turenas*
Bart Howard,: "In Other Words"

Chapter 49

Schubert, Fantasy in C-Major

Chapter 56
Beethoven, *Moonlight Sonata*
Debussy, *Au Claire de Lune*
Chopin, *Fantasy in F-Minor*

Coda
Schubert, *Lieder*
Dvorak, *Rusalka*
Kan Ishii, *Sinfonia Ainu*
Blas Galindo, *Sones de Mariachi*
Frederick May, *Sunlight and Shadow*
Carlos Morales and Nicholas Vecchio, *WaterLight*

Printed in the United States
By Bookmasters